Money-Grip

A Novel By Divine G

Website: www.streetknowledgepublishing.com

Money-Grip®

Published by: **Street Knowledge Publishing**
Written by: **Divine G**
Edited by: **Charlene McNiff**
Cover design and Photos by: **Marion Designs**

For information contact:
Street Knowledge Publishing
P.O. Box 345
Wilmington,DE 19801
Email: jj@streetknowledgepublishing.com
Website: www.streetknowledgepublishing.com

ISBN: 0-9746199-3-0

Dedication

This novel is dedicated to my family – my mother Gloria Whitfield, I love you like no other, my sisters Sharon Whitfield and Sandra Whitfield, my children Divequa, Karron Dantzler, Dinasia Whitfield, my aunt, Norris Gray, my # 1 cousin, Latasha Gray, my nieces and nephew Quiona Whitfield, Sasareeka Whitfield, and Kasiem Whitfield, my G-child Shayla, and Rashawn. Thanks for the love and support.

Acknowledgements

To Linda Williams, thanks for having faith in me, for being a friend, and for having my back. You have truly earned the title of being my Godsend.

I also want to give a supreme thanks to Street Knowledge Publishing, in particular, brother JoeJoe and staff for allowing me to become a part of the Street Knowledge Family. Love for Life!

Chapter One

Rasheen Smith sat on the bed with both hands clamped to his bowed head as he listened to the blood curdling screams of his mother being beaten mercilessly by Black Bob in the adjacent room.

"Okay Bob!" Barbara shrieked. "I didn't mean it." A vicious punch to the jaw dropped her to the floor. "I'm sorry, please!" Black Bob began stomping her with his Timberland boots as Barbara curled up into a ball trying to protect her high yellow skeleton face by tucking her head close to her chest. She was hollering and screaming as loud as she could while clutching the crack pipe, keeping it close to her bosom for extra-added protection. Normally her screams would slow Black Bob down, but tonight she noticed it wasn't working.

Rasheen fought desperately to tame the blinding rage circulating through his body. He looked up and saw his 11-year-old brother Lameek pacing like a caged Cub. His infant looking features no longer gave off accurate images. Lameek was so infuriated it looked like steam was seeping from his ears. His light brown complexion, dark brown eyes and rigid overall facial features, brought a deep pain to Rasheen's 17 year old heart as he observed his baby brother in a state of utter distress.

"He's gonna kill momma!" Lameek shouted as the tears finally started to drip from his eyes. "We gotta do something, Rasheen."

Rasheen got up and hugged Lameek in an attempt to comfort him while looking around at the roach infested bedroom. Although most of the roaches were hiding at the moment, it was evident an army of them would come out and play the second the lights went out. He glanced over at the dresser and saw a roach crawling on his old Spiderman doll, an antique toy of his that he possessed since he was five years old. His mother's agonizing screams re-ignited the extreme hatred and utter disdain he had for black men who abused women. Images of a river of blood rolling down the gutters of the Hood, all initiated by his own hands, flashed before his third eye.

The sound of breaking glass unhinged both Rasheen and Lameek, forcing them to break their brotherly embrace. Rasheen sat back down on the bed shaking his head, trying to tell himself that his patience would pay off.

Lameek was breathing hard with panic. Suddenly he ran to the closet, snatched a baseball bat and headed for the door.

Rasheen sprung to his feet and intercepted him. He snatched the bat from Lameek's grasp. "We tried that already!" He grabbed Lameek by the collar. "Black Bob's too fuckin' big for us!" He pulled his brother back towards the bed and made him sit down. "How many times he gotta beat flames out of yo' dumb ass for you to realize we can't whip his ass head up?" Rasheen sat listening to the screams while humming the new rap tone by Biggie Smalls.

Lameek was squirming as he sat listening to his mom now screaming for help. "We should call the cops on Black Bob's ass!"

Rasheen felt a jolt from Lameek's remark; he turned in slow motion, faced Lameek and stared at him. "What the fuck did you say?"

Lameek saw the rage in Rasheen's eyes and inched away from his big brother, who acted 10 years older than his real age.

Rasheen jumped up and slapped Lameek damn near across the room. "You ain't ever 'pose to call the cops! Ever!" He bolted for Lameek and slapped him again. "That's snitchin'! The worse motherfucker in the world is a snitch!" Rasheen sat back down and refocused himself. "I told you I got a fuckin' plan, didn't I? Now come yo' ass over here and sit the fuck down."

Lameek reluctantly sat next to Rasheen and a few seconds later they could hear the worse of Black Bob's ass whipping started to die down. They could still hear their mom, weeping, moaning and groaning so they knew she was still alive. After a moment, Rasheen put his arm around Lameek's shoulder and said, "Sorry for wigging out on you like that, but you know better than talkin' about snitchin' on somebody. We straight from the Hood man. We don't get down like that. You my baby brother and you gotta be thorough. Let me show you somethin'." With a smile, Rasheen lifted his shirt and pulls the huge 9mm from his waist. Rasheen's 17-year-old hand gripping the weapon made it look much large than it really was.

Lameek's eyes lit up with something much stronger than glee. An observer would have thought he had just laid eyes on the biggest toy store in the world. "Is it real?" He reached for the gun with awe gripping his entire being.

Rasheen pulled the Browning 9mm out of his reach, took the clip out of the weapon and handed it to his baby brother. Rasheen's smile grew two inches larger as he watched Lameek dancing around in the room pointing and playing with the gun. After a moment, Rasheen said, "Come on now, that's enough, give me it." Lameek handed it back reluctantly.

"I'ma show you how to use it soon. After, I blaze Black Bob." Rasheen said without the slightest hint of insincerity.

"Can I come with you?" Lameek said hopefully, "I wanna shoot him too." Lameek's expression was more serious than the crack epidemic of the mid-1980s, a plague that was supposed to be whining down according to a recent news report dated November 12, 1993.

"You can't come with me on this, but you can help me out." Rasheen saw Lameek's serious face grow into a network of smiles and wide-eyed delight. "When Bob breaks out, I'm gonna follow him. I need you to fill my bed with clothes to make it look like I'm sleep. If mom comes in, act like you sleep and she'll leave. I need you to stay up so you can open the window back up when I come back, alright."

"Where you gonna get him at?" Lameek's 11-year-old mind was gearing up for an onslaught of questions.

"Dirty Ricky said Bob be at his house with his mom. He comes here, takes mom's money and be usin' it to get high with Ricky's mom. Ricky told me earlier he heard his mom and Bob talking and he said he was gonna come over tonight after he came from here. I'ma try to beat him over to…." Rasheen heard his cue.

"I'm gettin' the fuck outta here." Black Bob said, "When I come back tomorrow afternoon, bitch you better have my money. You laying up around here smokin' up all my money when you supposed to be bringing that cheddar to me . . ."

Rasheen shot to his feet and grabbed the brown coat he recently took at gunpoint from some unknown cornball cat caught in the wrong Hood. The moment he laid eyes on the coat he knew it would be just right for this very special occasion. He raced to the window with Lameek on him as close as a shadow.

Rasheen opened the third floor window and the vicious January winter cold lashed at him with unrelenting anger. He turned to Lameek and said, "Remember what I said."

Lameek nodded as he excitedly ushered his big brother on, savoring the thought of Black Bob finally getting what he deserved.

Rasheen raced down the fire escape of the old, decrepit tenement building on President Street near the corner of St. Mark's Street, the tip of the heart of do or die Bed-Stuy. He jumped from the last ladder step and landed wrong, hurting his heels. Rasheen hastily took flight down President Street on his way to Dirty Ricky's crib over on Pacific Street.

Black Bob exited the tenement building and headed in the direction Rasheen had just run. He was completely oblivious of the small figure running in front of him with his bangy Guess blue jeans and the unfamiliar brown coat. Black Bob had a crack craving as angry as a full-blown hurricane, plus he was still infuriated by Barbara's audacity to try to hold out on him. That bitch and them two dirty ankle havin' ass gremlins of her's owed him their life when it came right down to it. He helped Barbara find an occupation that allowed her to work at home and stay as high as she liked. He hated ungrateful niggas with severe cases of amnesia.

Moments later, Black Bob entered the crack spot on Fulton Street and Rogers Avenue, copped four nickel vials of crack with half the money he got from Barbara and wondered should he go straight to Darlene's crib. Darlene was one of his newest mules he was currently in the process of breaking in. She had a gigantic ass that was destine to bring him in suitcases full of money. A huge wind lashed out and helped Bob to decide to stop at the pool hall over on Chancey Avenue to check on two of his other broads he had on the stroll. Candy Cane and Sarsaparilla were straight hood rats that would fuck a freak in the circus if the price was right and they were definitely his kind of hookers. He reached into the pocket of his Alaskan Parka to warm his hands. In ritualistic fashion, he caressed the 38 snub nose revolver and felt that familiar sense of security sweep over him.

Rasheen paced back and forth near the entrance of the dark garbage littered alleyway on the side of Dirty Ricky's house on Pacific Street between Franklin and Bedford Avenues. He sucked on the last of the Blunt and tossed the butt to the ground. The tingling sensation of the weed racing through his blood system instantly started taking affect. For what he was about to get into, there was no question he had to get his head right. Every so often he would peek out down the street to see if Black Bob was coming. Despite the wind cutting about the small area, the wretched odors were so unbearable that it easily masked the smell of the weed. At times when the shitty diapers and rotting food got too deep inside Rasheen's nose, he had to come out of the alleyway and stand near the curb in order to catch a whiff of fresh air. When he heard movement inside the building or saw a crack head approaching, he would snatch a lung full of fresh air as if he was about to submerge himself in water, then retreat back into the stomach curdling sea of horrible smells. His teeth were chattering and his whole body trembled with uncontrollable intensity. He didn't know for certain whether or not it was from the cold, or due to the fact he was about to use the gun on Black Bob. Despite the weed in his system, he was scared out of his mind, but the fury in his heart was too powerful to push him to seriously consider any other options.

Rasheen was fighting with that voice in his head, the one that kept telling him not to do it. The other voice, the one telling him to do it in order to save his mom and the other women under Black Bob's iron fist, wasn't as loud as it was earlier. The dark cloud of doubt and indecisiveness was growing, but all the brutal beat downs he received at the hands of Black Bob was just as powerful. His vindictiveness was even more pronounced and even if he wanted to turn back, his predisposition for always having to come out on the top with everything he did wouldn't allow him. To keep his energy fully charged, Rasheen started reminiscing. The time Black Bob knocked him out cold when he came to his mother's aid, sweeping a baseball bat at Black Bob was a very memorable moment because it was the first time Rasheen was ever knocked out and it was like a part of his life was cut away. The only thing he remembered was swigging the bat, Bob blocked it and everything instantly when black. The numerous other times Black Bob beat him, slapped him, kicked him in the ass, threw him down flights of stairs, and even made him and Lameek watch him fuck his mother in the ass while she was sucking on a crack pipe. He could still remember that sickening odor of shit that fumigated the room.

Rasheen was scared, but he was a man-child who had reached a point of no return and was pushed completely over the edge. He was beyond traumatized, brutalized, victimized and there was no one to turn to, so he did what he always did, turned to himself. His Hood had rules and he'd been mastering those rules since he was old enough to throw rocks at the bodega and run and hide when the storeowner came out and chased him. Whoever dished out the most violence was the most respected was the top rule on the list. He seen so many shootouts, murders, stabbings, and violence of all varieties he was practically immune to it. Not to mention he had a very violent up bringing of his own to say the least, but so far he hadn't killed anyone...Yet. Even his six-month stay in DFY wasn't enough to derail his antisocial attitude and behavior. From the moment he learned how to operate a switchblade, he'd been wondering how it would feel to kill another person. As Rasheen looked around the cold, smelly alleyway, he realized tonight he was going to finally find out. His cherry was gettin' popped tonight fo' sure! Rasheen thought with an inward smile.

Rasheen suddenly felt dizzy; he stumbled slightly and started to panic. What was wrong with him? He was so cold and he'd been out here so long, he realized he couldn't think straight. He wondered, was this woozy feeling caused by the brittle cold? He knew he wasn't properly dressed for a long distance stay out here, since he thought this would be a quick run and assumed there was no need for any extra clothing, but he didn't think it would have him feeling like this. About twenty minutes ago, he realized Black Bob was taking way too long to get here. It definitely didn't take an hour to walk eight blocks, Rasheen said to himself as he paced on unsteady feet trying vigilantly to keep his blood pumping. He wished he had a watch to see exactly how long he'd been waiting.

After what seemed like another twenty minutes slipped by, Rasheen was as numb and weather beaten as great grand mom's decrepit quilt hanging on a cloth line in the Artic Circle. His willpower to stay out in this treacherous cold was rapidly fading. The reality of knowing that Black Bob had turned his mom out on heroine, crack and angel dust, then made her a prostitute who he abused every time he laid eyes on her, was the only force capable of holding Rasheen out there in that brutally inhuman cold, and allowed his thoughts of hatred to run amuck in his mind. But his instinct was telling him he would kill himself if he remained out there any longer. Then, right on the heels of this premonition came that little voice, reminding him that it really didn't matter because by all standards he was already dead.

Rasheen decided to exit the alleyway for another whiff of fresh air. As he took his position near the curb and began walking in place to keep his blood circulating, Rasheen didn't realize a limousine had turned onto the block. Since Rasheen's head was turned in the opposite direction, and the vehicle's headlights weren't turned out, he didn't notice the Limo until it was dead upon him. When Rasheen turned and saw the Limo slowly cruising by, he almost panic and was about to bolt back into the alley, but common sense told him it was too late. Whoever was inside the Limo that had very dark tinted windows had apparently seen him. Rasheen watched the Limo until it disappear down the street and convinced himself it was nothing. It was probably some dudes showboating and getting high. He knew it was common practice for dudes to rent Limos, ride around the Hood with a carload of homies and girls getting high. Shit, he and his ace homie Jack Mack had done it twice before. Rasheen went back into the alleyway not giving the incident another thought.

After other thirty minutes crept by, it became obvious that Black Bob wasn't gonna show. Rasheen realized Bob must've changed his mind or something and went to another one of his whores' houses. Rasheen, with tears of defeat in his eyes, decided to head back home and try it again another day. Half delirious with hypothermia, Rasheen stepped from the alleyway and strutted down the street. After taking a dozen wobbly steps, he looked up ahead and saw a figure down the block and it looked like Black Bob and another man. While squinting and refocusing his eyes, Rasheen noticed the green Alaskan Parka and that was enough to confirm the ID. Lightening bolts of mind swirling adrenaline rushed to Rasheen's head, making him completely forget about the cold. Although he was trembling profusely as he held the 9mm in his pocket, it was apparent his shakes had nothing to do with the cold. Suddenly, he saw horrifying images flash across his mind; one of them was of him dying, the other was of him going to prison, leaving his brother alone to fend for himself, and another vision was of his mother dying. It seemed like everything was going in slow motion as Black Bob and the other man drew closer and closer and his heart started beating faster and faster. He was so glad he had on the new coat, since it was highly unlikely Black Bob would recognize him as long as he kept the hood on his head and in a position that blocked his face.

Rasheen started breathing faster when he was within a few yards of the two men. As he walked pass Black Bob and the other man, Rasheen's shoulder brushed the other man. In an instant, Rasheen pulled the 9mm, walked after the two, took careful aim at Black Bob's back in the same way he target practiced on empty Old English 800 Malt liquor quart bottles in the back of an abandon building on Halsey Street, and began squeezing the trigger. The loud ear-tormenting roar of the gun and Black Bob's body jerking from the impact of the four carefully placed bullets brought a thrill to Rasheen that had him in an elated state of mind.

The moment the first shot was fired the other man walking with Black Bob took off running while reaching for his weapon. He heard Bob hit the concrete with a hard thud as he made it behind a small red car and took aim.

Rasheen was so embroiled in the fact he was finally getting his revenge on Bob, he completely forgot about the other man. He fired two more shots into Black Bob's chest as he lay motionless on the ground and looked up at the other man behind the car. When Rasheen saw the man aiming a gun at him, he learned first hand why the saying, "my life flashed across my eyes" was used quite frequently because he saw it was true. Rasheen focused his vision and saw it was Killer Kato, the second biggest drug dealer in their Hood.

Killer Kato held the position as the thick smell of cordite faded rapidly. He instantly recognized the shooter was crack head Barbara's little crumb snatching rug rat. A smile began to creep on his face as though he was a proud father watching his son successfully ride a bike for the first time. His huge brown eyes, and his distinctly African pug nose could barely be seen beyond the hood covering his head. Killer Kato lowered his gun and said, "Little Nigga, you can't be creepin' like that. Boy, you about to get you damn wig peeled back." Kato was scanning the immediate area and saw there were no peeking toms in any of the windows. At least that's the way it looked. He looked over at Black Bob; he shook his head pitifully with a half-cocked grin. He had repeatedly told Black Bob he was going overboard with all that domestic abuse on those women, and he warned him that abusing them kids growing in the hood could definitely be hazardous to one's health. But, some folks had to learn things only one-way; the hard way. Killer Kato looked up at Rasheen. "Tomorrow, I want you to come see me about this shit, you hear me?"

Rasheen's heart was about to burst from his chest as he was stepping away. "Yeah, Killer Kato. I...I...I ain't mean to diss you, man, but that fuckin' nigga there be..."

"Get outta here!" Killer Kato shouted as he started heading down the street. "Come see me tomorrow!" Killer Kato took off running and shouted over his shoulder. "Don't make me come lookin' for you."

Rasheen bolted back towards his apartment. His brain was throbbing with so many different emotions, stressors and physical distress, he felt like he was on the Cyclone at Coney Island. He was trembling uncontrollably from both a mixture of cold, fear and delight. The closer he got to his house without being picked up by the cops, the more intense his thrill of victory grew.

When he arrived at his fire escape apparatus, he was breathing hard and realized that the run back to his crib had warmed him up to the point a small sheet of sweat was forming on his forehead and under his armpits. He climbed up the ladder and when he got to his bedroom window he saw all the lights were out in the room. Rasheen peered into the room and saw Lameek was in the bed asleep. An episode of rage was about to burst from his voice box, but he quickly curtailed the reaction. He couldn't blame Lameek for falling asleep, since he'd been gone probably three hours. Rasheen lightly tapped the window with his numbed fingernails. He saw Lameek didn't budge. A few seconds later, he tried it again, this time tipping a little harder with the same results. Rasheen sighed, took a seat, pulled his hood tighter over his head, and prepared himself for the long wait. As he savored the thought that Black Bob was laying dead over on Pacific Street with crazy bullet holes in his body, he realized the brutal cold wasn't that bad after all.

Chapter Two

Rasheen woke up to the screams of his mother. Yeap, she got the inevitable news. Word traveled fast in the Hood. Rasheen opened his eyes with a struggle as last night's drama entered his mind. He looked at the clock on the nightstand and saw it was 10 minutes after eight, and noticed Lameek wasn't in his bed. Hearing his mother's cries, he didn't know if he was more upset with her or Lameek? How could she be so distraught over this foul, low life, sadistic motherfucka, who didn't give a rat's ass about her! At times he wanted to slap some fuckin' sense into his mother. He also realized he was still upset with Lameek. This morning at 4 o'clock Rasheen had finally woke up Lameek when he shifted in his sleep and Rasheen tapped on the window just at the right moment. When Rasheen entered the apartment, he couldn't help but slap Lameek across the room. Without saying another word, Rasheen got undressed and went straight to sleep with Lameek begging him to tell him all about what happened.

Rasheen rolled over in his bed and clamped his pillow over his ears. Suddenly, Barbara burst into the room.

"Rasheen!" Barbara said in a whining voice with genuine tears in her eyes accompanied by huge bags under them; each eye had a bluish texture to them. "Somebody killed Black Bob."

Rasheen got out of bed with an attitude. He snatched his pants and put them on as he spoke with hostility in his voice. "That's good for him! I don't know why you be buggin', mom! Why should you care about that nigga! All he do is…"

Barbara charged at Rasheen with her pointer finger inches from his face. "That nigga was paying the fuckin' rent! Now, what the fuck am I supposed to do! Huh?"

Rasheen wanted to tell her to wake the fuck up and smell the coffee, since she didn't need a pimp to regulate her money. She could fuck and keep the money for her fuckin' self. But that would only inflame her even more, so he said, "I don't know, mom."

"You need to get your sorry ass out there and find a fuckin' job! And help me with some of these damn bills!" Barbara stomped out of the room, huffing and puffing. She needed a hit to calm her nerves; she raced into her bedroom, slammed the door, and found her crack pipe. She had two dime vials left and the usual thought of running out of crack terrified her. As she tapped a white rock into the stem of the pipe, she assured herself that everything was going to be all right. When she flicked the lighter, placed the flame to the stem, and the rock sizzled as she sucked in the cloud of smoke, all doubts vanished. Not only was everything going to be all right, but she also was instantly feeling all right as the cocaine raced through her system.

Rasheen finished getting dressed, brushed his teeth, drank a glass of kool-aid and was ready to walk Lameek to school. Twice he had to give Lameek the look of death when he started inquiring about the shooting adventure in a whispering tone of speech.

The moment they got out the apartment Lameek started up his inquiries like a nosy madman, since he knew outside was their usual place to talk about things that were meant to be safe from mom's omnipresence ears.

As they walked down President Street, Rasheen kept the story short and sweet, deliberately leaving Lameek fending for a blood gripping hood tale of blazing guns and baggy pants heroes with rap tunes swirling in their minds.

"When you gonna show me how to shoot yo' gun?" Lameek inquired.

"When you stopped fuckin' up in school." Rasheen said as he waited for the storm to follow.

"You ain't say that before!" Lameek's eyes were wide with anger. "You said you was gonna show me after you shot Black Bob."

"If you could learn that school stuff the way you know those raps, you'd be alright." Rasheen said. "You know damn near every rap song under the sun, but if I ask you what you learned in school you dumb out on me."

"That school shit is for the birds," Lameek said. "Rapping is real and that's what I wanna be, a rapper. I write good raps too and you know it. My shit is thorough. Look at you, you ain't in school."

"That ain't got shit to do with it," Rasheen knew this was coming since his baby brother always seem to latch on the theory that if Rasheen could do it, so could he. "Listen Lameek, I done told you my shit is different. I'm out here making shit happen so you don't have to do what I'm doing." He knew this was game at its best, but it always seemed to work. "Don't I be hitting you off?"

"Yeah, but you actin' like I gotta be on some white boy stuff, like I gotta be a brainy act or..."

"Ain't nothing wrong with being smart," Rasheen shouted. "And that ain't no white boy shit. Black folks is smart too. You see, that's why you shouldn't be getting crazy with the rap game because you gettin' shit all twisted. Now, for saying that dumb shit, I ain't teachin' you how to shoot my gat. I don't fuck with dumb niggas."

Lameek was shattered; he was on the verge of tears. "That's fucked up! Why you always gotta flip the script every time when you wanna make me do stuff."

"I'm only messin' with you." Rasheen punched Lameek in the shoulder with a brotherly smile. He loved the shit out of his baby brother and it tickle him silly at the way he was always able to push his buttons. "Stop whinin' like a little girl, nigga. You know my word is bond. Anything I say I'ma do I do it."

Smiling, Lameek said, "So when you gonna show me?" Lameek saw images of himself blazing away like the Terminator in the Movies.

"This weekend, I'll let you hang out with me and Jack Mack. We'll go shoot up some beer bottles and shit." Rasheen saw Lameek's face gleaming with happiness, and he wished he could find a way to make that look stay on his mug permanently. Seeing his brother happy always had a way of making him happy. There were only four people in his world he had any love for; mom, Lameek, Jack Mack and himself. He had Aunts, Uncles, first cousins and other distant relatives all over New York City, but he didn't care about them, since they didn't care about him.

After dropping Lameek off, Rasheen headed for Jack-Mack's crib. He could never understand why his mom, who was a straight up crack addict, wouldn't let him hang out in the crib during school hours, while Jack-Mack's mom would let him do whatever Jack Mack wanted, and she wasn't on crack. Although she drank like a mad Russian on the weekends, she never touched any other mind-altering substances. Rasheen made a pit stop at the weed house over on Hancock, brought two nickel bags and continued on his way. As he strutted down the street, his thoughts were running wild. He'd just smoked a muthfucka and it felt dam good! The nagging thought of having to go see Killer Kato came to mind, and the anxiety came to life. Killer Kato was one of the most thorough ballers in their Hood and he definitely earned the name Killer. Rumor had it that Killer Kato killed so many people even he lost count. Rasheen didn't want any drama with him; at least not now.

His mind started imaging all sorts of possible reasons why Killer Kato wanted to see him. Did he violate by killing Black Bob without putting him on point? Rasheen heard that in some situations, a cat wasn't supposed to get laid down without getting permission from the big dogs; that was the way the mafia did it; this led him to wonder was there some secret code he had missed. After tossing around a few more potential scenarios, he pushed the issue to the back of his mind and started focusing on other more pressing matters, like what was on his and Jack Mack's agenda for today? Who would be the unlucky victim to get robbed? Ever since Rasheen dropped out of school last year in the middle of the 8th grade, he'd been trying to come up with ways to make money.

There weren't many occupations in the Hood, and the choices were very limited. Drug dealing was at the top of the list, but everybody was doing it and Rasheen didn't have the stomach for it because it reminded him of so much pain; his mom came to mind every time he thought about slinging a few bags and that was enough to make him seek out a different line of work. There were other ways of getting paid like pimpin', boostin', jostlin', credit card scammin', and burglarizing people's homes. But for Rasheen the next best moneymaker was sticking up. This line work thrilled him because it was more action based than all other Hood occupations, and it took a lot of heart to role up on a person and take his shit. Although it was a naïve expectation, Rasheen vowed to get rich from robbing folks and move his mom out of this fucked up world of drugs, prostitution, rat and roach infested apartments and all the crabs in the barrel bullshit that came with poverty stricken people stuck in the ghetto. Ever since he was a child and was able to understand the pain and misery black folks were experiencing on a broad scale, he had always wanted to get his momma out of the hood and make her happy.

For years Rasheen had been doing an in-depth analysis of the power of money. Everybody needed it. Everybody wanted it. Some folks would kill for it. Other folks would flip on family for it. And money earned its title hands down as the root of all evil. If there was some drama in the air, you can bet money was behind it. Even if money wasn't the main cause, if you looked beyond the surface, beyond the underlying layers of facts, you can rest assured that money had its claws in there somewhere. Rasheen, like everybody else, loved money. He worshipped, cherished and praised that mean green. It was like the God of all Gods in his world. Another love was women. However, if there were a toss up between women and money, Rasheen would take the money every time. He'd learned when he was only seven years old that if you had the money you could get anything else after you got your pockets fat. Money was the epitome of power! Whenever he thought about this topic of money, he always remembered the lyrics in Whodini's rap song, One Love, which said, "I know what the Beatles were thinking of when they said that Money can't buy me love", and he wanted to meet Jalil so he could tell him to his face he was a motherfuckin' lair. Money could buy anything! Love, peace, happiness, and harmony! You name it money could buy it. Most of the celebrities had plenty money and from the way it looked to Rasheen they were well loved; they seemed to be happy and they were living in a state of peace and harmony. The complete opposite of what he saw all around him in a money deprived community.

But Rasheen also knew money was one of the strangest forces around. It seemed like the more money you got, the more you spent it and the more you needed it. In his Hood there was never enough of it. It wasn't an addictive drug, but once you started indulging in the acquisition of money you couldn't stop. This craving for money was almost as powerful as a crack addiction for some, and Rasheen fitted perfectly into this particular category.

Rasheen broke his daydream as he looked up and realized he was approaching Pacific Street. His heart started to beat a little faster even though the scene of the crime was about three blocks away. As he entered the intersection, he slowed his pace and looked down the street. He wasn't surprised to see a blue and white police car and a dark blue DT car in the middle of the street with stripes of yellow tape flapping in the wind. Rasheen caressed the 9mm in his coat pocket, grinned animatedly and picked up his pace. For the first time it struck him that his piece was hot; his baby had a body on it. According to the rules of common sense, he had to get rid of his precious 9mm and get a new one. He would have to go check out Bishop and see if he could workout a trade or something.

After some additional pondering, Rasheen realized that his 9mm was probably already hot as hell fire when he got it from that kid Kendu from East New York. His baby probably had a dozen bodies on it. There were very few guns running around the Hood that wasn't used in some kind of shooting, whether it was a murder or an assault. Rasheen also knew that most gun dealers in the Hood usually bought guns that were filthy with bodies from a distant Borough, like the Bronx or Queens, and then sold them to ballers in Brooklyn and visa versa. Very rarely was a gun thrown in the River. To the average money hungry gun trafficker it didn't matter who got caught with a gun with crazy bodies on it as long as it wasn't him.

Rasheen climb up the stairs of 345 Macon Street and, as usual, Jack Mack was playing his music loud with the bass rattling the walls. It was about 9:30 in the morning and Tupac was waking up the neighborhood. Rasheen couldn't believe how Jack-Mack was able to pull this off without anyone calling the cops. He never got around to asking how he did it, but one could obviously assume the neighbors either liked the music or was scared out of their minds of Jack-Mack and his thuggish antics. Rasheen hit the doorbell and a moment later the music was turn down only a few notches and Jack Mack opened the door with a blunt in his hand.

"Rasheen!" Jack Mack gave Rasheen some dap (tapped his clutched fist with Rasheen's fist) and ushered him inside. Jack was all smiles and his dark brown, chiseled facial features and his muscular physique was in accord with harmonious mood. "We was waitin' for you man."

Rasheen entered the living room, saw Lisa, Diana and Carmila, three classical chicken heads who all had sheer freak in their blood sitting around with cups and blunts in their hands. Quart bottles were all over the place. Rasheen smiled, snatched the blunt from Jack Mack and sat next to Carmila. She was three years older than him; she had a heart shaped ass and was drop dead gorgeous. Jack-Mack knew he had the hots for Camila and he gave Jack a big up for making moves to get her here. As he sparked up some petty conversation with Carmila, Rasheen realized he was slipping; they were supposed to be constructing a run for the day, but after seeing these fast boards, all that instantly became history. There was no doubt he very rarely put business in back of bullshit, but after last night's adventure and the anticipated meeting with Killer Kato, Rasheen knew he just had to get his skeet on, get his lady lovin' rod wet, get his freak on or any other phase you wanted call it.

As he got deeper into the dialog with Carmila it suddenly dawned on him. This was unusual. Why was Jack Mack celebrating? He played his music all crazy in the morning, but never did he party at this hour of the day. When he looked over at

Jack-Mack and they made eye contact, he instantly realized Jack-Mack knew about last night's run and was celebrating the fact he popped his cherry. By the smile on Jack Mack's face, Rasheen saw he was acting like a proud big brother. Jack-Mack was about three years older than Rasheen and had laid down two hood renowned thugs. No good, Rasheen thought. He had no intentions of ever telling anyone about the body; not even Jack-Mack, his best friend. After a moment of other facts coming into play, it hit him. Everybody knew Black Bob was beating flames out of him, Lameek and his moms. And if he was murdered, Rasheen definitely had a damn good motive to want to do it. Rasheen suddenly started to perspire. He never took any of these factors into consideration until now. That panicky sensation started to take hold of him.

Camilla looked Rasheen over. "Rasheen, you all right?"

"Yeah, I'm a'ight," Rasheen drew in a deep breath and let it out hard. "I was just wondering, why don't me and you go in the back room and kick it on another level?" He stood and squared off like a real live thug. He had to do something to clear his mind and fuckin' worked for him every time. He patted his back pocket to make sure he had the four packets of condoms.

Camila smiled, she'd always wanted to get with Rasheen on the sexual level. He was a little shorty, but he was fine! "Let's do this, boo." Camila rose to her feet and followed Rasheen.

Rasheen saluted Jack-Mack with a raised clenched fist and headed down the hallway to the bedroom. As he moved towards his destination, Rasheen made a note to have a nice long talk with Jack-Mack to find out if his assumptions were correct.

The moment Rasheen entered the bedroom he saw Camila was stepping straight to her business, peeling out of her clothes with a unique gracefulness and a golden smile. When Camila's huge, voluptuous breasts sprung from the confines of her bra, Rasheen's manhood stood at full attention and was practically ripping a hole in his pants, trying to make its presence understood. He went to her without further adue and started kissing, caressing her body, and navigating her towards the bed. By the time he fell on top of her, the only garment left to be removed from Camila's banging body was her thong style panties.

As Camila slid her panties off, Rasheen hastily undressed and resumed the kissing routine. Meanwhile, his hand began to explore Camila's womanhood; he was young but he knew it was wise practice to liven up that thang thang before going deep sea diving. His finger probed, swirled, dipped and dived energetically in and out, up and down, toying with her super slippery gee shot while his tongue danced with her tongue. Her moans and groans were causing the blood vessels in his joint to throb with a vibrant urgency. After the lovely fragrance of her womanhood was in the air, Rasheen knew she was ready and so he mounted Camila, determined to show and prove that a three year age difference didn't mean shit when it came to a fast cat like himself growing up in the Hood. When he began to pound deeper inside of her, he knew that she understood that the only thing that mattered was exposure; and since Rasheen had been exposed to sex at the age of nine, he had plenty experience by now, which showed in the way he rode Camila. When Rasheen exploded inside of her, she was convinced that he was a man-child in her promise land.

Chapter Three

After riding Camila for thirty-seven minutes, and busting off two nuts in the process, Rasheen exited the room buckling up his pants with a crazy smile. He sat next to Jack-Mack and kicked up a conversation while Lisa and Diana were in the kitchen cooking hamburgers and French fries.

"I gotta kick it with you, sun," Rasheen grabbed the bottle of Ballantine Ale, took a huge swig and said, "I need you to hold me down. I gotta go see Killer Kato about some shit."

"Killer Kato?" Jack-Mack was now at attention and was all ears. "What's the deal with that? You think it got something to do with Black Bob?"

Rasheen locked eyes with Jack-Mack. It was a fact; Jack-Mack knew what time it was. "What you heard about this Black Bob shit?"

Jack-Mack smiled. "I ain't hear shit. I just know you, sun. You a real live nigga, who ain't gonna let a mufucka keep dissing him."

Rasheen sighed, took another swig and said, "After we eat we gotta get rid of these boards and hit the bricks, sun. Before we figure out what we gonna do today, I'ma go check out Killer Kato. See what's happenin', you know. I need you to lay low outside his place…"

"Man, fuck that!" Jack-Mack said. "I'm going in with you. We been bangin' together with everything we do and this ain't no difference."

Rasheen suddenly realized he was acting real stupid trying to keep Jack-Mack in the dark about him bodying Black Bob. Jack-Mack had been rolling with him every since he was in public school, and it would be futile to continue trying to play dumb with him. "Alright, if you wanna roll we roll."

After Rasheen and Jack-Mack ate an earlier lunch with Camila, Lisa and Diana, they were out of Jack-Mack's crib. Rasheen and Jack-Mack told the girls they would meet up with them later at 8 o'clock tonight at the Abee Square Mall. Camila gave Rasheen a mean, exotic tongue kiss that announced to everybody that he had hit that thang really right, and everybody laughed jokingly while cracking jokes as they departed.

Rasheen and Jack-Mack headed towards Gates Avenue on their way to Killer Kato's game room over on Gates Avenue and Nostrand Avenue. They both had 9mms with an extra clip concealed within their baggy attire. As they strutted down the street, Jack Mack kicked up a conversation.

"Yo' you know that nigga, Kato got his hands in other shit besides drugs," Jack Mack said caressing the extra clip inside his coat pocket. "He got cats stepping to them rappers, pushing up on them on some security shit."

"I heard." Rasheen said looking at an elderly lady struggling with a shopping cart, feeling the urge to go help her because she reminded him so much of his deceased grandma. "It's supposed to be on the down low, but it's touching certain people's ears."

"That nigga got skills, sun; he pressured L-Cee and Big Willie Moe to put his people down with they security team; got on some real Al Capone shit. He basically told them cats that if his people ain't a part of that work force, won't be no peace at nobody's concert."

"I'm feelin' that," Rasheen said, remembering all the recent news reports of riots at various rap concerts, and wondered did Kato have his hands in all that drama. "So what you saying, that nigga be sending in motherfuckers' to fuck up shit unless his people eat?"

"That's exactly what I'm saying," Jack Mack said. "If the rumors are right and exact, he be running up on rappers, squeezing them to let his people eat and if they flip out, he shut they concerts down. One of them if we don't eat, nobody eat type thing."

Rasheen nodded his head and went into a silent cocoon as they turned the corner and were several dozen yards from the game room; he saw Jack Mack put on his screw face and zip lip expression. This was one of the reasons Rasheen enjoyed working with Jack-Mack; he was all business when it came time for work, and very rarely caught diarrhea of the mouth when it was time to do the do. Even when he was red from the trees they smoked, Jack Mack had the ability to stay focused, an attribution Rasheen had long since mastered and knew it was an ingredient needed to survive and flourish in their Hood.

Rasheen was the first to enter the game room. Wu-Tang's Thirty Six Chambers was booming on the jukebox and Rasheen saw the thirteen cats inside were officially thugged out, wearing screw faces and baggy clothing; some were showboating Rikers Island razor scars on their faces; they all wore their pants hanging off their behinds, and Rasheen had seen a few of them before at parties, hanging on various street corners and other places. Almost all of them were known heat-handlers and strong-arm specialists. A short, husky brother with a missing tooth approached Rasheen and Jack-Mack; his hard walk told everybody he was running things. After a moment, Rasheen recognized it was Ramrod, one of Killer Kato's top Lieutenants.

Ramrod gave Rasheen and Jack Mack hood style handshakes and said, "Killer's in the back waitin' for you," he gave Jack Mack a suspicious snare." He ain't say nothin' about you Jack Mack. I gotta ask him if it's cool for you to roll..."

"Killer Kato know how me and Ra role." Jack Mack said.
Rasheen chimed right in. "Whatever he got to say, he can say it to both of us."

Ramrod instantly locked eyes with Rasheen. This little mufucka think he the real deal, huh? Ramrod thought as he decided to lay his grill face game on Rasheen.

Rasheen stared back, handling the stare down, intimidation tactic like a veteran, not blinking or wavering once. He saw Ramrod's locked jawed grimace bounced back and forth between him and Jack-Mack. Then suddenly, he gave one of his nearby soldiers a head nod, and the soldier went through a blue door.

Meanwhile, Ramrod, Rasheen, Jack-Mack and the dozen other brothers inside the game room silently eyeballed each other the whole time it took for the soldier to return. The soldier came out the door, went to Ramrod, and whispered in his ear. When the soldier finished, he stepped back into his earlier position and Ramrod stared at Rasheen and then said, "He only wants to see you Rasheen."

Right on the heels of this comment all thirteen of the brothers inside the game room pulled out weapons, most of them had Mack 10 Uzis, while a few had Desert Eagles. They didn't take aim, but their grandstanding gestures made it clear the issue wasn't open for discussion.

Rasheen and Jack-Mack knew better than to even think about reaching for their weapons. Rasheen gave Jack-Mack a nod and headed for the door.

Jack Mack was smiling good naturedly, and then raised his hands playfully, "Hey dog, I'm in line, our all mighty emperor has spoken." He laughed to try to break the tension without much luck.

Rasheen stepped through the blue door and into the back room. He saw Killer Kato sitting behind a wooden desk with an ultra fine, light skinned sister massaging his shoulders. On the right side, he saw a muscular brother counting so much money it made Rasheen's head spin. There must've been at least five hundred grand on that table. Next to the stacks of bills was a huge assault rifle; it had to be an AK-47 Rasheen realized. Then on the left side was a huge bar with two men sitting with drinks in their hands. Rasheen didn't see their weapons, but any sane person knew they were heavily armed, and probably had a body count as high as any front line Vietnam veteran.

"Rasheen," Killer Kato said with a smile. His huge brown eyes, his distinctly African nose and his smooth, golden brown skin twinkled with a deceptively friendly glow. On first observation, no one would image he was a mass murderer and had brought a whole new meaning to the word ruthlessness. He rose to his feet and extended his hand and Rasheen shook it. Killer Kato waved for Rasheen to have a seat in the chair positioned in front of the desk in hot seat fashion.

Rasheen took the seat and was surprised he wasn't scared out of his mind.

"Listen Rasheen," Killer Kato sat back down. "I was feelin' you last night. You handled yourself like a genuine hitter. I also know you had every right to do what you did. But, in the game there are rules, and where there are rules there are consequences for those who break those rules." Killer Kato paused in order to allow his point to sink in.

Suddenly, Rasheen's heart started to pound. The word consequences told him he had fucked up and there was going to be a backlash.

Killer Kato continued, "Now, don't get it twisted, I don't give a fuck about that nigga Black Bob. He was a foul, bully ass nigga that loved beatin' up on the weak. He wasn't no coward, but a real nigga don't beat up on folks who can't fend for themselves. So, Black Bob, basically got just what he deserved. My problem is this. Black Bob owed me a hell of a lot of money. You killed him and now I can't get my money because the dead are not known to return from the grave. You feel me?" Killer Kato paused again, staring at Rasheen all the while.

Rasheen wondered was this the part he was supposed to say something. He was about to speak, but Killer Kato cut in.

"I don't take losses. I ain't took a loss since I was in public school about twenty five years ago. But, you Rasheen, got some choices here. I always give people choices. It's always healthy to pick and chose, cause then we have some control over our lives." Killer Kato smiled and paused again.

Rasheen swallowed hard and said, "So you saying I gotta cover Black Bob's tab he owed you?"

The room was deathly silent.

After a moment Killer Kato said, "That's it in a nice sweet nutshell."

Rasheen sighed, "So how much was it?"

Killer Kato saw he had him a nice little herb. Although Black Bob owed him five grand, Kato knew he could milk this kid for at least ten times that amount and also run those chumps out of that Miller Street spot he'd been trying to get his hands on for the last eight months. He liked Rasheen and saw this little shorty had mad heart, and he was definitely capable of killing. He also noticed he wasn't stupid and reckless like most young ass knuckle heads roaming the streets, doing some of the dumbest shit one could possibly imagine. He knew Rasheen was smart enough to know he couldn't go up against him and expect to win. Rasheen had independent thinker written all over him and his loyalty to whatever cause he got involved in was visible by the way he handled himself. Yeah, Killer Kato always kept his eye on any new raising star and made sure he found a way to make them understand who was boss around this motherfuckin' Hood. For what it was worth, he was gonna test the waters with Rasheen and Killer Kato said, "That bitch ass nigga owed me a hundred grand."

Rasheen almost passed out upon hearing those words. He was a vet at masking his inner responses to disturbing information, but this was way too much for him. "A hundred thousand dollars! Where…How the fuck you expect me to pay a tab like that?" Rasheen blurted out the word, not realizing what he said until the statement had rolled off his tongue and he couldn't take it back.

The room was engulfed by another deadly wave of silence. The vague sound of Method Man and Mary J. Blige's song, "You're All That I Need" was sliding under the crack of the door.

Rasheen quickly refocused himself; he felt subconscious by the way he just reacted and scolded himself inwardly for such a hasty, shook looking response. He hated to look weak and now he suddenly felt he had to prove he wasn't shook or soft, so he said in a too calm tone of voice. "That's a real big tab, man."

"Yes, it is." Killer Kato rose to his feet walked around to the front of his desk and sat on it. "I'm a realist, so I know this is something that can take time if you're dealing with petty, bullshit robberies like you're used to doing. But, before I go any further, I need to know are you gonna straighten out this thing? Ain't no sense in me laying down the important parts of the run, if you ain't down with it."

Rasheen was about to stare Killer Kato down, but his instinct told him Ramrod and Killer were two totally different people. He might be able to pull that shit off with a soldier, but not with the man who was running shit and bodying motherfuckers like murder was perfectly legal. After a moment, Rasheen said, "Do I really have a choice in this thing? I either play or pay is the way it's going down. But it would be nice if I can hear how I can fix this thing before I start picking and choosing."

Killer Kato smiled; he liked a young brother who was sharp on his toes and knew how to flip the bullshit back at the person dishing it out. "Check it, I hear you and your man Jack Mack like sticking up shit. It's sad ya'll two are letting those talents go to waste, crumb snatchin' petty ass shit like coats, gold chains and other silly ass kid shit. And after what I saw last night, you got a damn good handle on playing with them burners. Take it from me, Rah, you got the gift. Ain't many cats in the street built for handling hardware. Most of these cats out here don't think or plan shit, and that's why most don't survive."

Killer Kato paused as he went back around the desk and took a seat. Killer Kato then said, "Here's the deal. I got a run that could solve this thing in one nice smooth hit. You ever been to East New York?"

"Yeah, I been to the East." Rasheen said, hoping it wasn't to move drugs because he was not going bent and would have to try his luck.

"Well, I got a little headache over on News Lots and Miller Avenue. There's a drug spot in a building with a green door. It's the only door on the block with a green door and you can't miss it. On Fridays this place brings in at least a hundred and fifty grand. You hit it, bring me my hundred gees, and whatever's left is yours. Now, don't get it twisted, them niggas are heavily armed. If you ain't going in there to lay down a couple of mufuckas don't even think about fuckin' around."

The silence returned and Rasheen allowed his eyes to take in his surroundings as he thought about what was presented to him. After a moment Rasheen said, "No disrespect, but this sounds like a drug spot shut down. Sounds like those cats are taking all the business from you in that area and it's hurting your pockets. Why don't you just send a crew over there and knock 'em off? Why all the stick up kid stuff?"

Killer Kato was shocked but didn't show it. Shorty was sharp ass a Gillette razor. That's exactly what he was up to, but he didn't think his approach was that blatant. Killer Kato had to laugh it off in order to disguise the embarrassment he felt in front of his crew, since he'd told them earlier that Rasheen wouldn't figure it out. His crew, in robotic fashion, joined in the laughing charade. After ten seconds of laughter, Killer Kato stopped laughing suddenly and everyone stopped on a dime.

Rasheen felt a sheet of sweat forming on his forehead; he wanted to wipe it away, but didn't want to make any nervous gestures. Never let 'em see you sweat was what the voice in his head was saying as he humbly and respectfully allowed his eyes to wander.

Killer Kato said in a smooth voice. "You got a good eye, but contrary to your belief, the real reason I want you to do it is because I can kill two birds with one stone. Knock out a pain in the ass and get my mufuckin' money. How that sounds? Sounds like a wise move, wouldn't you say?"

Rasheen nodded his head, "Yeah, that make sense, a whole lot of sense."

"So what's it gonna be, Rasheen?" Killer Kato said point blank and then locked his eyes on Rasheen.

Now it was Rasheen's turn to hold the silence. Rasheen rode this soundless wave until he was certain it had irritated everyone in the back room and then said, "I'm in." He paused for a moment and then said, "I'm rollin' with just me and Jack Mack. I'm gonna need some serious hardware. Hey, dog, you know I'm only seventeen and I ain't used to fuckin' around with the big boys, so I'm gonna need all the help on the fire power tip I can get."

Killer Kato smiled, and realized he had to find a way to get this little smart-ass nigga on his team. He could be a major asset. But, then, that little voice in the back of his head was telling him Rasheen was the type you didn't want around you because he was the kind that could knock you off your throne if you weren't on top of your game. As usual, Killer Kato's arrogance wouldn't allow him to seriously entertain such a scenario on a serious level and decided he was going to get Rasheen down with his team one way or the other. He would be an excellent clean up man. Pulling him out and cutting him lose on the competition, only at times when there was a need for major cleaning. It kind of reminded him of how he came up the ranks from street thug to drug king pin, with hopes of soon turning it all into a legitimate empire. "Say no more. I'll get you whatever you need."

Rasheen smiled, and from that point forth his world took off like a rocket escaping the earth's atmosphere. But, the only difference between the rocket and Rasheen was that when the rocket ripped through the several layers of the atmosphere it burned away most of the spacecraft; with Rasheen it would work in the reverse.

Chapter Four

Rasheen sat in the back seat of the stolen blue Ford Taurus, scanning the late night streets of East New York. Dirty Ricky was behind the wheel and Jack-Mack sat next to him. Humming through the car speakers in a low volume was the song 187 on an undercover cop by Snoop Doggy Dog and Dr. Dre. Dirty Ricky was a fanatic for west coast rap songs and never went anywhere without some west coast rap tape in his pocket; he was so caught up in the west coast fervor, he even wore jerry curls, dark shades, and could easily pass for an Easy E wanna be. It was about 2 o'clock in the morning on a Thursday night in the month of March, and just as it was during their several dry run rehearsals no one except a few crack and heroine addicts were roaming Miller Street on the corner of New Lots Avenue.

Rasheen was still a little apprehensive about Dirty Ricky's involvement with this run, since he had a notorious history of gossiping and loved to brag and boast about the things he'd done. Although they made Ricky promise not to talk about this run ever, Rasheen knew once a bragger, always a bragger. If they could've found someone else who knew how to drive a car and who they trusted beside Dirty Ricky, they would have enlisted him. Rasheen vowed that after this run he would learn how to drive. Rasheen pulled from his front waist the Glock 9mm with the screwed on silencer and admired the weapon for the hundredth time. Killer Kato sure knew about guns, and the crazy fuck even had an arsenal like the guy in that movie he saw last week with Arnold Schwarzenegger in it. In his back waist, Rasheen also had a mini Tech 9 with a twenty-five round clip, but it was a weapon he was used to seeing, so he didn't have to constantly savor the sight of this particular weapon. This Tech 9 also had a makeshift silencer that Ramrod said was good for one complete clip; after this one clip was consumed, the silencer "probably won't work anymore."

In fact, the Tech 9 silencer looked like some shit the neighborhood Uncle Earl, chop shop butcher mechanic had concocted in his basement with rinky-dink parts he found in the local garbage dump.

Looking at the Glock silencer, another thought entered Rasheen's mind. He'd heard that if a person got caught with a silencer he could get life in jail. The prospect of going to jail for life was an extremely disturbing reality, and would have the power to make most folks pause with the intent of reconsidering whatever it was they were doing. But not Rasheen; the need for money was just far too overwhelming. If anything, the prospect of not having money was far more disturbing than going to jail. In any event, life was all about taking chances. Shit, whenever a person stepped foot out of their home to go to the store, there was a chance he or she could be murdered, so why not take a chance getting rich?

Rasheen picked up his miniature binoculars and peered through them. The lookout, a Latino man wearing a forest green hoody, was leaning against a light post, looking like he didn't have a care in the world. Rasheen put the binoculars down and the fact that Killer Kato had a dope and coke spot just a few blocks over on Bradford and Hegeman came to mind. They had drove pass that spot several times and Rasheen could see why Killer Kato was uptight with these green door cats. They were taking all the business. Rasheen wanted to tell Killer that maybe if he got some better product, he'd boost the number of his customers, but he didn't want to offend him with a suggested solution that even a retard should know. Plus, in Killer Kato's world there was no such thing as free enterprise, or fair trade and competition. Rasheen also wasn't feeling the way Killer Kato wanted them to run up inside the spot. It was obvious Killer Kato maneuvered the plan so that there would have to be some major gunplay. At first Rasheen resisted the idea of them catching the runner just as he walked out of the spot, but upon further scrutiny, he realized it was not only a workable plan, but it also was the safest way to guarantee that they would get inside the spot. Either way, it really didn't matter to Rasheen or Jack-Mack how they did it, or whether or not there would be heavy gunplay, so long as they got the money, Rasheen was down for any plan.

The most pervasive issue that hung around with lingering enthusiasm had to be the one dealing with Black Bob owing Killer Kato a hundred gees. Rasheen had been tossing this enigma around in the deep regions of his mind ever since Killer dropped that bomb on him. How the fuck could a dope fiend, fake ass pimp end up owing a gun slinging drug dealer all that money? Ain't no way Killer would let a dude like Black Bob run up a tab that big. No sane baller would allow credit to reach a level of a hundred gees. Rasheen wasn't no drug dealer, but he knew enough about the drug game to know it would be hustling backward to start giving a hardcore dope addict huge credit of that nature. Black Bob loved to get high, but ain't no way in the fuck he smoked, sniffed and drunk up that much shit. Rasheen wondered for the umpteenth time was Killer Kato playing him? In the Hood, everybody was always trying to hustle someone; especially predators like Killer Kato, who lived at the top of the food chain when it came to the acquisition of fast, dirty and bloody money. Rasheen shook loose of this particular reverie because it was getting him real tight and right now he needed to be focused.

No sooner than Rasheen re-harnessed his attention to the situation at hand, the cranberry Cadillac pulled up carrying the two targets. Dirty Ricky turned off the car cassette player, cutting off Snoop Doggy Dog in mid-sentence. Rasheen immediately put on his black leather gloves as he watched the Cadillac park on the corner of Miller street and Vermont Avenue in ritualistic fashion, and a man wearing a black hoody and baggy blue jeans got out the passenger side of the car, long strutting down Miller Street towards the spot. Rasheen was glad most drug runners usually did not park in front of their drug spot when picking up money and dropping off drugs; they usually tried to pretend they were customers just in case the police were watching from some nearby location. This ploy had its good points, but it also had its down side because it obviously allowed stick up kids like Rasheen, Jack-Mack and Dirty Ricky to maneuver more effectively.

Rasheen felt that familiar surge of anxiety circulating through his veins; his heart began to pound in his chest, his breathing increased, and the palm of his hands were becoming clammy. It was going down and the biological reactions in his body knew it was going to be a night to remember. When Rasheen saw the runner enter the intersection of Miller Street and New Lots Avenue, he started getting out of the car. By the time he was heading towards the parked Cadillac, the runner had entered the spot. In accordance with the plan, Jack-Mack waited until Rasheen was half way down the block and then got out the Ford Taurus and followed.

Rasheen gripped the Glock tucked inside the pocket of his hoody as he casually headed towards the Cadillac. Redman's song, "Time for some action" was coursing through his mind as he walked in step with the booming beat of the bass inside his head. "Ti-Time for some action! Ti-Time for some—Time for some action!" Redman's unique lyrical voice replayed itself in Rasheen's head. When Rasheen was feet from the Cadillac, he pulled the Glock 9mm and held it to his side. He took four more paces and in a flash Rasheen aimed and fired two shots through the passenger side window hitting the man sitting in the driver seat with both bullets. Rasheen loved the way the silencer equipped 9mm sounded and how the strips of fire violently flicked from the barrel as the bullet tore out of the gun and into the intended target. Little glass cubelets were strolled all over the immediate area the second the bullets cut through the car's window.

Jack-Mack was moving up the rear closely observing all the nearby tenement buildings. By the time Jack reached the car, Rasheen had opened the door, pushed the dead black man to a laying position and was fumbling inside the glove compartment. Suddenly, the trunk opened with a barely noticeable buzzing sound.

Rasheen sprung out of the car, quietly closed the door, and rushed to the truck as Jack Mack stood guard watching in every direction. Rasheen opened a brown paper bag. Bingo! There were stacks of bills wrapped in rubber bands. Rasheen hastily searched the trunk and within seconds he realized the brown bag was the entire stash from the drug runner's earlier cash pickups from drug spots all over the area. Rasheen snatched the bag, closed the trunk and headed towards the spot. About ten paces later he saw the trash can, quickly left the lid and sat the bag of money inside. Rasheen and Jack-Mack continued down the street. Rasheen looked at his watch. It was five minutes to three. The first part of the run went perfect. With hands tucked in the pockets of their hoodies, they crossed the street and saw the lookout staring at them in his usual nonchalant fashion. About two weeks ago, they had sent Dirty Ricky to attempt to cop some drugs while the runner was inside, so they currently knew how the lookout might react as they approached, and they had devised a plan for that as well.

Unbeknownst to Rasheen and Jack-Mack there was another lookout stationed in a third floor apartment #3D in the tenement building directly across the street from the green door spot. The big difference from this lookout from the street lookout was that this one had a 30.06 sharpshooters rifle with a hi tech scope. As Rasheen and Jack-Mack crossed the street, seconds from confronting the street lookout, the back up security man, as his employer called him, was dozing off as he struggled to keep his eyes opened. He sat by the window, but had a portable TV nearby where he could watch TV and with the mere turn of the head he could also watch the streets below.

Rasheen and Jack-Mack continued walking as though they weren't interested in entering the drug spot, walking right pass the lookout without saying a word. After ten paces, they quickly slid inside the green door and the lookout came running after them shouting, "Yo! Yo! Hold up, bro!"

In the third floor apartment, the back up security man woke up and looked out the window just as the street lookout entered the building. He yawned, sighed and now started watching the TV with sleepy eyes.

Inside the hallway of the drug spot Rasheen and Jack-Mack had their weapons in their hands. Jack Mack was positioned behind a corner near the staircase about twenty feet from the door, while Rasheen was on the side of the door. The lookout barreled through the door moving rapidly towards the staircase, Jack Mack stepped from behind the corner and opened fire.

SZK! SZK!

The two silenced shots struck the lookout square in the chest and Rasheen raced up behind him and caught him in a bear hug embrace just before he was about to fall to the floor. Rasheen dragged the dead man over to the staircase and tucked him underneath it. Rasheen looked at his watch, hoping this wasn't going to be a long wait.

The security man in the third floor apartment across the street looked out the window again and wondered why Jose was still inside the spot? He'd been inside almost five minutes; the security man knew this extended delay was definitely unusual. The 30.06 totting security man instantly concluded that Kano, the runner, was probably chewing another ass hole on Jose for leaving his post earlier. He'd warned Jose about doing that dumb shit and now he had to pay the price for that fuck up. He decided to wait a couple of more minutes and then he would call Kano on his cellular phone to remind him that Jose needed to be on his post, not inside getting a verbal lashing of his life.

Inside the hallway in front of the steel gate Rasheen and Jack-Mack stood with guns in hand, ready and waiting. Rasheen kept looking at his watch every minute and he had to force himself to stop fidgeting. Just beyond the steel gate Rasheen and Jack-Mack could hear two men speaking Spanish. Rasheen also kept his eyes on the door in back of them; he was hoping and praying a customer would not enter because there was no doubt he or she would be killed. Another thought entered is mind and turned his blood to ice. What if the police decided to do a full blown raid and found them standing in front of this door with guns and a dead body several feet away under the staircase? Rasheen had to force himself to stop thinking all these pessimistic thoughts because they were unfocusing his mind.

Suddenly, the heavy locks on the steel gate started unfastening, sounding like huge bolts on a prison gate slamming open. Rasheen and Jack Mack took aim as they held their breath. Rasheen saw everything suddenly moving in slow motion. The second he saw the face of the Latino runner, the fireworks went off like a Chinese New Year celebration. Rasheen shot the runner twice in the chest as Jack-Mack shot the other man but only one of the two bullets fired made contact and only grazed him at that. The grazed man frantically ran inside screaming while reaching for the Uzi tucked in his waist. Rasheen ran after him firing at the fleeing man's back. Just as the man turned with the Uzi in his hand, Jack-Mack came up along side of Rasheen firing his weapon. The man with the Uzi was doing a crazy dance of death, and it appeared as though the 9mm bullets from both Rasheen and Jack-Mack's weapons were holding him up in the same fashion as a puppeteer does to his doll attached to the strings. Suddenly, the man dropped to the floor and literally had smoke oozing from his body.

As Rasheen and Jack-Mack frantically searched for the money and the drugs, the smell of gunpowder was heavy in the air. Rasheen retrieved the bag full of money the runner was carrying and electricity swirled through his body when he opened it and saw all that money. He saw himself getting his momma that house he always promised with just this one run; then as he ran towards the back rooms to make absolutely certain they didn't leave anything, reality hit him. He had to give a hundred gees of this money to Killer Kato and then Jack-Mack and Dirty Ricky had to get their cut. It didn't take a mathematician to figure out after the smoke cleared he would barely have enough money to have a good time with his girl Crystal. He quickly shifted his thoughts and pulled his mind back to the mission at hand.

Suddenly, a buzzing sound came from the drug runner laid out on the floor and both Rasheen and Jack-Mack nearly had a heart attack as they spun around locking their aim on the man on the floor. After a moment, Rasheen realized it was the runner's cellular phone.

In the apartment across the street the security man was now becoming very worried. He instantly grabbed his 30.06 while he had the cellular phone glued to his ear. Something was wrong. Very wrong. Jose hadn't come back out. Kano wasn't answering his fucking phone. This shit is fucked up, the security thought with terror racing through his system because if he let something happen, Cowboy was going to kill his ass for sure. He slammed the phone down and tried to calm down without much luck.

Rasheen and Jack-Mack concluded they found all the drugs and the money. They had a tote bag full of drugs and a black plastic garbage bag half filled with money. They exited the apartment with lightening speed. As they raced for the green door, Rasheen suddenly felt weird and he stopped in his tracks just as his hand touched the doorknob. Jack-Mack stopped and stared at him with squinted eyes. Rasheen's instinct was turned on full blast. There was something about that cellular phone suddenly ringing and it was getting under his skin. All sorts of crazy scenarios were tumbling around in his mind. Could there be another backup roaming around? Could there be another lookout?

"What's wrong, Rasheen?" Jack-Mack was looking around the immediate area as if he could find the answer to his question within their circumference.

"I…I don't know." Rasheen cracked the door and peeked out looking everywhere and he instantly saw the open window across the street with a man in the apartment; he looked agitated and had something in his hand. From Rasheen's vantage point he couldn't make out what it was, but common sense told him to assume the worse. Rasheen pulled back and quietly closed the door and said to Jack-Mack, "They got somebody across the street on the third floor."

Jack-Mack stepped in front of Rasheen and peeked out the door in the same fashion Rasheen had done. After a moment, he pulled back as he quietly closed the door. With a cocky grin, Jack-Mack said, "I say we rush out with blazing guns."

Rasheen smiled back, "Fuck it, let's do it!"

They both reloaded their weapons.

"On the count of three," Rasheen said, "One, two, three!"

They burst out the door firing silenced bullets at the window while running towards the intersection.

The security man was caught completely off guard and the only thing he could do was duck down out of the path of the silenced bullets. The explosive realization that the spot was being robbed and he had let these two motherfuckers get inside, catapulted him up and into a terror-stricken charge to the other room window where he could get a clear shot at the two guys in hoodies running towards the intersection.

Rasheen and Jack-Mack were seconds from entering the intersection on their way to get the brown paper bag containing the money stashed in the trash can when loud shots rang out. Rasheen felt a savage gust of wind zoom pass his head and knew it was a bullet that had just missed him since the breeze was felt at the same moment he heard one of the loud explosions.

Rasheen and Jack-Mack scrambled for cover behind a black car as the bullets tore at everything near them. By the shocked look on their faces, it was evident a surge of panic was racing through their minds. Rasheen instantly realized they weren't able to get to the brown paper bag without getting shot. With some relief, he saw they could duck walk to the end of the block behind the park cars until they got to the corner and then could zip down Bradford Street and get to their get away car. Rasheen saw Jack-Mack detected this only escape route as well and didn't have to be told the plan, since he led the way and Rasheen followed.

Seconds later, Rasheen and Jack-Mack were running at top speed down Bradford Street and looked as though they were competing in the Olympic 100 meter race. They reached the Blue Ford Taurus in thirty seconds flat, jumped in the car and Ricky hit the gas pedal.

"Hold up!" Rasheen shouted, breathing extremely hard, "We gotta get the bag of money!"
Dirty Ricky slammed on the brakes, stopping the car with a head-jerking jolt.

"Hold up!" Jack-Mack spitted the words out in sheer exhaustion. "After...after all them shots, the...the police'll be here any second!"

The thought of losing all that money had Rasheen utterly shattered. It would drive him insane knowing he left all that money. But sanity did call for a hasty escape. Rasheen knew he had to do something very fast, and whatever he intended to do, he'd better do it in a now or never fashion.

Rasheen frantically opened the car and spoke just as frantic. "I'ma get the money! Meet me on the next block over! I'll cut through some backyards and meet you there." Rasheen bolted down Miller Street.

Dirty Ricky decided to wait until he saw Rasheen was second from his destination. Just when he placed the car's gear in drive, he saw a blue and white police car turn down Miller Street.

With flinching speed, Jack-Mack and Dirty Ricky crouched in their seats.

Moments earlier, Rasheen reached the trashcan, snatched up the lid and the second he seized the brown bag, he saw the beam of the car headlights sweep over him from the direction he came. In one smooth motion, Rasheen dropped the lid back on the trashcan, and charged into the nearby alleyway in between the two brown stone three stories houses.

Rasheen moved rapidly to the backyard. When he arrived at the tall, wooden fence, Rasheen panicked; the fence was virtually impenetrable. It was about eight feet tall and there was no way to climb it.

Suddenly, Rasheen heard the car on the street come to a stop. He was expecting whoever was driving the car to continue on their way, but it apparently didn't. Rasheen ducked behind the house and peered around the corner. He couldn't see whomever it was getting out of the car. Suddenly, the sound of a walkie-talkie crackled, and Rasheen flinched as though he was stabbed with a sharp object. Terror gripped him; it was obvious the vehicle that just pulled up was a police car. He was trapped and now he had to make the decision of his life. Should he shoot his way out of this situation? Or should he hide his Glock and the money, and hope and pray the police didn't find it and make the connection that he was the culprit responsible for the four nearby homicides? It took a fraction of a second for him to figure this one out. Rasheen would take his chances with a blazing gun.

Moments earlier, the police officers inside the patrol car had turned onto Miller Street to investigate a report of gunshots. Just as the headlights of the car lit up the street in front of them, they say a figure dash into the alleyway. They both decided to check it out.

In the third floor apartment across the street from the green door, the security man was having a genuine shit fit. His bowels were growing weaker by the seconds, and he had to keep his butt cheeks clamped very tightly, since he knew he was facing a death sentence if Kano was dead. Kano didn't answer his phone and this meant he was apparently incapacitated or dead. The fact that the two men he shot at moments ago had silenced weapons made it difficult to hold on to the possibility that Kano and Jose were still alive. Trembling with mind twirling distress, the security man knew if he allowed the stick-up kids to get away and he was unable to kill even one of them, the wrath might even spill over onto his family. Suddenly, the security man saw a crack head approaching the spot. It was foul, but he needed to lay a body out in the streets to at least show he was on his job. With that, the security man took aim, lined his infrared sights on the straggly dressed Latino man's head and let his trigger finger ride.

With flashlights in their hands, the two cops were less than twenty paces from turning the corner of the houses where Rasheen was standing with his Glock 9mm aimed when the loud gun shot went off. Both cops frantically retreated out of the alleyway and into their patrol car with hysterical haste. With tires screeching the patrol car barreled towards New Lots Avenue.

Rasheen ran to the entrance of the alleyway, saw the patrol car racing away, and he fled in the opposite direction. With the brown paper bag filled with money tucked under his arm as if it was a football, Rasheen ran as fast as he could.

Twenty minutes later, Rasheen was in the back seat of the Ford Taurus breathing hard as the car turned onto Atlantic Avenue, heading back to do or die Bed-Stuy. During the twenty-minute ride back to Jack-Mack's house, there was a limited amount of talk in the car. They all wanted to celebrate, pull out the champagne and bring on the dancing girls, but they all knew this run wasn't complete until they ditched the car and was in the confines of Jack-Mack's crib, counting all that lovely money.

They ditched the car over on Bedford and Gates Avenue, wiped it clean of all fingerprints and walked back to Jack-Mack's house on Macon Street. When they entered Jack-Mack's house, they saw Jack's mom was gone as usual. She practically lived with her boyfriend and always left Jack along, and Jack-Mack loved it just that way. When they dumped the money and the drugs on the living room coffee table, Rasheen, Jack-Mack and Dirty Ricky finally started celebrating. "Yeah!...It's on!...We hit the mufuckin' jackpot! It's gone be a party up in this here mufucka! Believe that shit!" They screamed in delight with smiles, hugs, hi-fives, and even crazy awkward dance skits, while imaging all the fun and partying they were going to soon be embroiled in.

It took them an hour to conclude they had came off with $110,035 in hard cash, and 2,543 bags of coke and heroine.

This was the part Rasheen had been dreading the most. How as he going to take a hundred gees of this money after they murdered four men and risked life, limb, and life bids in prison, and then turn it over to Killer Kato? Rasheen leaned back on the sofa while Jack-Mack and Dirty Ricky continued counting the money with mad cool-aid smiles plastered on their faces. Here again was the part where he had a choice. According to Killer Kato choices were a healthy way to give people the illusion that they had some control over their lives. Rasheen easily assessed that he had three options. Option number one; he could pay Killer Kato and get this chump out of his hair. Option number two, he could say fuck Killer Kato, don't pay him shit and deal with the consequences, which would probably be a death sentence for him and his family as well. And finally, option number three, he could pay Killer Kato a major chuck of the debt, and split the rest with his team; that way everyone got something and it could avert the worse of the drama. Killer Kato was a foul cat, but if he thought he was getting most of the money they came off with, he would hold tight. Rasheen knew this choice had a down side to it because now he had to do another run to finish paying Killer. Plus, knowing this cutthroat nigga, he would definitely want interest. After two minutes of contemplation, option number three won by a landslide.

Rasheen shot the idea pass Jack-Mack and Dirty Ricky, and surprisingly they both agreed without a debate. Killer Kato would get fifty gees, while they each retained 20 thousand dollars. They decided to sell the drugs to Dirty Ricky's cousin Kamron who had a few spots over in East Flatbush. They haggled over the price, but after a short debate they agreed to sell the whole bag for a straight five gees that would be split three ways.

Rasheen looked at his watch and saw it was 4:30 in the morning. He decided to call it night, took his share of the money and Killer Kato's and left. Dirty Ricky decided to stay back and smoke a few blunts with Jack-Mack. Before leaving, Rasheen made a note to the both of them to go real easy on the splurging because they had to make it appear as though they only got a little over 3 thousand each. Rasheen planned to tell Killer Kato that they only caught the green door for a grand total of 60 gees and he was giving Killer Kato the bulk of the money, 50 gees. Jack-Mack and Dirty Ricky adamantly agreed they would control their spending and Rasheen left.

Rasheen got to his house at about a quarter to five, entered the tenement building, and heard noise coming from upstairs. Rasheen pulled his Glock and crept up the stairs. The pungent odor of crack attacked his nose as he ascended up the stairs. When he reached the third floor, several feet from the door of his apartment, Rasheen saw two, crusty looking crack-heads sitting on the steps with crack pipes and Bic lighters in their hands. They had the flames of the lighters glued to the tip of the glass pipes while sucking feverishly on the other end.

"What the fuck is this?" Rasheen asked with pure venom in his voice. "This ain't no mufuckin' crack house."

The closest crack head, who was as black as tar and hadn't combed his hair for what looked like at least three months, looked up as though he just realized Rasheen had appeared even though he'd been standing there for a few seconds. His eyes were wide and crazy looking. He was as skinny as a piece of straw and his clothing were utter rags. His partner was a virtual carbon copy, but the only difference was his complexion was much lighter and his hair was wavy, as if he was mixed with Latino or something.

The black, nappy head crack head was staring at the black garbage bag in Rasheen's hand as he rose to his feet. "Hey, little man, what you got in that bag, bro?" He towered over Rasheen when he was fully erected. The other crack head rose to his feet while stepping on the third step and was also smiling crazily; he too had Rasheen by at least a foot.

Rasheen smiled as he looked up at the dusty black crack head. These fouls were planning to jack him for his shit, huh? He felt in the mood for a nice little mind game, so he took a few steps back, opened the bag, reached in and pulled a stake of hundred dollar bills, waving it in the air and said in his most innocent voice, "Well, let's see here, I think it's a bag full of money."

The crack heads eye grew larger than the hubcaps on an 18-wheeler.

Rasheen instantly tossed the bundle of money back in the bag, and tossed the whole bag in back of him, pulled the Glock from his waist and took aim. "Nigga, you wanna die tonight?"

Both crack heads looked liked they suddenly became sober and their eyes had shrunk almost to the size of a squinting Chinese.

Rasheen stepped up to the tall crack head, and pushed him into a sitting position on the first stair. With a wave of the Glock, the other crack head sat down as well. Rasheen grabbed the black crack head and tried to stick the barrel of the Glock inside his mouth, but his clinched teeth were blocking its entry. "Nigga, if I gotta tell you to open your mufuckin' mouth I'ma shoot my way through them yellow ass teeth of yours."

The crack heads month snapped open and the barrel eased its way in until he started to gag.

With the gun barrel caressing the crack heads tonsils, Rasheen said, "Listen up, mufucka!" Rasheen eased up on the crack head's tonsils when he started gagging to the point of throwing up. "That includes you to, bitch!" He said to the wavy hair crack head, who flinched into full attention. He saw smirk appear on his face and Rasheen spit dead in his face. "Twist up your face one more time nigga, I'll kill..." Rasheen snatched the Glock from the mouth of the nappy head crack head, and slapped the wavy haired crack head in the face with the weapon; the blow was so hard the man's head collided with the hand railing. As the crack head cringed in agony, Rasheen reinserted the gun inside the mouth of nappy head. "If I "EVER" catch you smoking that shit in this building again, I'ma blow your mufuckin' top!"

The apartment door in back of him was snatched open and Barbara and a man who was fastening his pants rushed out. When

Barbara saw it was Rasheen, she rushed over while shouting, "Rasheen, what the fuck are you doing?"

The wavy hair crack head lit up with hope as if a life raft was thrown to him just in the knick of time, "Barbara, we was just sittin' here waitin' for you to call us in, and this little nigga here came…"

"Waitin' for her to call "YOU" in?" Rasheen felt a lightening bolt strike his heart. His finger almost pulled the trigger on the Glock still cramped in the crack head's mouth at the thought of these mangy, diseased looking crabs having any contact with his mom. "What the fuck you mean you was waitin' for her to call YOU in! In for WHAT, nigga!"

Barbara heard the rage in Rasheen's voice and ran to him, "Rasheen, no, don't do it, please, baby let him go, don't shoot him." She caressed his arm and wasn't totally surprised he had a gun since almost every kid in the neighborhood had one.

Rasheen felt something snapped inside his mind as he imagined these dirty dudes throwing a train on his mom; one hittin' her from the backside, doggy style, while the other had her performing a blowjob on him. He held the Glock inside the crack head's mouth as he clinched his teeth so hard he heard ringing in his ears. He had to do something about his mother, since this was about as low as she could go. In that moment, he decided this shit was going to STOP! Rasheen let his rage guide him. "Get the fuck up, Nigga!" He grabbed the black crack head by the collar, yanked him to his feet and planted the Glock to his back as he ushered him to the flight of stairs leading down to the second floor. Rasheen took several steps back, charged and kicked the man down the flight of stairs. The man didn't touch a single stair as he glided down to the next floor and crashed landed in a sickening, bone breaking fashion.

"Stop it, Rasheen!" Barbara screamed and pleading, but she saw Rasheen was in the zone. "Oh, God, Rasheen, don't do this!"

The crack head moaned and groaned as he struggled to his feet and stumbled down the next flight of stairs and out the building.

Rasheen turned with the gun aimed at the wavy hair crack head, "Your turn, nigga!"

Remarkably, the crack head came to Rasheen with his head bowed and stood at the same location where his partner stood moments ago, waiting for the inevitable.

"I said stop it!" Barbara pleaded, trying to pull Rasheen away, but he viciously snatched his arm away.

Rasheen took several steps back, ran and kicked the crack head with everything he had in him, catapulting the crack head down the flight of stairs; he too didn't touch a single stair as he glided down the flight of stairs and landed with a thunderous crash. He stumbled to his feet and limped out the building, muttering a series of incomprehensible remarks under his breath.

Rasheen turned with the Glock aimed at the black man who exited the apartment with Barbara. "Let's go, bro, ain't no discrimination 'round here!"

With a trembling voice, the man babbled, "Barbara, calm yo' damn son down now. Come on, man, I didn't come here to…"

Rasheen rushed towards the man and placed the Glock on his forehead. "You got a choice mufucka! A bullet to the head or trip down the stairs? You gone fly or die, believe that shit!"

The man rushed over to the same spot where the others stood. Rasheen was boiling with rage now, and since this particular crack head had the audacity to challenge him, Rasheen decided to teach his a lesson or two; he ran and kicked him even harder than he did the other two. The man took off like a rocket, his head struck the bottom of the staircase leading up to the roof, twirling the man into a reverse back flip as he glided down to the second floor, crash landing on his back with nerve wrecking force; the thunderous impact even made Rasheen cringe. By the way the man slammed to the floor, Rasheen just knew he had catch a body, but he was furious and didn't give a fuck.

Rasheen yelled down the stairs as the man staggered to his feet, "If I ever see you in this building again, I'ma push yo' mufuckin' wig back, yah heard?" He turned, glaring at his mom like a raging bull. With flinching speed he grabbed his mom by the collar of her raggedy housecoat, scaring her clean out of her mind. Her eyes were wide with a genuine fear; she knew she had fucked up royally, and thought it was her turn to get kicked down the flight of stairs. Rasheen snatched the black garbage bag and practically dragged her inside the apartment.

Once inside the apartment, Rasheen tossed his mom onto the beat up sofa. He saw Lameek was now up, looking like he'd just been snatched out of a deep sleep.

Rasheen tossed the black garbage bag on the table, and said, "Lameek, you might as well hear this shit, since it deals with all of us."

Barbara didn't know what to do; she couldn't believe her son was acting like this; he'd always humble himself to her. What in the world got into him? She was literally afraid of him. But, then suddenly she realized after struggling to clear her mind of the crack surging through her bloodstream, this was her son and she was the parent. She rose and said, "Rasheen, now you know better than to be disrespecting me like that…"

"Disrespecting you!" Rasheen screamed as he came at her. Upon seeing her flee from him in a terror-stricken fashion as though he would really do serious harm to her, he felt real bad. He stopped and drew in several deep breaths as he stared at his mom. Suddenly, all the memories of how she used to be the most loving and caring mom in the Hood had flooded his mind. Those times she took him and Lameek to the movies before she started getting high; the times she would help him with his homework and would always give him encouraging kisses and hugs. The time she would cook meals and they all would sit at the table and eat, talk, laugh and have a damn good time. His mom was always broke as hell, but her love used to be colossal and made up for the lack of money. He felt himself about to cry and he fought back the tears like an angry trapped animal. He hated crack! That shit was the worse thing to ever hit the Hood. There were so many bad things roaming the neighborhood, but nothing could come close to outdoing crack in its ability to devastate and destroy everything he loved!

Rasheen sat down in the armchair and clamped his hands on his head as though he had a splitting headache. Why his mom had to turn out to be a tramp? He could hear the distant voices from his childhood taunting and teasing, calling his mom foul names. It hurt him deeply because they were all true. His mom was a cold-blooded crack head! A welfare bum! And a two-bit prostitute! After a moment he said softly, "Momma, this is gotta stop. You went from worse to super worse." His voice started to rise several degrees. "What the fuck can them mufuckas do for you besides giving you a hit of crack for some…" He felt self-conscious about saying pussy to his mom, so he skipped over the comment. "I know you don't wanna hear this, but there's gonna be some heart breaking changes around here." Rasheen locked eyes with his mom. He knew she wasn't gonna like the fact that there would be no more fuckin' in apartment #3A from here on. Rasheen, in this moment, decided if he had to lay his thug game down on every John that even entertained the thought of sliding up in his mom, the red rivers would flow as the bullets would fly. As he watched his mom fidgeting uncontrollably from the crack craving that was eating her alive like sulfuric acid rapidly gnawing away at a piece of metal, he knew he had to do more than just stop her from fuckin' for money and crack. After a moment, the solution hit him.

Rasheen got up and sat next to his mom; he saw she was crying heavy tears and he embraced her.

Barbara spoke through her tears, "I'm sorry, Rasheen. I'm just trying to make it through this fucked up shit." She cried even harder.

Rasheen said, "Momma, do you wanna live like this?"

"I…I don't wanna live like this!" Barbara felt a heavy wave of anger as her tears increased. "Hell no! I don't wanna live like this! Damn! Damn! Damn it! I don't wanna live like this!"

"I know momma," Rasheen said as he waved Lameek over and he joined in the familial hug. "Listen, mom, I got a whole lot of money. And I'm gonna help you stop using crack. You gotta promise us you gonna stop."

"I wanna stop, but I can't!" Barbara said in a whining voice. "I tried to stop, but I can't!" She pulled from the embraced and stared Rasheen in the eyes. "I tried twenty times, but…but I just couldn't do it. This stuff is too powerful. Maybe with help I could do it."

Rasheen rose to his feet. "If I pay your way to go to one of those places that help people stop using drugs, will you go?" Rasheen stared down into his mother's eyes; it killed him to see how weak and fragile that crack had made her. Six years ago when she was drug-free, he saw his mom as the strongest person in the universe.

Barbara smiled, "Yes, I'll go, baby." She saw Rasheen's smile and it made her feel strong for a change. "But what y'all gone do with me gone. You know yo' aunts and uncles ain't gone let…"

"The hell with them," Rasheen headed for the table, snatched up the black garbage bag and returned to his initially position. "If you wanna get clean, I'll stay here and watch over Lameek and keep everything in order until you get back."

Barbara was looking back and forth at the black bag and Rasheen's eyes. "It cost a whole lot of money to put people in them rehabs, Rasheen. We talkin' thousands of dollars. We ain't got no money like…"

Rasheen dumped the money on the nearby raggedy coffee table and Barbara and Lameek's eyes lit up like the North Star in the sky. When Rasheen saw his mom picking up stacks of money with an exaggerated look of sheer awe on her face, it brought a huge smile to his face. Seeing how the sight of this money made his broken family instantly start to change back into the happy family they used to be, he vowed to turn up the volume on his money making exploits, at least a couple of notches. He figured right then and there he was going to be a millionaire before he reached twenty-one . . .even if it killed him.

Chapter Five

Things started to look reasonably good for Rasheen during the next few months. His meeting with Killer Kato went as good as expected. He gave Killer 48 gees instead of the 50. After the promise he made to his mom to put her in a rehab, he realized the extra two gees were going to be needed to hold him over. Killer Kato took the cash with the quickness and made it clear there would be interest for failing to pay the tab in full; a prospect Rasheen suspected all along. When Killer Kato claimed Rasheen now owed him seventy grand, Rasheen had to fight not to respond in a disrespectful manner. Although Rasheen had a choice, the reality of being unable to pick the one he really wanted to select made it a no choice situation. Rasheen subconsciously knew he was being played when he realized Killer Kato already had another spot lined up for a robbery. Alabama and Livonia was another steel gate drug spot and was ran and operated by Columbians who were making tens of thousands of dollars daily even on a bad day. This time Killer Kato wanted Rasheen to make the hit on a particular runner, and Rasheen knew this was personal. Deep down, Rasheen welcomed this new job, but the thought of having to give Killer Kato seventy gees of it was forcing Rasheen to take a hard look at other options.

Rasheen also kept his word with his brother, Lameek, and began taking him to Jack-Mack's newly constructed soundproofed, shooting gallery in his basement for target practice. The whole team was amazed at how Lameek was a better shot than Dirty Ricky and was dead on Jack-Mack's heels. None of them could hang with Rasheen on the shooting tip, but there was no doubt Lameek was destined to take his crown if he continued getting enough practice. Meanwhile, Rasheen, Jack-Mack and Dirty Ricky, in between casing the Alabama and Livonia spot, were partying up a storm. Weed smoking, drinking beer and sexing out hood rats became a daily activity and often got in the way of the business. At times when the partying got too extreme Rasheen would snap out of his weed and beer induced daze and start spazzing out on Jack-Mack and Dirty Ricky and things would shape up for a while.

About a month after the green door run, and when their money started looking a little shabby, Rasheen, Jack-Mack, and Dirty Ricky started doing petty stuck ups, like robbing dice games, number runners, pool halls, after hour clubs and Bodega stores on the other side of Brooklyn and in Queens. During a pool hall robbery, Dirty Ricky had finally popped his cherry when he shot and killed a man who failed to follow instructions when they entered and specifically told everybody not to move. As Jack-Mack was retrieving the cash from the cashier and Rasheen was working on the manager in the back trying to get him to open the safe, a fat, gruesomely ugly man pulled a shot gun from under a pool table and Dirty Ricky blew the top of the man's head clean off. Afterwards Rasheen and Jack-Mack teased and taunted Dirty Ricky for days because after the shooting Dirty Ricky couldn't stop trembling until he got blasted on weed and beer.

During these petty robberies, Rasheen and his crew decided to expand their horizons; Lisa, Diana and Carmila wanted to get down with them on a few runs. They were excellent boosters (stealing clothing from stores), and it was clear they had plenty of heart, but did they have what it took to handle a gun and take things straight up instead of stealing by the means of sneaking (boosting). The answer to this question was answered in the affirmative during a stick up at a Greenpoint Brooklyn Numbers Spot when they allowed the three fine looking hood rats to regulate the whole robbery. The only support Rasheen and his crew provided was their gun totting presence. Rasheen gave them a grade consisting of a B minus. If it weren't for their failure to properly tie up the workers before fleeing the establishment, they would have received a perfect grade.

Rasheen was shocked when he heard a dude named Big Cee got arrested for the Black Bob homicide. Despite the unfortunate situation, it wasn't totally an earth-shaking revelation, since it was common knowledge there were a whole lot of folks from the Hood in prison for crimes they didn't commit. It also didn't take genetic physicists to figure out that if Black and Hispanic folks were still socially, economically and politically disenfranchised and in a state of enslavement in most other areas, innocence folks going to prison would be an obvious side-effect. According to the word on the street, a crack head name Randy Doylson had got arrested for burglarizing an apartment in Park Slope, and decided to cut a deal with the DA by making up a story in order to escape incarceration. In the past, Randy had successfully beaten two cases by falsely claiming he was an eyewitness to two unsolved murders, and couldn't help but try it again; especially when that gorilla on his back (crack cocaine) was demanding to be fed, and in any event he had a life-long beef with Big Cee, who was a well-known drug dealer.

From Randy's standpoint this was an all win situation; he was getting his freedom and revenge for that time when Big Cee pistol whipped him because he tried to steal a bullshit bag of groceries from Big Cee's sister's car. Randy Doylson also learned many years ago that most District Attorneys didn't care whether or not he was lying, since they always helped him get his far fetched stories in tip top shape. Randy was fully aware that racism was alive and well in the New York City Court System and DA's were concerned solely with acquiring convictions when dealing with defendants who were people of color; all that jive talk about constitutional safeguards, Civil Rights and Due Process protections didn't apply in most cases when it involved "those people" and Randy had no problem taking full advantage of their willingness to bend the facts and the law in order to cover up glaring flaws, inconsistencies and full-fledged flagrant fabrications.

July rolled in with a smooth bang and Rasheen was taking it in stride. It was the day after the 4th and Rasheen laid on the sofa in Crystal's crib with his feet propped comfortably on a pile of pillows watching the 6 o'clock news. Today's reports were the same as all the other news reports from the previous days; violence, corruption and the false promises from cutthroat politicians and backstabbing corporations, made up the bulk of the news agenda. In the background Rasheen could hear Crystal in the kitchen preparing the evening meal. Crystal was his main squeeze, the only woman he ever entertained the thought of being with in a husband and wife way. Not that he was planning to get married anytime in the near future, it was just if he had to describe how he felt for her that would be the closest description.

He couldn't hear Lameek, but Rasheen knew he was somewhere in the back area of the apartment listening to rap songs on Crystal's stereo set or writing and practicing his own rap lyrics. After his mom entered the rehab, Crystal offered to let Rasheen and Lameek stay with her. Since Crystal's mother owned the entire Tenement building (872 Koskisoko Avenue) and Crystal had her very own apartment, there was no major conflict with them staying there.

Suddenly, the phone rang. Rasheen was about to get it, but Crystal was heading for the phone on the second ring. Rasheen laid back and enjoyed the view; he watched the junk in her trunk jiggling in the yellow shorts she wore. Her smooth muscular legs in conjunction with her small waist, shapely breast, drop dead gorgeous facial structure made Rasheen feel like a king on a Platinum throne, and even though he was sexing her out constantly, he could never get enough of watching her walk. Just savoring the way she threw her hips as she strutted along was worth its weight in gold.

"Hello," Crystal said into the receiver, her flawless voice was replete with a sensuous tone that matched her banging body.

Rasheen resumed watching the news. The reporter was now talking about the unveiling of a price gouging scandal involving a waste disposal company and two city council men. When he heard Crystal say, "Mr. Finkelman, our only concern is that she returns home off drugs", Rasheen rose into a sitting position, now all ears. This was the rehab people calling about his mother.

A few weeks ago he had got Crystal to do some serious investigation in order to find a rehab to put his mom in. After dozens of phone calls, Crystal found the Daytona Drug Rehabilitation Group in Queens, who claimed they were the best in the field of saving lives from the ravages of drugs. That sounded good to Rasheen ears, but he was never the type to take things on face value; show me, don't tell me was one of his many golden rules. Rasheen was hoping they weren't pulling his leg, as he agreed to give up over five thousand dollars of his hard-earned cash. He could still remember as he handed a portion of the money over to the white man named, James Finkelman, who was dressed in a black business suit, the images of him emptying an entire Uzi clip in this chump's head if he found out a sham was being ran on him. If momma duke didn't return from that place completely resurrected, there was going to be hell to pay. However, he did feel extraordinarily good when he saw, during the ride to Daytona, his mom's spirits were running high and her strong disposition was already starting to regenerate.

"Okay, I understand," Crystal said into the receiver. "Thank you for calling, goodbye." She hung up the phone. By the time she turned around Rasheen was already on her back.

"It better be good news," Rasheen said calmly, hoping he wasn't going to have to raise some hell.

"Relax, Rasheen," Crystal headed back to the kitchen with Rasheen on her heels. "They called to let us know that your mom is still refusing to take her medication; she feels she can do the rest of the time there without the meds. Other than that they said she's over the worse of it; the first few weeks are the hardest, and it should be all progress from here on end."

"How much longer before the food is ready?" Rasheen took a seat at the table, and opened the Jet Magazine that Crystal was reading. "I gotta break out by 7 o'clock. I definitely want a hit of that chicken of yours…"

"I thought you said we was gonna chill together tonight?" She poured the Weston oil into the frying pan.

"I know, I know. But you know how shit is with this fast cheddar."

"No, I don't know. But what I do know is you're not spending time with me, and I'm not feelin' that Rasheen. You run in, hit the skins, and you back on the run. You out all night, you eat and run. I barely get a chance to be with you for any extended time. Come boo, all this ripping and running ain't healthy for you or our relationship."

"All this ripping running is keeping money in both our pockets. You know we can't have it both ways. I'm either in the streets getting paid or I'm here with you not getting paid. You know how this thing goes. If I sit around bullshitin' we ain't gonna be eating the way we do. And you know I got a plan. This ain't something I'm planning on doing for the rest of my life." Rasheen lied, but he knew this was all she wanted to hear. "If I can pull off that knock out score, I'll leave this shit and get a business or some shit like that." He caressed her soft butt cheek and went back to the living room to finish watching the news.

Crystal was flaming with anger; she knew he was just talking, running his mouth to make her feel good. He was talking about starting a business, but he never even read any of the books she bought for him dealing with businesses. She was furious with him, but deep down she knew he was right. No work, no money. Somebody got to put that work in; why not let it be him? Since she was a full time college student at Medgar Evers College, and merely had a weekend, part-time job, it apparently couldn't be her bringing in the money.

As Rasheen watched the news, his mind was wandering about. He knew it was time to hit Crystal off with a huge piece of loot. Whenever the beefing and bickering started the only cure was to hit her off with a few hundred dollars, which was usually enough to keep her content for about a week or two. This was a tale tell sign that her purse was just about on empty. Another reason for the tension he knew subconsciously was that she wanted him to go down on her. Crystal would go down on him every time they had sex, sucking the life out of him every time, but he wouldn't do it for her. Twice he came close to doing it, but each time he backed down just as his lips reached the base of her belly button. Crystal had asked him did he think she wasn't clean enough to eat and he adamantly told her it wasn't that. When asked what was the reason, Rasheen was stuck. He wanted to tell her, but couldn't; that if there was any girl he would eat, it would definitely be her. He wasn't a hood rat, she wasn't cheating on him, (at least as far as he could tell), and she very rarely hung out; she was the embodiment of a brainy act; she was destined to do great things and was the epitome of wifey material; not to mention she kept her apartment as clean as an Egyptian palace. In the back of Rasheen's mind he knew his apprehension was primarily because of the saying in the street that if a man had to eat pussy, it was because he wasn't long dicking it, and had to compensate by laying his tongue game down. According to the old timers the reason white boys ate so much pussy was because they weren't holding in the dick department. With this in the back of Rasheen's mind, eating pussy became an ordeal even though he really wanted to try it out. Rasheen decided to hold off and make a big event out of his pussy eating adventure; maybe put it off until Crystal's birthday, which was coming up soon, on August 17.

About an hour later, Rasheen exited Crystal's second floor apartment and was glad he kept his word that he would learn how to drive a car. He got behind the wheel of the rust colored Nissan Maxima he purchased for seven thousand dollars on his way to Jack Mack's crib. Since Crystal was 19 years old, two years older than him, and already knew how to drive, he convinced her to let him buy them both a car. As he turned the ignition key and the engine revved to life, a smile crept on his face as he remembered Crystal's reaction when proposed this car purchase to her. It didn't take a scientist to see that Crystal was not only thrilled about being able to show "her man" how to drive, but was ecstatic about being part owner of her very own ride.

As Rasheen pulled the car onto the road, he also realized he never knew how bad he had an ego issue until he got behind the wheel of their used vehicle with Crystal as his driving instructor. There was no doubt he had a patriarchal mindset and felt awkward having a woman, other than his mother, give him a direct order to do this or do that. If he didn't truly love Crystal and recognized that her bossy way of teaching was just the way she was, it would've been impossible for him to swallow all that "Didn't I tell you to turn here?", "don't turn that way!", "God, Rasheen, you're not listening!", "Hit the brake! Hit the brake!", "I told you to turn right at the corner!" The thought brought on a case of unintended laughter as he stopped at a red light.

The following two weeks slide by with remarkable ease. The date was July 21, 1994 and tonight was the big night. It was time for the final discussion regarding the Alabama and Livonia run. Rasheen, Jack-Mack, and Dirty Ricky had been scoping out the spot for the last three months and felt confident they had the whole plan laid out perfectly. Killer Kato wanted to have this last minute briefing, but Rasheen sincerely felt it was a waste of time. They had everything they needed as far as weapons and the getaway car were concerned, and that's all that really mattered.

Rasheen and Jack-Mack entered Killer Kato's game room at a little after 8 o'clock that evening, and the new TLC jam was blurting through the jukebox while the regulars were roaming about. Hood love filled the atmosphere. Compared to the way Rasheen was greeted in January when he first came to see Killer Kato, he was now embraced by Killer's team as if he was straight family. After giving all the super thugs some dap, handshakes and Hood style hugs, Rasheen and Jack-Mack entered the blue door.

Rasheen saw Killer Kato was sitting behind his desk counting a stack of money. Crazy B, Killer Kato's right hand man and personal bodyguard, was watching TV on the other side of the room, and as usual, he had his trusty old AK-47 with the crazy banana clip laying on the coffee table in reaching distance. He gave Rasheen and Jack-Mack a raised clenched fist salute like in the days of the Black Power Movement, and resumed watching the tube.

Killer Kato rose to his feet with his unique half-cocked grin. "Bring the noise!" He shouted, trying to sound like Chuck D of Public Enemy, but did a terrible imitation of the rap Icon. He gave both Rasheen and Jack-Mack some dap, gestured for them to have a seat, and they sat in the nearby cushioned chairs in front of the desk as Killer Kato sat back down.

"Rasheen!" Killer Kato said, "I been wantin' to kick it with you on a much deeper level. Jack-Mack you too. I'm even feelin' your man Dirty Ricky too. Man, y'all got a nice little team. You're keepin' it real, and y'all got a good handle on keepin' the bullshit and the business in there proper perspective, unlike so many of the brothers in the Hood."

"Oh, shit!" Rasheen thought to himself. He saw what was coming next as clear as a flashing red light in a dark room; this nigga wanted to strap them up to his wagon and work them like government mules. Rasheen cleared his throat and said politely, "I thought we were here to do some last minute planning with this run tonight?"

"Yeah, that's comin'," Killer Kato said as he leaned back in his chair. "We gonna talk about that. But first lemme get something off my chest." Killer Kato let those words hang in the air as he silently stared at Rasheen and Jack-Mack. Killer Kato was still riding high on the success of his Bradford Street spot. He always knew this tactic would work, but he didn't think it would succeed as well as it did. When they dropped those four bodies, plus, the body Cowboy's hitter dropped, it was more than enough to slide the green door spot right out of the game. Yeah! Ever since those bodies dropped, the 75th Precinct had been entrenched in that building and the immediate area. As planned, this was just enough drama to enable him to lock that whole section down, since there were no other heavy slingers in that section, all that beautiful business had to come his way. Yeah!

Killer Kato sighed as the familiar image of his short and long range goals gyrated across his memory bank. Short range goals: Lock down a major portion of Brooklyn's drug world, make millions, flip the money, invest in a rap label, and become a rap mogul. Long range goals: Become a rap mogul, make money, make money, make mo' money, and if possibly become a billionaire. However, the bear minimum level of success he was shooting for was absolutely attaining multi-millions, at least in the range of 300 to 700 million dollars. It was a long ass reach, but every innovative-minded man had a dream. Hey, Martin Luther King had a dream, why couldn't he too?

With regards to the success of his short range goals, he saw the evidence of victory was as glaring as the racism in America; he had a real live squad of intellectual knuckle heads that were more than glad to interrupt rap concerts; he had his hands on the security teams of two prominent rappers; he purchased a recording studio that had qualified cats about to make a grand entrance into the rap scene, and he had found a twist to throw into the drug game (more like a black eye, but what difference did it make when he really wasn't violating any of the cardinal rules of the game?). Knocking the competition out of the picture with indiscriminate acts of violence wasn't a brand spanking new tactic, but Killer Kato had every intention of taking it to a level that would awe-stricken all the others who had done it before him, whomever they may have been. The crazy thing was that he needed Rasheen to help him complete this particular aspect of his dream. Rasheen was a natural-born killer, he was sharp on his toes, he was young, he had a heart like a little Lion, he was trigger-happy, and full of a lust for money. He knew and obeyed the codes of the Hood and he had no visible connections to him, but most of all he was disposable. If Rasheen and his crew were killed or arrested, they could not link any of them to him. But most of all, since Killer Kato was hoping to taking a huge step into the rap game before this year was out, he needed to turn up his cash intake to its maximum level.

Rasheen sighed extremely loud and he saw this pulled Killer Kato out of his reverie.

Killer Kato nodded his head and said, "I'ma lay this proposition on you without gassing it up or taking you up and down and round the block. After this run here, I want you to get down with my team. But, this'll be a different and unique kind of arrangement. You'll be with me, but not with me, you know what I'm saying. This drug spot robbing thing is big business, Rasheen, and I know we can perfect it to where we can become millionaires. Every Hood got drug spots, and there's money all over the place. We'll never run out of work." Killer Kato sighed for dramatic impact. "I know you're saying to yourself. Shit, why should I fuck with this dude when I'm doing all the dirty work? Just think, with both of these runs I was able to give you inside information that would've been nearly impossible for you to get without me. I got a mean gun connect. Whatever run you do, you rock with a clean burner . . ."

As Killer Kato went on and on pointing out why Rasheen and his crew needed him, Rasheen wondered if Kato realized there was a second man in a building across from the green door spot, who was fully armed and they weren't forewarned of this? If this failure to communicate was due to his so called retrieval of inside information, Rasheen knew he would hate to see the results when he really made a blunder. Rasheen instantly saw this whole conversation for what it was: a bunch of all out bullshit. Basically, Killer Kato wanted to pimp them, lay some raw dick on them without the grease, and play them like they were crab ass puppets. Rasheen struggled to control his temper as he sighed humbly and then said, "No disrespect Killer Kato, but we ain't tryin' to make drug robberies our forte." He lied; they definitely were going to continue hitting drug spots, but it would be on their own terms. Rasheen continued, "Fuckin' with drug dealers is dangerous work, man, and ain't no guarantee the money will be all that. With the green door run, we only caught them for 60 gees. We thought there was way more than that in there and look what happened." Rasheen let that hang in the air.

Killer Kato smiled because Rasheen just reminded him that they had lied to him about the amount of money they snatched from the green door run. He was certain there was at least 100 grand in that spot; his man K-9 worked for Cowboy and knew exactly what, when, where, and how much money was being moved within that crew, because K-9 was the accountant. He wasn't mad at Rasheen for cutting him short, since all it did was extend his grip on the situation. However, his failure to accept his offer to get down with him did make him mad; real mad. He didn't want to do what he was about to do, but business was business. Killer Kato said, "Check this out, Rasheen. I'm into that choice thing for real. I respect your choice about not wanting to keep this drug spot robbery shit in motion. It's fucked up, but I respect that. But, you should know that all choices have consequences. For every action there's an equal and even reaction. Sometimes there's good consequences, and other times there's bad consequences." Killer Kato forcefully drew in a deep breath of air and let it out with equal force. He let this tad bit of info simmer for a while.

Rasheen hated when people threatened him. There was no doubt this was a threat, and it came as no surprise that Killer Kato was going down this pressure path. With a struggle, Rasheen rode the silence and even allowed his eyes to make firm contact with Killer Kato's.

Killer Kato rose to his feet and spoke as he moved to the bar. "I been wanting to give you a pat on the back for that thing you did for your mom. I wish I had a mom worth laying damn near seven grand on the table for." Killer Kato grabbed the bottle of Hennessey and started preparing himself a drink. "Now, that was some real loyal shit there. Seven gees for a six-month in house stay at Daytona is a little steep. They got a place in Manhattan a lot cheaper, but it's all good, cause it's the thought that count. Helping mom get it together ain't got shit to do with money. Man, your little brother, Lameek, is a little dude you need to keep your eye on. Yeah, you don't need him pickin' up any of them badass habits. You and I both know the bad ones are hard ass hell to break. Plus, I heard he got some rap skills; now that would be an unforgivable waste to throw talent like that away." He sipped on the drink and the strong liquor brought warmth to his mid-section. "You should hone them skills of his. That rap shit is blowin' up! And Crystal, oh man, now she's a straight dime piece, Rasheen. Nigga, you got good taste. Just make sure you be easy, cause you don't wanna get her fine ass caught in no cross fire on account of your line of work. Imagine you bumpin' heads with one of your Vics and they decide to do the dance with her standing next to you? You know in the Hood, whoever's on the scene gotta get a piece of that thing. She's too damn fine and got a lot going for herself to be gettin' shot up over some dumb shit. I really dig the fact she's in college for business management." He nodded approvingly, and took another swig of the Hennessey.

The silence returned with explosive force.

Rasheen couldn't stop staring at Killer Kato. The rage in his heart was mounding. He felt himself about to slip and say something or even do something he would regret. He made eye contact with Jack-Mack, and saw he too was just as disturbed by Killer's remarks.

Rasheen and Jack-Mack both glanced over at Crazy B, and saw he now had his AK-47 cradled in his lap. He was still watching TV, but it was apparent this was a sign that he was ready and waiting for some action. His other gestures and behavior were sending a clear subliminal message: Go ahead, play yourself.

Rasheen tried to swallow his anger. It suddenly became hard to stay focus, knowing this motherfucker was threatening to do some foul shit to his family and Crystal. He couldn't believe this foul motherfucker was talking about doing something to the only people he truly had love for. They ain't have shit to do with what he and Killer Kato were doing, and it wasn't fair to start throwing innocence people into the mix of all this bullshit. Rasheen would've never even thought about doing something to Killer Kato's family, (even if he knew where they were). What they did was between them; innocence bystanders ain't got shit to do with any of their dirty dealings, but deep down Rasheen knew the code of the game. And with a game where the cardinal rule was to survive and make it to the top by any and all means, these sort of foul tactics came with the territory. Rasheen sighed because he hated to bend under pressure; it made him feel weak and that was a feeling he absolutely despised. But, bending in order to protect the people he loved was something he could do with his head held high, since he would not jeopardize the lives of the only people he truly loved.

Chapter Six

Rasheen sat in the back seat of the stolen green Chevy Impala. Ricky was behind the wheel and Jack-Mack was in the front passenger seat. Ice Cube's rap lyrics whispered through the car speakers, talking about a Hood rat "giving up the nappy dug out". The car was parked in the middle of Alabama Street and they had a clear view of the Spot. The Alabama and Livonia drug spot was a six stories dirty beige brick apartment building infested from top to bottom with drug addicts, crack fiends and welfare recipients. It was the tallest building on the block and next to it were two burnt out three story Tenement buildings. The # 2 and 3 train line stood like a monolithic giant next to the building and covered Livonia Avenue for blocks. Across the street from this apartment building was an empty lot where similar apartment buildings once stood. This drug spot was a diehard, hold over from the great crack epidemic of the mid-80s and looked every bit of it.

Rasheen and his crew knew this run would be a lot different than the last run because the runner didn't park his vehicle blocks away from the spot; he pulled right up in front of the joint, got out the car, entered the spot while the driver took off. The car would then circle around the neighborhood until the runner was finished, and then the driver would return, pick up the runner and whisk away. The plan they had mapped out called for plenty of gunplay, and under the circumstances, they didn't have much of a choice. The good thing was that there definitely weren't any sharp shooters laying in the cut in any nearby apartments. This was something Rasheen and his crew went to great lengths to confirm, and all their evidence conclusively established that the only shooters were the players on deck.

Like all operations, there was bad news, or as some like to call it, unfortunate circumstances. First off, Rasheen didn't like the fact that these were Columbians with international connections and ties. If they were exposed, or caught by the police, even if they lived to make it to court, it would still be a death sentence. The Columbians had money that was simply too long to expect to fuck with them and not pay with your life. Another disturbing fact was that they discovered that the cats in this spot were working with military weaponry. From what Rasheen found out they had an anti-aircraft machine gun that was so big, it took two motherfuckers to operate it. It was a gun used to shoot down jets and planes and all kinds of other big shit, and according to the rumor, if a person got hit with one of those bullets it would rip off limps and even cut a person clean in half. Yeah, this was some scary shit for Rasheen and he made it clear to Jack-Mack and Dirty Ricky that when they stepped on the stage to open the curtains for the drama to begin, they had to hit hard, fast, and with absolute deadly force. One mistake, or even the slightest miss would mean lights out for all three of them.

A brown beat up Toyota Corolla was parked on the corner of Alabama and Dumont, about a block away from the green Chevy Impala. Inside this vehicle sat two Columbian men. They both had a set of binoculars in one hand and Uzis in the other. After receiving reports a week ago of a strange car casing the spot, they had been driving around looking for any odd cars parked for an extended amount of time that had passengers watching the spot. Two hours ago, they drove down Alabama Street and noticed the green Impala with three men sitting in the car. That's when they decided to park down the block and watch the men in the green Impala as they watched the spot. When the green car remained there for another twenty minutes without anyone getting out, and the time for the runner to arrive was growing near, the driver of the Toyota made a call to the runner who was at their Saratoga Spot, and warned him that there were some suspicious guys parked near the spot. After he hung up with the runner, he called the worker inside the spot and put him on point. The worker in turn, put the lookout on point. They instantly started pulling out the big guns.

    Rasheen, Jack-Mack and Dirty Ricky were staring at the lookout and the customers as they entered and exited the spot. They hadn't said a word since they parked and the only person doing all the talking, or rapping for that matter, was the West Coast rappers on Ricky's cassette tape. Suddenly, they saw the Burgundy Jeep come to a stop in front of the spot. Rasheen and the others jumped at attention with their eyes glued on the runner as he got out of the Jeep and the lookout came running to him and started talking. The confusion forced Rasheen to squint his eyes because they both looked extremely excited and they were looking around as if waiting for something. Suddenly, Rasheen's inner voice screamed, "They know!"…"Pull back!"…"Pull back!" Rasheen started breathing hard and felt a strange wave of intense fear sweep over him. All of a sudden he felt claustrophobic as if he was trapped inside a coffin, buried alive and couldn't move or breathe. What the fuck is going on? Rasheen wondered as he wiped the perspiration from his forehead. After a moment the weird sensations subsided and he brushed it off as a side effect of the weed he smoked last night.

    They saw the runner enter the spot and as planned Rasheen and Jack-Mack exited the car, headed across the street and entered the six-story apartment building directly across from where the car was parked. Rasheen and Jack-Mack raced up the stairs to the roof. They then raced across the roof heading towards Livonia, going from roof to roof. Since the buildings were connected they made it to the last building in twenty seconds flat. They raced down the stairwell and came out the building through the back way. They were now on Georgia Avenue. With a fast pace walk, Rasheen and

Jack-Mack scurried across Livonia Avenue. Just before entering the back of the building they were just watching, Rasheen pulled both silencer equipped mini Dessert Eagles from his waist, while Jack-Mack pulled two Tech 9 Uzis with silencers and they braced themselves. Suddenly, the sound of an approaching train could be heard at a distance and Rasheen wished it had come a few moments later. Rasheen gave Jack-Mack a head nod and they quickly entered, still grateful because the noise from the overhead train as it passed was loud enough to conceal their entry.

A man with his back turned and a handgun in his hand, but pointed downward, didn't even see it coming. Both Rasheen and Jack-Mack pumped two bullets a piece in his back, dropping the man to the floor. Jack-Mack dragged the fallen man out of the building and stashed him amongst the trashcans while Rasheen moved towards the front of the building, listening for any movement.

Earlier, the two Columbians saw Rasheen and Jack-Mack get out the green car and entered a building directly across the street from where they were parked. Because this occurred right after the runner entered the spot, the alarms in their heads instantly started ringing. It was confirmed that this was a stick up in progress. The driver started the car and both Columbians decided there was no need to wait for the robbers to start the fireworks, so they figured they might as well go pay the third man in the green car a little visit. The car pulled from the curb and cruised towards the green car.

Moments earlier, Ricky had the cassette tape turned off and he was looking at everything moving. He looked at his watch every couple of seconds. He had to wait another four minutes before he moved the car to the back of the drug spot on Georgia Avenue.

Ricky's heart was pounding and his eyes were taking in everything. He even kept his eyes on the side view and rear view mirrors. Ever since he was a kid, he'd always made it a habit of looking behind him. "Watch your back", was a rule of thumb in Ricky's world and when he was doing something he had no business doing, he especially watched his back. He'd known many ballers who fell victim to the game by only watching their front and neglecting the art of watching their back. To Ricky, watching your back was something to be taken literally. Ricky had his two silencer equipped weapons close by. One was in the back waist of his pants and the other was tucked underneath his leg, specially positioned for swift retrieval.

Suddenly, through his rear view mirror, he saw a car way down the block pull onto the street. This instantly got his attention because he didn't remember seeing anyone enter a car earlier. His attention started really percolating when he realized the car's headlights were off and the vehicle was drawing closer and closer in a very slow fashion. Dirty Ricky's West Coast mentality screamed, drive by! In a frantic hast, Dirty Ricky slid across the front seat, opened the passenger door, slid out the car, and remained in a crouched position as he closed the car door. He was glad as hell they made a habit of disconnecting the light switch that activated the inner light in the car when the doors opened. Dirty Ricky was shaking like he was having an epileptic fit or something and he made no attempt to control it.

Seconds later, the Toyota pulled to a stop next to the green car and the empty vehicle baffled the two Columbians. Dirty Ricky's heart pounded vibrantly in his ears as his fear of death gripped him. They were there for him! They stopped and were apparently looking for him! He braced himself, fighting to control his breathing, while wondering what Rasheen would've done in a situation like this? Would he spring up from behind the car with both guns blazing? Or would he wait for them to get out of the vehicle to investigate and then start blazing? There was no question a gun-blazing response was in the making, but when to start the blazing was the question. Dirty Ricky decided to start blazing when they got out the car, since this would allow him to hit his targets more accurately. Then, suddenly, realization hit him. What if the men in this car were detectives? Killing cops wasn't a lightweight matter, and everybody knew when you killed a cop the weight of the entire country would come crashing down upon the culprit. He quickly decided to go out with a blazing gun, whether they were cops or not.

With both guns in the ready, Dirty Ricky held his ground, listening for a sign that would tell him who he was dealing with. He heard the car door open and when he heard one of the men speak Spanish, he smiled; the vast majority of cops didn't speak Spanish, at least not the ones from the 75th Precinct. With these facts in mind, Dirty Ricky sprung to his feet with both guns blazing. His first wave of bullets missed, since he had to get his bearing on where his targets were exactly positioned, but the second pull of the triggers hit home. However, this split second lapse was all the Columbian man that was in the driver seat needed to effect a swift response, and as Ricky loaded up the man's chest with three silenced bullets, the man aimed and held his finger on the trigger of his Uzi, spraying a bombardment of bullets at Ricky. The Columbian that was in the passenger seat was struck twice in the face and was instantly knocked out of play.

When the smoke cleared all three of them laid sprawled out on the pavement.

Dirty Ricky had dropped one of his guns and was now clutching the upper right chest near the top of his shoulder. Shit! The first thing he wondered was, did he hit both of the men? Within seconds, he instantly felt certain he hit his targets. He struggled to his feet and realized the wound wasn't as bad as he initially thought it was. He eased around the car with the gun pointed. He saw one of the men moving and fired another shot to the man's chest. Dirty Ricky limp back to the sidewalk, picked up his other gun, tucked it in the front of his waist and realized the Columbians' car was double parked next to his, thus, blocking his car inside the parking space. Suddenly, he saw heavy commotion down the street in front of the spot. Ricky looked at his watch, and saw he was late. Panic started to grab hold of him. He ran, dragged the Columbians onto the sidewalk, looked up and saw people looking out their windows. The police! They called the police! His mind screamed and he increased his speed to a hysterical pace.

Within minutes, Ricky backed the Columbian's car out of the way and was in the Chevy racing down the block.

Earlier, Rasheen moved down the dimly lit corridor on tip toes; both guns in his hands were pointed in full ready mode. Jack-Mack came up the rear imitating Rasheen's gun stance. Loud talking could be heard up ahead around the corner; it was a mixture of Spanish and English alternating back and forth with confusing fluidity. When Rasheen reached the light bulb responsible for the inadequate lighting, he tucked a gun under an armpit as Jack-Mack allowed Rasheen to climb on his cupped hands in order to unscrew the light bulb.

The small corridor was instantly hurled into darkness. Rasheen and Jack-Mack then continued towards the end of the corridor. Rasheen stopped when he heard a man say, "Tell Manny to escort us to the car with the beast; whoever these guys are, will be in for a big surprised." Heavy laughter followed the comment.

Rasheen gave Jack-Mack a knowing expression; somebody had put them on point about the stick up. The man's comments were unmistakable, but it really didn't matter to Rasheen because they still had the element of surprise. Rasheen got on his knees and peeked around the corner to determine the exact number of men they had to bang out with. He saw five men, but sensed there was at least two more roaming around in a location he couldn't see. Rasheen smiled when he saw a man wearing a Hawaiian style shirt with a huge tote bag on his shoulder. He could almost smell all that lovely money as if he had money radar in his blood. Rasheen pulled back and then heard the same man who spoke earlier say, "Oh, yes, that is beautiful!" The sound of something huge being dragged out of an apartment was heard. The man continued, "Rico's doing the next pick up, Okay."

Rasheen knew this was their cue as he rose to a standing position. Red man was now in his head, "T-Time for some—Time for some action!" Rasheen drew a deep breath, gave Jack-Mack a head nod, and with graceful and proficient speed, he and Jack-Mack hit the corner as though they rehearsed this maneuver a thousand times.

All four of their guns were spitting bullets and silenced flames.

Rasheen and Jack-Mack mowed down any and everything that moved or had the potential to move. The six-men went down in a torrent of grunts, moans and terror stricken screams of pain. Suddenly, two of the men who were hit in the back frantically went for the gigantic gun on a stand with wheels. Rasheen realized they were wearing some kind of lightweight body armor, since the men who received headshots were immobilized.

Rasheen and Jack-Mack continued firing, but one of the men made it to the super gun. When his finger hit the trigger on that monstrous machine gun, the explosions from each bullet fired was like rapid thunder. The machine gun they called the beast was pointed at the door when the gun went off and it disintegrated. As the man held his finger on the trigger while spinning the beast towards Rasheen and Jack-Mack, gargantuan holes were appearing on the walls as huge chucks of concrete, plaster and other materials flew every which a way.

With hysterical speed, Rasheen and Jack-Mack fled back around the corner while firing at the three men who didn't fall victim to their bullets.

Rasheen and Jack-Mack made it behind the wall and kneeled just as bullets tore huge holes in the wall just about their heads. Instantly, the shooting stopped. In a kneeling position, Rasheen sprung one of his guns back around the wall and sprayed the remaining eight bullets in one of his Desert Eagles, hitting the man behind the beast dead in the head. The 9mm bullet swept the man clean off his feet.

The two remaining men were lying on their stomachs and had returned fire just as Rasheen opened fire. Rasheen pulled back around the wall as a wave of small caliber bullets battered the nearby wall. Rasheen hastily reloaded his Desert Eagles with frantic speed; he was glad he was dealing with dudes who assumed he and Jack-Mack had continued running out the back door like a bunch of scary ass cowards. This fatal mistake cost them the man operating the huge anti-aircraft machinegun his life. Rasheen was listening closely for the two remaining men to attempt to run for the big gun. He saw that the two sole survivors were several yards from the big gun, and if they attempted to go for it, they would make plenty of noise when their feet crunched on the scattered concrete, plaster, glass and other debris on the floor.

Rasheen heard movement, sprung around the wall and sprayed one of the two men who stupidly went for the big gun. The other man opened fire just as Rasheen appeared from behind the wall. This time Rasheen held his finger on the trigger while waving both Dessert Eagles laying a heavy sheet of bullets at the two remaining men. Rasheen decided that time was now of the essence, and bold and daring actions were needed if they intended to retrieve the tote bag full of money wrapped around the shoulder of a dead man dressed in the Hawaiian shirt. Rasheen felt bullets breeze pass him as he blazed away; silent flames were leaping from the Dessert Eagle with remarkable speed. Suddenly, Rasheen felt a huge blow to his stomach that shoved him back a few inches. As Rasheen mowed down the two men with carefully placed headshots, he felt a searing burning sensation where the impact had appeared. Rasheen had never been shot before, but he instantly knew he was hit by a bullet as he collapsed to the floor.

Rasheen suddenly felt a scorching sensation as if the site of the bullet entry was literally on fire. He shouted, "I'm hit! I'm hit! Ah, shit!"

Jack-Mack rushed to him as he fired several more bullets at the motionless bodies.

Clutching the gut wound, Rasheen shouted, "Get the money! Hurry!"

Jack-Mack ran to the man with the tote bag, retrieved the bag and as he returned he heard a stampede of footsteps coming from the staircase on the side of him. A mob was running from upstairs. Jack-Mack ran back to Rasheen with one Uzi aimed at the staircase, waiting for someone to appear.

With the use of the bullet-ridden wall, Rasheen struggled to his feet. Stars and waves of dizziness were taking a firm grip of his whole being. He made it to his feet and took aim at the staircase with the other hand clamped to the gut wound.

Rasheen and Jack-Mack were as quiet as a Library during the witching hour. The men were talking frantically and it was evident this was the back up.

The minute Rasheen and Jack-Mack saw the three men with automatic handguns appear they opened fire. Thanks to the silenced bullets the first two men had no idea what hit them until it was far too late. The third man would've had a chance of escaping if only he had known the reason his two comrades were falling down the stairs face first was because they were being hit with silenced bullets and not because they had tripped and fell; an assumption that cost him his life.

After the three new comers tumbled down the last flight of stairs, Rasheen and Jack-Mack rushed to the back of the building. Rasheen gestured to Jack-Mack to get his other Dessert Eagle he dropped moments ago when he grabbed at the bullet wound. In one fluid motion Jack-Mack tucked one of his Uzis in the makeshift holster, snatched the Dessert Eagle and continued for the back of the building.

Rasheen was on Jack-Mack's back and was now operating solely on willpower, fear and the thought of getting away with that humongous bag of money.

Earlier, Ricky brought the Chevy Impala to a screeching stop in back of the apartment building. The moment he stopped, he couldn't believe his ears upon hearing the thunderous machine gunfire. He instantly knew the caliber of the bullets being fired were not your regular run of mill military weapon. Dirty Ricky could've sworn he felt the car vibrating as the explosions went off; this machine gun fire reminded him of cannon blasts, but fired almost as rapid as a standard Mac 10.

Dirty Ricky kept looking at all the blood that was running down his chest. He even felt dizziness starting to come over him, but he knew the last thing he wanted to do was panic. He told himself repeatedly that the bullet wound wasn't life-threatening or else he wouldn't have been able to move his right arm. However, when he breathed the pain was telling him other wise.

Suddenly, he heard the monstrous explosions come to a stop. Ricky's mind was running wild. What if Rasheen and Jack-Mack were dead? If they got hit with one of those big ass bullets, they're lights were out for sure! He scanned the late night streets in all directions, hoping no police decided to show up. He even started checking out the windows in the apartment building. After a minute went by, Ricky felt the temptation to panic becoming unbearable. The blood was now running down into his boxer shorts, and the dizziness was growing by the seconds. You're bleeding to death! A voice shouted in his head, shoving Dirty Ricky two steps closer to the panic zone.

As Ricky started rocking back and forth to calm his nerves and to keep the dizziness in check, he saw Rasheen and Jack-Mack barreling out the back door. He instantly noticed Rasheen was badly wounded.

Earlier, a Latino man had burst inside his third floor apartment as he heard the gunfire downstairs. He was one of the back-up shooters, who's job was to lockdown any movement in the back of the building, if and when, the spot ever underwent what it was currently experiencing; a robbery. He had a Mac-11 Uzi with six clips in his back pocket. He reached the window and frantically started looking for any intruders. Then he saw the double-parked green Chevy Impala. Upon closer scrutiny, he saw someone in the driver seat. He opened the third floor window all the way and took aim, about to open fire, but realized the man could be an innocent bystander.

He put his trigger finger on hold. Then suddenly, he heard the back door to the building slam open and saw two men, (Rasheen & Jack-Mack) racing for the Chevy. When he saw the man in the Chevy become excited and slammed the gear in drive, he opened fire spraying the man in the car (Dirty Ricky) with carefully aimed Uzi bullets.

Seconds earlier, Rasheen and Jack-Mack moved rapidly towards the Chevy. Rasheen felt himself fading fast, but upon seeing their get away car the sight sparked a surge of super human energy.

Then, all of a sudden, machine gunfire exploded from a window just above their heads. Rasheen and Jack-Mack turned right, scrambling for cover as the bullets tore at the Chevy with gruesome force. They heard Ricky scream "What the fuck!" As an entire Uzi clip pulverized his body. Ricky had hit the gas pedal, jettisoned the car forward, but the bullet to the temple area of his head had knocked his lights completely out. The Chevy crashed into a parked Mitsubishi, scattering glass all over the asphalt.

Rasheen and Jack-Mack returned fire at the window as they hasty headed down the block. Rasheen felt a fear that almost buckled his knees; they lost their ride; there was no doubt Dirty Ricky was dead; he had a bullet in his gut and was seconds from passing out; they were in enemy territory with a bag of stolen drug money with a mob of crazy, pissed off Columbians on their ass. He could almost feel the Grimm reaper caressing the back of his neck.

Rasheen noticed the shooter in the window couldn't get a clean shot as they raced down the street towards Riverdale Avenue. He didn't have to be told that this particular shooter was on his way down the stairs and would soon be on their ass. Rasheen had no plan for this predicament; there definitely was no back-up ride and now they obviously had to carjack the first ride that came their way. With their luck, it was the wee hours of the night, and traffic was practically non-existent.

Rasheen and Jack-Mack hit the corner of Riverdale in full stride. Rasheen stumbled and said, "We gotta hotwire one of these cars. I can't go no more! Hurry!" Rasheen knew the more he moved the faster his blood would race and the faster he would lose his blood. As Jack-Mack broke the driver side window on a red Camaro, Rasheen kept his eyes on the street for any pursuers. Just as Jack-Mack opened the car door, a police car appeared down the street.

Rasheen took off down Riverdale towards Alabama Avenue, while Jack-Mack ran towards the police and then cut down Georgia Avenue. When Jack-Mack saw the police car about to pursue Rasheen instead of him, Jack-Mack did an about face and ran back in the middle of the street with his Uzi pointed, then fired a shot that cut through the front end of the patrol car.

The officers didn't hear the shot, but the flame that leaped from the Uzi and the impact of the bullet ripping at the hood of the patrol car told them all they needed to know. They immediately pursued Jack-Mack.

Jack-Mack's legs were pumping with frantic force as he raced down Georgia Avenue towards New Lot Avenue. Shooting at the police to save Rasheen from imminent arrest seemed like a good idea when he reacted on impulse, but now that he heard the police car's engine open up and was gaining rapidly on him, he wished he could've taken it all back. Jack-Mack shook loose of the negative thoughts, imaged all the shit he could do with this heavy ass bag of money, and with a smile he decided he would take these chumps on an urban goose chase that would make their minds twist, twirl and tumble.

Rasheen moved as fast as he could and now his mind surged with dizziness, desperation and dread. He had seen what Jack-Mack had done. If Jack hadn't drawn the police to himself, Rasheen knew he would've been done off. He saved him, and that was the ultimate proof of true thug love. Rasheen was some what surprised Jack-Mack had saved him by putting himself in harm's way, since if the shoe was on the flip side he might not have went there, especially when he was holding all the money. Indeed, this was the ultimate test of realness, and it clearly determined whether or not they were truly Homies for life, and Jack-Mack passed the test like a true blue brother. Despite this little touchy moment that ignited a wave of introspection within Rasheen, he also knew it definitely wasn't over, since the police had radios and by now they probably had the whole damn police force on the way.

Just as Rasheen hit the corner of Hinsdale Avenue he saw the beaming headlights of the car approaching from Livonia Avenue. The thought of sweet salvation gave him an adrenaline rush of energy. Rasheen stepped in front of the car not fearing the car striking him. The car tires screamed as the white Buick Regal came to a head-jerking stop. With his Dessert Eagle aimed, Rasheen shouted, "Get out the fuckin' car!"

There was a pause as the middle aged black man had both hands raised above his head.

"If I say it again..." Rasheen tried to shout louder, but the blinding pain became too intense when he tried to increase his volume. "Get out the fuckin' car!" He adjusted his aim, and the man hastily rushed out of the car.

When Rasheen saw the man about to attack him; apparently because he saw Rasheen was severely injured, Rasheen cracked the man up side the head with the Desert Eagle, dropping him straight to the pavement. The temptation to spray him with a few bullets was strong, but his yearning to get away from the police was a whole lot stronger. Rasheen jumped in the car, and spun off. He turned right on New Lots Avenue and went easy on the gas; there was no need to attract any unwarranted attention considering the fact he escaped the worse of the situation. Now, he had to decide what to do next. He wanted to go back for Jack-Mack real bad. Jack had all the money and the fear of losing it was eating Rasheen alive. But common sense was telling him to go back would be utterly foolish and straight suicide. He couldn't pull off a rescue with Five-O on Jack's ass. This wasn't a Hollywood movie script, this was real life, and under these circumstances to go back for him would end in disaster. But the thought of Jack-Mack having all the money in his possession was toying with his sense of rationale and he had to fight not to U-turn and go back into the area of drama. He calmed his nerves down by convincing himself that Jack-Mack was familiar with East New York, since he spent a lot of time hanging out in this Hood, and if anybody could out maneuver the cops, it was definitely Jack-Mack.

A sudden sharp pain in his chest took his mind off the money and on the state of his current condition. The minute he started contemplating what he should do with himself and how he would get medical attention, he felt his head spin with violent fury and his vision blurred. He almost ran a red light at New Lots and Rockaway Avenue. Now that his adrenaline rush was slowly subsiding, his body was being bombarded with all sorts of agonizing pain and he noticed the seat of his pants was soaked with blood; he realized for the first time he had a hole in his back. The bullet apparently went in his gut and out the back, since both holes were perfectly aligned. There was so much blood it started scaring the shit out of him.

As Rasheen drove pass Brookdale Hospital, he knew this place was definitely out of the question because it would be the equivalent of jamming himself; this was the nearest hospital to the scene of the crime and connections would obviously be made. Cruising down Rockaway Avenue, Rasheen noticed he was becoming very sleepy; it was a knock down drag off fight just to keep his eyes open. The thought of him having to drive for at least twenty more minutes, seemed like an eternity. As he made it to Atlantic Avenue, he felt a major sense of accomplishment mixed with nervousness. The police roamed this four-lane freeway on a regular basis, and the last thing he needed was to get pulled over for erratic driving; something he noticed he was doing a whole lot of as he fought the relentless urge to fall to sleep. Crystal's crib was his destination; he'd forewarned her that something like this could happen, and he hoped she was paying attention when he told her what to do if such a thing ever happened.

Rasheen stopped at a red light at Utica Avenue and slipped into a snooze. When the light turned green, a car horn in back of him snatched him awake and Rasheen hit the gas pedal. He started blinking his eyes rapidly hoping it would get rid of the severe case of blurred vision.

Five minutes later, the white Buick Regal came to a stop in front of 872 Koskisko Avenue, and Rasheen barely had enough energy to open the door of the double-parked car. When he slid out the car, and applied pressure to his feet, his legs collapsed under the weight of his body and he fell crashing to the asphalt. He looked punch drunk and as though he was half asleep. He laid on his stomach in the gutter breathing hard in between a blue and a beige car. He wanted to just go to sleep and be done with the whole dam thing, but he knew that would spell death. He didn't want to die and his iron-will to live was the only thing that had kept him going this long.

He crawled to the sidewalk. Although he crawled about seven feet, the energy exerted felt like he ran at top speed for two miles. He tried to scream Crystal's name, but nothing came out. He tried it four more times and the most that escaped his voice box was a scratchy voiced whisper.

Suddenly, the ever-present sleepy sensation grabbed him like an angry Vulture and when his eyes closed he saw a bright light. No! I don't wanna die! Rasheen screamed inwardly, surprising himself because it sounded like he shouted the words out loud, but it was apparently inside his head. He rolled onto his back, found his Dessert Eagle, unscrewed the silencer (a task that seemed to take hours), and fired three loud shots into the sky. He was desperate now and didn't care who came, just as long as someone came. As his hand with the Dessert Eagle flopped to the pavement, Rasheen saw he couldn't fight the craving to sleep any longer. The extremely comfortable sensation of lying on his back was just too relaxing to fight it. He closed his eyes and the bright light returned with the force of a nuclear detonation.

Chapter Seven

Crystal Walker sat in the Woodhull Hospital's Operation waiting room with a distressed facial expression. There were six other people in the room and everybody had twisted mugs. Crystal's smooth, golden brown, flawless skin complexion and those intriguing hazel brown eyes, clearly reflected the tension she was experiencing. Rasheen's blood was all over her clothing and her hands. She gazed at the blood and the incident replayed itself inside her head. The three shots had pulled her and half the neighborhood out of their sleep. She ran to her bedroom window and when she saw Rasheen lying sprawled out on the pavement, she just knew he was dead. With frantic speed, she called 911, then threw on a pair of pants and sneakers and was out the door with her mother rushing out of her first floor apartment telling her not to get involved. When Crystal got outside she saw Rasheen covered in blood with the Dessert Eagle in his hand. The White car's driver door was still open and she knew she had some work on her hands. She first checked Rasheen's wrist and sighed with partial relief since there was still a pulse. She then snatched the gun, checked his body for any extra clips, found two, retrieved them, and ran back into her building with the gun and clips concealed under her shirt and stashed them in a garbage can in the back of her building. She returned, jumped in the white Regal and drove the car around the corner, not caring who the hell saw her. She ran back and held Rasheen in her arms until the ambulance and a police car arrived.

Crystal rose to her feet, giving into the urge to pace. Rasheen was currently in the operation room, undergoing surgery. She hadn't seen a doctor yet, so her anxiety was very high. She hoped what she told the police would suffice to keep them from arresting Rasheen. Rasheen had always told her if he was ever shot to make sure she got rid of his gun before doing anything. She was glad she followed those instructions. She had told the police that she heard gunshots, looked out her second floor window and saw her boyfriend lying on the sidewalk. This disturbing image of a black man laying in the street, dying from bullet wounds was an all too familiar image for Crystal, since her father was gunned in front of her when she was six years old. Her dad laid no more than a few feet from where Rasheen currently laid, and dejavu was working overtime on Crystal's mind.

Crystal sighed as she went to the vending machine and purchased another can of cola. Her thoughts were suddenly enmeshed in her schooling and she wondered for the hundredth time was she doing the right thing by getting bogged down with a rough neck? She took pride in the fact she was not only academically inclined, and book smart, but she was also a Hood child to the core. She came up like most children in her community; rough, rugged and raw. Very few survived in one piece if they weren't strong and had a knack for fighting, whether dealing with day-to-day struggles or knowing how to duck and weave stray bullets. Every negative force the Hood had to offer, Crystal was exposed to virtually all of it. Unlike the weak ones, she was blessed with the ability to avoid being swallowed up by these negative influences.

She didn't particularly like bad boys, but Rasheen was different. Even she couldn't believe he was only seventeen. Although it was not unusual for ghetto, urban kids to grow up much faster than rural or country kids, Rasheen didn't just grow up fast, he jumped and skipped pass entire stages of growth and development with such ease and grace it was a perplexing sight to see. The first time Crystal was compelled to take notice of Rasheen Smith was when they were in Public School. During this incident in question Rasheen was a 4th grader while she was a 6th grader. Even then, Rasheen was an aggressive child; he wasn't a mean troublemaker type, nor did he bully the weaker kids, but he had an aura that broadcast danger. Surprisingly, he was a solemn, very quiet, almost shy kind of kid who seemed content being by himself. But, everyone knew from his prior altercations that he was a genuine hell-raiser with a sadistic inclination. It took only three after school fights for everyone to see he wasn't the kind of person to be fucking around with.

In one fight, Rasheen had bit a huge chunk of flesh clean off the face of Fat Jerry, P.S. 118's top bully, and then stabbed him twelve times with a number two pencil. The Fat Jerry conflict was definitely a memorable moment for Crystal, since this particular day Jerry was brutalizing everybody in his path, including her, and Rasheen just happened to be in the area. Fat Jerry slapped Rasheen so hard everyone thought he had knocked Rasheen's head off his shoulders. The on-looking crowd immediately uttered silent prayers for poor little Rasheen who was skinny and so fragile looking. Fat Jerry towered over him like the Titanic ship compared to a one-man canoe. Within twenty seconds flat, Fat Jerry transformed from predator to prey. By the time two adults who had happened to be passing by had arrived, Fat Jerry was out cold, bleeding like a slaughter cow on its way to market, and Rasheen was stomping his bloody face while hurling curse words like a raving maniac. Every single on-looking kid was in a state of utter disbelief, even Loco Louie, who had seen a triple homicide, and was shot in the stomach by a stray bullet when he was only seven years old, had became squeamish at the sight of all the blood.

The second incident happened the following year when a gang of much older kids came to the school to rob, molest and terrorize the whole student body. Everyone thought Rasheen had finally met his match, even Crystal. Rasheen shocked everyone when he single handedly ran all eight of the bullies away when he pulled a 007 switchblade and charged at the gang of big boys shrieking like a deranged, wide eyed lunatic. Once he slashed out at the hand of the boldest dude in the bunch, drawing a sea of blood, everyone knew Rasheen wasn't playing any games. When the gang came back to the public school about a week later, they were acting as though they wanted to continue with the beef and one of them had a gun. Everyone was scared for Rasheen, and low and behold Rasheen shocked everyone when he pulled a gun and had a western style standoff with the gang. It was nothing short of a miracle that shots weren't fired and that the leader of the gang eventually tried to make peace with Rasheen and was even riding his jock like he was a celebrity. One of them said Rasheen had more heart than his whole crew and wanted Rasheen to hang out with them, but Rasheen didn't want to be bothered. To avoid getting him riled up again they pulled way back from Rasheen, giving him plenty space. Crystal's admiration grew and so did her infatuation for Rasheen.

Then, she watched Rasheen take a nose-dive from being a mild-mannered kid who simply had an aggression issue, and a knack for not taking any shit from anybody to becoming a common criminal minded Hood child with a case of severe sticky fingers and absolutely no respect for other people's property. Stealing and robbing became his middle name. Crystal could see that the moment his mother, Barbara, started hitting the crack pipe was the precursor to Rasheen's career as a stick up kid. This was about the time she formally got involved with Rasheen on a more intimate level. She saw dealing with Rasheen, and as a challenge, she secretly wanted to be able to say she was the one who could tame, control, and keep on her bra strap, P.S. 118's Hood renowned hell raiser. Not to mention, Rasheen kept a pocket full of money; she'd been with older guys and not one of them could match up with Rasheen when it came to making money; he needed a little work in the bed department, since biologically he still had the inner physical workings of a kid, he had a premature ejaculation issue and was afraid to go downtown, but his willingness to show her affection and to give her money easily made up for these deficiencies.

Crystal sat sipping on the can of cola when she looked up and saw a doctor enter from the door with the words "Operation Room" on it. He was a tall white man, clean shaved with stringy black hair and reminded Crystal of a hippie from back in the day. He had a clipboard and a pencil in his hands. Crystal and all the other people rose to their feet with pleading expression, hoping he was there to give them some news about their love ones.

The doctor said, "Anyone here for Rasheen Smith?"

Crystal's heart skipped as she rushed over to him, "Yes, I am." She tossed the soda can in the nearby receptacle.

The doctor escorted Crystal beyond the door labeled "Operation Room", stopped once he was on the other side of the door, extended his hand for a shake and said, "I'm Doctor Russell Weinstein."

Crystal shook his hands, and said, "My name's Crystal Walker; I'm Rasheen's girlfriend."

Dr. Weinstein then said, "There's some good news and bad news, which do you want first?" He turned papers on his clipboard.

Crystal heart skipped again and she said, "Let's get the bad news out of the way."

"Well, Mr. Smith lost a tremendous amount of blood, we had to perform a major transfusion. He'll be confined to a bed and will have to wear a colostic bag for quite some time. At some later point in his life, there may be a need for additional surgeries. And, the police believe Mr. Smith may have been involved in some sort of crime."

Crystal gave him a look and a shrug which said, well, where's the rest, then she said, "And the good news?"

"The good news is Mr. Smith is going to make it." He smiled. "He's doing fine considering all the blood he lost."

"So, can I see him?" Crystal eyes pleaded with the Doctor.

There was a short pause as Dr. Weinstein looked around as if he was about to say something very secretive, and then said, "Ah, I'll give you about ten minutes. The police said they'll be here in about twenty minutes to question Mr. Smith. Come on, follow me."

Crystal followed the doctor down the well-lit, ultra clean corridors, which had rooms on each side of the hallway; the smell of medicine and antiseptics was thick in the air. When she entered the room, Crystal saw Rasheen was hooked up to tubes and all sorts of wires. A heart machine beeped loudly, while an oxygen machine was making a weird, suctioning noise. Doctor Weinstein gave her a nod and exited. Crystal felt a surge of pain in her heart because Rasheen looked severely battered. She always viewed hospitals as of place of great pain and suffering, and she hated to even enter these depressing places unless she absolutely had to.

When Rasheen had heard Crystal and Dr. Weinstein enter, he turned his head with a struggle and saw Crystal smiling. He wanted to reach over and lay a crazy wet-one on her, slob her down like she was his Queen of the Nile! Whatever she did, she did the right thing, since he was still on this planet. He noticed he was extremely weak and was in dire need of an ice-cold glass of water. The thirst he was experiencing was so intense it scared him; the first thing he said was, "Give me some water." Tears instantly filled his eyes as his crackling voice box screamed with a dry, razor cutting pain. He tried to swallow down some saliva to sooth the pain without much luck.

Crystal found his hand, caressed it and said, "I don't think you should try to drink anything yet. The Doctor said I only got ten minutes. And he said the police are coming here to talk to you."

Rasheen eyes squinted as the wave of anxiety took hold of him. Police! He wanted to say, but he felt his voice wasn't ready for another try.

"You ain't gotta talk," Crystal said softly. "Just listen, Boo. I did like you said. I told them I heard shots and saw you lying there. I stashed the gun, clips, and moved the car around the corner."

Rasheen thought about the money, decided the hell with his soar throat, and whispered, "What's up with Jack-Mack?"

"I called his house, and he told me to tell you everything's gravy." She smiled because she knew this meant whatever they robbed they had at least got the money. Since Rasheen wasn't a petty dude she knew it was a nice piece of cheddar.

Rasheen tamed the smile that was trying to force its way to the surface. His thoughts shifted to his baby brother, who was at the apartment alone. "What about Lameek?"

"I'm keeping an eye on him," Crystal started massaging Rasheen's arm. "I'll go check on him when I leave here. If you want, I'll bring him here to see you tomorrow."

"What about your mom?"

"She beefin' about all the drama, but she'll get over it."

Rasheen looked around realized everything looked more alive, he felt re-invigorated, even though his energy was low. It was definitely a mental thing. Just knowing he had knocked on the door of death, rubbed elbows with the Grimm reaper, and escaped his deadly clutches, made him feel extraordinarily lucky. Gut shots were life threatening and he'd known at least a dozen dudes from his Hood alone who died with a stomach full of bullets. Even though the bullet went straight through him, Rasheen knew there was stuff in the stomach that was obviously important to life. His sudden urgency to take life much more serious was growing by the seconds. He started kicking himself in the ass, for not wearing body armor. Bulletproof vests didn't cost a lot and he knew they had clothing of all kinds made of bulletproof fabric. He'd heard the garments came in all styles like tee shirts, hats, jackets, pants, and so on. From what he'd heard, any garment could be made with bulletproofed fabric. Realizing how close he came to losing his life, he vowed to take stuff like body armor much more serious. He wondered why Killer Kato didn't offer them a few vests. He definitely had a few lying around, and even saw his people wearing them. Then he asked himself, "How could I have been so stupid not to protect myself?"

Crystal looked at her watch, rose to her feet, and said, "I gotta go, Rasheen. The doctor'll be in here beefin' in a second. And I don't wanna be here when the police get here. I ain't up to another round with them." She gave Rasheen a kiss on his crusty, water depraved lips, and caressed his face. "I'll be back tomorrow when I get off work." She headed for the door.

Rasheen nodded his head as Crystal turned, waved and disappeared out the door. Rasheen started working his story around in his head; he wasn't worried about the police too much, since all they probably wanted to know was how he got shot, who done it and all that other snitch ass shit. He knew they couldn't link him to the drama over in East New York, since Crystal already laid the ground work for saying he was shot in front of her crib. That was all good! The thought of all that money brought a smile to his face.

His mind flashbacked back to the size of that tote bag, and he knew there had to be at least 200 grand in of it. Oh, yeah, goddamn! It was on for sure! Then, suddenly, Rasheen sighed angrily because he had wanted to tell Crystal to tell Jack-Mack to get up here so they could talk about that money. Then he realized Jack-Mack should know to get up here without anyone telling him. Then, common sense told him Jack-Mack obviously had to lay low until all the heat subsided.

After a moment of mental aerobics about the things he could get with the money, Dirty Ricky's predicament came to mind. Damn, man! That was some real fucked up shit! He could image Ricky's mom bugging out when she got the news. Suddenly, the stark realization hit him! For the first time he realized, he and Jack-Mack could be connected to Dirty Ricky. Everyone in their Hood knew Dirty Ricky was hanging out hard and heavy with him and Jack-Mack. Ah shit, Rasheen mumbled to himself, as a nervous tension began to grow. After repeatedly telling himself that as long as there were no witnesses who could identify him and Jack-Mack as participants at the Livonia and Alabama shoot out they would be all right, he was able to relax. When the seventy gees he owed Killer Kato came to his mind, his relaxed demeanor disappeared. He and Jack-Mack had to come up with a way to get this dude out of their hair. The thought of giving this cutthroat nigga seventy grand was eating him alive.

A moment later, Rasheen saw two detectives enter his room. They both wore suits and this instantly made Rasheen nervous because the DTs who wore suits were usually from the homicide division. One DT was white, chubby with blonde hair and clean shaved. The other DT was a light skin black man with a Caesar hair cut, was bulky on the muscular side, and wore a neatly trimmed goatee. Rasheen instantly pretended as though he was groggy, making his eyes appear sleepy.

"Mr. Rasheen Smith," The black Detective said as he pulled up a chair and the white DT did the same.

No good, Rasheen thought, they were getting comfortable, which meant this was going to be a long, drawn out cat and mouse game. Rasheen immediately started gearing his mind up for the long haul.

The white DT said, "I'm Detective Gallo and my partner is Detective Robertson. I guess you know we're here to talk about your little incident. Ah, I understand you were shot in front of your girlfriend's apartment. Would you like to elaborate?"

Rasheen tried to pretend he was having problems with his throat; he pointed to his throat gesturing he couldn't talk.

With a fake smile, Detective Robertson said, "Doctor Weinstein said you should be able to talk to us. Your injury involves your stomach, not your throat. He also told us your girlfriend just left."

Rasheen sighed, realizing he was making himself look guilty by refusing to say anything. He decided to just tell them what Crystal had told them. In a whispering voice he said, "Listen man, I was going to my girlfriend's crib and a car drove by and some cats started shooting. I got hit in the stomach and that's all I remember. I ain't see no faces cause it was dark."

Both Detectives nodded their heads and had that expression, which said, come on, keep going.

Right then and there Rasheen decided to zip up, put a padlock on his lips and vowed he wasn't saying shit else. He even felt self-conscious knowing what he just told them. It wasn't snitching, but talking to the police about anything was taboo of the utmost degree. After reevaluating this line of approach, weighing the pros and cons of this plan of action, he knew he had to take a few steps back. Primarily because on the flipside, he knew he was supposed to be the victim, and if he got a little too belligerent it might draw unnecessary suspicion to himself. With this in mind, he made it his business to answer questions, but to remember to stay in character while doing so.

Detective Gallo cleared his throat, "Mr. Smith, how old are you?"

Rasheen wasn't surprised by the onslaught of questions that followed. He answered them concisely without any extra verbiage. They asked about everything, from why he was in the street at such a god-forsaken hour, to where was his mother. By the time the questions began to slow up a bit, Rasheen had developed a nasty, snotty attitude and decided he didn't want to answer any more questions. Rasheen said, "Y'all actin' like I did somethin' wrong. A mufucka shoot me and now y'all comin' at me all crazy."

"Who's Ricardo Sanchez?" Detective Robertson said with a cocky smirk.

Rasheen looked at the DTs as though they were crazy. He didn't know nobody by that name and decided not even to entertain the thought.

Detective Gallo chimed in when he saw Rasheen's facial expression. "You might know him as Dirty Ricky."

Rasheen felt shock waves erupted through his system. He tried to play it off, but he knew his phony facial smirk gave him away. This question caught him completely off guard because it was a loaded question. With the quickness, Rasheen said, "I don't know who that is."

Both Detectives knew Rasheen was lying; his nervous response told on him. They also knew they couldn't shake him up with all those little scare tactics; Rasheen was handling himself better than most of the veteran criminals they had interrogated. So, they decide to spring the bomb on him and see how he reacted, maybe this would soften him up a little.

Detective Robertson said, "Were you driving a white Buick Regal on the night you were shot?"

Another explosive shock wave shook Rasheen to the core, and he instantly realized they had been navigating him down a bomb-laden path all along. There was no question they knew something, but how much they knew was the question. Rasheen decided to flip the shit back on them, and also try to find out what was really going on. He said, "What's all these questions all about? Y'all accusing me of something?"

Both Detectives glanced at each other as if to say, should we let him have it now. They rode the ten seconds of silence like expert mind manipulators.

Detective Robertson leaned back in his chair, turned a page in his small notepad, glanced at whatever was written down and said, "Mr. Rasheen Smith, your blood was found in a carjacked white Buick Regal; the owner of that vehicle picked your picture out of a photo array and he claims you struck him over the head with a gun; besides the fact your blood was found in the area where the carjacking transpired, strange enough, your blood was also found at a crime scene a few blocks away where eight dead bodies were discovered, including the dead body of your good friend Dirty Ricky."

Detective Gallo cleared his throat for dramatic emphasis, and he said, "With those cards on the table, do you think we should be accusing you of something?"

Chapter Eight

Rasheen never knew he could feel so much distress until he was arrested for multiple counts of murder, carjacking, assault with a deadly weapon, and an array of miscellaneous felony offenses. He also discovered that incarceration and friendship didn't mix very well. After Rasheen spent two weeks in Woodhull Hospital with a cop posted in front of his room, he was officially arraigned in Brooklyn Supreme Court and transferred to Rikers Island's C-74 Infirmary Unit. Of all the things that were gnawing at his patience, the one that chewed away chunks of his tolerance was the fact that his ace Homie, Jack-Mack, was actin' up. Rasheen still had no idea how much money they made on the Livonia and Alabama run, but he did get word that Killer Kato got 50 gees of the 70 he owed him. Rasheen was locked in a love, hate thing with Jack-Mack. Every time he started plotting how he was going to kill him when his feet touch the bricks, he would realize that Jack-Mack had a right to stay as far away from him as possible. The court appointed lawyer even confirmed that the police were looking for another culprit, which was obviously Jack-Mack. Only after Rasheen put himself in Jack-Mack's shoes did he calm down enough to realize he was overreacting. But, whenever that money crossed his mind, a fury as powerful as twenty hurricanes swirl up in the pit of his stomach and Jack-Mack was called every foul name in the English language.

Years ago when Rasheen did six months at DFY (Harlem Valley) for slapping his sixth grade teacher for calling him a "dumb nigger" was nothing like what he was currently experiencing. This was the Island and everybody in the Hood knew about this notorious jail located in the East River, smack dap in between the Boroughs of Queens and the Bronx. If you were hustling, drug dealing, boosting, sticking up, or was doing anything considered illicit you had to at some point in your career contemplate spending time on the infamous Rikers Island. Everybody also knew if you could make it there you could probably make it anywhere, and the rap lyrics "You won't be smiling when you're on Rikers Island" was loaded with a whole lot of truth. Rasheen hadn't smiled one time since he'd been there. The shit bag (colostic bag) Rasheen had to wear was the most annoying, torturous thing he'd ever experienced in his life. Because of his condition he was placed in the infirmary surrounded by a bunch of sick crazy motherfuckers who got on his nerves every second of the day. The MO (mentally unstable) prisoners asked for cigarettes all day long; they smoked cigarettes from off the floor, pissed and shitted on themselves, ate just about anything thing from off the floor, and talked to imagery people constantly. Rasheen felt like he was released from hell when they put him in population four months later when he could shit without that smelly embarrassing ass shit bag.

Rasheen entered the cellblock like an atomic explosion. The main rule of survival in prison was clear all over the world; only the strong survived. To Rasheen's Hood oriented mind this was interpreted one way; bleeding knuckles and a home-made knife dripping with blood was the best way to demonstrate he was in accord with this universal rule of law. The first fool who would experience Rasheen's fury was some ugly cat named Wayno from the Bronx, who was running the whole cellblock Upper 5 with a ruthless iron fist, a crew of puppets, and a couple of homemade shanks, of course. Rasheen entered Upper 5 dragging everything he currently owed, which was a garbage bag full of clothes and a beat-up mattress. Rasheen placed his stuff in cell # 13 and went straight to work. He dug in his bag, retrieved two thick aluminum shanks he'd made while in the infirmary, tucked them in his waist, and stepped straight to the phone. It was also universally known that the phone was a main source of much conflict on the Island. Full-scale riot style wars were known to spark up over the "Jack" and this was a good way for Rasheen to get a situation going in order to let everybody know there was a new boss in town.

Without asking anyone, Rasheen picked up the phone, dialed Crystal's number, turned and watched the whole cellblock started forming Voltron (a term used to describe when prisoners gang up together to attack an adversary). Rasheen talked to Crystal for about twenty minutes and then said, "Listen, Crystal, I gotta go. I'll call you back soon, alright. Love you, boo." He hung up the phone and turned around.

"Yo' little nigga, you know you violated!" Wayno shouted. His eyes wide with rage; his bulky body and his twisted grill made him look like a baby Incredible Hulk. "In this house, you ask permission before you go touchin' shit."

Rasheen saw the nine other prisoners taking their places, trying to place him in a circle. Without further a due, Rasheen pulled both shanks, knowing there was no way he was going to allow them to box him in a circle. The first thrust of the shank caught a skinny dude wearing a blue tank top dead on the right cheek, causing blood to spray like an aerosol can as the dude screamed like a terrified little girl. As the dude scream with ear torturous agony, Rasheen zoned out and started stabbing, jabbing, poking, and plunging both shanks into anyone who came near him.

Within moments, five of his ten attackers were either lying stretched out on the floor, or clutching blood squirting wounds with no intentions of re-emerging back into the conflict.

The remaining five attackers were terrified, but prison egos were known to turn apprehensive bullies into suicidal maniacs, and all five of them acted accordingly, rushing at Rasheen wielding their weapons.

With several vicious swings of the shanks, Rasheen easily knocked four more of them out of the knife fight, since they didn't have what Rasheen possessed: an iron will and a deeply rooted fear of being dubbed a bitch. Not to mention Rasheen had a peculiar ability to unleash an ancient style savagery that was foreign in this day and age. This explosive fervor had actually compelled most of these attackers to simply take a stab or two, so as not to destroy their reputations too badly, and to go ahead about their business, but Wayno wasn't thinking along those lines. He was boss man of his squad and knew a thing or two about fighting with a savage viciousness as well.

Rasheen locked eyes with Wayno, breathing extremely hard with exhaustion as the two sized each other up. This was no good at all; the tiredness he felt was so overwhelming, it scared him, since his lungs were on fire and he felt faint. A nervous realization seeped into his thoughts; he was now weakened by the scuffle; his stomach wound was acting up, and he even felt dizzy. The dangerous voice of doubt was wiggling its way into his mind. Looking at the knife Wayno possessed Rasheen realized it wasn't a homemade shank. It was one of those folding knives with a stainless steel blade about six inches long. The doubt was growing stronger. The only thing Rasheen knew he had going for himself at the moment was that the other attackers had the fear of God in them and weren't about to take another crack at him.

Wayno charged at Rasheen swinging the knife with sincere malice. Rasheen saw the fear in Wayno's eyes and that was enough to give him something to feed off of, and to reverse the rapidly growing doubt and indecisiveness. Rasheen weaved out of the knife's path and stabbed Wayno in the side just above the hipbone.

"Ahhh!!" Wayno shrieked with horrifying force, causing Rasheen to follow up with a jab to Wayno's shoulder blade. Rasheen tried to jump out of Wayno's reach as he charge at him with his head down, but his luck had ran out. Terror rushed through Rasheen's body as Wayno caught hold of his shirt. Rasheen dropped one of his shanks and immediately grabbed Wayno's arm possessing the knife. With wide-eyed shock, Rasheen felt like a rag doll as Wayno manhandled him as though he was a helpless infant in hands of a deranged parent.

After Rasheen inflicted four carefully placed plunges of the shank, strategically aimed at Wayno's midsection, Rasheen saw all of Wayno's fight was instantly zapped from him. He let go of Rasheen and collapsed lifelessly to the floor.

Rasheen was now breathing even harder than before; he examined his handy-work, and by the look of Wayno's wounds and the blood rapidly escaping his body, he just knew he was now facing a jailhouse body. Suddenly, the riot squad crashed through the gate, pulling Rasheen out of the rage-laden trance. When he saw the dozens of bully clubs in the hands of the twisted faced goons, he bowed down gracefully, dropped his weapons and followed the riot squad's instructions.

This first impression and prelude to Rasheen's appearance on the scene cost him four months in the "Bing", otherwise known as solitary confinement, the box, the hole, or SHU (Special Housing Unit), depending on where the violator found himself. Since Wayno didn't die nor did anyone else, Rasheen was charged and found guilty of multiple counts of assault with a weapon. Rasheen took his vacation in the Bing all in stride. This knife battle forced him take notice of the fact that he was light in the ass on the weight side and his wind was totally twisted. He remembered how Wayno tossed him around like a rag doll when he got hold of his shirtsleeve, and it was apparent that with a little more weight on his bones, he could protect himself against such a combat deficiency in the future. Even before he got shot, he had a relatively average body weight, but after the stomach wound he'd loss about 10 pounds that wouldn't seem to come back. It was time to "pump up the volume" as brother Rakim would say, and Rasheen started an exercise regiment consisting of push ups, sit ups, handstand presses, deep knee bends, toe raises, jogging in place, and eating everything he got his hands on. When Rasheen stepped out of the Bing, no one could tell him he wasn't the top Gladiator in the whole joint.

Rasheen stepped inside Lower 10 and instantly saw that word traveled like a brushfire on a dry scorching hot summer day in the Dessert. The red carpet, the blue carpet, the green carpet and all other carpets used to show mad love for honorary folks were laid out for him. Single handedly going up against and taking down ten thorough jailhouse thugs and living to talk about it was no petty feat; any sane person knew he had to recognize a real dude who was about showing and proving. Now that Rasheen firmly established that he was not the one to be fuckin' around with, it was now time to straighten out his pockets. Empty pockets, echo chambers in the locker, and starving like Marvin was something that was not going be tolerated. It didn't take long for Rasheen to realize there weren't many hustles in jail. Cats who worked in the Mess hall sold the shit they stole, but Rasheen knew that was utter peanuts. Extortion was a possible means of income, but the cash flow wasn't fast enough for a cat like him. The only booming business that could get his pockets right in a reasonable amount of time was drugs.

This presented a dilemma for Rasheen. He hated drugs with such a passion, he avoided selling them when he was on the street; he hated them so much he made a short career out of robbing drug dealers, and now he couldn't believe he was seriously considering getting into that game. Money sure had a way of changing people, he realized because the bottom line of it all boiled down to getting money. After closely watching the drug peddlers throughout the jail do their thing, and seeing how fast they were bringing in the money, he couldn't simply look the other way. The thought of robbing them crossed his mind, but that wouldn't work because that would result in constant war, since he would still have to live with the folks he would be robbing. He had no choice but to get involved in the drug game. With his thirsty and zealous attitude, he knew this game could make him filthy rich. The more he thought about it, the more he found himself unable to pull back.

After two days of toying with the idea of selling drugs, he decided to break his vow not to sell drugs. When his mother's bout with crack surfaced in his mind, his stress skyrocketed to abnormal levels. While in the Bing, he received a visit from his mom informing him that she was forced to leave the rehab because the Child Welfare Agency was investigating her to determine if they were going to take Lameek from her, and possibly have her arrested for endangering the welfare of a minor. His hatred of the system grew in that moment to an inordinate degree because they knew his mom was in a rehab, trying to get her life together. They weren't even trying to consider the fact that her sister, Carol, vouched for the fact that she had left him and Lameek under her care. True to their destructive propensity for destroying black families they weren't trying to hear shit. Seeing her on the visit with her weight up, and her skin shining like polished bronze mixed with gold, was enough to make Rasheen smile. However, knowing full well that it was his arrest for serious felonies that had caused the Child Welfare Agency to begin investigating his mom was touching his heart in a fucked up way. Although she talked as if she was back in action and was here to stay, Rasheen knew how powerful the drama in the Hood combined with the annoying nature of the system could be on a person dangling from a thin string that could snap and land the person back in the pits of hell. Even knowing his mom's delicate state wasn't strong enough to compete with Rasheen's need for fat pockets, and he forged forward with full force, shifting his way of making money with his head held high.

Rasheen decided to make weed his first product, then cocaine, and eventually heroin. Wisely, he knew he had to crawl, walk and then run. He was never the stupid type, and trying to take on the biggest before the smallest would be the equivalent of tinkering with disaster. Plus, the heroin game was bonkers! The money he could make off this particular drug was sheer amazing. When he got to know a few heroin sellers and they taught him the game, he was drooling by the time he completed the course. No wonder Killer Kato was in to this shit, he thought on several occasions, and now he wondered what the fuck was on his mind for not getting down with this program earlier? He'd always known the money was crazy large, but now that he was in prison trying to make money he sensed his sudden enthusiastic openness towards drugs was a severe case of selective anemia; as long as it was conductive to his pockets he was willing to forget whatever it was that was getting in the way of him making that money. Phase one of his plan would be to slide all weed peddlers either out of the game or put them under his wing in such a way that he got a piece of all the action. Phase two would emulate phase one, but would apply to the cocaine traffickers. Phase three would be the same old song, but would involve heroin.

Rasheen was somewhat surprised at how fast it took him to formulate a team. People were dying to be led and Rasheen had no problem leading them. It was even more perplexing that some real official dudes didn't mind being led, but those were the ones Rasheen knew to keep his eye on, since they had the heart to bring the drama and the potential to flip the script when shit didn't go their way. Right now Rasheen was the man, he was a gunman to the tenth degree and people respected him as such. However, one slip up could result in one sneaky solid blow to the heart, which every thorough cat knew could end it all. That's why Rasheen ruled with an iron fist, but showed super love to the super hard hitters; not enough love for them to get it twisted, but just enough to let them know they all could and will continue to eat as long as they banned together, and Rasheen was the Captain of the ship, of course. Obviously, in order to maintain this position, every now and then Rasheen knew he had to put some work in. He'd find the newest terror to hit the Island and put either the knuckles or the knife on him. No question, this tactic worked every time and was so effective it was magical.

Rasheen realized he needed another component to his plan, and that was a mule. Although he'd found two cats in C-74 who had girls that were bringing in big balloons of weed twice a week, Rasheen needed his own source of weed. During a visit with Crystal in February of 1995, Rasheen was planning to make the proposition to her, but as he entered the C-74 visiting room and saw Crystal's face, he knew she was stressed out.

Dressed in a tight ass gray jumpsuit, Rasheen gave Crystal a tongue kiss, a firm hug, and they both took seats. Rasheen gazed into Crystal's eyes and noticed she had been crying. "What's up, Crystal?" Rasheen said as he reached across the small plastic table and caressed her hands. "Look like you got some crazy shit on your mind."

Crystal knew the best way to deal with Rasheen was to come straight up without all the mind games. She sighed and said, "Yo Rasheen, that nigga Killer Kato is on some real bullshit."

An avalanche of emotions covered Rasheen's mind with the purest form of rage. For a moment he couldn't breathe and instantly started perspiring. "What that motherfucka did? He did somethin' to you, Crystal?"

Crystal suddenly felt awkward because she was gearing up to tell it like it was, even though it would break his heart. "This nigga been pushin' up on me, flashin' his money all up in my face and shit. He beefin' about you owe him money, and since I'm your girl, I should break him off a piece of some pussy..."

"When did this happen?" Rasheen struggled to stay calm. He decided in this moment that Killer Kato would die. He didn't know when, where or how, but one day, some how, some way, he would slay that motherfucker.

"He's been tryin' to get at me ever since you left," Crystal sighed and saw Rasheen was in the fire zone. "Rasheen, I ain't wanna dump this shit in your lap while you in here, which is why I didn't bring it up. I...I'm down with you, Boo, but this nigga is... He told me to stop fuckin' with you or he's gonna..."

"He told you to stop fuckin' with me?" Rasheen's voice went up two notches. Crystal was his main girl and he knew she wasn't no ride or die chick. She was a good loyal girl as long as he was there beside her keeping her monetary and sexual needs fulfilled. But, the truth of the matter was, she was a genuine gold digger. As long as a nigga had cheddar and she was getting broken off, it was all good. He'd always knew this fact, but never really thought about it in depth until now; now that he was in jail and couldn't regulate the way he normally did. Rasheen decided to play along. "Crystal, you gonna let this nigga break us up?"

"Rasheen, you know Killer Kato be shootin' people for all kinda bullshit. He just shot Brent and his girl, Linda. They don't even know if Linda's gonna make it. I'm in college, Rasheen, and I can't live like this. I love you, but..."

"But, not enough to die for me," Rasheen said calmly and was tempted to reach across the small plastic table and slap flames out of her ass. Common sense stopped him from taking this approach because it told him he couldn't get mad with her. She wasn't a killer, and obviously couldn't be expected to stand up to a killer. He was infuriated by her inability to standup to Killer Kato, but he quickly got his anger towards her under control. He suddenly started to feel guilty because he owed her his life; she saved him and no matter what she did, he couldn't forget that. He cleared his throat and said, "So, basically, you telling me that's the end of you and me? You said Killer Kato's trying to push up on you? You fuckin' this nigga, Crystal?"

"No, Rasheen," Crystal said, but couldn't look him in the eyes. She tried it again, but couldn't do it.

Rasheen felt devastated; this feeling of sheer defeat was an emotion he could never handle quite well. Killer Kato was fucking his main squeeze and was treating him as if he was his worst enemy. Suddenly, Rasheen asked himself, "Why was this nigga doing this to him?" There had to be some ulterior motive besides money for all this shit. He'd given him most of his money, so that couldn't be a reason to start violating a girl everybody knew was his main chick and who he had mad love for. Fucking a nigga's girl while he was on lockdown was the ultimate form of disrespect in the Hood, and no matter how you cut it up, a head had to roll. He couldn't believe he didn't try to kill this chump the minute he tried to lay that pressure game on him. All sorts of ways of pulling off such a hit instantly came to his mind and he felt steam oozing through his pores, knowing he didn't think of them earlier. Yeap, everybody was definitely writing him off as dead and stinking, and rightfully so. Any mufucka charged with seven bodies was dead as far as the Hood was concerned. The Hood also knew the court system was so corrupt and racism was so rampant, it was virtually impossible for any black man to get a fair trial, especially if his money wasn't extremely long. Crystal was human like everybody else, Rasheen rationalized as he gazed into her water-ridden eyes, and he wasn't even mad she was counting him out too, since he counted himself out of the game as well.

"There's something else, Rasheen." Crystal said, locking eyes with him.

Rasheen sighed impatiently, shifting in his seat since he knew it was more bad news by the way she paused while looking into his eyes to see if it was safe to dump some more bullshit on him. "Well, what is it? Might as well open the flood gates."

"Killer Kato put your brother down with a rap group and he's supposed to be getting them a record deal." Crystal looked away. "And he got your mom's to go along with the program."

"When the fuck did this happen?" Rasheen was seconds from spazzing completely out. "How...But I..." He sighed frustratedly, realizing Killer Kato was now venturing into territories that would turn him into a suicidal lunatic. He now understood why his mom stopped bringing Lameek up to see him. This would also explain why they stopped responding to his letters, since normally his mom would encourage Lameek to write and she would insure that the letters were mailed.

"I didn't want to hit you with all this at one time, but I think you oughta know. Your mother begged me not to tell you. I didn't promise her anything, so . . . I'm hearing Lameek might be one of the youngest rappers to hit the market."

"That nigga is gonna pimp my motherfuckin' family!" Rasheen felt thunderbolts of realization smashing down upon him. "Is my mom back on that shit?"

Crystal said nothing as her eyes wandered.

Rasheen felt his whole world crumbling around him. She was back on the pipe. He didn't have to be told that Killer Kato had re-addicted his mom to crack in order to get to Lameek. It took every drop of hatred in his heart to hold back the tears. This wasn't the time to embrace weakness of any kind, and with remarkable efficiency, Rasheen snapped himself back into reality. His heart hardened while his will to obtain revenge grew even harder.

Rasheen and Crystal talked for another fifteen minutes about mundane, trivial issues and he gave Crystal her last kiss and departed as friends; before leaving she promised to be there for him, send him letters every now and then and a few dollars whenever she could, but Rasheen knew it was all game. He'd been locked up for over a year and hadn't received much love from her or anyone else, and it was only logical to conclude that things weren't going to change in the near future. In any event, he wasn't stupid enough to believe he would be immune from the reality of the out of sight out of mind prison syndrome.

It took Rasheen two months flat with an eight-man crew to lock down the whole weed business throughout C-74. If a bag was sold and if Rasheen's hands weren't involved in it, all violators had some serious explaining to do or had to pay the piper in blood. The money was decent, but it wasn't as splendid as Rasheen wanted. On a very good week, Rasheen was touching about two gees after his whole crew got their share, which was about a thousand less than Rasheen.

Rasheen was also witnessing a new phenomenon taking place right before his eyes; Gang proliferation was reaching its zenith. Gangs were springing up out of the dirt like weeds and dandelions in an unkept lawn. It seemed like every week there was a new gang appearing in the jails of Rikers Island, and Rasheen had no problem making it known to all of them that his business dealings were off limits to all. The most prevalent gangs to hit the scene were the Bloods, Latin Kings, Netas, the Smokes, the Lions, the Crips, and a few others Rasheen could never remember the names. Some were major threats to Rasheen's cash flow, like the

Bloods, Latino Kings and Netas, while others were just trying to copycat the real bangers and could easily be quieted down with a few senseless acts of violence. Almost every prisoner was affiliated with some kind of group or gang. There were also cultural and religious groups like the Muslims, the Nation of Gods, and Earths, the NOI, the Ansa Community, and even the Christians. In any environment where people were forced to survive amongst people of different ethnic, social, religious, and political views, grouping up was inevitable. Since no sane person could expect the prison guards to provide them with safety from the chaos of prison life, the very prison system not only encouraged grouping up and gang proliferation, but they made it a prerequisite to survival. Rasheen and his multi-racial eight man crew (Apache, Leo, Deadeye, Ice, Wink, El-sun, Carlito & Brownsville) could be viewed as a gang, since they operated from a strict code of unity and brotherhood, but pity the fool who tried to clump them into that "gang shit" as they so eloquently would put it.

Two months of weed peddling and Rasheen was ready to turn it up and proceed to phase two. Just when Rasheen was ready to sit his crew down and explain the way he intended to implement the logistics for locking down the cocaine in the joint, he got news from the street. He'd recently made Camila his girl and she was troopering for him now. Camila told him his mom was not only back on the pipe, but was fucking with heroin. According to Camila, she was worse than she was before. But what really got Rasheen's blood boiling was Camila informed him that Lameek was selling drugs for none other than Killer Kato. At 12 years of age he was doing hand-to-hand, street corner drug sales and had even dropped out of school. Camila was even aware of the fact that Lameek was still rapping and that Killer Kato was sponsoring Lameek. Rasheen almost cried upon hearing all this bad news and when Camila told him Killer Kato was sporting Crystal around the Hood like she was some kind of trophy or something, he couldn't take it anymore, and didn't want to hear another word about anything going on out there.

This was when Rasheen decided he was going to get out of jail. The facts indicated that in order to get out, he needed money for a real lawyer. He started shooting crazy game on Camila and she ate it up like free lunch. She became the best mule money could buy. Rasheen knew he was taking a chance having money sent to Camila, since she was the epitome of a Hood rat with a big heart and an unquenchable thirst for money, but there was no other way to get his plan off and running. He would have drug money sent to Camila and have her go find him a good lawyer. Just when she received the first wave of jailhouse drug money, good news struck. Rasheen went to court and found out that the DA was offering him a cop out. They were offering him a 12 to 20 for the carjacking and the assault. Since there was no evidence besides his blood at the scene of the murders, this wasn't enough to convict him, so those particular charges stood a strong chance of being dropped. Rasheen never felt this happy in his life. He told his lawyer that he needed a few days to think about the cop out offer and the Judge adjourned the case for two weeks.

For the first time since being on the Island for 20 months, Rasheen sat and talked to a jailhouse lawyer, named Victor Reid, and decided when he returned to court he would take the cop out. He would have to go up North for 12 years before he would see the parole board; it was a nice little stretch, but comparing it to where he stood a couple of weeks back, he could now see a bright light at the end of the tunnel. He was tempted to fight them to the bitter end, but with the owner of the white Buick Regal was ready to take the stand and knowing his blood was in the car, it would've been a losing battle.

On March 22, 1996, the day Rasheen appeared for sentencing, he entered the Court with a hidden smile and saw a group of strange people sitting in the courtroom. His Hood alarms went off registering danger was in the midst as he laid eyes on the four Latino looking men. When Rasheen saw one of them point a finger at him imitating a gun, he realized the fireworks were about to begin. The Columbians loss seven of their people in the Alabama and Livonia spot, and there was no way they were planning on wiping such a loss on their chest and just let it ride. They had been waiting to see if Rasheen was really the one. Now that he was copping out, it was all they were waiting for. Rasheen suddenly realized that this was probably the reason the DA was having difficulty prosecuting those homicides since the Columbians probably made sure the State had no witnesses. They always kept it funky; the streets always kept it in the streets.

Rasheen found himself in that all too familiar situation of having to make a choice. If he copped out he would be telling those Columbians in the court looking over his shoulder that he was the one who murdered their people, and if he took it to trial he would be found guilty and get the max, which would be a minimum of 25 years to life. It took Rasheen about a minute to decide. He'd take his chances with the 12 to 20 year prison sentence, since right about now his desire to put a few bullets in Killer Kato's head was far more overpowering than his fear of the Columbians.

Chapter Nine

On June 13, 1996, Rasheen entered Clinton as one of the youngest prisoners in the facility. He was 19 in a men's prison where the State's most dangerous criminals roamed. How he got to one of New York State's top three toughest disciplinary facilities (Attica & Comstock being the other two) was a mystery to Rasheen and even his prison Guidance Counselor. At Downstate Reception Center, when Rasheen heard he was going to Clinton, his stress levels skyrocketed. He was now rollin' with the super big boys. Since Clinton was only a few miles from the Canadian border and took over 8 hours to get there from the city, Rasheen saw major drama on the horizon with getting Camila to continue muling for him. Trying to imagine Camila spending 16 hours on a beat up bus just wasn't clicking in his mind.

All eyes were on Rasheen the moment he stepped foot in Clinton. From booty bandits to gang recruiters, Rasheen was in full demand, since he simply could not hide that baby face of his. After he got his hands on a shank, he answered everyone's inquiries. Shorty ain't having it. Rasheen heard so much about booty bandits, who brutally raped young boys entering the system, and he took great pleasure in collapsing both lungs of Clinton's top little boy chaser and breaker, Dirty Dick Shawn. Unlike the Island, upstate adult prisoners got a thrill out of "gettin' it on" with a "thumper" who fought back, so Rasheen had to lay down two more very worthy opponents in order to help the prison population get in their heads; shorty ain't having it.

This three month prelude taught Rasheen many valuable lessons; all of which he passed with flying colors. The main lesson was a man who can stand up to pressure alone will invariably attract people of like stature. The Nation of Gods and Earths gained everlasting eternity respect from Rasheen, because they were the only ones who made sure he got a fair one each time he had to do a knife dance. Without the backing of the Gods, he would have definitely been easily murdered. Rasheen knew he had a heart bigger than a hundred African warriors combined, but there was no way he could've survived a Voltron hit by a gang of experienced shank users. This wasn't Rikers Island where most cats were just coming off the streets who only knew how to shoot a gun, and couldn't handle a knife or fight a single lick. This was up north where almost every prisoner was doing very hard time and handling a knife was about as common as using eating utensils.

Thanks to certain Gods, (Rondu, Born Master, Everlasting & Divine Supreme), Rasheen was able to get wind of every Columbian sponsored contract hit on his head, and of the exact crew or individual picking up the track. Knowing the who, what, when and where of prison hits made life real easy, since Rasheen could strike first and baffle the sponsor into believing he was far more dangerous and influential than he really was. After three failed hits, the Columbians stop sending out hitters, but Rasheen knew they were just waiting for a more experienced hitter to get to the Facility. The only hitters Rasheen knew who had that kind of clout and skills were the Rat Hunters, but they had good relations with the Gods. Since Rasheen was under the wing of certain Gods, he knew he was partially safe as long as Rondu, Born Master and Divine Supreme were in the prison. When they left and a real Rat Hunter arrived, he knew the Columbians would send a hitter, the type that didn't fuck up hits, because for each blunder they made they often paid with their very own life.

After the tension started to subside, Rasheen began constructing his drug selling team. Unlike the Island where Rasheen was amongst dudes his physical age, Clinton was an adult facility where the average prisoner was between the ages of 23 to 31. Rasheen being 19 years old was considered a baby in the eyes of most, and as such, most prisoners' egos were too big for them to allow a young cat to regulate a flourishing drug business. Even though Rasheen was well respected, and even had many older cats under pressure, most prisoners just couldn't open the door for others to perceive them as weak, and allowing oneself to be regulated by a little kid was a sure sign of weakness. But Rasheen was persistent and wouldn't give up. It didn't take long for him to figure out that he had to play the background, something he hated. With the help of Rondu, Divine Supreme and Born Master, Rasheen got his weed business popping. Once things got established, Rasheen started expanding, broadening his horizons to both the east and west side of Clinton. He was hitting off workers on the down-low and made them swear not to tell anyone who their suppler was. Rasheen was also surprised by Camila's loyalty. She beefed, bitched and whined a mile a minute about the long ass rides up to Clinton, but she was there like clockwork. In view of the difficult ride, Rasheen agreed to receive a visit from her twice a month, each trip she dropped off about three ounces of weed.

Things were going fine for about two months of uninterrupted moneymaking ecstasy, but with all good things come drama. Rasheen saw snitching was something that was everywhere. He'd always assumed the big boys had more morals and principles and kept it real and funky, but the truth of the matter was that they were doing more telling than the younger cats. Rasheen got a major surprise when he started getting too big for his breeches. There were so many undercover haters Rasheen didn't know where to begin looking. Cats would smile in his face and literally stab him in the back by dropping snitch slips on him. For two weeks straight the C.O.'s stayed in his cell daily, searching for what they called "contraband", which was another name for "drugs" and "weapons". Thanks to all the tricks he'd learnt from so many people throughout his prison journey, they never found anything. Rasheen also discovered that when a person was hold it down on the pressure tip, things often times got worse, since they knew Rasheen could handle a knife and had no problem sticking it to anyone who violated. Unfortunately, Rasheen learned the hard way, that cats under pressure had no problem getting the guards to do their dirty work.

Killer Kato entered his new, plush office located on the East 83rd Street in Manhattan. His closest associate and bodyguard, Crazy B was in lock step with him as they both took seats. Killer sat behind the executive style desk while Crazy B sat in the seat in front of the desk.

Killer Kato leaned back comfortably as he sighed in an attempt to tame his anxiety. Things were finally taking shape. His dream was coming true and it couldn't have been at a better moment. "Yo' listen, B, I want you to turn it up, and keep it up."

Crazy B said with a smile. "Have I ever not turned it up? Now that you said that, I want you to be clear with what you asking me to do, cause I don't want you coming at me later talkin' about I went over…"

"Yeah, you right," Killer Kato said, realizing Crazy B was notorious for taking things way beyond reasonable bounds. "Let me clarify." Killer Kato pondered his words carefully. "I need you and the team to put a few cats inside Ja-King's concert. If you can't avoid the gunplay that's fine; let the concert get flowing, let them think everything's under control. When Ja starts his last rap piece, shut the show down."

Crazy B's thick eyebrows rose as though he was surprised, "Why wait so long? We gave that bitch ass nigga an opportunity to avoid this drama, but he got on some real arrogant shit. That nigga straight from our hood, we let that nigga do him, we opened mad doors for that chump, and now he's turning his back on the peoples. I say we shut down that nigga's concert before that bitch gets one lyric out of his mouth."

Killer Kato smiled broadly; this was the reason why Crazy B wasn't the man doing the thinking, he wanted to say, but he knew how sensitive he could get. "The effect is better. It sends a message that says you either roll with Hoodaroma or the next time ain't gone be no show. We don't wanna appear to be unreasonable. We trying to lay groundwork to lockdown a few up and rising rappers, not start a full-scale war with them. The last thing we need is to scare folks too much to the point we have to start using extreme measures."

Crazy B knew he was right and just nodded agreeingly.

Killer Kato hated the idea he had to use this apartment to discuss delicate issues with Crazy B, but this was the only place he was certain was clean. "Any word on the Feds?"

"As a matter fact there is," Crazy B paused, wondering if Kato was ready for this bad news. "They're planning to hit us in about three more months. I heard that U.S. Attorney Broad handling the case is trying speed up their investigation. The good news is that they still ain't got that knock out piece of evidence they need to put the mesh on you. That's the real hold up."

Killer Kato didn't like the feeling he suddenly felt. It was a mixture of fear, anxiety and frustration. He'd rode this drug enterprise until the wheel was about to fall off. It was over but he had no intention of taking his ten million and jumping ship. His dream was far from fulfilled, and if he had at least 500 million he might have contemplated throwing in the towel. For the past couple of years, he'd been laying groundwork to get his foot firmly in the door of the rap business. To date, he had two recording studios, three rap groups, two solo artists, his people were security personnel in two heavyweight rappers' camps, and two of the records he produced were being played on several radio stations, all accomplished under his newly constructed Entertainment Company called Hoodaroma. He was making noise, but it wasn't the kind of explosive grand entrance he needed to make his presence felt by the industry's big wigs. Despite the fast money of the drug game, he knew he had to bring it all to a nice, neat conclusion, at least as far as he was personally concerned. He'd been working out this plan for the past several months, and it was time to not only unveil it to his Chief Enforcer, but to also put it is full activation. He sighed, and then said, "As they say, all good things must come to an end."

"What's that, a joke?" Crazy B couldn't believe he heard those words coming out of Killer's mouth. "There's too much mufuckin' money to be made in the drug game to walk away from it. I don't give a shit how bangin' this Hip Hop shit is."

"We will walk away," Killer Kato leaned back in his chair with his hand massaging his goatee. "Without walking away." He saw Crazy B's confused expression, and then continued. "We gotta bring in someone we can trust to run this shit who don't got visible connections to any of us, move the spots, change the street name of our dope, and make it look like we just up and disappeared. We'll re-work everything, rebuilt clientele and all we do is supply the works and pick up money. It won't be as gravy as it was with us grinding, but I'm confident that this rap thing is about to take off. If we get Ja-King on our team, and get him and Lameek together, and they start writing songs and shit, we're gonna knock Def-Jam, Death-Row, and all the others into oblivion."

"You know my position." Crazy B said. "Give me my marching orders and let me make magic. So who you got in mind to run the show?"

"That brother from Brownsville, Bam Bam; he's about the best I can come up with at the moment." He saw Crazy B nod his head approvingly. "He's been rolling with us on the DL for a good minute. I did a bid with him and he's the straight loyal type, and he ain't the grimy, cut throat kind of dude Unless you get reserves, I want you to get on this immediately."

"Home-team is an excellent choice, since there ain't many others. All I got to say is he got a decent little team, and they got some heart. With the kind of money he's gonna be touchin', do you honestly think his head is not gonna swell up to the point he starts forgetting who's running shit around here? Hey, Tony Montana did it to Sosa."

Killer Kato smiled. "I ain't no mind reader, nor am I able to predict the future. But I do know he knows why they call me Killer Kato. If he thinks I'm losing my touch or getting soft, then to answer your question, yes, he just might play himself. And if he does, I'm quite sure you don't mind letting him know how you got the name Crazy B?"

Crazy B smiled broadly, the expression on his face was filled with a sincere wanting as though he was praying that Bam Bam would slip up.

Rasheen stood with his back to the yard fence, while his team Johnnie Rock, Raleek and Energy stood in front of him talking about a controversial dope transaction. A few yards away, a dozen or so prisoners sat on wooden benches looking up at the TV that was inside a wooden cabinet, watching music videos. The Fugees were on the tube and Lauren Hill and Jon Wycliff were displaying their talents in their 1997 smash single, "Killing Me Softly."

Rasheen was listening to his soldiers go back and forth while he kept his eye on a dark skin dude who kept eye balling him. The face on this cat looked crazy familiar, but his memory wouldn't bring up the confirmatory facts regarding the who, what, when, and where of this particular prisoner. He'd been in Clinton almost two years now, saw two birthdays slip by, had more knife battles than he had fingers and toes, been keep locked so many times he'd lost count after the fifteenth time, and long sense came to terms with the reality that dreams don't always come true, since he vowed to be a millionaire by the time he was 21. As it stood he had about 990 thousand more dollars to go. But, he did succeed in a small way, since the ten grand he managed to make over the two years had put him in the celebrity category and he took it all in stride. Not to mention a thousand of which came from Jack-Mack, who finally got in touch through some broad name Darlene Dickens, but Rasheen eventually discovered that the name was a front when he wrote to the address and the letter was returned to the sender. He was glad Jack-Mack was using his head and most of all he didn't forget him.

Rasheen flexed up when he saw the brother approaching while staring at him. When Johnnie Rock noticed Rasheen's surprised facial response, his hand went straight for the banger as he nonchalantly turned around to face the approaching prisoner.

"Rasheen?" Kendu said with his arms raised, signifying that there was no malice in the air. "It's me Kendu from the East."

Rasheen's memory clicked upon hearing the name while observing the face. "Oh, shit! Yeah, that is you, Sun." Rasheen rushed over to him, and gave him a pound and a standard Hood style hug. Rasheen introduced Kendu to his team and then pulled Kendu to the side several yards away to talk in private. After they brought each other up to speed with regards to what they been through during their prison journey, Kendu started reliving the old days when they were beyond the prison walls.

"Sun, the way you was handling heat." Kendu said with a grin. "I never thought you would end up in here, especially with a nigga like Killer Kato on your side."

Rasheen felt like he was slapped in the face. Just hearing that name almost pushed him clean over the edge.

Kendu continued talking, not realizing Rasheen was streaming with fury. "You know that nigga Killer Kato is one of them big time rap producers now, he's the one who started Hoodaroma Records. He got that kid Ja-King down with him. I heard he cold strong armed him from Def-Jam Records. Since that's your man, I know he settin' you out a little somethin', especially since he put your little brother Lameek on. Yo' Sun, your brother's video is straight off the mufuckin' meat rack, man! Your man, Killer Kato sure know…"

"Man, what the fuck is you talking about?" Rasheen was seconds from exploding on Kendu. "That bitch ass nigga ain't my man. When we was viding in New York I didn't tell you he was my man. What made you think some shit like that?"

Kendu was getting nervous now. He didn't realize Rasheen apparently had beef with Killer Kato. "That time you bought that 9mm, the Browning, from me when you was tight that time that dope fiend dude was dismissing your old earth, well, Killer Kato stepped to me personally and told me I better not be trying to get fast on you. He thought I was overcharging you and shit. The way he was kicking it, y'all were supposed to be mad tight. I mean, you know, y'all from the same Hood and your baby brother just dropped an album under the Hoodaroma label."

Rasheen struggled to contain his shock. "Did he ask you why I bought the gun?"

"Yeah, he asked."

"And you told him?"

Kendu hated to feel this way. The current vibe unmistakably indicated he had apparently done something he wasn't supposed to do. "Yo' Rah, man, he asked me and I told him what you told me. You and him are from the same Hood; he's a high roller, and I ain't know you and him had drama, Sun."

"Be easy, Kendu. I ain't tight with you over that." Rasheen lied and knew if the Pinocchio story were true his nose would've grown ten feet. "You ain't know what time it was."

Kendu sighed inwardly and immediately got on another topic.

As Kendu rattled on about his new gun trafficking connection in St. Louis, Rasheen was listening, but wasn't listening. A series of disturbing questions started screeching across his mind. Did that slim bucket ass nigga rig up that whole situation? Did he know he was going to get at Black Bob, and strategically put himself on the scene? Did Black Bob really owe that foul motherfucker all that cheddar! That little voice inside his head responsible for intuition assured him that all inquiries were answered in anyway that was detrimental to him, and as a result, his rage and thirst for revenge grew to even a higher level.

In the weeks that followed, Murphy's Law was hard at work, and Rasheen saw that he was rapidly running out of luck. All the tricks designed to circumvent the C.O.'s effort to undermine his drug dealings were just about at the end of the line. They couldn't catch him so they decided to transfer him to another facility, and the messed up part of it all, it couldn't have happened at a worse moment. After 19 months in Clinton, it was obvious that the prison administrator's rationale was that if they couldn't beat him at the game, then they damn sure had the power to at least disrupt the game. And boy did they disrupt Rasheen's flow; he had hundreds of dollars of work out on the street, credit tabs were all over the place and it didn't take intellectual stability to conclude that once he was gone those tabs would turn into instant headaches.

As he packed his belongings, he reflected back on those times when he seen how crab dudes started playing dangerous money games with even thorough hard ballers' when they got transferred. Since most folks in the prison system had all sorts of grimy hidden agendas, and whenever they knew a cat was leaving and couldn't reach out and touch them, they would gamble on the possibility that the cat's team players were undercover haters, and wouldn't keep it real, but Rasheen had a terrible surprise for any fool stupid enough to play games with his money. Although he knew his team would make sure the big debts were taken care of, he was still upset because all the crumbs had to go to the team players who were still putting work in. It was an unwritten rule that had it's good and bad components; he hated it, but had to respect it, and the main reason for this attitude was because his love for that mean green made him want every single penny of his, even if that meant preventing his team mates from getting a piece of his action. It was a foul way of thinking, but this was indeed an excellent illustration of the awesome grip that money had over him.

Chapter Ten

Jack-Mack pulled the money green Range Rover to a stop in front of the shabby looking one family house. He was wearing a black coogi sweat suit with a pair of gray Airmax's. In accordance with his survival instincts he closely scanned the late night terrain as he killed the engine, felt his 9mm in its special made holster, and exited the Jeep. After spending close to four years on the run from the police, the Columbians, and the countless ballers he and his girl Candy had been robbing, watching his back, sides and front came as natural as breathing.

But this evening, things weren't right. Earlier, as he was casing a spot in Trenton, New Jersey, he kept feeling as though he was being watched. He feverishly searched the immediate area for the source of his sensation, but detected absolutely nothing. Even after casing the dirty politician's crib for an hour, and as he drove down the Turnpike on his way back to Jersey City, he kept feeling like he was being followed, but the more he searched for the car responsible for that feeling the more he realized he was bugging out.

As he retrieved the key to the door, he heard a car turn onto the street. The vehicle's headlights sweep across the nearby houses and strangely Jack-Mack felt the odd compulsion to seek cover. The sensation of danger seemed to be everywhere. Instead of hiding behind nearby trashcans, he frantically opened the door and rushed inside.

Candy was lying on the sofa watching the Jay Leno Show and leaped to her feet with the Mac 10 in the ready as Jack-Mack rushed inside. Dressed in a brown sweat suit, Candy's strong, pretty Hood rat facial features took on a deadly aura as her big boned body moved gracefully towards Jack-Mack who was now

peeking out the window. Her high yellow complexion resonated
with ever readiness. She knew the routine, since she'd been rolling
with Jack-Mack for the pass year and a half, and enjoyed robbing
and sticking up with him. When she reached him, she whispered,
"Who it look like? Five O or the others?"

"I couldn't tell. Might even be a false alarm."

"I guess it's time to close up shop and break north once
again…"

A noise came from the back of house. It sounded like a
flower pot was knocked to the ground.

"This is it." Jack-Mack was in motion, since the noise
apparently came from the trip wire he had planted.
Candy was on his heels.

They both grabbed their hiking bags that were already
packed just for a special occasion as this one. Inside the bags were
thousands of dollars from their most recent robbery of an Atlantic
City drug runner who was working for some Russians who came
right off the boat. With efficient smoothness, Jack-Mack and
Candy were dressed, packed, armed and ready to abandon the
house within five minutes. It was apparent they had done this
before and were acting as though they had been expecting this to
happen.

Jack-Mack moved towards the back of the house, with his
backpack on and a fully loaded Intra-Tec 9mm compact
submachine gun in each hand. These weapons were specially
designed with 40 round clips. Candy had on a backpack as well
and was brandishing the Mac 10 with a 9mm handgun tucked in
her waist; she preferred to use the Mac with both hands, since it
allowed for more accurate shooting.

Jack-Mack struggled to hear any signs that would tell him who it was coming for them. Although it really didn't matter since he was going to shoot his way out of this predicament regardless of whom they were, knowing their identity served only to assist his curiosity.

When a barrage of silenced bullets tore at the window, forcing him and Candy to belly wop the floor, his inquiry was answered. Law enforcement very rarely opened fire in this fashion and definitely didn't use silencers. This was a solid indication that it was folks from the underworld.

Scurrying behind nearby furniture, Jack-Mack waved to Candy, who was crawling over to Jack-Mack, indicating to take it easy since there was a window close by. As she slid on her belly, a man crashed through the living room window, and Candy fired the Mac 10 at the intruder.

Jack-Mack allowed one of his weapons to spit fire as the bullets pounded the man's chest. On the heels of the brief exchange, the front and back doors were blown from their hinges almost at the same time.

Jack-Mack rushed over to the fallen intruder, firing strictly headshots. Two of the bullets ripped fresh blood dripping wounds into the Latino looking man's face. Columbians! Oh, shit, the Columbians had finally found him, Jack-Mack's mind confirmed. A flood of memories entered his mind.

Jack and Candy rushed to the bedroom as they heard the mob of men entering the house; glass, wood and other materials could be heard dropping to the floor. As Jack-Mack flung the carpet away from the hatch door in the floor, Candy stood guard at the entrance of the room door peeking down the short corridor. Jack-Mack pulled open the hatch door, and was hoping this old escape route trick of his would work as planned. The homemade tunnel he constructed with his bare hands would merely lead him to a sewage drain that would then lead to a man hole in the middle of the street about three houses down.

Candy saw two men turn the corner, now slowly approaching. She took aim and the Mac 10 started spraying violent strips of white-hot fire. Both men crumbled to the floor, falling backwards. Candy screamed over her shoulder. "Is it ready?"

"Let's go! Let's go!" Jack Mack said while digging inside his backpack. The hatch door was wide open. He pulled out a grenade and rushed to the door.

Candy peered down the hall and was shocked to see three men rapidly approaching. She again squeezed off a barrage of Mac 10 bullets, cutting the men down with ease.

Jack-Mack pushed her aside, pulled the pin on the grenade, flung it down the hall, slammed shut the special made reinforced steel door, and ran for the hatch. Candy was already down inside the tunnel as Jack-Mack quickly descended.

BA-BOOOM!

The grenade shook the whole foundation of the cheap house. As Jack-Mack slammed the hatch door and fastened the slide bolt lock, he could hear parts of the house tumbling down, just as he had hoped. After the lock was in place, he retrieved the flashlight hanging on a hook and ran after Candy, who also had a flashlight. Twice he almost tripped over some electrical wires. It took them about 80 seconds to reach the sewage drain. When they opened the door the toxic fumes of the raw sewage attacked their nostrils with savage fury. Despite the sickening odor they continued forward.

Within seconds Jack-Mack led the way as he climbed up the manhole ladder and pushed the manhole cover from its slot. He moved it just enough so he could see out. The late night streets were empty. At a distance he could hear the Columbians talking excitedly while screeching car tires coming to an abrupt stop could be heard as well. Although he couldn't see them, it was obvious they came with an army. After scanning the area in all directions, Jack Mack shoved the cover completely out of the way and climbed out of the manhole onto the street. He helped Candy out of the manhole, slid the cover back in place, and they both ran east in the opposite direction of the commotion. Jack Mack was thoroughly tight because the backup get away car was parked at a location he couldn't take a chance touching, since he saw the Colombians had soldiers on the adjacent streets.

No sooner than they turned the corner, about to start looking for a car to hotwire, a marked police car turned onto the block cruising slowly. Jack Mack and Candy frantically tucked their weapons, but weren't certain if the police seen their abrupt gestures.

As the car slid by, Jack locked eyes with the two white men in the cop car and looked away to avoid antagonizing them. When the cop car was several yards in back of them and hadn't come to a stop, they sighed, but the moment was cut short when they heard the car slow down. When Jack-Mack turned and saw the police car doing a U turn, apparently on their way to harass them. Jack-Mack gave Candy a look. When he saw Candy pull her Mac 10 while reloading the huge weapon with a dazzling smile plastered on her face, Jack-Mack smiled as he too pulled both of his weapons.

On January 27, 1998, Rasheen entered Elmira Correctional Facility with a serious attitude. It felt as though his whole house was tore down right in front of him and now he had to gather up enough new energy to rebuild it. The good thing, he kept telling himself, was that he still had Camila on his side. Rasheen stepped into I-Block and saw it was no different from Clinton; a cellblock in any state prison was the same as any other cellblock anywhere in the world he concluded, and got in line with the every day mundane routine. Initially the routine started out as Chow, Rec. Chow, Rec, Chow, Rec. When he got out of reception or orientation as the Correction Counselors loved to call it, the routine changed a bit, evolving into Chow, Program, Chow, Program, Chow, Rec.

Within two weeks in the joint, Rasheen had constructed a small, dedicated dope dealing squad. Due to the numerous dudes who knew him when he was in Clinton and on Rikers Islands, and his reputation was one of a die-hard, play no games kind of prisoner, he had his drug empire back on its toes in no time. True to the drug dealers MO, he took a gallery porter job, which was a highly degrading job from the prison prospective because it was another name for a janitor. Although the job was a no brainer, it did allow him to move around the cellblock in order to take care of business. With huge amounts of time on his hands, Rasheen started doing a lot of thinking. Besides the fact Killer Kato, his brother, his mom's worsening condition, and Camila stayed on his mind, his future would always seem to ease into the equation.

During these long thinking episodes, he would get the urge to want to read. He'd always knew reading made a person smarter, but he assumed that because he knew how to read and think, he didn't need any practice. But this particular misconception had long since began to change. He wanted to be smart at what he did, to be the best of the best, and that meant he had to be real sharp. He knew he wasn't a dummy, and consistent with this belief, he was smart enough to know that in order to be the best, he had to be an extraordinary thinker. When he was in Clinton he used to do a considerable amount of reading. And to his surprise it used to make him feel smarter. Now that he didn't have many other things to do, he started back reading. Thanks to Born Master, he learned to enjoy reading, and true to Born's manifestation, reading allowed him to go to unfamiliar places, and to learn about things that gave substance to who he really was. Born used to always tell him that he was God, and that all black men were Gods, because Black folks were the first people on the whole planet and everybody, even Chinese people, came from the Black family. This was some powerful stuff for Rasheen to digest, but at the time Born was saying these things, it wasn't new information. He'd been hearing that the Blackman was God in his Hood for as long as he could remember. But what made the way Born Master presented it to him so powerful, was that Born was able to actually show and prove it. These building sessions (as Born used to call them) inspired him to classify Black history as the topic that intrigue him the most, and started the process of opening up doors in his mind that he never knew existed.

For the first time he started reading academic type books on money. Stocks, bonds, and the stock market interested him, since he'd always wondered how people got so rich, so fast by playing with the stock market. After attempting to read two books, he found it to be an uphill battle trying to understand the information, and threw the books to the side. Plus, it sounded like too much work for him, and from the way it looked the money would come in far too slow to say the least, which was more than enough to turn Rasheen off.

On a dreary day in the month of May, Rasheen sat in the Mess hall eating a stale piece of pizza and soggy macaroni salad when he saw C-Rock enter the Mess hall. He hastily swallowed the mouthful of pizza, and waited until C-Rock was about to walk by.

"Yo C-Rock!" Rasheen shouted, his heart sincerely went out for the brother. He saw C-Rock didn't recognize him and knew it was because of the facial hair. "It's me, Rasheen."

C-Rock smiled, "Yo' Rah! Damn man, I ain't see you in ages, Sun. What gallery you on?"

"D gallery. Yo' what you doing tonight?"

"I ain't doing nothing. I'm chillin'"

"Yo, come to the yard; we need to kick it."

As C-Rock continued on his way towards the serving counter amongst dozens of other prisoners, Rasheen resumed eating his pizza. It was a weird feeling, seeing the man in prison with a life bid for the murder he had committed. It was a relief to see C-Rock was holding it down like a trooper, and Rasheen had to admit he could only image the pain C-Rock was experiencing every morning waking up in a cage when he was completely innocent. Now, that was a wicked form of cruel and unusual punishment, Rasheen concluded, but wasn't passionate enough for C-Rock's plight to even consider coming to his aide by stepping up and revealing the truth. What C-Rock was going through was fucked up, but not fucked up enough for Rasheen to add more time to his bid.

That night in the yard, Rasheen kicked it with C-Rock and ended up hitting him off with some weed and dope. At first C-Rock was wondering where he was going with this unsolicited act of kindness and when Rasheen informed him that he was dealing on a large scale and that he only wanted to look out for the people from his Hood, C-Rock's suspicions subsided. On the real, Rasheen was trying to tame his conscience, and since C-Rock was a drug dealer for life, he knew C-Rock would enjoy getting his pockets fats when a golden opportunity presented itself. When Rasheen offered to put him down with his team, C-Rock jumped on the offer like a starving skid row derelict being offered a drink.

After six months in Elmira, Rasheen ran into his first strong arm rape. Rasheen was helping his man, Kano move to another gallery, and when he walked by cell 27 he heard whimpering and smelled the strong odor of shit coming from inside the cell. He saw a sheet was covering the front of the cell, and was shocked. He also heard another person humming the Eric B and Rakim tone, Check Out My Melody.   Rasheen moved quickly to cell 39, Kano's new cell, dropped the garbage bag of clothing and other items inside the cell and headed back to cell 27. His mind was racing along with his adrenaline; there was one lesson he learnt well while in Clinton and took it to heart, and that was any motherfucker who took another man's manhood was public enemy # 1. That shit was tolerated and deemed socially appropriate behavior in those Midwestern and Southern US Prisons, but in New York, prisoners always looked down on that foul shit, and real steppers had an obligation to step to foul motherfuckers who ventured into that kind of foul behavior.

Rasheen decided he was officially about to demonstrate how well the God's at Clinton schooled him. Suddenly, Rasheen stopped in his tracks, realizing he wanted to go all the way with this run. He did a quick about-face and rushed back to Kano's new cell, dug through his bag and found what he was looking for: an extension cord. Rasheen stormed out of the cell. As he strutted down the gallery, past the C.O.'s office, he saw and heard the officer on the phone with his feet kicked up on the desk. It was always a beautiful thing when C.O.'s were slacking off on the job, since it made runs like this so wonderfully successful. Then he saw Kano entered the gallery dragging his mattress and a garbage bag.

Kano saw Rasheen's tight demeanor, "What's up, Rah?"

Whispering Rasheen said, "We got a booty bandit in cell 27."

Kano dropped his belongings and followed Rasheen.

Rasheen stopped and spoke with an attitude, "Take your shit to your cell. If the police see your stuff there it'll draw attention."

Kano hastily complied as Rasheen continued onto the cell in question.

On tiptoes, Rasheen stopped in front of the cell, the smell of shit was still heavy in the air, but now the cat was humming Rakim's Paid In Full. It was obvious whoever this fool was, he had a thing for Rakim's music. Rasheen pulled the extension cord from his back pocket, got it ready, and snatched the sheet from the cell bars while simultaneously pulling the cracked cell gate open.

As Rasheen rushed inside, he saw a young prisoner on his knees on top of the bunk with his pants down to his ankles, and a big, black muscular dude with his pants down in similar fashion and was riding the kid doggy style. Both their backs were to Rasheen as he leaped on the dude's back, wrapped the extension cord around the startled big black booty bandit's neck, and commenced to pulling both ends of the cord with blood curdling force. The booty bandit was jolted into a desperate response; he tried to reached for his knife laying on the bed near his knee, but Rasheen had saw the shank and jerked him out of reaching distance. The tighter Rasheen pulled the cord, the harder the bandit fought with savage force. Through gurgling sounds, the booty bandit was thrashing violently while slamming Rasheen into the cell walls, trying to break free of the death grip without much luck. Despite his frantic struggles, Rasheen was locked tight on his back, riding the big booty bandit like a rodeo cowboy. He was glued to him like a deprived leech on its last leg of life while latched on a blood throbbing vein.

Kano arrived and was about to get in a few licks, but saw Rasheen had the situation under control, since the booty bandit had stopped struggling and was now laying face down twitching as though the nerves in his body were short-circuiting.

When the bandit became motionless Rasheen snapped back into the world of reality and saw the victim of the rape was cowering in the corner of the cell, looking like a traumatized little girl. In that moment, Rasheen saw what would have happened to him if he had not been who he was. The thought that if he was weak and scared to kill, he would've been in the same shoes of this young dude, that touched a part of his soul which bought shockwaves to his heart.

"Put your shit on, and get out of here," Rasheen said to the terrified dude, who probably thought Rasheen was there to get a piece of his hind. "Hurry up motherfiucker!" Then realization hit, what if this is his cell. "Who cell is this? Is this your cell?"

When the kid nodded his head affirmatively, Rasheen knew he had a major situation on his hands, because now he had to move this dead body. He wasn't too much worry about the rape victim snitching on him, since the dude was probably getting his backside blown to piece on a regular basis and hadn't told yet, so it was highly unlikely that he would start telling now. In any event, everybody knew snitches didn't survive very long in this place. Thinking quickly, Rasheen said, "How it look out there, Kano?"

"So far so good."

"Go see if any other cell is open." Rasheen said, as he started dragging the booty bandit towards the entrance. "The closer the better." He saw Kano moved down the gallery.

Seconds later Kano returned, and said, "Cell 18 is open, but I thinks it's one of them Crip dude's cell."

"Fuck him," Rasheen said, dragging the booty bandit out of the cell and down the gallery. "Look like Homie got himself a brand new set of problems."

That evening, the whole gallery was locked down under investigation, and as predicted, Homie in cell 18, a dude named Bishop, did have some problems on his hands. After the C.O.'s found the dead booty bandit upon doing their periodic rounds, they went to the yard, snatched up Bishop, and transferred him to the box. The beautiful and the fucked up thing about prison was that no matter how crazy the situation was, the prison officials almost always snatched up the wrong prisoner, and often times knew they had the wrong person and simply didn't give a shit. But in this place, in their eyes, everybody was guilty, even when they were innocent. Also, everyone knew Bishop was in the yard at the time the dead booty bandit was found dead, but the C.O.'s still put the blame on Bishop merely because it was his cell, and the guy was a known jailhouse terror. Rasheen's conscious didn't act up the least with this situation for the simple reason, Bishop was a gang banger and had a vicithesaruous reputation for gunning down innocent civilians, so in essence, he got what his hand called for, since he got eaten up by that saying, "what goes around comes around".

About month later, Rasheen was walking the yard and couldn't believe who he saw coming out of the Reception Block. Rasheen had to blink his eyes several times to make certain he was seeing who he knew it obviously was. To confirm the identity, Rasheen eased up closer for a bird's eyes view as the dude began talking to two clean-cut prisoners; the three moved towards the building and were now posted up on the wall. When Rasheen was about several yards away, it was a confirmation. Yeap, it was him. Rasheen smiled wickedly as the thought of putting this bitch ass nigga through some serious hell crossed his mind.

When Rambo saw Rasheen approaching, he lit up with delight, stuntin' a mile minute since he heard Rasheen's name was ring bells all over the state and he knew he had been a little hard on the brother when they were in New York, "Rasheen! What's happenin', Sun!"

Rasheen wanted to walk right up to Rambo and slap flames out of him, solely on the strength that he was one of Killer Kato's closest solders. Then he realized this would be an excellent opportunity to squeeze Rambo for some vital information. "Hey, what's the science, Rambo?"

The two shook hands and gave each other Hood style hugs in accordance with standard Bed-Stuy operating procedures.

Rasheen pulled Rambo away from the other two prisoners and began kicking it about their Hood. Rasheen talked solely about ice breaking topics, softening him up for the real information that was certain to come. When Rambo laughed at one of Rasheen's jokes, he knew he was ready to hit him with the shit. Rasheen said, "So what's up with your man, Killer Kato, I hear he's blowing up, beyond imagination."

"Yeah, he doin' him," Rambo said with a sincere touch of venom. "Nigga blowing up crazy, Sun, but you know how extreme niggas with big heads, big hearts, and big dollars can get."

Rasheen wanted to smile, since he detected malice in this man's heart. Killer Kato had apparently shitted on Rambo.

Rasheen decided to ease in with grace. "So, you and him still doing the damn thang, I know. As tight as y'all was, I know he got you swimming in cheddar."

Rambo sighed with frustration, "That bitch ass nigga shitin' a mile a minute. I took a fall for that bitch ass nigga and he ain't even get me a lawyer. I had to dig in my own stash."

That was it; Rasheen saw there was no need to continue softening him up because Killer Kato had not only softened him up already, but had also made himself another enemy. "I been meaning to ask you, what ever happened to that tab I owed Killer Kato, did Jack-Mack give him…"

"Man, that foul nigga played you," Rambo said, "He set that whole shit up. I know if he knew I was telling you this, he'd probably string my ass up to the nearest light pole, but right now I don't give a fuck about that nigga. You know, that's one foul, slimy ass motherfucker…"

"Yeah, yeah, we all know that," Rasheen had to cut him off, since it was apparent he was about to go off on the deep end, and get enmeshed in one of deeply entrenched temper tangents. "You said he set the whole shit up? What you mean by that?"

What Rasheen heard rolling off of Rambo's tongue, changed him for the rest of his life; there was indeed a lot of truth to the saying that a man's transition can occurred at the snap of a finger; kind of like a love at first sight sort of scenario. But with this situation, Rasheen knew he had to get out of this place, and he knew when his feet touched the bricks his whole life would evolve around killing that snake, slimy motherfucker, Killer Kato. That night Rasheen was waiting in the alley for Black Bob, he did remember seeing the Limo with tinted windows, and now according to Rambo, Killer Kato was in that ride, and knew

Rasheen was planning to kill Black Bob. Not only did Killer Kato plan the whole Black Bob conflict, but had milked Rasheen in the worse way. Black Bob owed Killer Kato a thousand dollars, but pressured Rasheen to pay him a hundred grand. And then to top it off, he had sent him out on kamikaze missions to kill his rival drug dealers so that he could make more money, all the while lying to him that he had an inside man who was guaranteeing him that he was not walking into a death trap. It was all a lie! Every inch of it! In a nutshell, he raped Rasheen, pimped him, fucked him with no grease and spit dead in his face. But the part that almost killed him was Killer Kato enticed his mother to start shooting heroin, knowing she was struggling to avoid drugs for good, and he was laying crazy pipe to his girl Crystal. By the time Rambo got to the part about Lameek and Crystal being deeply involved in Killer Kato's Entertainment Company, Hoodaroma, Rasheen was numb with something far more powerful than fury, rage and anger.

Indeed, what he was feeling couldn't be found in the English Dictionary.

Chapter Eleven

Killer Kato sat behind the recording studio console with headphones on, rocking lively to the beat as he listened to Lameek who was inside the recording booth kicking rap lyrics that were destine to change the game. He was dressed in his standard casual attire; navy blue Sean John Slacks, a matching designer shirt and light blue Wallabees. Sitting next to Killer Kato was his top engineer, Karl "Break-master" Jones, who was mixing, blending and remixing the dials on the console while he was bobbing his head to the rhyme. The beat they were listening to was utterly off the chain and if there were such a thing as the epitome of pure raw magic, this beat was definitely it.

Killer Kato was floating on cloud ecstasy and the way he was moving to the slamming beat represented the emotional state he was currently in. He had reason to be enthralled with the state of his success, since Ja-King's new album hit number one on the rap charts, his R & B act, called "Class Reunion" was fourth on the R & B charts, all of his rap acts were being played on radios all across the country and in most other parts of the world. Hoodaroma had become a household name in households all over the world, and most of all, so much money was rolling into the company's bank account, he was already making plans to expand Hoodaroma into an Entertainment Distribution Company. He always knew the real money lied within Distribution. Now, after independent research and advice from several lawyers and ex-recorder company executives, which completely confirmed this fact, he was thoroughly convinced that Distribution was the only road to becoming a billionaire. His company was currently worth a little over 700 million dollars, and he knew he could get twice that much in a bank loan. Although starting up a Distribution Company come run in the billions, Killer knew if he slapped the whip a little harder he could make that kind of money appear, especially considering the fact Bam Bam was doing a wonderful job with the drug business. In other words, the fulfillment of his dream was well within reaching distance.

Although white folks had the distribution aspect of the business world locked down, and would get real grimy while utilizing extreme measures against folks for even thinking about tapping into that part of the game, Killer Kato always enjoyed a nice, knock down, drag out fight, filled with smoking guns, dead bodies littering the streets, and happy Funeral Home Directors. He'd lived that kind of life all his life so it made no difference if he continued this policy, but doing it while becoming filthy rich. It was all a part of what he was here to do; this was how he saw it, and it was virtually impossible for him not to venture into such a business. This new founded idea came instantly into existence when several producers and rap moguls told him that those were forbidden territories. Had this threat not touched his ears, he might have breezed right pass this project. There was nothing more enticing to Killer Kato than to be told he couldn't do something. Just the thrill of the fight was enough to give him a hard-on. He loved women and had dozens of them catering to him on hand and feet, but even that fringe benefit was nothing in comparison to the thrill of doing something that people said he couldn't do. It was on! It would soon be poppin'!

Killer was so into the beat he didn't realize Crazy B was trying to get his attention as he stood outside the recording room, waving his hand. When Killer turned and saw Crazy B, he deliberately made him wait until the song ended. Whatever it was couldn't be all that serious, and even if it were, making him wait a minute or two wouldn't make a difference. He loved Crazy B to death, but he had a serious patience problem that was taxing his serenity; his overzealousness was a good attribute, but it could become very irritating at times.

Killer Kato said to Karl, "If you want my option, I say put this one in the can, but make Lameek take another crack at it."

"But what about the four songs we're scheduled to bang out for today's session?"

"Hey, looks like it's gonna be a long day." Killer Kato said and exited the recording room. He saw Crazy B was tight under the collar as usual. "What the fuck is it now?"

Crazy B looked around at the various employees moving about to give emphasis to what he was about to say, "This is a behind door discussion."

Killer led the way to his office on the other side of this seven-story building he owned, located on Houston Street in lower Manhattan. He entered the room, went to the computerized box planted on the wall, and punched in a number, activating the specialized frequency scrambling devise designed to circumvent any hidden bugs, recording apparatuses, and listening devices. In light of the fact he had evaded the Feds with regard to his pass drug dealings, and knew they were apparently trying to get at him now that he was a rap mogul, he knew there were probably undercover agents all throughout the work force he employed. Since he was now a legitimate businessman, he had no substantial control over the people he hired. If he were not an equal opportunity employer in light of the tremendous nature of his company, he would open himself up for all kinds of federal charges.

Killer Kato took a seat behind his desk while Crazy B sat in the chair in front of the desk and crossed a leg over the other.

"That dope fiend bitch is buggin' again," Crazy B said. "She's threatening to take Lameek to another label, if she don't get more money."

Killer Kato wanted to start shouting, but knew that was a waste of energy. "What's up, you ain't hittin' this bitch off with that raw shit? If she was getting her head right, she wouldn't have time to keep her eyes on the cash."

"That bitch is like a Hoover vacuum cleaner. Ain't enough dope in the country to cool her heels. She's making me real nervous. Apache told me she's been coming down here to the City; said she's trying to reach out to an entertainment attorney. She's still hopping on that shit about Lameek wants her to be his manager for life. If she shows that contract to a lawyer, shit is gonna get out of hand."

Killer Kato had made his current discussion the moment Crazy B mentioned Apache's findings. There was no question the bitch had to go. The only problem was how was Lameek going to take it? The last thing he need right now was for Lameek to get locked in an emotional rut and become unable to complete this CD. They were days away from a completed masterpiece. Killer Kato sighed, "Well, you know what time it is. We definitely gotta cancel her contract. Keep it clean and free of any traces of foul play. Maybe we can give this bitch some 100% pure china white. I heard that shit could blow out the heart valves of an Elephant."

"Sounds like good clean fun to me," Crazy B smiled. "I got two more issues; one good and the other not so good. I'll give you the good first. Our investments in all those Hood oriented projects are producing damn good results. There's a few names you need to know, cause these cats are doing wonderful work. You got Poison Red, Butter, Cowboy, Jay-R, Big Gains, Baby Blue and Bobby G. Man, they turnin' it up some kinda proper. Soon, there won't be a bar, club, pool hall, barber shop, liquor store, number spot or gun trafficking ring in Hoods all across the country that ain't got our hands in it, and the good thing is that everybody eating love love, and ain't nobody steppin' on nobody's toes. "

"You said Big Gains?" Killer Kato inquired. "You talking about gold tooth Gains from our Hood, over on Stuyvesant Street?"

"Yeah, Big Gains. I forget to tell you I reached out to him. I heard he was trying to start up strip club, so I took some money from the slush fund and hit him off. I marked it down in the monthly financial report; I thought you seen it."

"Yeah, I saw that entry but I didn't realize it was my main man, Big Gains. Send him my regards. As a matter a fact, get with him and let him know we need to get together, some time next week."

Crazy B took out his notepad from the breast pocket of his Iceberg Jean suit, wrote the note down and tucked it back in his pocket. He sighed and said, "This next issue is the one you need to brace yourself for." He paused for dramatic effect. "Apache recorded a conversation you need to hear." Crazy B pulled the small, hand-held cassette player from his inner breast pocket, and pressed play.

Ja-King's thugged out voice oozed from the devices speakers:

"I'm tired of this nigga! Ain't no way in the fuck, my royalties are supposed to be this low! That's it! I'm out of here! Tell that nigga Mike over at Def-Jam, we need to talk. My records are selling like crazy in this mufucka, and this nigga Killer Kato is playin' me like I'm some dumb nigga, who can't count. I ain't going through all that lawyer shit, and court battles. He can keep that rinky dink shit he's snakin' me for. You can bet Def-Jam ain't stupid enough to play they self. Here I am the top rapper damn near in the whole country, and this nigga is clipping me for my cheddar, on some real petty, slime-ball shit . . ."

When the tape came to an end, Killer Kato felt the acid in his stomach starting to bubble up. This was no good. There was no way he was going to let this golden goose slip from his grasp. He knew this blow-up was coming, but he didn't think Ja-King would start talking about going to another label. That was definitely a no-no. He thought the little scare tactics were deeply engrained in Ja-King's heart and mind, but it was obvious the missing money was powerful enough to make him test the waters. Staring at Crazy B, Killer Kato realized he had to do something he didn't want to do, but all the facts on the table indicated he had no choice. After pondering the pros and cons, and looking down the line way into the future, he saw he would get it all back. He cleared his voice. "Bring Ja-King here tonight. We're gonna wine and dine him, and hit him off love love."

"Once we go there ain't no turning back. You know how this thing goes. If we give in once he'll expect us to always give in. Now, I know we schemed a little bit of his cheese, but he's been warned that once he lay down with us, he can't lay down with nobody else. The nigga loves his mom, done bought her a four million dollar mansion. If we give this chump a firm reminder, he'll get in line."

Smiling Killer Kato said, "Yeah, you right. But right now we need his heart in his work, cause we sure gonna put this nigga to work. We gonna make this nigga larger than life, and then take our agenda to another level."

Crazy B saw Killer was talking in riddles, and assumed he knew what the fuck he was talking about. It didn't matter either way, since he knew Killer with his grimy mind was up to something that would straighten it all out. "I hear you, dog. You know me. Give me my marching orders and let me march."

Killer Kato rose to his feet, talking as he approached the door, "Right now get on this Barbara thing. I'll start working on Lameek. Yo', B, I'm tellin' you, this little nigga is bananas!" As he opened the door exiting the room, he continued, "He's been holdin' out some type of crazy! . . ."

Barbara Smith sat at the dinning room table in her two million dollar mansion, located in up-state New York that Lameek bought her last year, wondering why she suddenly felt the urge to take an introspective look at her life. She just received a bag of heroin from Apache, and was preparing to mainline the bag. Apache was her personal gopher who made sure she got her medicine whenever she needed her hits. Although her supply as still heavy, Apache hit her off with this bag claiming he found a new dealer that assured him this stuff was the best shit in the state.

Most of the time she had enough product to last her weeks at a time, and she was happy as a free bird. Ever since she started shooting heroin, she'd been experiencing a high she really felt content with. Unlike that crack high, she could now get her head right and not get stupid and start throwing her morals and principles out the window. But the best part about heroin she noticed was that she didn't need so much of it to function, and the high lasted way longer before the cravings started. The only major down side was that upon coming down from the high, and the feinding started, it was a feeling that was scary. Another adverse effect was that she was content being without a man; she embraced loneliness as if it was an intricate part of life even to the point that sex meant nothing to her. All her life she'd known about the dangers of heroin and its highly addictive nature, but she didn't care because now she had money to support her high without fuckin' and suckin' and doing all sorts of dumb shit. Subconsciously, she even wanted to thank Killer Kato for enticing her to try out heroin, because deep down inside she enjoyed getting high. Indeed, she came to realize that she was a junkie for life. Be it crack, straight cocaine or heroin, she was destined to do drugs, and that was that.

Looking at the bag of heroin, she realized her son Rasheen was on her mind. As that all too familiar feeling of guilt started to creep in, she had to fight tooth and nail in order to shift her thoughts away from her son, but the battle was without much success. She hadn't written him a letter in years; she didn't even know what prison he was in, and didn't care. She loved him, but felt bad every time she thought of him because she knew she had let him down, and so she went to great lengths to avoid thinking about him. It was just too painful. What was done was done, she couldn't change it, and so, there was no need to waste time thinking about things that couldn't be changed. But it was strange how he had just popped up inside her mind as she prepared the bag of dope.

Sensing the pain about to bring on a wave of tears, she hastily tied the rubber strip tightly around her arm, causing the vein to bulge from underneath her skin. She tapped the vein in ritualistic fashion, retrieved the syringe, inserted the needle into the warm cooked heroin in the spoon, sucked up the liquid, cleared the air from the syringe, gently inserted the needle into her vein, and unleashed the substance into her bloodstream.

Barbara sighed in delight, noticing this shit was the bomb. If there was one thing a veteran dope fiend knew, it was certainly good dope. She instantly went into a vicious nod. Everything was going great until she noticed her heart was pounding in an unusually hard and excessively fast fashion.

Terror gripped her and her inner instinct told her that she was in a life-threatening crisis. Her heart started beating faster, and faster, and faster. Her bowels even began acting crazy. She felt a warm liquid escape from her grippers as she sprung to her feet in a state of desperation. The intense dizziness buckled her knees and she went down to the floor, realizing she was gagging on her own saliva; she tried to scream, but couldn't. Every nerve on her body twitched with violent fury and all she could do was ride it out while hoping and praying she would live to see another day.

Suddenly, as though the whole house exploded, she saw a bright white flash and was hurled into oblivion.

Rasheen sat on the bus shackled to another prisoner with a serious case of bad breath. The bus was parked in front of Sing Sing's huge gate, waiting to enter one of New York's most notorious and most famous prisons. Reflecting back on how he got to this point in his life, he came to understand that drama was his middle name. Beside the fact, the Elmira prison officials didn't allow him to go to his mother's funeral. They started a campaign of harassment that would put Hitler's Storm Troopers to shame. His 2 years and 7 months at Elmira indeed turned out to be one that he would never forget. But the real deal was that Rasheen knew there were bigger hands pulling strings, puppeteering things in order to put him in complicated situations. Money made things happen and since the Colombians had plenty of it, and certainly hadn't forgotten that he laid down several of their comrades, he knew this transferred was probably done to facilitate that beef.

The date was August 12, 2000, and Rasheen entered A-Block with his eyes, and ears open and his mouth shut. He'd heard so many foul things about this facility he knew he was treading into dangerous territories. Although the prison was flooded with drugs of all kinds, there was no widespread respect for standard prison etiquettes. Prisoners talked, ate, and literally hung out with the COs; snitching was everywhere, and frontin' was even more rampant. Cats who were upstate quiet as the heart beat of a fly were down here roaring like hungry Lions, and the minute the mesh was put on them in accordance with standard operating prison procedure, they would be sitting in a Westchester County Courtroom, pointing out standup dudes in front of an all white jury. But, the most amazing thing was that it never crossed most of these cats' minds, that they might have to go back up north, and when they did there was no running away from the past.

After his first two weeks in Sing Sing, he decided he had to come up with a way to reactivate his drug empire. Camila was so used to muling and receiving money at the P.O. Box, she was getting a little up tight that Rasheen wasn't making moves, since she saw this whole drug dealing drop off as a job, and rightfully so, because the money coming in was paying the bills, kept food on the table and a roof over her head. Rasheen knew mad dudes here at Sing Sing, but he also knew how the looseness of the facility had a strange way of poisoning the average prisoner, making him forget the way things were supposed to be done, which made constructing a team that much harder.

As Rasheen was formulating a team, he ran into a bump in the road that almost knocked him off track. He almost reacted recklessly and impulsively when he saw the ultimate snitch, Randy Doylson. Rasheen literally was itching to reach out and hit him right there in the school building. As he watched Randy through the corner of his eyes, he was hoping this foul motherfucker didn't recognize him, but there was no such luck. He not only saw him, but came rushing over, acting as though they were long lost Homies. Rasheen was seconds from wiring this chumps jaw as he approached him, and started frontin' like nobody knew what he'd done to C-Rock. For the moment, it was all good, and Rasheen played right along with a smile, pretending he knew nothing. As they departed, Rasheen knew this particular run would be his most well constructed Sun Tzu style murder that would make him famous, if people knew it was him. And the best part of all, Randy would do it to himself, since the rat motherfucker was still getting high. Oh, yes, he was going to enjoy this, Rasheen thought as he watched Randy walking away.

Within a month's time frame, Rasheen's team was in effect. It was a six man squad; two in A-Block; two in B-Block, and two in 5-Building. All Rasheen did was drop off product and count doe. He did no hand-to-hand combat, with hopes that this approach would keep the heat off of him, but to his disappointment that wasn't the case. The CO's were on him as though he had murdered their mom's or something, and twice Rasheen had to discard his package when shit reached critical levels. Even his workers were getting hit by the police as though they were terrorists or something; and half of them ended up abandoning ship, claiming it wasn't worth the headaches.

Rasheen sat in his cell one night trying to figure out what the fuck was going on. There was no way he should be getting this much tension from he administration. After going over everything he'd done since being at Sing Sing, realizing he had done everything right, the only logical explanation was that the snitches were on a rampage. The haters was hatin' at a level he ain't never seen before, and that type of hatin' had to be mixed with some other emotions, like fear, intimidation, or maybe even greed. After going over the various possible ways to rectify this dilemma, it was clear, in order to weed out the enemy he had to find out who had the most to lose by him prospering in the game. It took about a week to find out just about all the people who were selling drugs of all sorts. There were about 13 hard-ballers and maybe 20 small timers, who sold on an off and on basis, and did it primarily as a way to support their habits. Common sense told him he could exclude the small timers to some degree because most of them were just going with the flow. If they were snitching they had to be professional snitches, probably had a special card and the whole shit, and if they flipped out on a cat, it was likely because somebody pissed them off or they were trying to get around some keep lock time. In the end, Rasheen knew he had to watch the hard ballers very closely. For the time being, he continued supplying his workers with packages, the ones who were willing to continue selling, despite all the drama, of course.

Towards the beginning of the fall season, Camila came up on a visit with a suitcase full of drama, and she came to dump off straight in Rasheen's lap. He'd always been her shoulder to cry on, and was like her personal emotional advisor. The moment he stepped foot on the visiting floor and saw Camila's expression he knew this was drama of the serious kind. After he gave her a strong kiss, and sat down, he dove into the discussion.

"What's up, what's the matter? Damn, girl, it can't be that bad."

"You wanna bet?" She sighed, taming the urge to wipe her eyes. "You know my style Rasheen, I get straight to the point with what's on my mind. But I will say this; before I go there, you know I'm there for you no matter what happens . . ."

Rasheen felt shockwaves erupt throughout his body, because this sounded like one of those Dear John speeches. Oh, shit! She was leaving him!? With a slight struggle, he held his emotions in check.

Camila continued, "Rasheen, you know I got needs. I was even willing to marry you, but you ain't trying to go there. I respect that, you know. You know I always had a thing for you, and will always love you, Boo." She paused, as though collecting her thoughts.

"Come on, Camila, spit it out. You know you can tell me anything." He knew this was the truth only to a certain extent; there was one thing she couldn't tell him and that was she was leaving him. He wasn't trying to hear that, nor would leaving be tolerated.

"Yeah, you right," she sighed. "Listen, Rasheen, I'm pregnant." She looked him in the eyes and thought she saw a hurtful response. "Yeah, I know you tight, but I was willing to marry you so we can get some trailer visits, but you wasn't ready. I got needs."

Rasheen wanted to burst out laughing in relief, and did notice he felt something. This was what had her all nervous!? Realizing she wanted him to react a certain way, he put on a show. "Camila, I know you got needs, that's why I told you, you can do you. I know that thing starts itching and somebody gotta scratch it. If I ain't out there to scratch it, I'm not stupid enough to believe it ain't gonna get scratched by somebody else. I'm just surprised you ain't used protection. There's too much shit out there to be playing games, Camila."

"I did strap up," She lied, but knew the defective condom excuse was known to work. "We was doing us and the damn condom broke."

Rasheen was surprised. He felt like he was about to catch feelings. He'd brought her into his life strictly to mule drugs for him, but now he noticed his emotions had somehow got into this relationship of theirs. "I thought I told you, Camila, I want to marry you one day." He told her this to string her along; the old carrot and the horse trick and it worked perfectly. "And I want to do it the right way. Not in prison on some degrading shit. You deserved better than that." He paused for dramatic effect, feeling the urge to tinker with her emotions. "Damn, Camila, I thought you said you would wait for me?"

"I know, Rasheen," Camila said with a whining voice, loving the way he always made her feel needed, desired and appreciated. "I know I said that, and I'm sorry. And I meant it, Rah, I'm waiting for you. It just happened. Ain't nothing between me and this dude. And I'm getting an abortion anyway; I just wanted to be straight up with you, because that's what we promised to do with each other."

Rasheen couldn't deny the fact he did feel some pain in his chest, and had apparently developed feelings for Camila. When the visit was over and he returned to his cell, he did some intense introspection, and after thinking about what happened to his mother, and the current situation his brother was in, he knew now wasn't the time to start allowing his emotions to supercede his vow to get paid, and to stay paid. Camila was a mule, plain and simple and if she wanted to get her fuck on, that was her business. When the time came for his feet to touch those bricks on the other side of these prison walls, he would need a lot of doe to set the record straight and anything that got in the way of him attaining this goal had to be neutralized.

But the truth of the matter was that Rasheen savored the memories of their past sexual affairs and he had to admit that he wouldn't mind tapping that thing right about now. Camila was definitely a head turner, and had a crazy, humongous ass, just the way he liked his women. He could image himself hitting her from the backside, doggy style, with all that ass bouncing off his body. Even the sensuous smell of sex was still fresh in his memory bank, despite the fact he hadn't touched a piece of pussy in five years, and he noticed the mere thought was making his mouth water. Camila couldn't compete with Crystal when it came to facial beauty and a model shaped body, but when it came to straight fuckin' and suckin', Camila was the Queen Bee. Although Camila was picking up a lot of weight, her additional pounds were popping up in all the right places. When Rasheen's dick started getting rock hard, he had to shift his thoughts, since the urge to beat off was about to take control, and right now jerking off wasn't on the agenda for tonight.

As the weeks slipped by, Rasheen saw that Sing Sing was like being in another world. Even the Gods were bugging the fuck out. He couldn't believe there were Gods frontin' on other Gods, which was utterly unheard of up north. The incident that made Rasheen realize there was some truth to the saying, "that a black devil is the worse devil", occurred when he witnessed what boiled down to a crucifixion of a good brother who was one of those old militant Gods from the days when the God and Earth Nation was in their glory days.

Brother Dashien was the President of AAOU (African-American Unity Organization) an inmate organization ran by the Gods, and he had made a statement indicating that any man claiming to be righteous while selling drugs were hypocrites of the worse type. He didn't pull no blows and told every God selling any kind of drug to their faces that they were hypocrites. What followed was a sickening and disgracefully display of sheer cowardliness that would've resulted in a bloodbath had any of the ring leaders of this conspiracy had been around the type of Gods he was used to being around. The four co-conspirators were Pow Wow, Black man, Black Cream and Divine Eyes. These supposed to be righteous and civilized men tried to have the brother removed as the President and replaced with one of their personal flunkies. They tried to label him a snitch, they tried to get non-Five Percenters to stab the brother, and they concocted so much bullshit on the brother to the point that all their endeavors were subsequently recognized as a personal attack and their whole underhanded agenda backfired on them. Meanwhile, Dashein stood strong, and made one statement to all of them, "whoever you send, you better make sure he don't miss. Y'all just like little bitches, so I know if a hit go down it won't come from y'all hands." Since the four snakes behind this Coup D'etat were true blue cowards at heart, were trying to get others to do their dirty work in accordance with the standard way cowards do things, and most of the other Gods saw what was really going on, the situation didn't escalate into a full-scale internal war amongst the Gods.

Rasheen watched closely, and was pleased by all this drama that was taking place, because he now had an idea of who the undercover haters might be. A perfunctory investigation revealed that the snakes who attacked Dashein were selling product for years, and not one of them ever received a single scratch. He'd known two of the four were amongst the 13 hard ballers, but because they were a part of the God nation, he'd give them the benefit of the doubt. After what they had just done, he could no longer give them such a benefit. Although this didn't necessarily indicate conclusive that they were the culprits, merging the fact that everyone else selling drugs except them, went through some kind of scarring process with the fact they had been selling drugs for over five years, made this truly disturbing. It was virtually impossible to go five years doing anything in prison without some kind of turbulence, and for someone to pull that off in a snitch infested environment like Sing Sing, such remarkable success apparently had absolutely nothing to do with luck or skills. This had Quid Pro Quo written all over it.

Rasheen now started scrutinizing this whole situation from every angle, while simultaneously sending out his own spies to find out everything he could about these four snakes. Within weeks, Rasheen was not only surprised when the information started piling up on the table, but he was also appalled by the level and degree of frontin' that these snakes were doing. One of the snakes was an undercover male prostitute when he was on the street, taking dick in the ass in the wee hours of the night on the Streets of East New York; another one was a confirmed snitch who testified against a cat and had gotten the dude a twenty year bid, and another one was a master manipulator who had a history of sending young cats out to do his dirty work while he sat on his ass, pretending as though he was some kind of Don, when in fact, he was a cold-blooded bitch who couldn't and wouldn't fight a lick; because of his remarkable knack for frontin', he tricked the best of the best into believing he was a thorough dude, which allow folks to embrace him. There was only one cat he couldn't find any real dirty on, other than the fact he got knowledge of himself, became a part of the Gods and Earth Nation, only after he allegedly was sentenced to a life bid and that disturbed him because this dude was like a ghost; nobody knew much about him and that was strong grounds to really watch this cat very closely. Rasheen's highly precautious mind started pulling up scenarios from the black history books he'd read, and as sure as pussy smelled like fish, he felt it in his heart that this cat was some kind of CIA agent or a deep cover cop or something. He couldn't prove it, but his heart was telling him there was something real crazy and ultra foul going on with this particular dude.

Meanwhile, Rasheen was looking into the possibility of giving back some of the time on his back. There were numerous jailhouse lawyers in Sing Sing; some were good, some were reasonably good, while very few were exceptionally good. One that was in the last category just happened to be in the prison. It was a dreary day in October when Rasheen crashed the Law Library, pulled Alamo from the back and hit him with a proposition.

Rasheen and Alamo sat at the table in the far corner of the Law Library; Alamo with his Clark Kent glasses, wavy hair that he kept in a neatly trimmed Caesar style haircut, and his ever present good natured smile, sat across from Rasheen.

Rasheen stared him straight in the eyes and said. "If you can get me out of here, I'll pay you any amount of money you want." Without blinking, Rasheen maintained his locked jawed seriousness. He reflected back on all the stuff he'd heard about Alamo, who was dubbed a legal wizard and had a vicious track record for getting dudes reversals left and right. Rasheen had even heard of this cat, Alamo, when he was in Clinton years ago, and everybody classified him as being awesome with handling those legal books. Rasheen had no problem gambling, taking chances, or putting his money where his mouth is, especially if there was a chance he could win something that no amount of money in the world could replace: his freedom.

With a smile, Alamo said, "Yo' bro, I gotta see what you got first before I can let you know if I can get you out."

"What you need?" Rasheen said, allowing his eyes to wander some. "I can give you a rundown of what happened in my case."

"Actually, at some point I'm gonna need to see whatever paper work you got. But for right now, I can interview you to get an idea if I can even help you. Before I go there, I need to let you know, I don't take cases I can't win something. I pride myself, one my reputation for getting dudes out of here, so don't get all twisted up if I pull back from your case if I see I can't make it happen. My prices are very reasonable; I'm about fighting the system, so when I help folks win, I'm getting my shit off too, you know. You should also know that there are such things as the nail in the coffin. In other words, some folks are stuck here for the endurance of their sentence. Alright? Now that we got the ground rules all laid out, let's hear your situation. You can take it from the moment the police put the cuffs on you."

It took Rasheen about twenty minutes to explain his situation and when he finished he saw Alamo still maintaining the straight face he'd had on from the moment he started talking. Rasheen said, "So, how it looks?"

Alamo sighed hard; he hated when they copped out; he nodded his head and said, "There's a few things I gotta look into first, before I can tell you whether or not I can get you some rhythm. But looking at your case, there might be some things floating around that we can use to make it happen. Since you copped out, you waved a lot of your constitutional and statutory rights, so this is gonna be a touch and go kind of thing here. But, I will take your case. I think we can make something happen, even if it's just a time-cut. We gotta do a whole lot of FOIL requests, court document requests, and stenographer requests for the minutes and all the transcripts in your case, so you gotta be patient."

Rasheen sighed because he felt a good vibe about Alamo, and he saw he was definitely about his business. The way he took notes and listened closely, he saw brother Alamo was professional through and through and even reminded him of the lawyer he had when he was on the Island, but seemed to be far more into the case.

In the months that followed, Rasheen was gradually coming up with successful ways to circumvent the snitches and the money started trickling in slowly. His investigation into the four snakes was still progressing, and he'd finally come up with a way to solve the Randy Dolyson matter. He'd been buttering up this fool for months and now he was ready to lay the blows on him. This was something Rasheen knew he couldn't share with anyone, not even his closest comrades Rashango and Kojak, who were his running partners. This was only for his eyes, ears and hands. Rasheen even got a job in the vocational building as a porter, and as he did his cleaning chores, he would steal small portions of various chemicals; especially the ones that were locked away in specially secured cabinets and were only opened up to him while the C.O. would watch. Whenever the cop blinked, Rasheen would stash a small portion of the chemicals in a small plastic tube he kept with him. Half the time he had no idea what he was taking, but he took them anyway, and figured if he could mix enough of these chemicals that had skulls and bones on the labels and other large warning signs, he could brew himself up a nice poison that could easily knock Randy's boots clean off his feet.

In February of 2001, Rasheen blessed Randy with a real hot and banging package of dope. Randy was drooling from the mouth as Rasheen placed the bag in his hand, and even gave Randy a nice clean syringe. To ensure that Randy had mainlined the stuff in the bathroom in the school building, Rasheen stood guard. Rasheen smiled wickedly as he heard Randy sighing in ecstasy, and then sounded as though he was choking. When he momentarily cried out, Rasheen got nervous and had to walk away from the bathroom just in case the C.O. returned and saw him near the bathroom. As he walked away, he could hear Randy's delirious shrieks starting to subside. Rasheen rush back to the bathroom, checked his pulse and smiled when he detected his ticker had stopped. He pulled Randy inside the stall so that his body couldn't be seen if someone merely looked inside the bathroom without entering.

As Rasheen exited the bathroom, the C.O. appeared from around the corner and his heart nearly dropped to the floor, since the C.O. saw him exit the bathroom. As he headed towards the Law Library, he was literally praying that the C.O. didn't search the bathroom. There was no doubt the C.O. saw him leave the bathroom. Rasheen turned into the stairwell leading up to the Law Library, but stopped and peeked around the corner to see what the C.O. was doing. He saw the C.O. look in the bathroom and then suddenly and frantically rushed inside. Rasheen sighed as a wave of terror gripped him. He climbed the stairs up towards the Law Library, realizing very soon he might be sitting in a courtroom facing new murder charges, and maybe even the death penalty, since the crime happened in an institution.

Chapter Twelve

Lameek paced about the plush executive style office while huffing and puffing; the fury in his bodily gestures was apparent. Killer Kato and Crazy B were sitting comfortably on a plush tiger skin sofa as the Hoodaroma head lawyer, Philip Henderson, sat in an armchair with a laptop computer sitting in his lap.

"Man, fuck movin' to Cali!" Lameek shouted at Killer Kato. "I ain't gotta tag along with you. Yo' do you, and I'll do me."

Killer Kato spoke calmly. "I don't know any 17 year old rap stars doing them without an adult holdin' them down. Let me see you go buy yourself a ride without me, Phil or Crystal to sign for you? Lameek, bro, you being unreasonable."

"Unreasonable!" Lameek took a seat in the nearby matching armchair. "Motherfucker you be fuckin' with my money on the motherfuckin' regular. I be looking at my bank notes and I know that shit ain't right. My CD is third on the rap charts, it made gold two times over, and that means at least a couple of hundred thousand records were sold. Master-Con's CD ain't even make 7th place and he be seeing way more doe than me. You wanna talk about unreasonable…"

"The Distributor's hands are deep in our pockets," Philip said. Realizing this was his area of expertise, since Killer Kato hired him exclusively to keep the artists, and the workers content while he shammed, schemed and robbed them blind; this was definitely his cue to put some work in. "Lameek, I told you we've started a trust fund for you," he lied. "Putting money away for a rainy day is the way of the world. By the time you get 21, you'll have a nice basket of eggs to live quite well…"

"Man, fuck y'all! Put my money in my hands and let me handle my own shit!" Lameek locked eyes with Killer Kato; his love/hate emotions were strong. "When my mom was alive, she was taking care of my cheddar, and I still don't think she said she wanted you to handle the business dealing with me…"

"Show him the contract," Killer Kato said, clearly frustrated. "Let him read it for myself once and for all, so he can stop flipping out, thinking we're trying to pull some shit on him."

Philip retrieved his suitcase sitting next to him; he flipped it open, pulled the contract, and handed it to Lameek.

Lameek walked over, snatched it, and started reading it. Deep down inside, he'd suspected that Killer Kato had something to do with his mom's death, but he couldn't prove it. He sucked his teeth when he finished reading it. "This contract is bullshit, cause my mom told me, if she had to pull back from being my manager she would turn my business stuff over to my brother. Y'all ain't even talk to him before you started…"

"Your brother's in prison," Killer Kato said. "He ain't write your black ass back in years. What makes you think he wrote us back when we tried to reach out to him to fulfill your mother's wishes? You been writing him like crazy, and he won't respond. Don't you get the message?" Killer Kato smiled when he saw Lameek's defeated facial expression; his hurtful pain was so powerful, everyone in room felt it just by observing Lameek's shattered response. Killer also knew if Lameek had known that he had intercepted every single letter Lameek had mailed to Rasheen, he would have probably found another way to reach out to his big brother. Killer Kato had contacted the Post Office, informed them that he was Lameek Smith's legal guardian, and wanted all of Lameek's mail addressed to Rasheen, a convicted felon, to be held and not forwarded. After explaining to the Postal Officials that

Rasheen had a history of abusing Lameek, they reluctantly agreed to the arrangement. Killer Kato took great pleasure reading Lameek's letters since he now knew just about everything that was going on inside of his heart and mind. He certainly wasn't surprised Lameek suspected him of killing his mother, but he was surprised he knew that he was fucking Crystal on the side.

"I'm not moving to Cali," Lameek said pointblank. "You want to go out there to make movies and all that bullshit, and trying to drag me out there with you like I'm your fuckin' flunky like Crazy B here."

Crazy B lunged out of his seat, but Killer Kato grabbed hold of his arm, and Crazy B relaxed.

"Nigga, I ain't scared of you." Lameek stood up from the chair. "You ain't the only nigga around here bustin' his gun up in this motherfucker." He flipped his jacket open, revealing a 9mm.

"Lameek, I thought you agreed not to carry a weapon?" Philip said. "If you get arrested again, you can kiss your rap career goodbye. Keep that thug stuff for records. You seen what happened to Tupac and Biggie, don't follow in their footsteps."

"Yeah, yeah," Lameek said sarcastically. "Whatever."

"Like brother, like brother," Killer Kato said. "Here you are doing things that the average nigga in the Hood would kill to be in your shoes." The disgust in his voice increased ten folds. "You actin' like a straight dumb ass, petty minded nigga, you know that?" You getting high, going to parties acting stupid, you been arrested three times in the last year, you on Probation, and at the rate you going you about to fuck yourself up so thoroughly, even Houdini won't be able to get your dumb ass out of the trick bag you puttin' yourself in." Killer Kato rose to his feet. "And you think you a motherfuckin' thug? You wanna see a real thug? Hah!"

Lameek saw Killer Kato was about to go into one of his serious zone out episodes. At first his nervousness started to take hold of him, but in an instant, his rage and ego took control of his heart. He poked his chest out in defiance.

Killer Kato started shouting while approaching Lameek in a menacing fashion. He wanted to see if Lameek had the killer instinct like his brother. "Nigga, I'm a thug! Check my track record cause it speaks for itself. You young cats around here frontin' and stuntin', thinking y'all know what urban drama is. You wanna see a bitch? Hah! Go look in the fuckin' mirror, and you'll find the bitch! You ungrateful, clown ass, snotty nose, wanna be thug ass..."

Lameek pulled the gun with flinching speed. The rage circulating in his veins caused him to tremble. He never tolerated people talking to him anyway they felt like; not even the infamous Killer Kato. With a tight-lipped, trembling screw face, he aimed the 9mm at Killer Kato's chest. When Crazy B reached for his weapon, while Killer quickly held up his hand, Lameek's aim landed on Crazy B.

"Chill, Crazy B!" Killer Kato shouted, sensing Crazy B was about to show and prove how he got his name. Suddenly, Killer Kato allowed a proud smile to grow steadily into a gargantuan grin. "There you go!" He said playfully to Lameek. "I knew you had it in you. You like the way I pushed that button, huh? Now, be easy with that thing, you know I'm only fuckin' with you." Killer Kato sat back down.

Lameek slowly tucked the gun back in the waist of his pants. Suddenly, he realized he let his anger get the best of him.

"Alright." Killer Kato threw his hands up. "You win. You can stay in New York. Now, I don't want no shit out of you with the concerts and the tours. Starting next week your tour schedule is gonna be real hectic and off the chain. You and Philip can leave now, and start the rehearsal process."

As Philip and Lameek headed towards the door, Philip said to Lameek, "I suggest you start devising your tour routine as soon as possible. I spoke to Kevin, and he'll be here this evening to start rehearsals."

As Philip escorted Lameek out of the office, Killer Kato pretended to be completely undisturbed by what just happened. As he got up and went to his desk, he realized there weren't many folks alive who had pulled a gun on him and lived an extended amount of time to talk about it. He tried to recall the last person who violated in such a fashion, and saw he had to dig real deep. After a moment of shoveling through the cobwebs in his memory bank, he remembered the incident back in 1981 when a dude named Gizmo pulled a gun on him, but made the fatal mistake of not using it. The next day Gizmo was found dead in an abandon lot with twelve bullet wounds to the head. The police actually thought it was a decapitation, since the huge 44 magnum bullets fired at close range had a remarkable way of doing tremendous damage to a human skull.

Looking over at Crazy B, Killer Kato knew that he knew lines were crossed that were never supposed to be crossed. How he should deal with it was supposed to boil down to basic street etiquette, but Lameek was lucky because he was currently a golden goose, and also had one more thing going for him that even Killer Kato found to be of a shocking caliber. Put another way, Lameek had a lucky charm up his ass and didn't even know it.

As Rasheen laid on his bunk staring up at the ceiling with both hands tucked behind his head, he realized he had a lucky charm up his ass. By a remarkable stroke of good fortune the C.O. who found Randy Dolyson lying dead in the bathroom stall with a syringe stuck in his vein and a rubber band tied around his arm, had assumed it was a self-inflicted drug overdose. He didn't even mention Rasheen's exiting the bathroom moments before he found Randy dead in his Unusual Incident Report. The more Rasheen reflected on the C.O's course of action, the more he realized racism, and a complete lack of concern for black life was so deeply entrenched in the system, it literally reached levels of circus like portions. Rasheen remembered when that white dude had over-dosed on heroin in A-Block in his cell at about 3 o'clock in the morning a few months ago, and the next day they shut down the whole A-Block for half the day, while they tried to get someone to reveal who gave the white dude the drugs. But with Randy, they simply slid his ass out of the school on a stretcher, put him on the slab with a toe tag, and were back to business within hours. It was all-good for Rasheen, but it definitely made him stop, and look at the lopsided and unequal way the system functioned.

A week slid by and Rasheen saw his luck had in fact ran out when he saw the hit on him coming. Bad luck actually seemed to be everywhere, since the 9/11 attack on the World Trade Center had took place two weeks earlier, which spewed a contagious spell of utter chaos over the whole country, including the prison yards of Sing Sing. Rasheen was in the A-Block yard, standing near the handball court, kicking it with Rashango when he saw five Latino prisoners looking at him strangely. By the way they moved, and how they repeatedly eyeballed him while whispering amongst themselves, he instantly knew right then and there a hit directed at him was in progress and was about to go down real thick and heavy because one of the individuals was a known Rat Hunter with Statewide clout. He instantly knew it had to be the Columbians once again trying to get at him. Rasheen felt a nervous tension coming over him because all he had on him was a little rinky dink razor, and the number of the hit mob had increased to seven prisoners or may be even more, since others could be laying in the cut. He had a nice bone-breaker stashed in the bathroom, but from the way the mob of prisoners were moving it was highly unlikely that he would be able to get to it. This hit was going down, and if he moved in anyway that signified that he was preparing to defend against it, he knew that would only incite them to move with immediate, explosive, and unrelenting force.

Rasheen whispered to Rashango, "You got any hardware on you?"

Rashango had seen what was taking place moments ago, since it was a bold display of transgression. "You think they coming for us? Ain't no reason for them to step to us on this scale."

Rasheen didn't have time to explain that the Columbians were gunning for him, so he summed it in an economical way. "Believe me, they coming for me. No doubt about it."

Rashango didn't ask why as he pulled his ice pick that he kept tucked between his ass cheeks and got ready for the storm. Everybody knew the Rat Hunters didn't do any talking with their mouths; the components of their language consisted of knives, razors and fists.

Rasheen watched the seven hitters suddenly turn into nine. His nervousness grew; two against nine were some very dangerous odds. He'd gone up against three prisoners one time when he was in Clinton, but he was wielding a vicious bone crasher. Realizing his anxiety was starting to interfere with his overall attitude, he decided to open the curtains so that the show could begin. He'd learned from Master Born that bold behavior of a shocking nature had a strange way of throwing off an opponent enough to unhinge him, and right now he decided it was time to reaffirm that this tactic had some validity.

Rasheen headed straight towards the ringleader with the razor concealed in his hand. Rashango was flanking him on the left with the ice pick up his sleeve.

The drama went up like an atomic explosion. The nine hitters pulled their shanks and charged at Rasheen and Rashango with clear intentions to do deadly harm to them.

Rasheen pulled off his jacket, hastily wrapped it around his fist into a ball and Rashango did the same thing. Rasheen had full intentions of disarming one of these attackers, but the way they were handling their weapons he saw that was highly unlikely. When one of the nine attackers tried to get behind them, Rashango and the attacker started stabbing and jabbing their weapons at each other. Two attackers came at Rasheen; he weaved and caught one of the attackers across the face as he blocked the thrusting motion of the shank with his balled up jacket. With shocking speed Rasheen made certain the shank got entangled in the fabric of the jacket and jerked the knife clean out of the attackers grasp as he shrieked from the razor slash across the face.

Running backwards, Rasheen was forced to retreat as the remaining five attackers rushed at him swinging at him with savage fervor. Rasheen got hold of the shank entangled in his jacket and saw the gang of C.O.s running at them from the other side of the yard.

Suddenly, a C.O. shouted over a bullhorn from the gun tower. "Drop the weapons! Drop your weapons right now! This is your last warning!"

A warning shot rang out, but the attackers kept coming at Rasheen and Rashango and they kept defending themselves.

By the time the twelve C.O's arrived, Rasheen and Rashango were swinging their knives, unable to hold off the nine attackers any longer. Rasheen received two stab wounds to the lower back, and four stab wounds to his arms, while Rashango was stabbed in the stomach, the face, the shoulder and his left leg. The attackers received similar injuries.

Just as Rasheen stabbed one of the attackers in the upper chest and the green eyed Latino screamed with ear torturous energy, he felt a bully club come crashing down upon the back of his head. He stumbled as the stars swirled across his vision, but he was able to maintain his footing. He turned to see which cop cracked him over the head, but saw Rashango fall hard to the ground.

A shot rang out.

Rasheen saw one of the attackers hit the ground, and the riot style commotion came to an instant halt.

The C.O.'s overlapping shouts became even more frantic. "Everybody on the ground! Drop the weapons! Drop 'em! This is a direct order!"

All the prisoners involved in the conflict stood with their weapons in their hands, locked a vicious stand off; everyone was looking at each other, waiting for someone to rush at them.

Another shot rang out and the bullet sprayed up concrete causing everyone to obey.

Moments earlier, Rasheen held on to his weapon, despite the possibility of being shot. He wasn't going to be the first to drop his weapon, and it was apparent everyone else was thinking the same way. However, upon seeing the effects of the second bullet as it tore through the concrete, spraying a thick mist of pulverized cement, everybody dropped their weapons, and so did Rasheen.

Two weeks later, Rasheen was in SHU, working out in his cell, shadow boxing; he realized this situation couldn't have happened at a worse moment. Things were starting to take shape with his legal work, and trying to do it from the box was far beyond difficult. He was glad he and Alamo went through the proper channels by getting administrative approval to have Alamo assist him with his legal affairs. This helped tremendously, but everything was delayed by days. He would send Alamo the FOIL materials or other Court documents that came from the courts, Alamo in turn would read the materials, prepare responses, send them back to him for his signature, and then he would mail the stuff. It was frustrating, but Rasheen took it all in stride, since he'd learned years ago that there was no need in stressing himself out by brooding over a SHU stay; he was sentenced to one year in SHU, which he could do standing on his head; the only down side was he had to allow his head soldier, Kojak to run the drug business with Camila visiting him to make the drop offs. Box time was indeed a part of the bid, especially when he had world-class drug dealers gunning for him. In any event, he was grateful he was alive to fight another day.

Rasheen also surprised himself when he saw he was able to get beyond his distrust for Latino prisoners. Although he wasn't on some racial nonsense (his man Dirty Ricky was the epitome of a Latino honcho), Rasheen very rarely opened up to Latino prisoners, in view of the fact the Columbians were of the Latino stock. Dario Montero was his next cell neighborhood in SHU, who was much older than him, was an old time Dominican gangster, and had apparently been watching Rasheen very closely. At first Rasheen got on the defensive when he saw Dario knew shit about him that most prisoners weren't supposed to know. He knew Rasheen was a stick up kid, who specialized in robbing drug dealers, and he was in prison for robbing the Columbians. This obviously wasn't information that was hard to find out, but the way Dario was going about it did make Rasheen wonder what his true intentions were. All sorts of questions were popping up in his mind as Dario worked hard to tear down Rasheen's shield. Could he be working for the Columbians? Could he be a snitch working for the state or feds? Every prisoner with some degree of intelligence knew the government was notorious for planting snitches next door to a target; the agent provocateur would then befriend the target with hopes that the target would reveal a series of unsolved crimes, preferably homicides, because there was no statute of limitations for murder.

But what broke down Rasheen's protective shield to a level that allowed him to open up to Dario occurred when he detected Dario was genuinely bitter with his crew; it was obvious by his tone, he was disgruntled and wanted revenge against his people who turned their backs on him after he caught a life bid for them. When Dario kept hopping on the fact that he had Alamo working on his case, and that there was a good chance he might be leaving this place, Rasheen egged him on to lay down his agenda. As Rasheen walked the SHU yard with Dario, listening to Dario share with him all the inner intricate workings of one of the most prominent Dominican drug gangs in the New York City area, revealing the who, what, when, and most of all, the where of at least 6 stash houses that were overflowing with that wonderful, all might mean green, Rasheen knew that his presence in SHU was a preordained event. Kind of like a sign from heavenly forces that were giving him the tools and materials he needed to fulfill his mission. His assumptions were confirmed when Dario asked him to hit his crew, rape and rob them royally, give him a reasonable cut, and with a grateful grin Rasheen accepted the offer.

About a year from the day Randy Doylson took his last shot of dope, Rasheen got a motion and a kite from Alamo, informing him that he believed that he had finally found a solid issue. According to Alamo, the DA had presented false testimony to the Grand Jury, and even when it became obvious that the testimony was false, the DA failed to obtain a superseding indictment on proper evidence or to disclose the facts and seek permission from the Court to resubmit the case. When Rasheen read the motion and the exhibits attached to the motion, he saw that the cop named Robertson who was investigating the murders and the carjacking had testified at the Grand Jury that a witness identified Rasheen in a line up as the culprit fleeing the scene. This was a flat out lie, and during the pretrial hearing it was discovered by the DA to be a lie when the same cop testified that there was no such identification. Even though Rasheen copped out, it didn't matter because perjured testimony did not foreclose his right to challenge the error. Under the law, errors of this magnitude were "nonwaivable, jurisdictional prerequisites." Rasheen wasn't familiar with all the legal jargon, but he did understand the term "rhythm", and Alamo seemed to be confident that the issue would do the trick.

Rasheen got the CPL 440.10 motion papers notarized and mailed the motion on April 30, 2002. After going through the formalities consisting of the court acknowledging receipt, setting a calendar date for the motion, receiving the DA's opposition, and Alamo did a reply, the waiting game was all he could engage in.

Then one day in July, Rasheen received legal mail. When he read the Kings County Supreme Court's decision and order by Judge Garrison (his original Judge had died of a heart attack), stating that his case was reversed and the indictment dismissed with instructions to the DA to obtain a superceding indictment, he was literally dumfounded with utter delight. He read the seven-page court document eight times before he finally convinced himself that it wasn't a dream.

After spending 7 years in prison, there were no words that could describe how enthralled Rasheen felt when he was on the bus, cruising back down to Rikers Island. When he stood in front of Judge Garrison, his joy reached levels not of this world. His elated attitude grew even higher when the DA offered him time served and he jumped on the offer with the quickness. Smiling from ear to ear, Rasheen looked around the courtroom, saw Camila as his contentment continued growing, and when his eyes landed upon the four Latino men wearing evil snarls on their grills, his smile disappeared instantly. At that moment, he realized the real drama had just officially begun.

Chapter Thirteen

Rasheen stepped off the Rikers Island bus and saw Camila running towards him with her arms extended for a hug. He looked around the parking lot for the car he knew was out there somewhere. As he hugged Camila, she secretly tucked the 9mm into his waist while whispering in his ear, "I got a surprise for you," sounding like the Jones Girls from the record "All Night Long."

Upon returning to Rikers Island from Court, he had spoke with Camila over the phone and instructed her to come pick him up and to come ready for action. She insured him that she was bringing her younger brother, Amar and his thuggish friends who would be on the scene with her in a green Jeep. She also said she was working on some sort of surprise. When Rasheen saw the Jeep he felt a small ping of relief. He continued searching as he and Camila headed towards her blue Toyota Acura, but was perplexed by the fact he hadn't seen any of the Columbian hit men. Nobody could tell him as he got inside the Acura on the passenger side, that there wouldn't be a wild-wild west shoot out the moment he stepped foot off the bus, and he now realized how Camila tried to tell him the men in Court weren't there for him, but he wasn't trying to hear a single word of it. Reflecting back on the four men in the courtroom he realized he may have misread the situation and overreacted by assuming the worse. After spending years in prison with Latino prisoners trying to take his head off, it was only natural for him to perceive those four men, who all were sporting vicious sneers on their faces, to be there to step to him.

When Camila started the car, Rasheen began to realize that this drop off area was just across the bridge from Rikers, and common sense told him that wise hit men wouldn't rush the job.

Now that he was no longer behind bars, they could obvious allow their own folks to step to the business the proper way.

As Camila pulled away, Rasheen was looking in all directions at all vehicles with the gun ready for action. He saw the green jeep and a black Chevy Impala following them.

"Be easy, Boo," Camila said. "The black car is down with us. We checked this area, and ain't no drama around here. And the eyes we got checkin' it out are the ones that don't make mistakes." She smiled teasingly at Rasheen.

He saw Camila was hinting at something big. "What's the surprised you got for me? Right now if it ain't a winning lotto ticket for millions, that big grin on your face is out of place."

"Well, it ain't a million dollar ticket," Camila took the turn onto the BQE, seeing through the rearview mirror the headlights of the two cars were still on her tail. "But I see something like that on the horizons."

"Come on, Camila," Rasheen said seriously. "Lay it on me."

She paused and then said, "Jack-Mack is in the black car following us."

Rasheen smiled, realizing this was very good news. "How the hell you pulled that off."

"Don't get mad, but a couple years back Jack-Mack gave me a number to his cousin's cell phone down south in Florida, and told me if I ever needed him strictly for life and death situations to call and leave a message in a code he gave me. He said it might be safer if I kept this between just him and me. I used it only once to see if he was frontin', and he shocked the shit out of me when he called the next day. I couldn't think of a better time to use it than right now."

Rasheen couldn't stop smiling. It was surely going to be a beautiful day in the neighborhood, at least as far as he was concerned. It couldn't get any more beautiful. When they reached their destination, a private house in Nassau County Long Island, and Rasheen and Jack-Mack conversed after not seeing or talking to each other for 7 years; Rasheen's head spun with pleasure when Jack-Mack revealed that he had his cut of the money from the Livonia Avenue stick up stashed in a locker at Grand Central Station in the amount of 50 grand.

"My motherfuckin' brother!" Rasheen shouted; he gave Jack-Mack a pound as he reached out and hugged him in Bed-Stuy fashion. "Love is love for real, Sun!"

"Nigga, we know how this thing goes!" Jack Mack sat down gearing up to roll up a blunt. He was a little self-conscience about the fact he had clipped Rasheen for about twenty grand, but he couldn't get up the nerve to share this with him. He knew how much Rasheen loved money, so he decided it would be best to let this particular bone in the closet stay in the closet. "If shit wasn't so hot, I would've showed way more love. I would've went up in them mountains and visited your ass, you feel me? But I know you got all that cheddar I was blessin' Crystal with. I was hittin' her."

"You gave Crystal money for me?" Rasheen felt something stronger than rage forming in his stomach. "She ain't hit me off nothing coming from you."

"Ah, shit, here we go. All together I gave her damn near four gees. I told her make sure she keep your commissary right."

Rasheen felt steam rolling off him; he'd always knew Jack-Mack was stepping to his business, and now he'd just added another snake to his hit list. He'd known Crystal was a gold digger of the first kind, but he'd never imagine that she was lying and stealing from him when he was at his lowest point. Disloyalty and stealing was grounds for a bullet to the head no matter who the violator was and now it was time to set a whole lot of records straight.

"Don't worry about that shit, dog," Jack-Mack sucked on the blunt, pulling in a huge cloud of smoke. "We's about to blow up like the motherfuckin' World Trade, bro." He passed the blunt to Rasheen as he slowly let out the smoke.

Rasheen took the blunt just as Camila and Candy entered the room. He drew on the blunt and coughed explosively. This shit was as raw as atomic fuel! While in prison he smoked only on occasions, since he was never the type to hustle backwards, and getting high on your own supply was clearly a example of that, so he'd learned to discipline himself.

Rasheen was pleased with Jack-Mack's new girl Candy; she was most definitely a ride or die chick, and looked good too. He was surprised to see Camila's brother Amar, had grown tremendously. The last time he saw him, he was in the street playing skelly, with a snotty nose and big crusty lips. He even remembered Amar's homeboy, Dapper D, who was also one of those little badass gremlins from the Hood that stayed into shit. Rasheen saw he had himself a nice little mob, since they all looked up to him as the leader, the chief, the general, and he was eating it up like White Castle burgers.

After they all got treed up, and their heads were buzzing with Hennessey, they brought Rasheen up to speed with all the current events, then Rasheen and Camila were on their way to the bedroom.

Rasheen entered the room and noticed Camila was all over him. She peeled out of her clothing so fast Rasheen thought she just performed a magic trick. His dick was pulsing with rock hardness and had been standing at attention the minute Camila give him the cue that it was time to hit the sack. Rasheen flopped down on the bed on his back and just when Camila snatched his pants off, he remembered the vow he made when he was in Sing Sing after he took an AIDS awareness class. He promised to strap up no matter who it was, since HIV was murdering folks without the slightest inkling of mercy. Camila climbed up upon him, grabbed hold of his wood and was about to insert it into her watery world of pleasure.

Breathing hard with excitement, Rasheen grabbed her arm, startling the shit out of her. "We gotta get a condom, Boo."

Through her accelerated breathing she was trying to figure out if Rasheen was serious, "What you saying Rah? I'm clean, I ain't been fuckin' around, letting any ole nigga run up in me."

Rasheen sighed, knowing this was going to happen. Already his hard-on was fading. He sat up in the bed. "Listen, Camila, don't get what I'm saying twisted. I know you clean, but I took an AIDS awareness class, and I know anybody can have HIV. People walk around infected for years and don't even know it. They look, and feel healthy, but they can pass it on to people and don't even know it."

Camila wasn't feelin' this kind of talk because she viewed AIDS as a disease for fags, dope fiends, and dirty people. "I don't know where you going with this, but right now let's find us some condoms, so we can do this dam thang. If you want we can go to the clinic and put both our cards on the table."

Rasheen reached over and gave her a deep kiss, designed to inform her that she said the right thing. He let go of the kiss and said, "Now, go get about three of them condoms."

Camila was all smiles as she grabbed her robe, put it on and was out the door. She was back in two minutes flat with five condoms.

When Rasheen entered Camila with the rubber on, he noticed it was the blandest, and most boring sexual episode he'd ever engaged in; the sensation was so unstimulating he realized he had to concentrate in order to bust a nut. Prior to his incarceration he never used a condom, and when he fucked it was raw head or nothing.

As they cuddled, Rasheen was anxious to get to the Clinic, so that they could put their cards on table; he wanted to touch some raw, uncut, no-chaser, unadulterated pussy so bad, he was tempted to take a chance sliding up in Camila raw head. Had it not been for all those graphic images of dying AIDS patients, looking shriveled up with pus oozing sores all over their bodies, he might have fail victim to his lower desires.

Chapter Fourteen

Killer Kato and Crazy B sat comfortably at the conference table in Killer Kato's multi million-dollar mansion, talking.

"I think the time is right," Killer Kato said. "This beef between Ja-King and Money-Man is being played out all over the country. And it got a good ring to it; New York versus the Dirty South."

"Yeah, but Ja-King is pulling blows," Crazy B said, and took a sip of his Jack Daniel's. "He told them reporters at Vibe Magazine that he's not going to response to Money-Man's concert battle offer. The way he's pulling back is gonna make it hard to create a situation where all evidence point to his death being linked to a lunatic fan."

Killer Kato sighed because he was tired of waiting to take his plan to the next level. "I think this plan is ready; we got ownership of his masters, and the three albums we got planned will make us major millions. Just look at it, he is worth more to us dead than alive. Ja-King is at the top of his game. The rap game is shinning mad love on him. The fans are feelin' him like a mufucka! If he dies right now, he'll be even more famous than he'll ever be. Don't forget, most rappers don't got staying power like R&B artists. Usually they blaze onto the rap scene, make crazy cheddar, and fall back a little; they may make a weak ass come back, and then you don't see them ever again. Whatever happened to Big Daddy Kane, Special Ed, EPMD, MC Lyte, Stetasonic? The list could go on and on. That's cause the fans are always looking for new blood. Nobody wants the same old shit over and over again. If we smoke Ja now, fans all over the world will get behind anything we put out of his. Look at Tupac, Biggie, and Marvin Gaye. You read the figures; their record sells quadruple when they died."

"I think Marvin's was a little bigger than that."

"Yeah, you right, and the doe is still rolling in," Killer Kato saw Crazy B was totally unemotional as he nursed his drink. "I say now is the time to set it off. We don't want this nigga getting too crazy with his own security either. It's bad enough he fired our peoples and got his own peoples doing the bodyguard work."

"The niggas he snatched up are amateurs," Crazy got up and headed for the bar to refill his glass. "A bunch of cornball ass niggas riding his dick for attention."

"Yeah that may be so, but cornball ass niggas with guns can put up a fight and may fuck this thing up if it ain't done right."

"We got this," Crazy B returned to the chair. "My gun don't miss when it goes off. When we hit this chump he won't see it coming." He clinked his ice cubes around. "If his team wants a piece of the action they can get some too."

Killer Kato sighed impatiently. He hated Crazy B's cockiness, but loved his overconfidence. "And we can't overlook the fact he violated when he cut some undercover track with GBE Records behind our back. I guess he think we selling wolf tickets when we told him he's stuck with us for life."

"Yeah," Crazy B shifted in his chair. "I will admit played himself with that dumb shit."

"I can make this call straight up, you know, but I need your heart in this one; you the one on the frontline."

Crazy B downed the remaining portion of his drink, and sighed, "On the real, Killer, you preaching to the choir right now. It don't make me no never mind whether we kill this chump now, next week, or next year. I just feel we could milk another CD out of this nigga before we flush him down the toilet. Once we go there ain't no undoing this thing. But, hey, if you feel the time is now, give me my marching orders and I'll march."

Killer Kato smiled proudly. "Good. You can step to this thing as soon as possible. I got only one reserve and that is . . ."

Ja-King sat in the VIP booth of the Ecstasy Club, nurturing a drink as the hip hop tune had Fred and Lamont, his two personal bodyguards, bobbing their heads to the rhythm as they stood nearby and watched the area for any funny business. Sitting across from Ja-King was his new girl, Vanessa, who was an aspiring actress who just got a part in a feature film starring Samuel L. Jackson. Ja-King's chiseled muscular physique was tensed with stress that could clearly be detected in his baby face. His smooth, could never hurt a fly facial structure, took on a flare of deadly seriousness.

Something was wrong. The air was saturated with it. Ja-King could almost reach out and grab hold of it.

Ja-King's mind was on one thing. The beef between him and Money-Man. Rumor had it that Money-Man had peoples that were planning to take it to the next level. They didn't say exactly what that next level was, but in the Hood everyone knew what that meant. He sighed as he watched the folks dancing on the huge dance floor, realizing he tried desperately to dead the beef. The way those music industry wolves were using this as a moneymaking gimmick solely designed to sell records, and how they were dumping barrels of gasoline on the fire was beyond sickening. What angered him the most was that Money-Man was playing right into this bullshit without considering the inevitable consequences, after what happened to Biggie and Tupac, one might think it would be utter insanity to start tinkering with full-scale disrespect battles that pit geographical locations against other geographical areas. Rap fans were very serious about their rap icons and had no problem letting a few bullets fly to show just how much they cared. Ja-King didn't want to give any fuel to this thing, but at the same time he wasn't about to allow any motherfucker to hurt him in anyway, including scarring his reputation he worked so hard and so long to build up.

Ja-King felt his response in his new CD would put an end to all this drama. He checked Money-Man properly and respectfully, while at the same time dropping some vicious jewels about Black unity, and made it clear that he was wise enough not to allow a rap battle to escalate into a bloodbath. He even dropped a thing or two about how industry executives were instigating the drama in order to sell more records. That was a potential hot spot, but truth was truth, and if some backlash for making that statement was coming, then bring the noise. But he did have to agree that this new CD was craftly done in such a way that keep it real for the streets, while showing the world that he was the better man for trying to dead the conflict before bullets started flying instead of words. Although he made this CD on the side without Killer Kato's knowledge, and with a new record label named GBE, he knew it was the best way to do it because Killer Kato was one of those folks encouraging him to go for the jugular and to keep the beef going. He also knew Killer was going to be furious when he found out, but because he was Hoodaroma's heaviest and most prominent rap star, he also knew he would get over it.

Ja-King looked at his watch, and decided it was time to put a conclusion on tonight's festivities. His mind simply wasn't there.

He massaged the 18 shot 9mm he had tucked in his waist, and felt reassured. Growing up in the streets of Crown Heights Brooklyn had taught him to never trust his life in the hands of anyone. Sure he had gun-totting bodyguards, who were trigger happy criminals, itching to show how loyal they were to him. In fact, his current crew was Homies straight from his own Hood, and he had kept Fred, Lamont, Rondu and Leo on the DL for special situations like the one he was currently embroiled in. Even despite the fact they were from his Hood, he wouldn't even fully trust them with his life. He was so intent on holding himself down he went to great lengths to keep the 9mm he was carrying concealed from everyone, including his current bodyguards.

"Come on, Vanessa," Ja-King stood, brushing away imaginary lent from his two piece Marc Ecko suit. "Let's get up outta this piece."

"Where to?" Vanessa grabbed her purse as she rose to her feet. "I hope it ain't another night in the crib."

Ja-King wrapped his arm around her shoulder as he led the way towards the door. "What's wrong with my crib? That mufucka cost me over six mill." He saw Fred and Lamont were on point. Fred was in the front on the cell phone, apparently informing the Limo driver, Calvin, that they were coming out while Lamont was behind him and Vanessa.

"I thought this was supposed to be our night out?" Vanessa said, "It's not even 12 o'clock and we calling it a night?"

Ja-King was intercepted by the fans that started showing him mad love; some fans asked for his autograph, which he signed without the slightest hesitation, while others were inquiring about his upcoming concert and new CD. When he finished, he stepped out of the club and saw his Limo across the street. This was very odd because Leo and Rondu were nowhere in sight and the Limo wasn't parked in front of the club in accordance with standard Limousine procedures. Ja-King's alarms went off with the explosive fury of angry hornets. His hand instantly went for the 9mm.

Suddenly, from his peripheral view, Ja-King saw movement. Two men were approaching fast wearing ski masks. Just as the gunshots rang out from the two-armed men, Ja-King dove onto Vanessa, knocking her down to the ground.

In a flash, pandemonium took control of everything.

Lamont pulled his compact Uzi the moment he saw the two men and just as he took aim at the two masked men, several shots from across the street rang out; two bullets ripped through Lamont's head, spraying brain matter and blood. Despite the deadly injuries, Lamont reflexively held down on the trigger, unleashing a barrage of Uzi bullets that struck one of the masked men.

Meanwhile, Fred fired his 9mm at the two men while crouching on one knee, making sure the car in front of him blocked him from the shooters across the street. When Lamont hit the ground, Fred continued firing his 9mm at the other masked man who attempted to retreat behind a nearby car, but was cut down by Fred's bullets. Fred then slid to the nearby car and saw four additional masked men creeping towards them and opened fire, causing them to retreat behind the nearby parked cars.

The people inside the club were screaming and running in terror, hiding behind the closest things to them.

Ja-King had the 9mm in his hand while Vanessa was curled up in a fetal position; he screamed to Vanessa, "Crawl inside the club, hurry!" He saw she was galvanized with fear, which prevented him from screaming on her with malice. Calmly he said, "Listen, Vanessa, stay on your stomach, and crawl inside the club. If you stay here, you will be shot!"

Vanessa obeyed; she trembled with sheer terror as she slid on the pavement inside the club.

Ja-King scurried to the nearest car to get a visual of what was going on across the street. He saw Fred was exchanging gunfire with four masked men. Then it dawned on him that Leo, Rondu, and Calvin must be dead because they hadn't appeared on the set.

Out the corner of his eye, Ja-King saw another men creeping towards him from down the street in the opposition direction of the first two shooters. Ja-King crouched down, pretending as though he didn't see this masked man, waiting until he was just a little closer. When the man was positioned perfectly, Ja-King hastily took aim and pumped off four shots, dropping the men instantly.

Ja-King hastily duck walked to the fallen men as bullets fired from across the street pulverized the cars he eased pass. Ja-King saw the man twitching and fired a shot to the man's head. He had to see who it was behind the mask; the overpowering urge to know who was coming to murder him was irresistible. Ja-King snatched the ski mask off the dead men's head, and nearly passed out when he saw who it was. Oh, hell no! He saw it was Crazy B's man, Anthony. Realization slapped his mind wide open. Killer Kato was trying to kill him! Ja-King was immobilized with disbelief and shock, but why? Why would this motherfucker want to kill him? It couldn't be because of the work with GBE; there's no way he could know about that! When no answer jumped in his mind, he struggled to pull himself back to reality.

The sound of sirens shook him loose from his galvanized state. He wanted to do something, but didn't know what to do. Suddenly, he saw frantic movement; he spun with the gun aimed and fired two shots. As the individual he shot collapsed to the ground, Ja-King instantly sensed he had made a major mistake and had jumped the gun. He stepped closer to the fallen person to inspect what he'd done. When he saw it was a white lady, apparently an innocent bystander, who was probably fleeing for safety, he hit the panic lever. He was calling himself every foul name in the English language as he saw his rap career fizzing away like water escaping down a drain. How the fuck could he zone out and start firing before looking at what the fuck he was shooting at? But common sense told him that any person in his shoes with a hit mob coming to kill him would've done the same damn thing. Kill or be killed was law right about now. Plus, this dumb bitch was in the wrong place at the wrong time and should've stayed her stupid ass off the fuckin' streets, especially with bullets flying around, he told himself.

As the sirens grew louder, and he noticed the four men across the street that were locked in a gun battle with Fred started leaving the scene, Ja-King realized his whole life had just been snatched from under his feet. He felt like a dead man walking. Reality surge through his mind, and he knew there was no getting around this, even with a multi-million dollar bank account. He'd just killed two people (one a white innocent bystander) with an illegal firearm and he was a black man.

Instinctively, Ja-King took off down the street, running as if he was a world-class track star. To be honest he didn't totally understand why he was fleeing the scene, but he sensed it was in his genes. When he was a nobody, running the streets and robbing everything moving, he'd always felt the urge to run whenever he heard police sirens, so it was only right that he maintain this life sustaining tradition, especially when he knew if they caught him under these situations it would be lights out. Like most sensible black men surviving in an inherently racist country, he'd decided to take his chances running.

Chapter Fifteen

Rasheen sat in the front passenger seat of the blue cable TV van, listening to the radio news-report regarding the Ja-King shooting incident last night. Camila sat behind the wheel. They were in Trenton, New Jersey watching the large colonial style mansion about two blocks away. Both dressed in matching "Eco-view Cable Company" uniforms, they were waiting for Manny's wife and his three children to leave the premises to go to work and to school before they entered. The same "Eco-view" symbol stenciled on their uniforms was also posted on both sides of the van. The facial disguises they wore were quite convincing and could've fool each other had they not known the deal. Rasheen wore a fake moustache and beard, while Camila wore cat woman glasses and a wig. After casing this Dominican stash house for several days they figured out the family's daily routine, and knew in about five minutes the pretty brunette and the three adolescent children would be on their merry way.

"You hear this shit?" Rasheen said to Camila rhetorically, as the news-report about the Ja-King shooting came to an end. "Ja-King murdered four people!" Out of habit he turned off the radio and turned on Lameek's CD. "Naw, I can't go for that one. That nigga got millions dripping out of his ass, and ain't no way he shootin' motherfuckers over a rap battle. With that kind of money, you can pay a whole lotta dudes to do the shootin' for you." He glanced at the mansion, and saw no activities. "That shit is game. I know Ja-King personally. He wasn't no gunman when we was ripping and running in them streets. All that thug shit he be talkin' on wax is all show. Handling hardware like that there wasn't in his blood. If he laid down four bodies, somebody put his back up against a wall." Rasheen took another sip of the Tropicana orange juice and sat it back on the dashboard. "With all that fame on his back, I don't know how he plannin' on out running Po-Po. I bet Killer Kato's grimy ass hands are all in that shit."

"Ain't no doubt about that," Camila said as she sat the binoculars down. "That nigga so foul, a dark cloud of death and destruction swallows up everything around him. I still can't believe that foul, cut-throat nigga blocked your brother from showing you any love." She shook her head in disgust. "Before Lameek blew up, and Killer had him under the wing, all he did was talk about how he was going to become a big time rapper and get you out of jail one day. I tell you that motherfucker poisoned Lameek's mind."

Rasheen was catapulted into a deep reverie by Camila's comment. His hatred for Killer Kato flared up with the speed and force of a fatal allergic reaction. That nigga twisted his whole life upside down! He'd long sense concluded that his life wouldn't be worth shit until he put Killer Kato where he belonged: six feet under. That day Judge Garrison announced his release, Rasheen reaffirmed his vow that his entire life would be dedicated to killing Killer Kato. Although he'd made that decision many years ago, it was truly a pleasure to see that instead of his desire for revenge weakening, it had actually grew stronger. Thanks to Killer's willingness to drag his family and loved ones into the beef, he transformed this conflict into one that could only be resolved when one of them were dead. The only thing that came close to competing with this vow was his promise to become rich beyond the average person's imagination, and after comparing the two, it was obvious they were interconnected. Without money there was no way he could go up against Killer Kato and be successful; that chump was probably worth mega-millions by now, and at the snap of a finger he could move a good size army of people to do his bidding. Also, there was no way he could enjoy any amount of money with Killer Kato walking the planet, so either way it went the acquisition of one required the completion of the other.

Rasheen turned off the CD player when he saw Manny's wife and only two of the children exit the mansion. He threw his binoculars to his eyes, joining Camila as she watched the events unfold. This was not a good look. He sighed, "Did Amar mention anything about the other kid spending the night elsewhere?"

"Nope, he said they all was in place as usual."

Rasheen saw major drama on the horizon. He was hoping this run wouldn't get as crazy as the hit they did two nights ago on the previous Dominican stash house, but the missing kid said it was going to one of those days. During the previous stick up they ended up killing three men who apparently felt it was better to engage in a suicidal resistance instead of explaining to their superiors how they allowed 1.2 million dollars to be stolen from a secured location that no one was supposed to know about. In reality it really didn't matter since the three men saw Rasheen and Jack-Mack's faces, and that in and of itself meant they had to go whether or not anyone wanted it that way.

Watching the wife and kids drive away, Rasheen realized he hadn't anticipated this happening, and felt tension brewing in his mid section. One thing for certain he didn't give a shit about Manny; he was getting knocked out of the game no matter which way the cards were dealt. It was the kid that got under his skin. Rasheen sighed frustratedly. Killing innocent people touched him in a crippling way, but killing innocent children was utterly unthinkable and completely unforgivable.

That voice reminded him that nobody respected a baby killer, not even the most unscrupulous of prisoners; he flashed back to that time in Elmira when he saw that dude Juan Batista hanging from a cloth rake in his cell. Although the "Unusual Incident Report" wrote it off as a suicide, Rasheen knew the real deal. Scram Jones was lynched; once the word touched the right ears it was just a matter of time before true justice would be served, especially in light of the fact Juan was in prison for hanging his 2-year-old son while in a fit of jealousy and revenge. Even sadistic prisoners found it hard to fix their minds to believe Juan killed his own son in order to get back at his common law wife when he saw her with another man, but the newspaper clippings were floating around the jail as irrefutable proof. Once this kind of ultra-foul information seeped into the prison population, it was just a matter of time before the self-appointed clean up crew would start cleaning up.

When Rasheen saw the car disappearing down the street, he got on the cell phone. "Jack-Mack, we in motion."

Camila started the van and headed for the mansion. "So what's the deal with the kid? We taking hostages or what?"

Rasheen ejected the CD from the CD player and placed it in his breast pocket; he said nothing for several seconds, since he was still working out a plan. He didn't want to kill a five or six year old kid, but there was no way he was going to allow himself or anyone in his crew to be identified in this robbery, which would automatically link them to the others. "We stick with the plan. I'll deal with the kid if and when the time comes."

Two blocks behind the Eco-view van sat a green SUV with two men inside. Antonio and Remmy had been watching the van closely. About twenty minutes ago, Remmy had turned the SUV onto the street leading to Manny's mansion and saw the van, which instantly set off both of the men's alarms. They were on their way to drop off the money from last night's pick-ups.

As they drove pass the van, they saw a black man and woman inside; instead of making the drop off, they circled around the block and parked a few blocks behind the van and watched. Antonio immediately called Manny and informed him of the situation. Surprisingly, Antonio discovered that Manny did in fact call to have his cable repaired, since it had just went on the blink the day before. Now all three of the drug dealers' alarms were going off like crazy.

After what happened to Paco and Peto's stash house, there was nothing else to talk about. Antonio immediately called Ramon, requesting that a heavily armed crew report to Manny's mansion immediately. They all agreed that even if it turned out to be a false alarm, it was always better to be safe than sorry, especially when dealing with money in the million-dollar range. That was about ten minutes ago, and Antonio was a bit disappointed as he watched the van approach the mansion moments after Manny's wife and two children drove off. The van pulled to a stop right in front of the front door. There was no way the back up would arrive in time for the fireworks. But then again it really didn't matter since Antonio and Remmy had two Uzi's concealed in specially constructed hidden compartments in the floorboard of the SUV. They also knew Manny had an arsenal of the finest military weaponry that money could buy. Without uttering another word, Antonio started getting the guns ready as Remmy started the car and approached the mansion.

Rasheen hit the doorbell again. He and Camila exchanged nervous glances as they tugged on the straps of their leather tote bags dangling from their shoulders. Rasheen welcomed his nervousness and saw it as a healthy emotion as long as it didn't hinder the ability to think quickly and efficiently.

Suddenly, he heard someone approaching the door. As the locks were being unfastened without the person on the other side asking who it was or even looking through the peephole, Rasheen felt the compulsion to go for his gun and gave into the urge. Nobody opened their doors in this city in this fashion unless they were expecting the person on the other side or there was a trap being put in motion. When the door swung open, revealing the small child who had not left with the wife, Rasheen allowed his hand to relax. For safekeeping he had tucked his thumb inside his belt so that his hand would've been within inches from the 9mm.

"Good morning," Rasheen said with a huge smile, sounding professional. "We're here to repair your cable. Are your parents around?"

"Yes," The kid said. "My daddy says to come inside." He opened the door wide and stepped to the side as Rasheen and Camila entered.

Just as Rasheen's eyes were taking in the extremely elegant interior of the mansion, he heard the frantic commotion of the kid rushing out of the house. Without having to look to see what the hell was going on, Rasheen was already in motion, fleeing towards the partition while retrieving his 9mm. He saw Camila responded as though she was inside of his head, since she too scrambled for cover while pulling her weapon.

Almost exactly on the heels of their rapid response the massive machine gunfire exploded from the top of the spiral staircase, which shattered the early morning tranquility.

Every member of Rasheen's crew went straight into the contingency plan.

Jack-Mack and Candy were sitting in a tan Ford parked in back of the mansion when the machine gunfire sounded off. They both jumped out the car and ran towards the mansion.

Earlier, Amar and Dapper were waiting amongst the thick patch of trees and shrubs surrounding the mansion when they saw the green SUV racing towards the mansion. The urgency in which the SUV approached told them instantly that the plan was out the window. As they got their Uzi's' in the ready position, machine gunfire went off inside the mansion and jolted them both into instant action. The contingency plan was now in effect. Amar lead the charge towards the mansion; he was surprised when he saw the kid running across the courtyard.

Just as Antonio and Remmy brought the SUV to a screeching stop, and rushed out of the vehicle, Amar and Dapper's silencer equipped Uzi's came to life almost at the same moment. The dozens of bullets pounded both men in a merciless and brutal manner, collapsing them to the pavement before they got off a single shot.

Inside, Rasheen and Camila fired silenced shots at Manny who was hiding in a position that shield him from their bullets.

Amar and Dapper arrived at the entrance and were prevented from entering when they were met with a wave of Manny's machine gun bullets.

Rasheen saw that he and Camila were in a quagmire; if they moved from their current location they would be easily gunned down, and if they stayed here any longer the police were bound to arrive before they even got in place to implement the contingency plan, but the part that disturbed him most was the possibility of leaving without getting the money. This was definitely not a good look.

As Jack-Mack and Candy entered the house from the back as planned, they knew what they had to do without fully knowing all the details. They swiftly glided across the carpeted floors in cat burglar style in accordance with their instructions. On tiptoes Jack-Mack and Candy split up, Jack-Mack headed towards the front of the mansion to find Manny while Candy started looking for the loot.

Jack-Mack flinched when Manny's machine gun rattled off a wave of huge caliber bullets, but he was grateful because he now knew exactly where the shots were fired. With the 9mm aimed in a shooting stance, Jack was moving extremely fast. When Jack reached the side of the balcony, he looked up and saw Manny as clear as day holding the AR-16. He smiled and thought this was too good to be true; Jack had a clear shot since Manny had left himself wide open and apparently didn't expect someone to come from the back. Jack took careful aim and squeezed off six rounds into Manny's unsuspecting flesh.

Rasheen heard Manny's startled cries and the swooshing sounds of Jack-Mack's silenced gunfire; he sprung into a frantic charged towards the spiraling staircase, knowing Jack had entered from the back. Rasheen shouted, "Check everything! Hurry! Hurry! We out in four minutes! Hurry! Move! Move!"

Camila, Amar, and Dapper rushed inside and split up as though they had rehearsed this move a thousand times.

Ten seconds later, Candy shouted, "I got it! I got it!" She had found a safe hidden behind a huge fake fireplace.

Within seconds, Rasheen and Jack rushed inside the dinning room.

Rasheen slapped a slab of C4 on the safe's dial, inserted a detonator, rushed out the room and pressed the bottom.

BLAAM!!

The explosion shook damn near the whole neighbor.

"Let's go!" Rasheen shouted as he saw the safe's door was blown open and money was raining down to the floor as though confetti was being tossed at a parade.

Jack, Candy, Camila, and Dapper rushed to the safe hysterically dumping stacks of money into their tote bags.

Rasheen and Amar ran to the front of the mansion. Just as Rasheen arrived at the entrance, he saw three police cars pull into the circular driveway and came to a stop. He pulled a detonator from his bag. Peering from behind the entrance, Rasheen watched as the cops rushed out of their patrol cars with guns drawn, and slowly approached the van. Just when the six cops were within the C4's peak zone, Rasheen hit the button of the detonator as he ran towards the back of the mansion.

BLLAAMM!!

The C4 disintegrated the entire van, gulfing the area in flames and falling debris. The cops never knew what hit them. Their deaths were swift and painless.

Rasheen and Amar reached the back and saw Jack, Camila, Candy and Dapper were still stuffing their bags with money; they were even picking up the scattered money from off the floor. Rasheen loved their energy, but it was officially time to go. He shouted in drill sergeant fashion. "Let's go! Let go!" He led the way out the back.

Ten minutes later, Rasheen was in the passenger seat of a red Camaro; Camila was driving. Now stripped of their disguises, they cruised down the New Jersey turnpike with Jack and Candy behind them; Amar and Dapper were in back of the tan Ford. Dozens of police cars zoomed passed them with their sirens blaring.

Rasheen felt alive with energy. He smiled since the thrill of the moment was mind tingling. This run was a success in every sense of the word. Although they had to utilize the contingency plan, and killed a few cops, the good thing was that they got away with more money than they retrieved during the last Dominican stash house hit. It was time for a celebration. He pulled Lameek's CD from his breast pocket and popped it inside the CD player. When the song, "Keepin' it real" came through the speakers, Rasheen started bobbing his head energetically to his baby brother's rap lyrics.

They arrived at their hideout located in a backwater town in Camden, New Jersey, not far from the Delaware River and the Pennsylvania border, and immediately began counting the proceeds from the robbery. By the time they counted a million, and saw there was plenty ways to go, they started celebrating. By the time they finished, and it was determined that there was a little over two million dollars, champagne was floating around as though it was water, and everybody with the exception of Rasheen was jumping for enjoy as if they were the richest people on the planet.

Rasheen watched them with a smile plastered on his face, and a glass of champagne in his hand. He was tight because after this money was shared evenly amongst the entire crew it was nothing more than peanuts. He reflected back on what everyone had got after splitting the 1.2 mill evenly and as far as he was concern it was straight bullshit; crumbs. Two hundred grand was good money, but wasn't big enough for Rasheen's future plans.

Even after adding this current cut and the fifty gees from the Livonia Ave hit to his grand total, which brought his total worth to about 700 hundred grand, he still wasn't content. If there weren't so many members on his team, the returns would be much greater, he concluded as he downed the rest of his drink.

As they partied that night, Rasheen was watching Dapper and Amar closely. As the liquor worked on his mind, he figured that the only member in their bunch who was disposable, was Dapper; Rasheen needed to see if Dapper and Amar were really close like that. He had even found where Dapper had his four hundred gees stashed and thoughts of strong arming Dapper for his shit, was toying with his mind. After pondering all the drama that was bound to follow, Rasheen decided to abandon the whole issue, at least for the moment.

When Rasheen and Camila hit the sheets it was raw head city. Two days ago they both got their HIV test results and they both were negative. Rasheen must've skeeted a hundred times inside Camila since receiving the results, and the thought never crossed his mind that protection from disease wasn't the only reason for condoms. Pregnancy was the furthest thing from his mind, nor did he think to ask Camila if she was using birth control. Had he known Camila wasn't on the pill or using any other birth control, and dreamed of one day bearing his seed, he might've used some precautions.

As Rasheen pounded inside of Camila, her head banging rhythmically on the bed board, the thought crossed his mind that he had never eaten pussy. In an attempt to shift his thoughts about going downtown, Rasheen look down at his joystick going in and out of Camila's super moist pussy. But that didn't help because for the umpteenth time he wondered how did it taste? Was it sweet, bitter, sour, salty? It had to taste like fresh Tuna fish since the two smelled similar he concluded as he felt himself about to blasted off and slowed down the pace of his hip grinding thrusts. His hormones and the liquor were raging through his body and the combined effect was egging him on to go downtown. He was literally seconds from chowing down on Camila's fur burger, but reality was fighting its way into his mind as his lips crept downtown, dancing across Camila's caramel colored skin; the more she moaned and groaned in ecstasy, the stronger his urge to do it grew. Just as his chin touched her pubic hairs while his tongue did a slow dance inside her belly button, that voice reminded him that Camila was no church girl. She obviously did her rounds up, down and around the block and back; she wasn't the average hood rat, but she wasn't an angel either. His vow indicating that the only woman to get that out of him had to be someone he intended to marry recaptured his senses, and he immediately pulled back. Unfortunately, Camila didn't have hold of his heart in that fashion.

In the weeks that followed, Rasheen vowed to turn it up to a new level. After casing the three remaining Dominican stash houses, (one in Ozone Queens, one Paterson, New Jersey, and the other in Williamsburg Brooklyn), it became evident that they had burned it out. Security was literally off the chain; it was way too strong and well organized to penetrate. God damn it! Rasheen cursed inwardly, realizing he should've hit three of the houses simultaneously. Rasheen couldn't stop brooding as he watched the two-family house in Williamsburg Brooklyn that had several cars circling it. Looking at the security as it was beforehand, he seriously believed they could've hit all of the stashes at the same time.

In no time they bounced back, agreeing to move on since there was no need in crying over split milk. However, there was one more thing that had to be dealt with before the topic regarding the Dominican drug dealers could be deemed closed, and that was Dario Montero. So far Rasheen hadn't given Dario one single cent for the addresses and other crucial information regarding the Dominican stash houses, and had no intentions of doing so. This was a serious matter since Dario knew Rasheen and had to know by now that they had hit the two stash houses. If he reneged on the deal he made with Dario, Rasheen knew Dario would do the same thing to him that he did to his own crew. The solution was simple; Dario had to go. At a meeting Rasheen explained to his crew that everyone had to kick out a few dollars to pay for the hit. Rasheen figured he could save money by simply giving Rashango and Kojak a few gees instead of giving Dario twenty percent of the money taken. Since Dario knew the amount of money taken, there was no way to pull a fast one on him. Camila immediately went up to Sing Sing and informed Rashango of the situation, who jumped on the offer to do the hit on Dario with an obliged smile. While she was in New York, Rasheen instructed Camila to put 2 thousand dollars in Alamo's account and to send him a separate note thanking him for his superb jailhouse lawyering skills.

The next thing on the agenda was what they were going to do now that the Dominican stash houses was a dead issue. As it stood, they enjoyed hitting drug dealers, and nobody in the crew wanted to give this moneymaking activity a rest. With a smile, Jack-Mack said, "There's a whole lot of drug stash houses all over the country. Who said all these other ballers can't get a piece of the drama?" And with this obvious fact in mind, Rasheen coordinated investigating teams, each one required to do serious fieldwork in order to find out who was who in the drug world. With the entire crew working over time to keep that money rolling in, they succeeded in lining up twelve stash houses in the tri-state area, (New York, New Jersey and Connecticut), four of them were operated by members of the Bloods and Crips gangs. True to his equal opportunist spirit the only thing that mattered to Rasheen was the color of the target's money, and as long as their cash was green like everybody else's they all got treated the same.

Within a week they hit the first stash house in the Bronx, and came off with 700 grand. The run went well and inspired them to dive into the next run two days after the first. During this hit on a Jersey City Chapter of the Bloods gang, things got difficult when they had to shoot their way out of a tenement building. Rasheen was shot twice in the chest, but thanks to the bulletproofed vest, a garment the entire crew was required to wear, he survived with two bruised ribs and a duffle bag of money totaling close to 400 hundred grand. By the time the third run rolled around, Rasheen was becoming totally impatient. The money simply wasn't coming in fast enough, nor was it a sufficient amount. He was hoping to have at least five million dollars at his disposal before reaching out to touch Killer Kato, and he was dying to get at this chump within the next year. At the rate things were going, he wouldn't reach this goal for years. Plus, he didn't like the idea that he and his entire crew were living like nomads, and had based their entire lives around robbing, running, living out of a bag, stealing, killing, partying and fucking. He actually wanted a mansion of his own one-day; he even wanted to settle down on some family man stuff like the folks in the TV shows.

Rasheen especially had a major problem with the way Amar and Dapper were spending excessive amounts of money on flashy cars, clothes, jewelry, and were even bringing a lot of fast women and suspicious dudes into their tightly knit circle. They would get drunk and twisted on weed and have crazy parties with people from the surrounding areas they happen to be residing in; they didn't even know these people and the wild nature of these parties were attracting a lot of unnecessary attention. Although Amar and Dapper had rented their own place of resident, and were old enough to manage their own lives, because they were a part of a team, what one did automatically put the other members in jeopardy. Rasheen had forewarned them that if he caught anyone of them running off their mouths about what they did for a living, the punishment would be "swift and very severe". He didn't have to say the penalty was death, since Rasheen had made it very clear to everyone from the start of their relationship that he had no intentions of going back to prison, and if anyone attempted to put him in an awkward position that made that likely, he wouldn't hesitate to "get rid of the problem". He ended the discussion with one of Rakim's rap verses, which said, "No mistakes allowed!"

Things started to change for the better when Jack-Mack met a brother named Keith Ramsey from Atlanta City who was trying to find investors interested in investing in a security business. According to Keith, his security business would consist of several divisions; a bodyguard service, a satellite estate security component, and an on-site security personnel service. At first Rasheen was totally against giving Keith a million dollars until Jack-Mack pointed out how they could use this cat to help them find the addresses of super rich folks. "Drug dealers ain't the only motherfuckers with mad loot, you know. And when you get right down to it, legit folks with money are richer than drug dealers," Jack-Mack had said, which instantly turned on a bright light inside Rasheen's head. Rasheen countered this argument when he pointed out that robbing drug dealers was a more guaranteed come-off, because drug dealers didn't put their money in banks while "legit folks" did. Despite the few deficiencies in some of Jack's arguments in support of the security business investment, Rasheen gradually started to see this investment as a way to help him attain his ultimate goal. After two days of engaging in deep mental aerobics on the topic, he saw this security business as much more than an excellent idea; in fact, it was a perfect way to step to Killer Kato. Without further a due, Rasheen and Jack-Mack started working overtime on Keith Ramsey, blessing him with whatever he needed to get the business up and running.

No soon as things started to take shape, disaster knocked on the door. Rasheen and Camila were food shopping at the nearby 24 hour Pathmark on Hillcrest Road in Waterbury, Connecticut. It was about 1 o'clock in the morning, and there was no crowd inside the supermarket, just the way Rasheen loved it. It was a dreary, damp October night and the atmosphere fitted Rasheen's mood. They were in the frozen foods section, sifting through the dozens of brands when Rasheen got that strange feeling as though he was being watched. From behind the shopping cart, he looked around and saw a white man and a woman, but they looked harmless and weren't paying Rasheen and Camila any mind.

Unknown to Rasheen and Camila, that same couple along with two other men had been following them around the Supermarket. In fact, they had been following them ever since they received confirmation as to the make of the vehicle Rasheen and Camila drove, which was a sky blue Cherokee Jeep.

Rasheen forced himself to remember the last time he saw the couple and it dawned on him that they had been constantly popping up in the same aisle. When they were in the can goods section, the couple was nearby. When they were in the health food section, the couple appeared at the far end of the aisle. This was not a good look. Rasheen knew the way he felt was something not to be taken lightly, even if the couple looked like the epitome of a harmless middle-aged couple.

When Camila saw Rasheen cutting his eye at the couple and noticed the tension in his facial expressions, she inquired, "What's up with you?" She looked over at the white man and woman who were examining the items in the glass door refrigerator, and she instantly detected something wasn't right with the two. Even without being exposed to Rasheen's facial reactions she knew she would've felt the same way, since the couple needed some serious acting lessons if they were pretending not to be following them.

Rasheen wanted to slap Camila's eyes out of her head for giving away the fact that they were on to the couple. He inconspicuously grabbed Camila's arms as he pointed out a Swanson TV dinner. "This one here looks good," Rasheen said at normal volume, and then lowered his voice. "What the fuck is on your mind? You ain't supposed to stare. They been following us ever since they came in. Just be easy and keep your eyes on 'em without staring."

As Rasheen and Camila continued shopping, Rasheen was trying to figure out who this couple was. The more he observed his surroundings the more he realized this couple was not alone; in fact he detected two more men. By all standards he assumed they had to be Po-Po since the bullets hadn't started flying yet, and the couple was white. If it was the underworld, they would've gunned them down without all this cat and mouse shit.

As Rasheen and Camila approached the cashier, Rasheen gave Camila the signal indicating they were going to make a run for it. When the shopping cart touched the chaser counter, Rasheen and Camila were in motion. They both pulled their 9mm and ran for the electric doors.

The group following them instantly gave chase while opening fire. The sprinkle of shoppers and cashiers hit the deck.

Rasheen stayed down low as he ran, pumping off shots as Camila barreled out the electric door. The couple and the other men opening fire inside a supermarket confirmed for Rasheen that they weren't police, at least not the scrupulous ones.

Once outside, Rasheen and Camila ran towards their Jeep, their eyes darting about in search of the group's backup. Suddenly, machine gun fire rang out, shattering the windows of closed shops. Rasheen and Camila had ducked the moment they saw from their peripheral view, and returned fire at the two men hiding behind the parked cars. The dozen or so bullets dropped one of the attackers. When they reached their Jeep, and saw all four wheels were flattened, they continued running, responding as though they knew the area.

With his legs pumping frantically, Rasheen glanced in back of him just as they entered the housing complex comprised of sleek three story buildings and saw four cars approaching. A wave of gunfire was directed at them, forcing Rasheen to pick up speed as bullets whizzed pass him. Simultaneously, he heard Camila unleash a pain-stricken moan; he turned, noticed Camila had slowed down tremendously and was holding her left side. No! Shit! It was obvious she was hit. Seeing her run while holding her side brought back a flashback of the time he was shot during the Livonia Avenue robbery. As Rasheen saw the four cars drawing closer, while Camila was slowing down, he knew he had to do something, but unfortunately there wasn't a whole lot of things he could do, so he did the first thing that came to mind.

Chapter Sixteen

Killer Kato hauled off and slapped Charlie Johnson, a terrified brown skinned man who was sitting down in a wooden chair, with his hands bound behind his back. Charlie's head snapped back from the impact. Charlie's wife, Denise sat next to him and she was similarly situated, but her mouth was covered with black tape and she had streams of tears rolling down her face. Crazy B stood behind Denise with his arms crossed while his two assistants were on the sideline.

Killer yelled at Charlie, "Nigga, you sign this contract or your ass is history! When you went behind my back and recorded a CD with one of my biggest…"

"Ja-King came to me!" Charlie shrieked defensively. "He said his contract permitted him to do freelance work and I took his word on face value. I shouldn't be faulted…"

"Now's the time to pay the piper. You cut-throated me, now it's my turn to set the motherfuckin' record straight." This was a lie; Killer had been looking for the slightest reason to pressure GBE Records into becoming a subsidiary of Hoodaroma, and Charlie's work with Ja-King just happened to be a prefect excuse to justify his hostility towards Charlie, GBE's founder, owner and CEO. "Now sign this contract so we can move on with our lives."

Charlie screwed up his face as he spoke, "Please, this…this is not ethical, Mr. Gidson. You can't just go around…"

Killer Kato slapped him; this time the blow knocked Charlie and the chair over. "My name is Killer Kato, motherfucker!" He hated when people used his government handle. He despised that name and his mother for naming him Colin Gidson. Colin…How the fuck could such a ridiculous name even be considered a name? Sounds like a body part or something, he thought. "Listen here, Charlie." Killer reached down and snatched Charlie and the chair up. The two assistants helped Killer put Charlie and the chair back in its original position. "I'm finished talking." He pulled the 9mm from the shoulder holster, cocked it near Charlie's ear for dramatic effect, and pointed the gun at Denise. "Sign it or you can kiss your pretty ass wife goodbye."

Charlie couldn't believe this crazy motherfucker was actually trying to force him to agree to merge his record company with Hoodaroma. This is America! Things like this aren't supposed to happen here in this country! This is utter madness! He couldn't believe Killer Kato would kill has wife over this. Murder is a very serious offense. He was bluffing, had to be. "Listen, Mr. Kato, I'll sign this contract if you make a few minor revisions I told you. Take out the clause that says I don't own any of my masters. I'll bend to everything else, including the fact GBE will be a subsidiary of Hoodaroma, but I can't give up my masters. I…I…I just can't do it…"

BOW! BOW!

Killer Kato shot Denise in both legs.

Denise literally went crazy in the chair, trying to scream through the black tape covering her mouth while thrashing hysterically. It appeared as though the seat was on fire and she was trying to break free.

"No! Please! Stop it!" Charlie screamed as though he was in just as much pain as Denise. He was more shocked than anything else. This fool was really crazy! "This is not supposed to be happening! Please, don't hurt…"

"So what's it gonna be!?" Killer Kato took aim at Denise's head. "I'll take this bitch out of her misery, keep fuckin' around. Now, I'ma say it again. Are you gonna sign this contract as is. It's a non-negotiable contract. It is what it is, and it will be sign as it is. You're gonna sign it?"

"Yes! Yes! I'll sign the fuckin' contract!" Charlie was now in tears. His shock instantly transformed into rage, which had his mind spinning with suicidal thoughts of revenge.

One of Crazy B's assistants untied Charlie's hands while the other assistant handed him an ink pen. With a smile Killer Kato pulled the small table in front of Charlie and slammed the contract down on it.

With trembling hands Charlie looked over at Denise who was delirious with pain; her whole face was dripping with water from her eyes and blood was pouring from the two bullet wounds. All the years of mind breaking, back shattering, incalculable heartaches and headaches flashed across Charlie's mind as he looked at the contract. Once he signed it, he would be a slave to Colin Gidson, AKA Killer Kato. He looked around at Killer Kato and his bloodthirsty thugs. That voice inside his head and heart told him he couldn't go out like this! He'd rather die fighting! And with this thought surging through his body, Charlie grabbed the gun from the waist of the nearby assistant while simultaneously turning the assistant into Killer Kato's line of fire.

Killer Kato saw Charlie's frantic maneuver and fired several shots, hitting the assistant.

The whole room went up in pandemonium.

Charlie started firing the 9mm at Killer Kato and the other assistant.

BOW! BOW! BOW! BOW!

Killer Kato scrambled for cover behind the bar; the bullets just missed him as he dove over the top of the bar.

Crazy B returned fire as he crouched low. His bullets pounded the assistant that Charlie had positioned in front of him.

Peering from around the corner of the bar, Killer Kato took aim and held down on the trigger. The gun jerk rapidly as strips of fire leaped from the barrel. He saw a huge red cloud explode from the side of Charlie's head from the two bullets that entered his right cheek and exited the left temple. When Charlie fell dead to the floor, Killer Kato stepped from behind the bar. He saw Crazy B get up from the floor and fired a shot into Charlie's chest. He also saw both assistants were dead. Then he saw Denise was still alive. Her wide-eyed delirium was almost comical.

Crazy B took aim about to shot Denise in the head, but Killer Kato shouted, "No! Be easy!"

Killer Kato wanted control of GBE real bad. Now that Charlie was dead he saw this well-planned endeavor was in shambles. Looking at Denise, he wondered if she signed over her husband's company, would there still be a chance to get control of GBE? He figured if he at least had one of their signatures, there could be a chance of getting what he wanted. He said to Denise in a soft voice. "If you want to live you gotta sign the contract. Will you sign it?" He saw Denise shake her head frantically. He waved for Crazy to untie her.

When the rope was cut, freeing her arms, Denise signed the contract without hesitation.

Killer Kato examined the contract. He smiled, took aim and pumped off two shots into Denise's head.

Rasheen and Jack-Mack sat quietly in the stairwell on the sixth floor of the Marcy Housing Project building, located on Marcy and Park Avenues. Rasheen was still furious despite the fact two weeks had gone by since the major set back. He and Camila escaped the Connecticut fiasco by a stroke of sheer luck. As Rasheen hid behind one of the Waterbury housing complex building with Camila on his side groaning in pain, he was about to open fire on the approaching cars, when several police vehicles arrived and gave chase to their pursuers. Seeing this Rasheen knew he had a calling; he didn't believe in a mystery God, but after experiencing this remarkable get away, he wondered if a mysterious force was responsible for the perfect timing of the police. Afterwards, he hotwired a car, dropped Camila off at the nearby hospital, and returned to their hideout on Clarksville Avenue.

As Rasheen drove pass the hideout, he knew they were the subjects of a full-scale hit, since the area was crawling with police vehicles. In accordance with the back-up plan, Rasheen proceeded to the rendezvous location and was relieved when he met up with Jack-Mack and Candy. But upon being informed of what actually took place, Rasheen damn near cried genuine tears of rage when he discovered that Amar and Dapper had not only sold them out to the Columbians, but also had the audacity to steal all the money they came off with while in Connecticut as well as Jack-Mack's entire stash. They got everybody for their shit, every dime. The set back was so great, Rasheen and the others barely had enough money to get back to New York City.

Reflecting back on his overall handling of his money, Rasheen was grateful that he had continued utilizing safe deposit boxes to hold the bulk of his money; had he done what Jack-Mack did, (keep the bulk of his money on him), he would've lost month's worth of work. Rasheen felt sorry for Jack-Mack since he lost about 80 percent of everything he'd stolen. Indeed, Amar and Dapper had suddenly become public enemy # 1 in Rasheen, Jack-Mack, Candy and even Camila's book.

The damage Amar and Dapper caused was immeasurable since the police were now looking for Rasheen, and since his picture was inside the international database, he knew the whole game had just changed. After Camila came to after surgery the police arrived shortly thereafter to investigate the shooting; they had also investigated the shooting at the Pathmark and eventually arrested Camila after they matched her face to images on the surveillance cameras at Pathmark. As clear as day she and another suspect (Rasheen) were firing weapons at several unidentified assailants. When Candy slipped into the hospital pretending to be a family member and told her what had happened, she was beyond devastated; after hearing that her brother sold them out, her gunshot wound wasn't half as painful as grappling with the fact that she was going to jail as a result of her brother's greed for money. Chained to a hospital bed with a cop sitting outside the door, Camila wept intensely because she still refused to believe her baby brother, Amar tried to have her killed. Her own fuckin' brother! She also cried because the Doctor told her she was three weeks pregnant, and felt bad she hadn't told Candy about her condition. Since she wasn't certain whether or not she was going to keep it, she tamed her tongue. Rasheen didn't believe in abortions, so there wasn't any need to pile more drama on top of drama.

Rasheen was now determined to make Amar and Dapper pay for what they did. He was especially tight with Amar since he not only threw his own sister to the wolves, but committed the ultimate violation; he stole from family, he tried to kill family, and anyone who violated family in this fashion had to die. He showed this ungrateful nigga mad love, treated him like he was his very own brother, and for him to flip out like this, he was the worse kind of cat in the game. Because Amar was the dominant one when it came to his and Dapper's relationship, he knew Amar was the brains behind this supper grimy maneuver. Now he regretted he didn't strong-arm Dapper for his shit when he had the chance.

A noise came from inside the hallway, causing Rasheen and Jack-Mack to pull their silencer-equipped 9mm, and peek around the corner. They saw a woman getting off the elevator with a bag of groceries cuddled in her arms. They both settled down.

Rasheen's field investigation led them here. According to ,his sources, Amar and Dapper were living here in Marcy Projects with a chicken-head named Darlene, and were splurging money like they were celebrities. The fools were even bragging and boasting about all their robbery exploits. Rasheen was sizzling with a bitter form of rage, because these dumb niggas didn't even have the sense enough not to return to their own Hood. It sickened him to the bone as he realized he had allowed these dangerous idiots to do dirt with him. This was a tale tell sign that if they had gotten busted, these silly ass fools would've jammed up him and the rest of the team with their stupidity. Rasheen believed, once a dumb motherfucker, always a dumb motherfucker.

Rasheen also decided that once and for all, he and Jack-Mack had to come up with a way to bring this beef with the Columbians to a head. This shit had been going on for over a half a decade, and with each attempt they made on their lives they got closer to succeeding. It was obvious if they didn't do something real drastic they were bound to slip up. This was readily apparent based on the law of averages. Instead of running and hiding, they decided they had to bring the noise straight to their front doorstep.

Rasheen surmised that no man who walked the planet was untouchable. And even if this person was theoretically untouchable because of the amount of security hovering around him at all times, there were always cracks in the armor of even the best. Since no human being was perfect, the cracks had to exist; it was just a matter of knowing where to look, and how to capitalize on them. This crack theory proved to be one of substance when Rasheen got word that Rashango successfully knocked Dario Montero out of the game. Rashango had done such a wonderful job, Rasheen was planning to send him additional payment once he straightened out this situation with Amar and Dapper.

Rasheen and Jack-Mack also were wise enough to know that they had to start diversifying. After the Amar and Dapper fiasco, they decided to go full blast with the Security Business, and went so far as to give Keith Ramsey any amount of money he needed to solidify the business. Not only was this decision provoked by a need to lay low for a short moment, but they saw a way to get crucial information in order to rectify their problem with the Columbians. According to Keith Ramsey, once the security company obtained federal approval, and passed the many security clearances, the company would have access to very sensitive information. Keith also pointed out that he had several associates in several Federal Agencies who promised to help him in whatever way they could. Upon hearing this, Rasheen and Jack-Mack gave Keith 150 thousand dollars cash, and the next week Keith produced the paperwork showing that the company was well on its way. Keith was so thrilled by the sudden movement of the company, he offered to introduce Rasheen and Jack-Mack to the company lawyer, who was Keith's cousin named Steven Ramsey, but they declined the offer. When Keith said, "What do you think about the name Supertech Securities Services being the company's handle?" Rasheen had reminded Keith, "We silent partners, Bro. You the man with all them degrees in Security Management; if you say that's the name, then that's the name. Basically, all we want is a job and to know when them motherfuckin' checks are gonna start rollin' in."

Rasheen and Jack-Mack heard the elevator come to a stop and got in the ready position again. When the elevator door, swung open, revealing Amar and Dapper, Rasheen and Jack-Mack smiled and waited until they headed towards the apartment. Three seconds later, they rushed out of the stairwell with their 9mms aimed at their targets backs.

Amar and Dapper spun around startled.

"Put your hands up," Rasheen said calmly as he moved swiftly towards the two.

Amar was high on weed, Hennessey and coke, but realized he wasn't high enough to make a run for. The moment Rasheen slapped him against the wall, he started copping a plead. "Yo' Rah, man, it ain't what you think, Fam. We didn't go out like that."

BLAAM!

Rasheen stuck him on the head with the 9mm. "We want our money!"

"Is it in the crib?" Jack-Mack said as he had Dapper spread eagle against the wall.

"Most of it is!" Amar said. "Rah, please, don't go there with us. Most of the money's there…"

"Let's get it." Rasheen grabbed Amar by the collar and shoved towards the apartment, while Jack-Mack held on to Dapper with the barrel of the 9mm pressed up against the back of his head.

Rasheen detected Amar's procrastinating gestures as he searched his pockets for the key. "Go ahead and get crazy, and see how fast I light your bitch ass up."

After Amar unlocked the door, they entered the apartment. Rasheen sighed in relief when he detected Darlene wasn't home. Now, they didn't have to kill her.

After Amar laid the duffle bag of money at their feet, and Jack-Mack ransacked the apartment for additional moneys, Jack-Mack counted the money as Rasheen kept the gun trained on Amar and Dapper who sat on a nasty looking sofa that was covered with every stain imaginable.

"It's short 25 grand." Jack-Mack said, disappointed. "Not including their cut and my money."

Rasheen stared at the two, wondering if it was worth squeezing them for the missing 175 grand. There was no question they needed every penny they could get their hands on, but was it worth the headaches of moving these two cutthroat niggas to wherever the money was located. He knew they couldn't have fucked up 175 grand in two weeks; or could they? Reflecting back on the way he saw them wigging out when they were with the team, he instantly altered his views. Rasheen took aim.

"No! Please! Wait Rah!" Amar shrieked as he stupidly threw up both hands as though he could block the bullets. "We got the rest of the money at this girl's crib in the East." He was hoping to get in a position where he could make a run for it.

Rasheen held his aim; he was surprised by Dapper's unflinching response and locked jawed stare; this nigga wasn't afraid to die, or maybe he was high on some real powerful shit. He glanced over at Jack-Mack who had his 9mm aimed. "What you think Jack?"

Jack-Mack was stuck. He wanted his money back real bad, but he knew it was dangerous to be playing games with Amar. He said to Amar. "What's the address of this crib?"

"Let me show you," Amar said, sensing some hope at the end of tunnel. "I'll even give y'all the info on those Columbians who tricked me and Dapper into doing this."

Rasheen was about to pump off a shot. Just hearing Amar trying to shift the blame was enough to irritate him to the core. It was like a slap in the face for him to even imply that the Columbians tricked him into flipping out on them. "Yo' Amar. I'ma say this once, and only once. You hear me?" When he saw Amar's head nod, he continued. "Don't talk to us like we some dumb niggas. You motherfuckers had a choice, and y'all chose, so don't try to act like you a motherfuckin' victim in this thing."

"Give us the address!" Jack-Mack shouted. "You ain't in no position to be bargaining a motherfuckin' thing!" He took aim at Amar's forehead.

"I think this nigga's trying to play us," Rasheen said to Jack-Mack as he watched Amar's reaction, and saw what he was looking for. "He's grabbing at straws." Then he said to Amar. "This is how we gone do this. Give us this broad's address. Me and you'll stay here while Jack-Mack and Dapper go to the crib. When they get back with the doe, we'll talk about the Columbians."

Amar saw his only life raft slipping from his grasp, and panicked. "I gotta go! Dapper don't know her like that! We...he...I gotta be the one to get it!"

Silence gripped the whole apartment. Rasheen and Jack-Mack received the answer they were looking for, since the subtext was clear; Amar was trying to hang onto every minute of life he could squeeze them for. The thought of torturing them was very tempting; they spoke about this earlier and agreed not to go there after looking at the apartments on the floor; if it wasn't for the strong possibility of the neighbors calling the police, because of the inevitable hollering and screaming, they surely would have gotten medieval on Amar and Dapper. Rasheen gave Jack-Mack an inconspicuous signal to play along.

Rasheen sighed. "Okay. You can go, Amar. You and Jack can go get the money; me and Dapper'll stay here. What's the address? I need to know that up front for obvious reasons." He saw Amar was about to speak, but continued talking while holding up his hand like a traffic cop. "I don't wanna hear shit! This is a take it or leave it offer!" He took aim.

"Okay, okay!" Amar said. "1241 Cleveland Street. It's right off the corner of Hegaman Avenue."

"Apartment number?" Jack-Mack said.

"Ah…it's…ah…apartment 2D. The chick's name is Shanequa Williams."

Rasheen and Jack-Mack's eyes met each other's. They both started firing their 9mms at about the same moment. Rasheen shot Amar three times, twice in the upper chest in the heart region and once in the head. Jack-Mack shot Dapper four times, two shots to the head, and two to the chest.

A half hour later, Rasheen and Jack-Mack were in their cranberry colored Toyota Corolla cruising down Linden Boulevard on their way to Cleveland Street. From behind the wheel, Jack

Mack brought the car to a stoplight at the intersection of Pennsylvania and Linden. Lameek's CD blazed from the car's speakers.

Rasheen sat scanning the streets remembering how he used to run these hard Streets of East New York with his man Kendu back in the day. A lot had changed; the Wendy's was gone, as well as the Galaxy Restaurant. He was surprised the gas station was still there. Then, suddenly, he saw a dude that looked just like Ja-King walking towards the intersection. The closer this cat got to the intersection the more he looked like Ja-King. Just as the Ja-King look alike stepped into the street about to walk pass the Toyota, Rasheen saw it was absolutely Ja-King, no doubt about it. He yelled out the window, "Yo' Ja-King!" When he saw the Ja-King look alike hand go for the weapon, apparently in his waist, the reaction confirmed the identity. "Be easy Ja! It's me Rasheen." He saw Ja-King stopped reaching as he slowed his pace scrutinizing the occupants inside of the Toyota. Rasheen was enthralled by the fact he could now get access to inside info on Killer Kato. "Come on, man, get in the car. We need to kick it."

Jack-Mack said, noticing Ja-King's apprehensiveness "Come on, Ja-King, we got beef with the same nigga. Three heads is always better than one."

Ja-King didn't know what to do as he stood on the highway divider, realizing it really was Rasheen and Jack-Mack. He hadn't trusted anyone every since that day he banged out with Killer's hit crew and had no intentions of ever trusting anyone else, but he, Rasheen and Jack-Mack was fam for real when they were vibing back when they were teens. Then again he knew Rasheen was Lameek's big brother, and since Lameek was still moving with Killer, he didn't know what to think. "Yo' listen, Rasheen, I know y'all probably heard what time it is. I'm about as hot as the motherfuckin' Taliban, man."

The light changed; a white man in a green Cadillac in back of the Toyota started honking his horn.

"Get in the ride, man," Rasheen said as he opened the door. "We can talk about that and some other thangs." He understood what Ja-King was going through and knew he had to first put Ja-King's mind and suspicion to rest. "Fam, we both got beef with the same nigga. Killer Kato fucked me, he fucked you, he's laying mad dick on my baby brother and my child-hood sweet heart Crystal, and he's been fucking over every other motherfucker whose hand don't call for it. Now get in this car so we can talk about what we gone do about it."

Ja-King smiled; it was a pleasure to know there was someone else with just as much hatred in his heart for Killer Kato. This was an opportunity he couldn't dare pass up. The way Killer was fucking over Lameek, he knew if he told Rasheen what was going on behind the scenes, while spicing it up a little here and there, he would definitely have another ally to help him get at Killer Kato. Ja-King hastily got in the car and Jack spun off.

Ten minutes later, they arrived in front of 1241 Cleveland Street, and shortly thereafter, Rasheen and Jack-Mack weren't surprised to discover that Amar's assertions were all game. Although there really was a crack head name Shanequa living there, her crib was so fucked up there was no way close to a million dollars could be stashed anywhere in that raggedy ass apartment. For safekeeping, Rasheen and Jack-Mack tore up Shanequa's crib looking for the money while two filthy, pitiful little children, the girl was no older than ten years old and the boy looked even younger, watched them with sad eyes. After searching the apartment from head to toe, Rasheen gave the two children twenty dollars each and made them promise to buy themselves something to eat and to not tell their mother about the money.

They left Shanequa's little shop of horrors, pissed off by the fact the remaining portion of their money wasn't there.

Within the months that followed, Rasheen was feeling good about the things that were starting to take place. Rasheen, Jack-Mack, Candy and Ja-King decided to move to Atlanta Georgia to be close by Keith. The two family house Rasheen and Ja-King rented was off the chain, and Rasheen couldn't believe the reasonable price the rent cost. Jack-Mack and Candy got a similar house several blocks away. As Rasheen and Ja-King started kicking it in depth, he realized meeting up with Ja-King was the best thing that could've happened to his plan to touch Killer Kato. Homie knew things that would make the mission a success, but he also knew shit that was tearing Rasheen's emotions to pieces. For instance, when he heard the way Killer Kato was fucking Crystal's brains off, and how he was robbing Lameek for all his money, he felt fire erupting inside the pit of his stomach. One of the major down sides with their relationship Rasheen saw at the movement was Ja-King's rap stardom had gone to his head; he had a thing about calling shots and was talking to Rasheen and Jack-Mack as if they were on his payroll or something. Rasheen told him straight up that if he was going to survive hanging with him, he had to tone it down and get in line. Rasheen checked Ja-King when he said, "It's a good thing you finally popped your cherry when you laid down a few of Killer Kato's crimies. Just cause I'm showing you some love don't make the mistake and think shit is sweet this way. I been dropping bodies so long ago I stopped counting after my sixteenth homicide." After Ja-King refreshed his memory of the fact that he was dealing with career thugs, with a genuine ability to massacre, maim and murder, he quickly got off his high horse and stayed off of it.

Another critical problem was Ja-King was too well known; despite the disguises he wore, he had one of those faces and body frames that were unique. Not to mention the way he swaggered was a walk that was his and only his. Rasheen had his own issues and started having second thoughts about letting Ja-King tag along with him, especially after retrieving everything he needed on Killer Kato. The temptation to throw his ass to the waste side like an old wore out shoe was very strong. If it wasn't for the fact that Ja-King had found a way to get access to some of his money, and had various under world connects, he might have dumped him. The connect that particularly interested Rasheen was the one that enabled him to get them phony ID.

Rasheen was still struggling with the fact that his ride or die chick was no longer at his side. He got word that Camila copped out to a two-year bid; Candy found a way to communicate with Camila through a P.O. Box in a bogus name. Rasheen wasn't a letter writing kind of person, but after all the shit Camila did for him he forced himself to write her a scribe every once in a blue moon and sent her a couple of hundred dollars every other month. In one of her letters, she revealed that she was pregnant with his child and Rasheen was prancing around with his chest poked out, proud as hell to be a father, even though he wouldn't be able to see it until Camila got out.

Rasheen and Jack-Mack started their first legitimate job ever in their lives. They walked into the headquarters of SSS dressed in casual attire and within hours knew this wasn't for them. Keith agreed to let them work at SSS, helping out wherever needed. Had he known Rasheen and Jack's only concern was to find out the locations and other delicate information about filthy rich folks (potential SSS customers) in order to rob them, things would have turned out differently. As a way of preparing themselves for their future moneymaking endeavors, Rasheen and Jack-Mack started learning about various security alarm systems and other aspects of the security business. They immediately befriended the head computer specialist, Sharon Walker, and made it clear to her that they were part owners of the company. As expected, Sharon was more than pleased to assist them in their effort to "learn" about the "critical functions of the company." Rasheen even took Sharon out on a few dates in order to make it clear that he was serious about this Security Business thing. During their second date, Rasheen discovered Sharon was totally with the program; she even gave him a specially designed laptop computer that was hooked up to SSS's mainframe computer.

When Rasheen and Jack-Mack got on the SSS computer, they were like little kids playing with a new toy. This extremely high-tech computer was hooked up to a satellite and various Federal Agencies; with Keith's special password they were able to tap into all sorts of sensitive areas of information. To their surprise they couldn't believe they were able to obtain a listing of well known Columbian drug cartels; they were really shocked to discover the government not only knew where most of them resided, but also knew what they were doing, when they were doing it, where they were doing it, and were turning a blind eye. Rasheen and Jack-Mack honed in on the two top Columbians, Emanuel Gomez, and Raul Hernandez. Within weeks, and after getting Sharon Walker onboard with their hidden agendas, they were all smiles and grins as they realized they had something real big in the palm of their hands. Where they could go with this thing was literally limitless.

Rasheen's biggest challenge by far was keeping his hormones from causing him to make bad decisions. With him and Ja-King living in the same house, while both fugitive of justice, who had a problem keeping their dicks in their pants, disaster was looming heavily on the horizon. Rasheen was able to snatch up Tracy Hicks, a local girl, and worked overtime convincing her they could only he friends, and there would be no serious relationship. In other words, they were bed buddies, plain and simple, and to Rasheen's delight Tracy Hicks had no problem with such an arrangement.

Ja-King's situation, on the other hand, was like a Vietnam minefield; Rasheen couldn't keep him hidden in the basement forever, and surely couldn't stop him from leaving the house. After four weeks of being cooped up inside the house, Ja-King was becoming stir crazy; one night after smoking some weed and drinking two pints of Jack Daniel's, he went out and snatched up a drop dead gorgeous prostitute named Robin Woods, who he thought he had convinced that he wasn't that famous rapper the police all over the country were looking for. After Ja-King blew Robin's back out, fucking her for a straight hour, Ja-King fell asleep. Robin, the kleptomaniac that she was and the professional police informant who had two open cases for credit card fraud that she was trying for months to get off of her back, saw a way to kill two birds with one stone. As Ja-King slept, she stole the five hundred dollars from Ja-King's pants pocket and fled the house on her way to call the police to get the ten thousand dollar reward for Ja-King's capture.

Chapter Seventeen

Killer Kato entered the Hotel room with Crystal in tow. Killer Kato was totally in a fucked up mood, and the only thing on his mind at the moment was to release the tension. He started peeling off of his clothes as he watched Crystal do the same thing. When he saw her huge, shapely, and voluptuous breasts spring from the bra, he felt himself rising to the occasion.

Crystal felt like she wanted to cry and scream; she felt like a cheap tramp, and a prisoner in a world where there was no conceivable escape. She hated Killer Kato, even though he paved the pathway for her to drive expensive cars, style exotic clothing, maintain a huge bank account and run a multi-million company, was everything she use to dream of doing. Despite all this money, power and respect, she was unhappy; often times she didn't totally know why, but logic linked to Killer Kato and the way he used her strictly for sex and her other skills. He even had the gall to be a jealous lover who didn't allow her to have relationships with other males, while he had a harem of lovers. As she took off her panties, and tossed them at Killer Kato, while forcing herself to smile playfully and pretend like she was enjoying this sexual excursion, just the way he liked it, that hidden region in her mind where that logical voice resided, began reminding her that she was nothing more than a cheap prostitute allowing herself to be used. But when the other voice spoke out, demanding that she fight back, put her foot down and not tolerate it anymore, the rational component intervened as usual and told her to let lying dogs lay, since she knew Killer was killing people left and right, and she didn't want to be anybody's statistic. She even knew his hands were involved in the murder of the owners of GBE, and he was strong-arming any and all independent record labels to merge with Hoodroma. It turned her stomach knowing she was fucking a psychopathic, sadistic, power-hunger maniac. However, she was glad she was able to convince Lameek to move down to California, but even this small scrap of good news was rendered insignificant by Killer Kato's usual foul way of doing things, since he immediately started tormenting Lameek. It was bad enough that he was robbing the kid blind, but to play a series of mind games with him was like rubbing salt into an open wound. When Killer Kato approached her, she smiled and giggled playfully, just the way he liked it.

Killer Kato wasn't in the mood for any foreplay, so he embraced Crystal as he gently laid her down on the silk sheets and navigated his manhood inside of her womanhood. Although he wanted immediate gratification, he decided to enjoy this special moment. Going inside of Crystal was always something special. Even when his emotions were tortured, her smooth, super soft, youthfully tight, and blistering hot pudding had a way of making him feel content again. Unlike his other women, Crystal knew where, when and how to please him, and she had a way of taking him to a place that was saturated with bliss. But as he dipped in and out of Crystal, twirling and swirling around inside of her, their bodies' movements gorging each other in a synchronized dance of delight, Killer Kato's mind couldn't completely neutralize the setbacks that were taking place. The GBE endeavor blew up in his face in the worse way. According to Philip Henderson, the contract was worthless in view of the Will that Charlie and Denise Johnson had secretly constructed that superseded "any and all contracts." Had at least one of them remained alive the superseding clause in the Will could have been overridden. Even Lameek was making matters worse, since he was acting the fool, threatening not to make any more CDs or do any concerts until he got all of his money. The little smart-ass bastard was talking about taking him to court; if he didn't have mad love for him, he would've shot his ass a long time ago. Other bad news came when Killer got word that his feature film, "Urban-Drama", wasn't doing well in the theaters. Lion's Gate Film Distribution Company was even contemplating pulling the film all together and sending it straight to video; had it not been for Philip Henderson's various connections with film industry heavyweights, "Urban-Drama" would have been pulled. Killer was devising a way to get people into the theaters and needed a few more weeks to put that plan in effect. The "Urban-Drama" setback was also wreaking havoc on his second feature film, "Hell up in Red Hook" and he knew he needed some strong medicine to bring some life to this project as well.

Killer Kato felt himself about to explode inside of Crystal and slowed down his rhythm. In accordance with her expert abilities, despite her ohs, ahs and other orgasmic displays of pleasure, Crystal read his body movement and readjusted her flow. Killer Kato's mind went back to the issues he was momentarily trying to get away from; there was big drama brewing in LA. His workers in his studios and offices in LA were confronted by mob affiliates, supposedly Italian and Russian organized crime figures. Put in a simple way, they were demanding punk dues; they wanted their palms greased in exchange for police protection and other protection they assumed the Hoodarama workers were able to figure out by reading between the lines. Upon hearing the news, this revelation brought a smile to Killer Kato's face because he'd been expecting them to show up at his doorstep last year when Times Magazine did a short article on Hoodarama. In this business this was a sign indicating he was not only moving up in the Entertainment world, but was also making major strides within the corporate world. This was like a good/bad situation; good he was worth approaching because he was making enough noise to be seen and heard, bad because now he had to expend value time, energy and resources thumping it out with two worthy opponents. Surprisingly, Killer Kato had always wanted to go toe to toe with the Italian and Russian mob, but didn't dare be the one to initiate the beef. Now that they stepped to him, trying to treat him as though he was a sheep, instead of a wolf, they opened themselves up to whatever backlash that would follow. And rest assured there was going to be plenty of spillover effect, which was why Killer

Kato needed to be in between Crystal's legs right about now. Once he skeeted a few times, he would be in the right state of mind to devise his response to the Italian and Russian invasions.

With this in mind, Killer Kato let his juices flow, and Crystal rode the movement with her usual force and energy that made Killer feel as though he would never stop coming.

Rasheen pulled his new Mustang GTX to a stop in front of the house in College Park in Atlanta Georgia that he and Ja-King had leased and saw Robin rushing out of the house. Her reaction to the car told it all; this conniving bitch was up to no good. This was not a good look. Rasheen didn't know what she did, but whatever she was up to, wasn't going down the way she thought it was. Rasheen rushed out the car and caught up to her just as she was walking down the walkway, about to make the turn.

"Ah, excused me miss," Rasheen said as he grabbed her arm. "What're you doing coming out of my house?"

Robin panicked and tried to bolt down the street, but Rasheen had a firm lock on her arm. She tried to unleash a blood-curdling scream, but Rasheen's hand slammed over her mouth as his other arm maneuvered her into a strong bear hug.

Rasheen was now certain something had just happened as he casually dragged the squirming woman back to the house. As he moved down the walkway, his eyes scanned the immediate area, looking over at the windows of the Simms household, since they were notoriously nosy neighbors. He saw the coast was clear as he turned the doorknob and was surprised the door was unlocked. He entered the house and yelled, "Yo' Ja! Ja!" He waited a few seconds and heard no response. "Ja! Get the motherfuckin ass up here nigga!" Rasheen was furious now, since this bitch was trying to gorge his eyes out and he had to bless her feisty ass with a few firm wallops to the head.

Ja-King heard someone calling him and he pulled himself from the alcohol induced deep sleep. Oh, shit! Rasheen was calling him! But why? He frantically grabbed his 9mm and stumbled up the basement stairs. He burst through the basement door and saw Rasheen manhandling Robin. "Oh, be easy Rah, that's my girl Robin. I brought her here."

"I just caught this bitch creeping out of the house," Rasheen said, his hand still clamped over her mouth. Then he said to Robin. "I'm gonna let you go; if you scream, I'll knock your ass out. You hear me?" When Robin nodded he let her go.

ERRRR!...

Robin screamed. Rasheen hauled off with a blow that came way from down in the boondocks, and damn near knocked Robin's head clean off her shoulders. The blow instantly killed her lung-bursting screech and catapulted her several feet; she crashed landed to floor as though Mike Tyson had hit her.

Ja-King cringed at the awesome sight. "Damn, man!" Ja-King went to her, feeling sorry for her as he remembered how good that pussy was. He became squeamish when he saw a piece of bone protruding from her jaw as the blood began to flow from the wound. "Did you have to hit her like that?"

"This bitch was robbing your dumb ass!" Rasheen said, massaging his bruised knuckles. He shook it, hoping he didn't break a bone or something. "Look at her, the bitch was sneaking out behind your back."

As Ja-King stared down at Robin, realization clicked inside his head. Rasheen was right; she was dressed as though she was leaving. He reached down, dug into her coat pocket and found the five hundred dollars. "Ain't this a bitch." He rushed back down the stairs, checked his pants pockets and discovered his money was gone. Ja-King rushed back up the stairs, and said to Rasheen, who was now tying Robin's arms with twine rope. "This bitch tried to rob a nigga."

"This is your mess," Rasheen said as he placed tape over her mouth. "You can do the honors of putting this bitch out of her misery." He grinned wickedly at Ja-King.

"You wanna kill her?" Ja-King was stunned. He hated it when fine bitches get smoked, and he especially despised it when a broad with good pussy got killed. "But...But she might not..."

"Say it and I'll air your ass out," Rasheen said calmly as he folded his arms, staring at Ja-King. Now that voice in the back of his mind was really telling him to get rid of this clown ass nigga. "If this bitch goes to the police our asses is through. The way this bitch was sneaking outta here she was up to something, and it wasn't just stealing. You fucked this bitch without a disguise and you think she don't know it's you? Ja-King, Hoodaroma's finest and top notch nigga!" His anger was mounding by the seconds; he couldn't believe this fool could be so naïve and reckless. "A thug, gangster rapper who got a ten thousand dollar reward over his head, and you think this bitch don't know what time it is! Huh? And what you think she's gonna do when she wakes up with a broken jaw?"

Ja-King saw the logic as clear as a sunny day. After a moment, he sighed and said, "You right, Robin gotta go." As Ja-King went to get dressed, his mind was doing somersaults; he hadn't had a good piece of pussy in so long he was thinking about fucking Robin one last time before he knocked her off. Then he scolded himself for thinking this way. As he wondered how he was going to kill Robin, he noticed with dread circulating through his mind, body and soul that he had become someone he'd never dreamed of becoming; a cold-blooded, heartless murderer.

Two weeks later, Rasheen, Jack-Mack, Candy and Ja-King were in a customized blue Dodge van cruising down highway 40, on their way to Winslow, Arizona. Candy was behind the wheel while the others were in the back compartment, putting polish on their plan. Operation step to the Columbians was in full swing, and this endeavor couldn't have come at a better moment. And the top man in the Columbian crime family, Emanuel Gomez's ten million dollar mansion, where he lived with his spoiled rotten family, couldn't have been in a better geographical location. Besides handling the Columbian problem, they were about to find out just how efficient and effective Supertech's information database and its satellite universal computer link really were. In other words, after they dealt with the Columbians, they were planning to rob a few super rich folks while enjoying the blazing hot Arizona sun.

A week later, they were in place. They had been watching the Gomez family's routine for two days straight. The security Gomez had around the mansion made it clear that they could not penetrate that kind of shield. Going inside in commando militia fashion was out of the question unless they had a 25 man hit team equipped with top grade military weaponry, so they went into plan B. Rasheen didn't like what he was about to go, but the game of life was always filled with these kind of moments, and he learned many years ago to roll with them as they came.

The date was August 16, 2003, and the heat rays were beaming down upon the planet as though the sun was trying to swallow up the earth. It was 110 degrees, and Rasheen hated every minute of it. Rasheen and his team were hiding inside a wooded area on top of a hill within a huge mountainous area that overlooked a valley below. They were watching the Gomez mansion with their high tech binoculars.

From a specially concealed crevice within the forest area, Rasheen saw the Gomez family exiting the mansion. He saw the wife and the young daughter who looked about nine years old approaching the family Limousine. "It's show time!" He said excitedly into their small communications device as he raced towards the van.

Minutes later, the van raced down the mountain and caught up with the Limo that was being escorted by two black SUVs; one in front of the Limousine, and the other behind. Rasheen and the crew had been practicing this mission in their heads for countless hours; now it was a matter of making it work according to the way they perceived it, which was a difficult feat in and of itself. They stayed well behind the Limo and its escort vehicles so as not to alert them. If only they had known for certain where the Limo was headed they could've had someone waiting at the arrival point, but either way, Rasheen was praying they could pull it off. It was a Saturday, and the only place the Gomez family could be going was shopping or to a family outing.

Twenty minutes later, the Limo pulled into a small Shopping Mall, and Rasheen practically jumped for joy; he put on his disguise, causing the others in the van to do the same. The timing was good, since it was early in the morning and the crowd hadn't grown yet. This was what they were hoping for and now they got their wish. The Limo parked and the woman, the child and a huge man dressed in a suit exited the vehicle. Rasheen watched from the van, and the minute the two entered the Mall, Candy was in motion. Candy entered the Mall and followed the woman, the child and the bodyguard around the Mall while Rasheen contacted Sharon Walker at the SSS headquarters on his laptop computer and told her the location of the Mall. Once Sharon locked in the Mall's coordinates, the satellite would disable the surveillance cameras in and around the Mall. About an hour later, the group approached the cashier with a shopping cart full of merchandise, and Candy whispered into her communications device, "They're on their way out."

Jack-Mack and Ja-King were hanging out in different locations near the Mall entrance. Rasheen was inside the Limo, behind the wheel. Earlier, they had killed the occupants of the escort vehicles and the Limo driver with silenced weapons. When the Gomez family exited the Mall, Jack-Mack and Ja-King followed them. Just as the three were entering the Limo, Jack-Mack opened fire killing the bodyguard with three carefully placed silenced bullets, while Ja-King shoved the woman and the child inside the Limo before they could scream. Jack-Mack dragged the dead bodyguard inside the Limo and slammed the door. Rasheen pulled off while Candy rushed to the van and followed the Limo.

That night the negotiations began and to Rasheen's surprise, Emanuel Gomez spoke as though he was used to this kind of drama. During a phone discussion, while speaking through a voice-altering device that made him sound as though he was suffering from throat cancer, Rasheen had said, "We don't want your money. All we want is for you to leave us alone."

"I don't even know who the fuck you are!" Emanuel said, seriously, sounding well educated with a mild Spanish accent. "You say my people are hunting you, but I have no fuckin' idea what you are talking about!"

"Well, I guess it's in your best interest to find out who the fuck we are and what the fuck we talkin' about. Back in 1994 a Columbian drug spot in Brooklyn, East New York was robbed and a few of your people were killed. One of the robbers was killed, one was caught and the other got away. Ever since then y'all been trying to kill the two survivors. Call off your hounds; contact all your honcho and call off the hit. You do that and you can have your wife and daughter back. I'll call you back in 6 hours; I hope you'll have some good news. And if you get the police involved your family will be murdered." Rasheen hung up.

The next time Rasheen called, Emanuel was all talk. "I now know what this is all about." Emanuel was genuinely disturbed by his investigation. "Unfortunately, my people are not the ones who are pursuing these people. I had nothing to do with any of the contracts you speak about."

"But you know who they are, and you have the power to call them off," Rasheen said. "Unfortunately, you are now involved. We will release your family only if you can guarantee us that those contracts are dead. Can you guarantee us that?"

"I told you, those contracts weren't orchestrated by…"
"I hope you kissed your family goodbye. Have a nice day, Mr. Gom…"

"Wait! Wait a minute!" Emanuel saw he was about to lose control of the situation. Plus, the FBI agents were waving to him to keep the caller talking. "Okay! Okay! I'll make efforts to call them off. Just give me…"

"Don't make efforts! Call them off! I'll call back in 6 hours. If the problem isn't fixed your family is dead." Rasheen hung up.

Emanuel sighed angrily as he hung up the phone.

FBI Agent, Donald Mooney, a clean shaved white man with sandy brown hair, who woore a sleek business suit said, "I find it hard to believe this guy doesn't want any money. We checked out his allegations regarding that robbery, and the person arrested is not even in the minor leagues. He's nothing more than a two bit hip-hop, wanna be thug whose been listening to too much gangster rap. I hope you're not playing games in an attempt to get out of wearing that wire at this upcoming meeting of the minds?"

"You know, you people never cease to amaze me!" Emanuel was furious. "You have this remarkable knack for turning the victim into the violator. My family is in danger and all you can think about is your fuckin' case?"

Six hours later, the phone rang and Emanuel snatched it up, and said, "Hello?"

"So what's the deal?" Rasheen said.

"It's done," Emanuel lied; the Hernandez mob wouldn't even entertain the thought of dropping the contract. "I called the person responsible. Mr. Hernandez has assured me that the contract as been suspended."

"Good," Rasheen said, his voice now sounding as if he was talking into a fan. "Just remember; if my people even sense you have misled us, the next time there will be no discussion, no phone calls. Your entire family will be killed. I'll call back with the location where you can pick them up." He disconnected the call.

The return of Gomez's wife and daughter was a simple procedure. The drop-off went smooth. Rasheen and his team had dropped them off at a secluded location in the dessert, fled the area and an hour later informed Gomez of his family's whereabouts.

As Rasheen and his team cruised down highway 40 in a new burgundy Ford van, Rasheen was in the back compartment with Jack-Mack and Ja-King looking at the screen of the laptop at various road maps. Rasheen was trying to figure out why he felt as though something wasn't right. But he was certain what was eating at him didn't have its roots with the performance of the kidnapping, because Gomez's wife, Mary, and his daughter, Carmen, never saw any of their real faces. It couldn't be an issue with the tracking of the cell phones, since the phones were bogus, and couldn't be traced to them. Each time they called Gomez they used a different phone, and even though each phone had a built scrambler devise, they discarded them anyway.

His instincts reassured him that they did everything right with the kidnapping. In fact, Rasheen was satisfied to such a degree he was even contemplating making the kidnapping of drug cartels' families a part of his many illicit approaches to making money. As he examined the map to get a bearing on how far they were from the house they were planning to rob, Rasheen was wondering if he should have went along with Jack-Mack's suggestion to squeeze Gomez for a mill or two. Initially, Rasheen believed the money pick up was where things always got good and crazy, and almost always ended in disaster, at least that's what the research said. But in light of how smoothly things went with this run he was second-guessing his decision not to go for the money.

As Rasheen pen-pointed the house with the help of his laptop computer and determined that it was about a two-hour ride, his cellular phone rang, and he answered it. "Yeah, what's up?" He said into the phone, and upon hearing what the person on the other end of the line was revealing to him, he found out exactly why he was feeling the way he did, and the news was far worse than bad; it was cataclysmic.

Chapter Eighteen

At about the same time Rasheen and his crew arrived in Arizona, Crazy B sat in the passenger seat of the brown Range Rover with his most reliable assistant, Jamaican Jim, behind the wheel. They were parked on Crenshaw Boulevard, one of LA's busiest streets, about two blocks from the targets place of employment, a construction company that was more like a hang-out for wops and guineas who did bad imitations of the Sopranos and other mafia oriented TV shows and movies.

Crazy B nodded his head approvingly when Joey "Gum Shoe" Gabozenni and two of his flunkies exited the storefront. Joey wore a huge pinkie ring and was waving it around in showboat fashion as he talked to his soldiers. When the men were inside the four-door black Lincoln, and the engine roared to life, Crazy B pulled the detonator from his tote bag and turned the power supply on as Jim started the Jeep. Just as the Lincoln pulled onto the roadway, Crazy B hit the red button.

KA-BLAAM!!

The Lincoln exploded into thousands of fragments.

The Range Rover pulled off, heading for the next target.

That evening when Crazy and his miniature army returned to Killer Kato's mansion in Hollywood Hills, they had succeeded in knocking off the two most prominent under bosses within both the Russian and Italian crime families. Big Bill Colicchio met his maker when he entered a parking garage with a stomach full of pasta and meatballs. After enjoying a wonderful dinner at his favorite restaurant, four gunmen opened fire on him and his personal bodyguard. Victor Stavisky never knew what hit him when two sniper bullets struck him down as he stood near the window of his restaurant cursing out two of his soldiers for failing to extort more money from a new client. Several miles away, Victor's first cousin, Karl Stavisky, was in the back room of his nightclub counting the proceeds for the day, when two masked men kicked in his door (after silently killing his four bodyguards) and pumped his body fill of 9mm copper jacket bullets.

After hearing how well the runs went, Killer Kato decided it was time to give his crew a well deserved party equipped with strippers, tons of alcohol, and any kind of drug the participants felt the urge to get lifted with. Once the celebration was underway, Killer Kato took Crazy B to his private study to discuss their next move and other crucial matters.

Killer Kato took a seat behind his desk and kicked his feet onto the desktop. He took a glance at his Rolex watch with 200 white diamonds flooded around the bezel and band, and saw it was 10:20 pm. He was indeed feeling really good. The sudden shift of his luck was truly mind tingling. His feature film projects were developing well. Hoodaroma was back on top with five number one singles, and was the number one record label in the country due to astronomical record sales. Lameek was back onboard thanks to Crystal who, once again, talked him into behaving. He watched Crazy B take a seat while nursing his favorite drink, Jack Daniel's on the rocks. Killer sighed and said, "If this doesn't get us the attention we earned I don't know what will."

"Fuck the attention," Crazy B took a sip of his drink, swooshed it around in his mouth and swallowed it. The taste was exquisite. "What we need is big cheddar, baby."

"You know what attention I'm talking about. Crime families all across the country understand one thing and one thing only; and that's violence. Whoever can dish it out and knock down opponents, and put the fear of God inside the hearts of these men will invariably make money. And I'm not talking about any kind of money. I'm talkin' the billion dollar kind of money; maybe even trillion dollar money."

"Well, I'm ready to see that kind of money."

"It's coming." Killer Kato slide his feet off the desk, sprung his body forward and took a sip of his drink, a vodka and grape juice. "So what's up with the seeds we been dropping; it's about time we start seeing and feeling the fruits of our labor. There should be sprouts of wild fruit by now."

"A lot of that stuff I can't shoot off the top of my head, but I'll give you a detailed report in the morning after we whine down some. But shit is looking damn good Killer. Shit starting to look so sweet, got me thinking there's some funny business going on. They say if it's too good to be true, then maybe it ain't true. But anyway, all the love we been showing in New Jersey, Ohio, Oakland, Alabama, Oklahoma, Baltimore and a few others is taking off.

Man, niggas are lining up to get with the program. You a motherfuckin' genius, bro, cause you saw this shit could work. Who'd ever thought a mainstream celebrity could open up hundreds of businesses in the Hood and get niggas to honor payment. That's some ground breaking shit."

"So how are the money pick up procedures going? Are there any issues developing?"

"None at all. We can get the books and see for ourselves," Crazy B said as he was getting up from the chair to go get it.

"Naw, chill B, we'll look at it tomorrow."

Crazy B sat back down and took another sip of his drink.

"I really called you in here so we can talk about this next move. We drew first blood, so it ain't no turning back. Not only is there no turning back, there's no turning down the pressure until these motherfuckers understand that there's a new entity in town and we want a piece of the action. We ain't trying to stop them from eating, but we ain't tolerating any motherfucker interfering with our right to eat at the table as well. As it stands they probably don't know who hit 'em. Tomorrow I'm gonna step to Nick and Frankie, I'm gonna need a full backup mob. There's no telling how these chumps might take it when they find out it was us that hit 'em. I'm hoping they realize we ready to die if need be to make our mark, and we're also ready to lay down motherfuckers everyday until the sun burn out, or until they bend."

"They ain't stupid. My assumption is that they gonna wanna talk about whose territories is whose, who don't go here, who don't touch that, who can't touch this, who should fuck this, who should fuck that. But in the end it's all about the money. Money can't be made with bodies dropping all over the place, so I think they'll play ball and wipe those losses on their chest and start the business back as usual. Since we ain't trying to slap 'em in the face or kick 'em in the ass and take all their shit, they'll bend."

"You may be right." Killer Kato leaned back in his chair and kicked his feet back up on the desk. "But I don't like to take losses. Whether big or small, a loss is loss. If they decide to bang out with us, we will take major losses. Fighting two fronts at the same time ain't a small feat, and world history is proof that it can't be done. Germany tried it; Russia tried it; Roman tried it; Egypt tried it. If they all failed the odds say we will fail."

"Yeah that shit sound good, but them niggas ain't have what we got. We got standby divisions in damn near every major city; we got niggas anxious to bust their guns against worthy opponents. These thug hunger cats would come running if we told them we about to go head up with the two most infamous crime families in the country. Man, I say we murder all them crackers and take our rightfully place in the sun."

"That sounds good as well, Crazy B, but don't underestimate them crackers. This is a country ran by crackers, and you can bet all crackers stick together and take care of other crackers."

Rasheen felt faint as Sharon Walker rattled off the cataclysmic news. His mind was convoluted with an unadulterated form of stress. He spoke excitedly into his cellular as Jack-Mack and Ja-King looked on with anxiety-ridden expressions. "Did they say why they were looking for me?"

On the other end of the line Sharon said, "No, they showed their FBI badges, and told us to inform you when we see you that they're looking for you and that you should turn yourself in. I did my own investigation; that's how I found out they raided your house; Keith mentioned something about them finding your safe deposit boxes."

Rasheen was now devastated beyond description. "You got an idea what caused this?" He sensed he knew the answer, but needed to hear someone else's assessment.

"Gomez was a FBI informant. When you stepped to him it was like stepping straight to the feds. How they tracked you to us I don't know. Listen, Rasheen, I gotta go. If it's any consolation to you, I got your back. Call me only on this secured line. I know I don't have to tell you not to come back East for a while. Okay, talk to you later."

"Hey Sharon," Rasheen said, and then went silent for a moment. "Thank you, sis. When I come out of this, I will never forget how you holdin' me down."

"Take care, Rah," Sharon said and hung up the phone.

Rasheen sat silently for a straight minute, staring at the maps; it was as if he was locked in a catatonic trance.

"Let's hear the whole thing," Jack-Mack said, knowing disaster had reared its ugly head.

Through a daze Rasheen told them everything. The feds were now looking for him; the FBI hit his house in Atlanta; they came to Supremetech looking for him; they hit his safe-deposit boxes and got all his money. And the part he struggled to get out, was that all this happened because Gomez was working for the FBI as an informant. This was absolutely not a good look.

The revelation was so disturbing everyone was speechless; they decided to make a stop at a secluded Diner to get something to eat and to discuss their next move.

Rasheen sat next to the window, while Ja-King sat next to him; Candy sat across from Rasheen while Jack-Mack sat next to Candy. The white, redhead waitress with a huge smile and freckles, said with a southern drawl, "May I take your order?"

As they ordered their meals, Rasheen was in his own world. He was literally sick with a mixture of rage, frustration, confusion, and regret. Even doubt and indecisiveness was inundating his thought process. What the fuck was he gonna do now? Most of his money was gone, damn near two million fuckin' dollars! And the feds were on his ass! He shook his head struggling not to cry; even his money stashed under a fictitious name in a grand central station deposit box was untouchable, since he definitely couldn't go back to New York, at least not anytime soon. Then he wondered, did the feds also get to that money? Naw, they couldn't have gotten that stash, he concluded because he had taken extra precautions to cover his tracks.

As Rasheen stared at an old pick up truck in the parking lot, noticing his crew was waiting for him to say something, he reaffirmed his vow that he was not going back to prison. He would die before he would allow himself to be put back in a fuckin' cage. He further vowed that he was going to set the record straight with Killer Kato, even if he died in the process. Killer Kato had to pay for all the fucked up shit he'd done to him. When Ja-King's statement indicating that he believed Killer Kato had killed his mother because she was about to pull Lameek to another record label had entered his mind, Rasheen received the clincher reminder that put an end to the matter. Killer Kato had to die.

The waitress returned with several plates of food (hamburgers, french fries, tuna fish, hot dogs, potato salad, and sodas) and handed them to Rasheen and the others.

As they dressed up their food with salt, pepper, ketchup and other condiments, Candy said to no one in particular, "Where we go from here?"

Jack-Mack took a huge bite of his burger, and spoke as he chewed the food. "If they onto you Rasheen, then it goes without saying they onto all of us. Since we can't go back east, we might as well set up shop out here."

"I'm with whatever," Ja-King said, savoring his hot dog. "Plus, I ain't got no where to go anyway." He smiled, hoping the crude joke would lighten the tension in the air.

"One thing that is for sure," Jack-Mack said, "we gotta put some major work in, and real soon. Our money is mad low, and we can't touch the doe back in the East." Jack had put what was left of his money inside a safe deposit box, and was hoping the FBI wasn't onto him like they were on Rasheen.

"Whatever work we decide to put in can't be in this State," Candy said as she took a sip of her Ginger Ale soda. "You can bet the feds in this State are looking for us right now."

Rasheen was chopping down his tuna fish sandwich, listening closely to the suggestions. Every one of them was right on target, and they all had to be incorporated into their next move. "Yoh, Ja-King, how familiar are you with Cali?"

"I know a lot about L.A. and San Diego. I've been to Santa Barbara and San Francisco a few times."

Jack-Mack nodded approvingly, "Now, that's a good idea. Sound like big cheddar is coming our way. Shit, Cali is one of the top money states in the country. Hollywood folks got money dripping out the ass. You ain't gotta ask if I'm with it."

Candy swallowed a mouth full of masticated hamburger and said, "You think Home Girl got hook ups in Cali?"

"Yeah, I saw 'em with my own eyes," Rasheen said, wiping his mouth with a napkin, and then said to Ja-King, "You know a way to get some hardware and fake ID?"

"I know some cats who might can help us."

Ten minutes later, Rasheen and his crew were ready to leave. The moment they rose to their feet an Arizona State Police vehicle entered the parking lot and the two patrol officers headed towards the Diner. Rasheen gave everybody the signal to stay calm, don't start reaching and panicking until they absolutely had to. As Rasheen headed for the cashier, Jack, Candy and Ja-King moved towards the door. The waitress who served them handed Rasheen a bill for $22.50, and he gave her a twenty and a ten dollar bill as the officers entered; the officers inspected Jack, Candy, and Ja-King as they exited the Diner and proceeded towards the van. Rasheen's heart beat picked up speed when he saw these cops were straight red necks, looking for trouble; he changed his mind about waiting for his change.

As Rasheen walked pass the officers, the waitress said, "Excuse me Mister, you forgot your change."

"Keep it," Rasheen said politely as he slid pass the two officers who were now looking at him in their usual locked jaw, hard-nosed fashion.

As Rasheen approached the van, he could feel the officers' eyes burning a hole in the back of his head. He struggled to stay calm and to not look back. Just as his hand touched the van door, he heard the door of the Diner open, and before he could turn around to confirm what was going on, he heard Jack-Mack and Candy about to spazz out.

Keith Ramsey sat on the sofa in his Peachtree Street Condo counting stacks of money piled on the coffee table. Another man sat next to him watching the 11 o'clock news with a TV remote in his hand; his name was Aaron Wilson and he was the epitome of a rogue agent, second in roguishness only to his ex-partner Keith

Ramsey. Aaron was leaning back comfortably with his feet propped up on the coffee table, wondering why Keith was so worked up over these pennies. Although Aaron was extremely handsome and had good-natured attributes, he was probably the most toxic person in the whole FBI agency. Sort of like a beautiful fruit that looked too good to be poison, but was deadly enough to kill any living organism with just a single drop of its inner contents.

Keith completed the stack of ten one hundred dollar bills; his count was now at nine hundred thousand; he stopped counting and said, "I knew this nigga Rasheen would be the best thing to happen to us. This is better than that time when we had those Albanians on the take, and that was long and strong money."

"I still don't know what all the whoop and holla is all about." Aaron changed the channel. "Your man is just about on his last leg. If that safe deposit box is all he got, me and you got beef. You know how many corners I had to cut and the number of procedures I had to violate just to get my hands on that money? Looking at it I would say it's barely a mill. I thought you told me this nigga had three mill?"

"I just found out it's more than three. By now it should be close to four mill. It's obvious he got his money scattered around. He probably got several different deposit boxes under several different names, probably in several different banks. What we need to focus on is finding those other safe deposit boxes, including Jack's stash. He's got one too, I heard him talking about it. He probably got a mill or two."

"I don't know how we gonna throw Jack in the mix," Aaron said. "Unless we can confirm he's committing crimes with Rasheen, I don't know how I can get Klingaman to agree to include him with the Rasheen investigation."

"The man's a fuckin' fugitive. He's been on New York's most wanted list for years. New Jersey's looking for him as well. NYPD records confirm he was Rasheen's co-defendant in that murder case Rasheen did time for, but Jack was never apprehended. With a track record like his it shouldn't be too difficult to convince Klingaman to include him in the net. Didn't you say they're aware that Rasheen had accomplices during the kidnapping? Well, tell 'em you're 100% certain Jack is his accomplice. Believe me Aaron, it's worth it. These guys been robbing drug dealers for years, and they been stacking crazy paper."

There was a moment of silence as Keith picked up a handful of hundred dollar bills and resumed counting the money while Aaron's attention was pulled to the news report about a shooting.

When Aaron saw the broadcast was unrelated to the case, he said, "I'm definitely not feelin' the fact that we had to do a last minute rush job. I'm not trying to get myself jammed up…"

"You act like I knew this nigga was going to Arizona to kidnap a federal informant," Keith said frustrated, and realized Aaron made him lose his count. "It ain't like I'm his baby sitter. They're under the assumption that I'm on the straight path. They go out of their way to keep their livelihood concealed from me, and we know that's the way it supposed to be."

"We gotta find a way avoid these kind of surprises." Aaron said with a touch of aggravation in his voice. "We partners for life, but I'm not ready to take the same road you took."

Keith stopped counting again, made a mental marker of where he stopped, and said, "So what you trying to say? You know damn well the Bureau is racist through and through. I was fired because I wouldn't bow down to the bullshit. Yeah, I did a little scheming here and there, but name me one agent who's been with the Bureau for a decade or more and has not schemed at some point in his career. If I was willing to sell my soul to the devil I wouldn't have been fucked over the way I was and you know it."

"Okay, okay, let's not rehash that again. I'm not trying to pick a fight with you. I'm just pointing out the fact that we have to be on top of our game. The smallest mistake can cost us dearly. In fact, I suggest we close this project. You've just about squeezed these two bone dry; you've got 'em to invest in Supremetech, we got ourselves a nice piece of cash." He gestured towards the money on the coffee table. "And it's a good chance we'll find those other deposit boxes. First thing in the morning I'll talk to Sally over in the Bank Fraud Department and show her pictures of Rasheen and Jack. I'll get her to check the surveillance tapes of all the local Banks. We're bound to come up with something."

"Well, in that case," Keith said with a half-cocked smile. "I concur. As long as we get the rest of the money, I'm with closing down this project. We came this far; it would be insanity for us not to get the rest of the money. I hope you can arrange it so that they don't make it to court. The last thing we need is a bunch of loose ends floating around. If one of your thorough fellow agents starts snooping around, and stumbles onto something, we don't want them linked to us in anyway. Although they don't seem to be the weak, snitchin' kind of criminals, we both know how the most notorious criminals will do a 180 degree flip when they start looking at them football numbers."

"Don't worry. I'm already on it. Today, I got Klingaman to assign me as the chief investigating agent on this case."

Chapter Nineteen

Rasheen sat in the back compartment of the moving van feeling totally relieved they didn't have to bang it out with those two state police officers. Earlier, when he was about to enter the van, and thought it was the police exiting the Diner, he had turned around and saw it was the couple that was sitting on the other side of the Diner. He had jumped in the van and Candy pulled off.

Their destination was San Diego, California. By the time they were ten hours into their journey, they had contacted Sharon and had setup a hit on a multi-million dollar mansion right across the California border in a small county called Tecopa, not far from the infamous Death Valley. The whole team was with it and even Sharon agreed to deactivate the mansion's alarms, provided that they agree to send her five thousand dollars within the next week. Rasheen was knocked slightly off balance by the high price and when he tried to haggle her down to three thousand, she said, "Four thousand is the lowest I'm going, take it or leave it." Rasheen took it without another word.

When they arrived at the mansion in Tecopa, they were extremely tired in view of the fact they had been traveling non-stop for twelve hours, and hadn't gotten a decent night's sleep in a nice comfortable bed in days, but their need for money was a stronger driving force. Rasheen saw it was after 1 o'clock in the morning as he called Sharon to get her to deactivate the alarms. Ten minutes later she called back and assured them that it was done.

Brandishing 9mms, while wearing ski masks, Rasheen, Jack and Ja-King entered the mansion through the front door. They were on tiptoes since they were aware that the owners were home. As they moved about, they were hoping Sharon's schematics of the mansion's layout were accurate. After locating the occupants, a man, a woman, and two teenage kids, then tying them up, Rasheen, and Jack-Mack decided to pressure the white man who had a head full of white hair into telling them where the safe was. They were convinced that rich folks like these always kept a huge stack of money in their house. It took the breaking of only two fingers to convince the man to reveal and open the safe. When Rasheen, Jack and Ja-King saw all those jewels (diamonds, emeralds, rubies, and some other things they had no idea what they were), stocks, and bonds, they were struck by mixed emotions. They were enthralled because it was obvious these rocks and money certificates were worth a lot of money, but they were frustrated because they needed instant cash. Ja-King pressured the man further and was able to squeeze him into giving up all the cash on the premises, which totaled a little over 75 thousand dollars.

By the time they entered San Diego, they had sent Sharon her cut via Western Union and had retrieved the addresses and structural layout of three huge mansions in and around San Diego. Before they began casing the mansions, they decided to hit the streets to find a buyer for the jewels. Meanwhile, Candy had also made some calls and found out that Camila had given birth to a baby boy weighing in at 7 pounds 5 ounces. Upon hearing the news, Rasheen was so proud and enthralled with happiness he didn't know what to do with himself or with the wonderful energy he was experiencing.

Around 4 o'clock that afternoon, they pulled up in front of a pawnshop on Julian Street called "Willie's Wares." Ja-King claimed he knew Willie very well and that he was a reliable, head-up dude who wouldn't flip out on him. Rasheen felt it was too risky for Ja-King to step to Willie in light of the reward money hanging over his head. After going back and forth for five minutes, Rasheen gave in. He decided to go inside the pawnshop with Ja-King. Upon entering the pawnshop, and to Rasheen's initial surprise, he saw Ja-King was right. Willie was straight from the streets and appeared to be genuinely concerned about Ja-King's well-being. He was a black man mixed with Mexican and European, the epitome of a mutt. He talked like he wasn't feeling the fact that the police was hunting Ja-King. When Willie said, "Anything I can do to help you just let me know," Rasheen started to open up a little.

Rasheen pulled the black velvet bag from his jacket pocket, spilled the jewels onto the counter and said, "We trying to get these off."

Willie started closely inspecting the jewels with a magnifying glass. He struggled not to display his amazement. After a moment he said nonchalantly, "I'll give y'all ten thousand dollars."

Rasheen said, "Look bro, why you trying to play us, we'll go else where if..."

"No, I'm not on it like that, brother!" Willie said, alarmed at the thought of losing these remarkable jewels. These things were sheer magnificent! "Listen, I'm not a jewel specialist, so all I can do is offer you what I think they're worth," He lied; he knew enough to know these jewels were worth over a million dollars. "Okay, okay, look here, I'll double my offer ..."

As Willie rattled on, Rasheen saw as clear as day that Willie was gaming them. The first thought was to shit on Willie, treat him like an old, decrepit two-dollar whore in a crack den. He looked around to see if there was anything worth robbing him for, and saw nothing that interested him. The more he looked around the shop at all the things on sale, and at the way Willie was acting, the more he realized they could use him on their team. At the moment they weren't in the position to push potential allies away. Rasheen sighed hard and said, "Check this out Willie. We got a price estimate before we came to you," he lied. Being from the Hood and all, and knowing game when it was mashed in his face, he knew how to react to it. Throw it right back in the gamester's face. "These jewels are worth over a million dollars. We came to you cause we thought you would treat us like fam..."

"Hey, Ja-King and me is fam!" Willie said defensively. "Right Ja-King?"

"No doubt," Ja-King said. "You always kept it real; I hope you keep it that way."

"I told you I'm not a jewel expert," Willie said almost whining. "Hey, if you say they worth a mill, then I guess they worth a mill. I ain't got that kind of money." His hopes and dreams were slipping from his grasp, but he felt the urge to keep grabbing. "But, I got peoples that's holdin' like that."

"Naw, Willie," Ja-King said, seriously. "We ain't fuckin' with that. I can trust you, fuck anybody else!"

"How much loot can you kick out?" Rasheen inquired.

Willie thought about the question. He hated situations like this, since the question was loaded with all sorts of pitfalls; anyway you answered, the answer it could blow up in your face. Plus, it was evident Rasheen was sharp on his toes and there wasn't any need to create any more turbulence. "Twenty grand tops."

Rasheen picked out two of the rocks and slid them towards Willie. "This should cover that much."

Willie examined them; shook his head. "No way, add two more and you got a deal."

"One more, take it or leave it," Rasheen said as he slid another rock across the counter.

Willie sighed as he rode the moment for all it was worth. "Deal. But if we fam, I want first dibs on the rest. I got more than just cash. You know that Ja-King. In your situation, y'all need a dude like me on your side. A man with good street morals, old time principles, and many connections, can make life on the run a lot bearable."

Rasheen gave Willie a smile and a head nod. He felt that good vibe again and decided to bring Willie onboard. Despite what his instincts told him, common sense overruled this vibe and he decided to keep Willie at a distance, but well within arms reach.

That evening Rasheen and his crew sat at a makeshift dining room table in the one family house they rented in Coronado County. They were eating Chinese food while discussing tomorrow night's run. By a majority vote they decided to hit the mansion located on the outskirts of Lakeside County. This was the second mansion on the list of the three in this area, and they chose this one because Sharon indicated that it was the most lucrative of the three and the most secured. Earlier, as they cased the premises, they saw this mansion was as huge as a prison institution, covering at least ten acres of land, and had three individual buildings on the compound. This place even had its very own security guards. They saw the guard who did foot patrol was doing his rounds every hour. They all agreed the moment they saw this place, that this level of security was a good indication that there was something of great value inside.

The following night they parked their van about fifty yards away from the mansion's huge outer gate. Rasheen, Ja-King and Jack-Mack got out of the van dressed in black clothing with backpacks in their black leather glove covered hands and 9mms tucked in their waists, and rushed towards the outermost gate. As usual, Candy remained in the van. According to Sharon, there was another guard inside the mansion, who sat watching the surveillance camera monitors. She informed them that she could cause the cameras to loop a particular visual moment only for ten minutes. Therefore, Rasheen and the others were forced to move extremely fast. When they arrived at the entrance, Rasheen pushed on gate as he looked up into the camera lens, knowing it displayed the image it picked up at 2:34 am, and it opened. They rushed towards the mansion. Rasheen and Ja-King rushed up the stairs towards the huge gold trimmed front door while Jack-Mack went around the house to find the guard doing foot patrol.

Rasheen pulled his 9mm, pushed open the door and entered on tiptoes. It was dark and the silence was intense. As they moved towards the hallway on their right, where the security guard room was located, Rasheen's eyes slowly began to adjust to the darkness; he could now see the dark images of elegant furniture, chandeliers and the spiral staircase.

When they got to the end of the hallway, they peeked around the corner and saw the security guard room. Rasheen felt relieved when he noticed the guard was sleeping in the job. He rushed towards the door, snatched it open, and fired two silenced shots into the sleeping man. Rasheen immediately began turning off the alarms, cameras and other electrical devices. He hit a red button and a loud beeping noise almost startled them into a frantic retreat; Rasheen hysterically started hitting any switch in sight, and the beeping stopped. They rushed out of the room on their way to the bedrooms, realizing the noise may have awakened the family.

Had they known that switch had activated the silent alarm connected to the Lakeside Sheriff's Department, they would have vacated the premises instead of rushing into the rooms and began tying up the screaming man, woman and their teenage son.

Jack-Mack heard the muffled beeping sound come from inside and the abruptness of the sound caused him to flinch. Right on the heels of the beeping sound came the foot patroller charging towards the mansion, while talking into a walkie-talkie. Jack-Mack kneeled behind a bunch of neatly trimmed bushes. When the guard was a few yards away and rapidly approaching, Jack sprung into a standing position with the 9mm pointed. In comical fashion, the guard came to a stumbling halt just as Jack's bullets ripped at his body. By the time the guard fell crashing to the lawn, he had four bullets lodged inside various parts of his center mass while the life in his body was running away from him with the speed of violent winds from a hurricane. Jack rushed over to the fallen guard, saw he was still moving and pumped a bullet into his head. Homeboy was as strong as an ox, he thought as he realized all four of his bullets had struck the guard but he was still moving. Jack ran towards the mansion, trying to figure out what that noise was, and whether it was safe to continue with the robbery.

When Jack burst through the front door, he saw Ja-King at the top of the stairs.

"Up here," Ja-King said waving excitedly. "We found the stash." As he saw Jack rushing towards him he said jubilantly, "And man is this one big motherfuckin' stash!"

Jack zipped inside the study and saw Rasheen kneeling in front of an open safe, dunking stakes of money inside the backpack.

Rasheen said excitedly, "I don't think our bags are big enough. Tell Ja-King to find some bags!"

Jack rushed out, conveyed the message, rushed back in and started helping Rasheen fill the backpacks with the money.

Rasheen was so excited by all this money, he felt as though he had to defecate. There were even ten solid gold bullions. This was the biggest hit to date, even bigger than any of the drug stash house hits. Looking around, he saw the white man who owned this establishment was some kind of architectural engineer. He could tell by all the small models of buildings, shopping centers, and other complexes. He also saw this man apparently didn't believe in using banks. Rasheen was feeling so good it scared him because usually when things went this good it was often too good to be true, and was followed by catastrophe.

Candy frantically turned in her seat when she saw approaching car headlights in the rear view mirror. She got down real low as her heart was about to beat itself out of her chest. Despite all the drama she'd been through over the years she still noticed her adrenal always got pumped up whenever trouble was amidst. She rushed to the back window of the van and peeked out. When she saw it was three police cars, she felt an electrical surge rush through her body. She rushed to the walkie-talkie, snatched it up, and shouted into the device "Get out! The police is here! Five-O! Five-O!" She dropped the walkie-talkie and grabbed the AK 47 and two extra clips. She slid out the van as inconspicuously as possible, and hid amongst the nearby bushes.

The driver of the first car saw someone get out of the van and brought the car to a stop, almost causing the other police cars to collide into each other's rear ends.

Candy decided not to wait for them to get out of their vehicles, and opened fire. Her first bombardment of bullets disintegrated the first patrol car's windshield and chewed away the deputy's face, causing every one of his comrades to scramble out of their cars.

Rasheen, Jack and Ja-King where rushing out of the mansion with huge backpacks filled with money and gold bars. Candy's frantic comments were still ringing in their minds, and the rapid gunfire from the AK-47 was confirmation that shit had gone wrong. As they drew closer to the front gate, the sound of more approaching police sirens blared, growing louder and louder, which told them all that things were about to get fucked up in the worst way.

Rasheen realized they couldn't get away in the van, because that was where the shots came from. He stopped, and shouted exhaustedly, "We can't get away with the van! We gotta find another ride."

"But what about Candy?" Jack spit the words out despite his intense exhaustion. "We can't leave her."

Rasheen was about to say fuck Candy, but the look on Jack's face was very serious. He had to make a hasty decision. If they went for Candy, they would be locked in a vicious gun battle with an entire police department, and probably wouldn't survive. If they retreated now there was a slim chance they could get away. That voice shouted at him, reminding him that Candy was family. Rasheen also remembered their collective promise to help each other if there was a chance that a fellow comrade could be saved; the agreement jolted his memory like a slap to the face, and Rasheen lead the group towards the van.

Rasheen, Jack, and Ja-King heard and saw the five additional police cars had arrived on the other side of the mansion; the officers were running about in an utterly unorganized manner, and it was clear that they had never been confronted with an ordeal of this magnitude. Considering this shortcoming, Rasheen knew they had a chance, if they moved extremely fast, and with extreme and unrelenting force. In guerilla warfare fashion, with the wooded area providing cover, they split up, got as close as possible to the police cowering behind their vehicles and started picking them off. Rasheen hit the two police officers hiding behind the third car, while Ja-King focused on the two hiding behind the second vehicle, and Jack-Mack knocked off the one cop behind the first patrol car. They opened fired almost at the same time from the forest like area and the police didn't know what hit them. As the police tried to flee for cover while squeezing off desperate shots, Rasheen, Jack and Ja-King's silenced bullets shredded their bodies with efficient speed and brutal accuracy.

As they moved precautiously towards the van, two of the newly arrived cops swiftly crept through the wooded area heading towards the van. Jack embraced Candy and was relieved she was okay. They rushed towards the van and just as they were about to get inside the van, the cops opened fire, striking Jack Mack in the back with several bullets, one of the bullets struck him in the back of his skull as Candy scooted inside the van. Rasheen and Ja-King pumped off shots towards the wooded area as they moved back towards the police vehicles.

From inside the van, Candy positioned the AK-47 and rattled off a volley of bullets. When she saw Jack-Mack lying motionlessly on the ground in a pool of blood, she screamed agonizingly and unleashed another barrage of bullets.

Rasheen and Ja-King saw what happened to Jack-Mack and their pain was exquisite; they also saw about dozen police moving towards them. The dozens of flashlights moved towards them with frenetic energy. Rasheen felt tears pushing their way to the surface; he wanted to run over to the van and join Candy in the attempt to punish the motherfucker who did this to Jack, but that would be suicide. Looking at the situation it was even impossible to save Candy. She was locked in a vicious quagmire; if she attempted to leave the van the cops could easily pick her off. He snapped out of his reckless state of mind, pulled on Ja-King's arm, and ran to the third patrol car. He jumped in behind the wheel as Ja-King got in on the passenger side and sped away.

With his foot flooring the gas pedal, Rasheen saw through the rear view mirror, the violent volley of flashes coming from Candy's AK-47, and he realized this was the part of the game that hurt the most. He knew causalities were unavoidable, since good fortunate, and misfortune were two forces that worked with each other hand-in-hand. But when these fatalities occurred, it was like they were never supposed to happen; what goes up must come down didn't apply until confronted with a major loss, and nobody seemed to respect these realities unless they felt the raw effects of their wrath. But as the flicker of flashes faded in the rear view mirror, Rasheen was truly grateful it wasn't him in Jack's or Candy's shoes.

Killer Kato ran out of the Boyle Heights studio towards the Limo with his Berretta blazing at the shooters behind cars as the machine bullets whizzed pass him from what seemed like every conceivable direction. Crazy B was in back of him cutting down the intruders with a CAR-15 Colt Assault Rifle. Two of his soldiers had similar weapons and were unleashing bullets in a similar fashion as their captain. The situation imitated a WWII battle scene of the likes of the opening scene in the movie, "Saving Private Ryan".

Killer Kato pumped off a barrage of bullets into the chest of a shooter just as the man took aim; surprisingly, Killer wasn't the least disturbed by this sneak attack even though the Russians and the Italians assured him two days ago that there was a cease fire agreement in place and that there would be no retaliation for the murder of each groups' under bosses.

As Killer stepped over his fallen soldiers and kneeled behind the now bullet-battered bulletproof Limo, he fired the 9mm until it was empty and rapidly reloaded it. He was riding this violent wave with an inward smile, already imagining the red rivers of mass chaos that would flow once he waved his wand.

Across the street on a rooftop, a Russian soldier fired upon the Limo with a M240B machine gun. The awesome power of the 7.62mm dum dum bullets chipped away at the Limo's bulletproof material with remarkable efficiency. But, in light of the ear-shattering loudness of the gunfire, the Russian soldier didn't hear when Crazy B's soldier crept right up behind him. The man with long dreadlocks took aim and blew the Russian's top clean off. Crazy B's soldier took control of the machine gun and began firing at the other Russians on nearby rooftops.

Five minutes later, Killer, Crazy B and the Limo driver were inside the car fleeing the scene with smoke oozing from the barrels of their weapons.

That very same evening, Killer made the calls. These calls went out all over the country. He would soon find out if all the years of preparation would pay off. He called Butter from Oakland, Cowboy in Baltimore, Jay-R from Cincinnati, Poison Red in New Jersey, Big Gains (Gold-tooth Born) from his hometown, Bed-Stuy, Baby Blue in Texas and Bobby G from Detroit. This was his standby street mob, and each one of these individuals had at least two-dozen reliable and dedicated soldiers. This was a group of associates Killer had been looking out for over the years, helping them set up shops, businesses and stores of all kinds, regardless whether they were legal or illicit, Killer financed them fully and completely with one stipulation (in addition to the 10% he would get of the profits); when that phone call came, they had to come running. In his speech to these brothers, Killer had said in broken record fashion, "I'll give you whatever funding you need to get your projects off the ground, and you don't have to pay me back in cash. You owe in services. Those services will consist of putting work in when the time comes when we lock horns with folks that will eventually attempt to put us under the wing. If you agree and you take this money, you will be murdered if you try to renege." Since these brothers were from the streets, they were loyal to the code of the streets, and believed in word is bond and bond is life, most of them answered the call. Baby Blue and Jay-R reneged and would become the example for all the others to see and remember. Killer Kato not only saw what they did as a slap in the face, but also as an attempt to steal from him in view of the fact he was just breaking even with these two particular hardheaded associates, and it was evident they were trying to play him.

Killer Kato also had several dirty cops working for him as well. Because L.A. was where most of his heavy business dealings took place, he made it his business to recruit from L.A's finest. It came as no surprise to Killer when he saw just how much police services long money could buy. Virtually everything from personal body guarding, head bashing campaigns and contract hits to turning over of delicate information and rigging up cases so that defendants could get their convictions overturned. If the price was right anything could be bought. As an extra-added precaution, Killer dug real deep into his treasure chest of aces up his sleeve when he called the dirty federal agent, Aaron Wilson, a long time associate who always made things happen as long as the price was right. The good thing about Aaron was that he had a crew of six fellow agents who were far more unscrupulous than him.

Two days later, after a five hour briefing in a warehouse in Pasadena, the Killer Kato bunch had set upon the streets of America with full intentions of hitting any and everyone who was someone within the Russian and Italian mobs. They all stepped to their business with a fervor that said it was finally their time to sit in the sun, and bathe in the glorious sunshine of the underworld as the Kings they once were in antiquity. But what they didn't realize or anticipate was that their opponents had not only made similar preparations, but had merged their forces together and had taken their endeavors to a level that could literally boggle the mind; they even brought in affiliates from all over the world; including ex-members of the IRA, international hit men, members of the Mexican mafia, sellout blacks from all across the country, and even ex-CIA operatives.

Chapter Twenty

Rasheen sat in a lounge chair in the backyard of the new house they rented over on Valley Pine Road, drinking an ice cold 40 ounce of beer (Colt 45). Sitting on a small plastic table next to him was the San Diego daily newspaper. Rasheen was dressed in boxer shorts and sunglasses; he was trying hard to enjoy the sun and to clear his mind of all the madness. It had been a very long time since he'd taken a moment to relax and take a breather, and it felt odd as hell. The Lakeside Mansion murders and robbery had been front-page news for the pass four days straight. Jack Mack was dead; a single shot to the back of the head was what did it. Candy was shot several times, but remarkably she lived. According to the articles, Karen Jamison, AKA Candy went out with a blazing gun, and held back the police to the last bullet. After expending her last bullet she started throwing things at the police, at which point the police opened fire upon her, filling her body with fifteen police bullets. They recovered fifty thousand dollars of the stolen cash and four bars of solid gold. The article further indicated that there were two other assailants that got away and were responsible for the six murdered police officers, the two murdered security guards and the remaining missing proceeds, which they capped at a little under two million in cash and twenty five gold bullions. Rasheen shook his head as he read this part of the article and saw how lying was standard protocol for life on this planet, because they were jacking up the losses. It was a little over a mill and sixteen gold bars that was taken. This was either an insurance scam in progress or the police had stolen the rest of the stuff, he had realized as he laid the newspaper to the side.

Rasheen took a huge gulp of beer and sighed. The fact that Candy lived really disturbed him. He knew she was strong and was a die-hard ride or die chick, but she knew too much. The things she knew could disrupt his and Ja-King's lives if she decided to suddenly become weak. Rasheen knew he was correct when he fled the Coronado County house immediately after the Lakeside Mansion robbery. The minute he and Ja-King entered the house, they dug up all of their money, including Jack Mack and Candy's money they had buried in the basement and fled the house on Valley Pine Road. With Willie's help they found this house. Rasheen was struggling with all the issues bombarding his drama-stricken life. He also realized his views, motivations and attitudes were changing. After losing Jack, and knowing he had a child on the way, he felt differently. He was also getting tired of his current lifestyle. Looking at the fact that he now had close to two million dollars, 8 gold bars, twelve jewels worth crazy money, not including his stashes in various safe deposit boxes, he wondered would it be wise to just get up and disappear to another country and enjoy his life. He had enough money to live extremely well for the rest of his life. Even Ja-King had just as much money as him, and if they merged their moneys together they could do great things.

He saw his next-door neighbor, a middle aged black woman, come out of her house and take a seat on her lounge chair to get a piece of the sun. She waved at Rasheen with a huge smile. Rasheen was surprised by her sincere kindness and waved back. Suddenly, his mother entered his mind because the woman could've passed for his mother. As he tried not to stare at the woman, the reality of his life came back to him. His mother was murdered. Ja-King confirmed it wasn't an accidental heroin OD. His baby brother was being enslaved, and the same person responsible for all of his pain and misery was the same motherfucker that shitted on him, robbed him, dissed him, fucked him over royally and took his child-hood sweet heart. With this reality circulating in his mind, he felt himself coming back; the hatred that kept him going for years regenerated itself. The vow he made to kill Killer Kato was once again an intricate part of his mind, body and soul. But he did wonder why he kept balancing back and forth as to whether or not he wanted to murder Killer Kato. He guessed it was the money and the fact he was a fugitive of justice that was pushing him to break out, and say the hell with everything and just enjoy life.

Rasheen picked up the paper to re-read the article on Killer Kato and the beef he was going through. Rasheen liked the fact that cutthroat nigga was caught up in a war with the Russian and Italian mobs. He instantly saw potential in that scenario. After reading the article again, he sat the paper down and allowed his mind to reflect on Killer's beef knowing an idea as to how he could use it to his advantage would eventually take shape. There was no question they had to get out of San Diego, and he had to get closer to Killer Kato. San Diego was too hot to complete the other two robberies, and in any event, he and Ja-King needed a few other hands if they intended to continue robbing mansions. Since Sharon was still down with the program, he knew if they moved to L.A., she would find other mansions to hit. He was glad he called Sharon in accordance with her instructions, that if they ever came close to getting caught, to let her know immediately so she could activate the self-destruct component in the laptop. Reflecting back on that moment in the police car, it was evident if Ja-King hadn't remembered, the police may have found the laptop.

Just as Rasheen reached from his 40 ounce, he saw from his peripheral vision the lady approaching his fence. He turned his head and saw the light skinned black woman was wearing a wonderful smile. If she didn't have that old tire around her gut, Rasheen realized he might have been aroused enough to press her for some airplay. But the one thing he saw she did have going for herself was that pretty face of hers. It had a touch of oldness, but it was obvious she used to be a vicious head turner.

"Good afternoon," Gina said. "My name's Gina Olson. Since we're neighbors I thought it would be neighborly to introduce myself."

As he got up and approached the fence, Rasheen wasn't certain how to respond, since he hadn't expected this. However, common sense told him to play it safe, so he gave her his fake name on his driver's license. "I'm Michael Baisley." He reached out and shook her extended hand.

"Michael," Gina repeated smilingly. "I have a brother named Michael." She couldn't control her reckless eyeballs.

Rasheen peeked her checking out his equipment, and realized he had him a desperate and horny housewife on his hands. "So how long you been living here?"

"About three years," She said, realizing he was about to hit on her. Her panties instantly became moist. "It's really a decent community . . ."

As Gina gave him the run-down of the neighborhood, Rasheen felt his hormones coming to life. He hadn't busted a nut in weeks and the mere thought of skeeting off had him ready to lay some serious pipe to momma Duke. He wanted to cut to the chase, but didn't know how to do it without scaring her off, since he was ready to get his grove on.

When Gina said, "Would you like to come inside and let me fix you something to eat," his dilemma was solved. Upon entering her house, he was impressed with its cleanliness; the whole house smelled like jasmine mixed with raspberry. Just the smell alone made the blood rush to his crouch area. He sat on the plush sofa as she went into the kitchen. When Gina returned, now wearing a see-through gown while carrying a serving tray with some sandwiches on it, Rasheen's rod stood at full attention. She laid the tray on the coffee table and Rasheen reached out for Gina and she absorbed his embrace as though she was aching for the touch of a man. Rasheen kissed Gina, eager to show and prove that a younger man could do a better job at foreplay than any old foggy could imagine. Before he could get a flow going, Gina started peeling out of her clothing and when she finished, she strong-armed Rasheen's cloth off like a big bully. As they resumed kissing while rubbing their bodies up against each other the electricity of the moment caused sparks to surge through both of their bodies.

Gina pushed Rasheen on the sofa commanding him to lie on his back and he obeyed. Just as she mounted him, and took hold of his throbbing penis, Rasheen spoke through his accelerated breathing, "We need a condom."

Gina acted as though she didn't hear him and inserted the tip of his rod inside of her. Just when she was about to apply the weight of her body, Rasheen scooted away.

"Listen, Gina," Rasheen said seriously as all the HIV/AIDS courses he'd successfully completed while in prison coursed through his mind. The lesson that currently stood out the most was the one that confirmed there was no way to tell whether or not someone was infected with HIV by merely looking at the person, and that most people infected didn't even know they were infected and walk around for years with the virus, unknowingly infecting everyone that dived in bed with them. "I use protection on first dates. Besides pregnancies, there's STDs. I hope you got a condom. If you don't, I got some in my crib."

"I like it raw," Gina said seductively as she kissed him insistently. "I'm clean, disease free and I'm on the pill." She sucked on his ear, and immediately went down on him.

Rasheen let her do her thing, since he knew it was difficult for a man to contract a disease from a blowjob. She slurped him up like a chocolate candy bar. Damn! He sighed in ecstasy as Gina polished and shined his knob to the point his toes were curling up like cheese doodles. He saw Gina was a super vet when it came to giving head; every time he was about to explode, she stopped until the sensation to release subsided completely while allowing her tongue to toy with his testicles every so often.

Gina allowed her tongue to twirl around Rasheen's wood while she had half of it snuffed in her mouth; she would then accelerate her in and out sucking motions, making slurping sounds as though she was smacking on a tasty piece of candy. Gina went back and forth with this routine for three straight minutes; suddenly, the blood vessels in Rasheen's wood became as hard as cobalt steel and Gina slowed her rhythm almost to a complete stop. When Rasheen signaled to her that he was ready for her to restart by shifting his hips, she resumed her slow rhythmic sucking and licking that made Rasheen realize he was missing out on some awesome sex by looking pass all them old broads. Oh, we! He sighed as Gina grabbed his butt cheeks, pulled his body towards her with great force and deep throated all 8 inches of him. He couldn't hold back any longer! The moment his helmet started caressing her tonsils and his nuts started tapping on her chin, it ignited an urgency that he couldn't contain.

Gina saw he'd hit the point of no return, and sucked on his rod as though she was trying to pull a golf ball through a straw.

The force of the ejaculation was truly ferocious. He thought Gina was trying to hurt him, in view of the intense way she sucked on his wood. If he were a cornball, he would've fallen completely in love with Gina after this magnificent head job.

For two days, Rasheen kept returning to Gina's house, and ran through several boxes of condoms. He saw Gina was a cold-blooded freak for the doggy style. During every sexual encounter, Gina's butt cheeks stayed clapping against his waist. There was so much doggy style fucking going on Rasheen started creating real funky clapping beats that he knew he could've made millions if he sold them to those beat makers that sampled beats for rap songs. When he met Gina's young daughter, Kela, he tried to hit on her. She was 18 and was definitely within the age range to get broke off something lovely, but he noticed she kept turning up her nose as though she was disgusted by the fact he was sexing out her mom. Initially, he thought it was because of their age differences until he was snooping around Gina's draws and found some ATZ, HIV medication, with Gina's name on it. He instantly concluded that this was indeed not a good look. His first thought was to murder this bitch. When he realized he had never had unprotected sex with Gina, his rage abated some. Then he recalled how she was so eager to have him raw dick her down, and he knew he had to get away from her because it was obvious this trifling slut was trying to give him the monster. The rage was so blinding he knew if he confronted Gina about this matter he would kill her on the spot. The only thing that really stopped him from blowing her wig back was Kela; shortie needed her mom, so he left the house and said nothing.

As Rasheen and Ja-King were packing up to start their journey to LA, Rasheen shared the experience he went through with Gina with Ja-King.

Ja-King looked at him crazy upon hearing he wasn't going to put that bitch's lights out. "Rah, is you buggin' nigga? That foul bitch tried to give you the monster and you gone let her live? If she was trying to give you that thang, you can only image how many other motherfuckers she done laced up with that shit. That nasty bitch is a threat to every nigga in this community. Sounds like she gone lace up every dude she can give that shit to."

Rasheen felt a light switch clicked on inside his head. Ja-King was right. Gina was a dangerous bitch; she was trying to give that shit to unsuspecting dudes. The way she pushed up on him was clear evidence she was going out of her way to bless cats with that shit. The thought of how many dudes were walking around with that shit because of Gina, and giving that shit to more people, who were giving it to even more people, alarmed him deeply. It was obvious Gina had to go.

The night after Rasheen and Ja-King had their van loaded up with the few things they owned, Rasheen snuck into Gina's house from the back door with his silenced weapon. He tiptoed towards the living room and saw Gina watching TV. As he took aim, an image flashed across his third eye; it was the image of his mother. He shoved the image away and whispered, "Gina." When Gina turned, and saw Rasheen, she sprung to her feet as a smile appeared. Upon seeing the gun she was about to scream, but Rasheen fired two shots; one struck Gina in the chest and the other in the head.

Killer Kato sat at the head of the huge conference table with Crazy B strategically on his right side while Butter was on his left. Occupying the twenty seats were all his Lieutenants from various parts of the country. It was progress-reporting time, and Killer Kato was on a roller coaster of mixed emotions.

"I want to commend y'all for staying focused," Killer said to no one in particular. "We ahead by at least twenty bodies. But, Cowboy, I got to give you a special acknowledgement, because that phone trick was real creative. That's the kind of shit that let people know we about our business."

     Cowboy, with the help of special agent Aaron Wilson and his team, had found a way to plant explosives in the cellular phones of various Russian and Italian mobsters. He succeeded in blowing off the heads of ten key figures in these groups. He had shook up both groups so thoroughly they started fighting and killing each other because they thought a spy was amongst them.

     Cowboy gave Killer a clenched fist salute. "I'm just glad you gave me the chance to showcase my skills, big daddy. But your man big A is the one who deserves the real big ups."

     Killer Kato liked to address the good news first, so he big upped all the Lieutenants that were victorious in their endeavors. Butter was acknowledged for running up inside a Russian shipping company with his mob and gunning down all eight of the workers. Poison Red was shown mad love for killing two IRA hit men who were planning a hit on Killer. As the two entered their hotel after doing a dry run of the contract hit, Poison Red and his crew pushed both of their wigs back. Big Gains got rave recognition from Killer for breaking into the homes of eight prominent mobsters, and leaving a message on the wall written in human blood, which said, "If we can't eat at the table, then nobody will!"

     Killer Kato took a moment to gear up for the storm brewing in the pit of his stomach. The losses were devastating because they were hurting his pockets. He said calmly, "It ain't about blaming and pointing fingers, but facts are facts. It was a major fuck up when these chumps were allowed to blow up all of the studios." The five Hoodroma studios were reduced to rubble in a synchronized hit that claimed the lives of seventeen employees. The hit even brought the feds in and now they were investigating him.

Crazy B said, "Tommy Gun, that was your post. You told me what time it is, but you oughta explain that to us all."

Tommy Gun gave Crazy B a hard look that said, why you gotta go there? His high yellow skin complexion turned a shade darker. He drew in a deep breath and said, "I spread my mob out too thin, you know. And I had a few dudes that were sleeping on the job. I straightened them out, and replaced them."

Killer Kato said, "But how was it possible for them to get inside all five studios? I could understand if they got inside three out of five, or even four out of five, but every single one? And you telling us, nobody in your crew saw anything?"

Tommy Gun started perspiring, and his throat became as dry as sandpaper. "I know this is a major fuck up Killer. The cats responsible paid for this shit."

"What you do to them?" Killer said, detecting the bullshit. "The last I saw, your whole team was intact."

"Well, I…I." Tommy Gun swallowed hard. "I gave Raymond a vicious beat down. And Spike even got lashes…"

"But none of them paid with their lives," Crazy B said. "Despite the fact their fuck ups cost innocent lives."

Tommy Gun didn't have to answer verbally because the answer was self-evident.

Killer Kato started theatrically sniffing the air. "Smell like an agent provocateur to me. I hope they paid you properly. Y'all smell that?" He sniffed again.

Everyone in the room played along, sniffing loudly and muttered agreements.

Crazy B sprung to his feet with the 9mm pointed and squeezed off three shots into Tommy Gun's unsuspecting chest. Tommy Gun's eyes were wide with shock as he slithered out of the chair and fell dead.

Later that evening, Killer Kato and Crazy B were in the Hoodaroma office building on Hollywood Blvd. They were in the executive suite and both had drinks in their hands when the phone rang.

Crazy B picked up the receiver, "Hello?" He listened. "Yeah, this is Hoodaroma. Can I ask who this is?" He nodded his head. "Yeah, he's here." He handed the phone to Killer. "It's Galucci."

"Yeah," Killer Kato listened emotionlessly. "We open for discussion. We've always been willing to talk. But I want to say one thing before we go any further, if we can't eat at this table equally, all talk is dead." There was a pause. "I'll be there." He hung up the phone and locked eyes with Crazy B.

"They ready to talk?" Crazy B saw Killer nod his head as he drank the remainder of his drink. He went to the bar to refill his glass. "You think it's a trap or what?"

"I doubt it," Killer said as he took another sip. "The one thing about these people you can bank on is that they ain't stupid when it comes to making money. Right now, their money flow is hurting. Yeah, we hurtin' too, but they hurting a little more. At the rate this thing is going, we'll both go bankrupt, but they'll go dry before us and they know it. Yeah, egos are caught up in this thing, but those big dogs don't give a fuck about egos because catering to motherfuckers' egos don't pay no god damn bills and it damn sure don't keep folks pockets fat."

"Yeah, that's what we thought the last time." Crazy B sipped on his Jack Daniel's. "Maybe they're trying to pull you out into the open to get a clear shot. In the game of war, if you kill the general the game usually comes to an end."

"Anything's possible. But my gut feeling is that they want to enforce a truce. How ever they come, we gonna be ready for whatever they dish out." Killer Kato took a sip and realized he was engaging in wishful thinking. He wanted this shit to be over with and as he thought hard about this upcoming meeting with the top Italian and Russian bosses, he subconsciously knew he was overreaching. He just hoped he wasn't allowing his over-zealousness to be the root of his demise.

Chapter Twenty-One

Rasheen, Ja-King and Willie entered the new house in Glendale, L.A. they purchased under Willie's name. The place was real neat and clean; it had pine trees lining the outer perimeter. There was a pool embedded in the ground in the back, and the place could pass for a celebrity's crib once the right type of furniture was placed inside it.

Rasheen went from room to room, examining the place. "It's nice. But, unfortunately, there's no sense in getting too comfortable."

Willie was shocked, "What you mean? This joint is top of the line."

Ja-King wanted to tell Willie to shut the fuck up because he was making him regret bringing him along, but instead he spoke politely, "We ain't planning on staying still too long for obvious reasons, bro. It's harder to hit a moving target. What's the deal, you ain't listening? We here to make some money; hit and run." He knew talk of money would get his mind back on track.

Willie realized he spoke to hastily, "Yeah, yeah, you right, you right. My bad; I'm just feelin' this place like a motherfucker." He looked around, still patting himself on the back for picking out this nice ass house. "When I pick it out, it met all the requirements y'all gave me. Don't it fit the specifications?"

Rasheen was nodding his head approvingly. "Yeah, you did a good job Willie." Rasheen reached in his pocket, pulled a huge knot of bills and peeled off two fifty-dollar bills. "Go get us some dinner." He handed the bills to Willie who was all smiles.

"What y'all wanna eat?" Willie was still smiling; he loved making runs for Rasheen because he very rarely asked for the change.

"Use your imagination," Rasheen said, still examining the place.

As Willie headed for the door, Ja-King shouted, "Bring me some seafood, catfish or something like that."

Rasheen went to their bags stacked near the front door and started rummaging through them, looking for the shovels. "I guess we might as well stash the bulk of this cheddar." He found a shovel and handed it to Ja-King. He found the other shovel, snatched up a huge duffle bag while Ja-King grabbed the other duffle bag.

Rasheen led the way out to the back door and into the yard. The sun was just making a dash down into the western horizon, and the image of the reddish orange sunset was breathtaking. Looking around Rasheen saw Willie did a damn good job at finding a place that wasn't too close to any neighboring houses, and had a huge, secluded backyard that led to a wooded like area. Rasheen found a spot about ten feet from the first tree leading into the wooded region and carefully started cutting a hole in the top part of the grass so that they could lift it up without disrupting this top layer. Once the layer was safety lifted and placed to the side they began digging.

Rasheen said, "This gang banger dude, what's his name again?"

"Rooster," Ja-King said. "I'm tellin' you, Rah, he got a serious team. I think they call themselves SCR, the South Central Rangers. This cat Rooster got mad beef with Killer, cause Killer tried to push up on him when he was trying to get into the rap game. The only reason Killer couldn't get anywhere with him was because this cat got hook ups with damn near all the gangs out here in LA. Killer saw if he pushed too hard and started touching the wrong folks, he was bound to get his hands burnt. Basically this cat Rooster backed Killer's ass down. But you know the type of nigga Killer Kato is. He couldn't wipe it on his chest, so all of a sudden Rooster's baby brother, Chicken Hawk, ended up dead."

Hearing Rooster's situation reminded him of Lameek; it was time to give his brother a call. He'd been planning on calling him when they were in San Diego, but after the first robbery turned into a fiasco, he was force to hold off. Now that he was in traveling distance it was as good a time as any to finally get a chance to see his brother. "Listen, I need you to get me in touch with Lameek."

Ja-King stopped digging, and cocked a smile at Rasheen, "So it's finally that time? I thought you'd never ask." He resumed shoveling dirt. "Man, Lameek, used to talk about you all the time. You ever listen to his rap lyrics?" He said rhetorically and sarcastically, since Rasheen played Lameek CDs every chance he got. "Yeah, of course you listen. And I know you remember the verse where he be talking about this dude. You know the part where he be talking about the savior of his world of reality. You hear him kick that same verse in damn near all his tracks. That person in that verse is you. He messed me up when he told me that."

Rasheen was touched by Ja-King's comment. He remembered that verse. How could he not, since it was the one that always got his attention? Rasheen started kicking the verse. "Grand narrative spectacle of a key element family, much love to the savoir of my world of reality."

After they dug about three feet into the ground, Rasheen and Ja-King laid their shovels down. Rasheen unzipped the duffle bag and pulled out a huge stack of hundred dollar bills; the amount in the stack was 150 grand, and he laid it to the side. Ja-King extracted the same from his duffle bag. They then placed each duffle bag inside an extra thick garbage bag, and placed them both inside the hole. They filled in the hole, and shoveled the excess dirty into a garbage bag and placed the left over dirt on the other side of the yard.

They re-entered the house, and Ja-King got on the cellular phone to make contact with Lameek, pretending to be Sammy Bones from the LA Chronicle. Ja-King convincingly changed his voice while speaking to Lameek's lawyer and manager, Philip Henderson. When Philip put him through to Lameek, he gave the phone to Rasheen.

"Hello," Lameek said.

"What's up man?" Rasheen said.

"Who this?" Lameek said frustrated. "Where's Sammy Bones?"

"Oh, so now you don't remember my voice, huh?"

Lameek strained his mind to recall that voice. Impatiently he said, "Come on, now, I ain't got time for this bullshit, I'm a busy man."

"Too busy for family?" Rasheen heard Lameek's knowing response. "Yeah, it's me. Be easy, don't blow it up if people are watching."

Lameek felt lighting bolts surging through his body. "Rasheen! On, shit! When you got out?"

"Anybody listening to you?"

"Naw, I'm in my office by myself," Lameek was elated with extreme and uncontrollable happiness. "So where you at?"

"Calm down, little bro. Pick a place where I can meet you. It's gotta be secured. I'm real hot, so it can't be where a lot of police are."

"So you in LA?"

"Yeah. Pick a time and place for tonight. I'll be there. But come alone."

"Ah, meet me at the Serenade on Beverly Hills Blvd. At 11:30."

"See you then," Rasheen said and hung up.

By the time Willie returned it was pitch dark outside; they ate the meal consisting of Mexican rice and beans, hot chilly peppers, fried red snapper and an assortment of other Mexican foods that Rasheen and Ja-King had no idea what they were, but enjoyed them nevertheless. The minute they finished the meal Rasheen, Ja-King and Willie were on the move. They exited the house and were on their way to Beverly Hills.

Sitting in the back seat, watching the California highway, Rasheen realized he was a little nervous about seeing his brother. The last time he saw Lameek, he was just a baby, no more than 12 years old. Now Lameek was 19 years; he was a millionaire and was a worldwide rap star. Although he still couldn't understand why Lameek never wrote to him while he was in prison, he knew there had to be a damn good reason.

They pulled up in front of the Serenade Restaurant, but they didn't see Lameek. Ja-King had made it clear that he didn't like this area because the police were notorious for pulling over black folks. He would've suggested they meet up at another location had he known Lameek suggested this area. They found a parking space and decided to wait.

Five minutes went by and Rasheen's patience was expended. He wondered was Lameek actually inside the restaurant. After pondering the situation, he realized that's where he had to be. Rasheen opened the door and said, "I'm going in. He's probably waiting for me inside."

Rasheen headed across the street. He was hoping this restaurant didn't have metal detectors because he had no intentions of going anywhere without his biscuit. He repositioned the 9mm in his waist and picked up his pace. The minute he pulled open the restaurant door, he saw Lameek get up from a nearby table and approach him. As Rasheen entered the extremely elegant establishment, his eyes swept across every face in the joint.

Rasheen and his baby brother embraced each other. Rasheen whispered in his ear, "Let's break out, and go somewhere safer than this."

"But..."

Rasheen pulled him by the arm and led him out the door.

As they were in the car, heading down Beverly Hills Blvd., the silence in the car was intense. Twenty minutes later they found a secluded area in front of a public park; they pulled the car to a stop, and Rasheen and Lameek got out. They sat on a nearby park bench.

"I'm proud of you, bro," Rasheen said. "Can't call you shorty no more. You a world-class rapper and your shit is tight too. I see you fulfilled that dream of yours."

"Yeah, you can say that. Damn, man, look at you. You all cock diesel and shit. Why you ain't write me back? I was writing you like crazy…"

"You was writing me? I never got your letters!"

"I used to write you at least three times a month. Word is bond. Even though you never responded, I was still writing. I was even sending you checks, but they were never cashed."

"Did you ever mention this to Killer Kato?"

Realization suddenly clicked in his mind. For the first time it dawned on him that Killer was tampering with his mail. "You know something, that nigga knew I was writing you. And he used to throw it in my face that you didn't care about me because you would never respond to my letters." Lameek thought hard about the situation, and suddenly it all made more than just good sense; after hearing that Rasheen never got one single letter of his, it was now unquestionable confirmation that Killer Kato had his hands in this shit.

"So what's up with Crystal?" Rasheen wanted to believe he really didn't care about her, but his heart was telling him otherwise. "I heard she's some kind of big wig with Hoodaroma."

"She's doing her. Killer got her handling all the company's management issues. I was never feelin' the fact that she walked off on you like that, but you know how it is; she her own woman."

"You ain't gotta justify any of that bullshit. She made her choice. Killer put pressure on her and she folded. And let's keep it real, she's always been a gold digger." He felt his anger being rekindled, and decided to get off the topic of Crystal. "I'm gonna ask you something. It's gonna spark up some emotions, but I need you to be honest with me." He paused for a moment as he looked around the empty park. "Did Killer kill mommy?"

"I think he did. I didn't see him do it with my own eyes, but at the time mom was talking about moving me to another label. And we know how Killer do shit. He was spazzing the fuck out and then all of a sudden she pops up dead. Ja-King knows what time it is. You see how he tried to knock him off when he started talking about leaving Hoodaroma."

Rasheen flashed back to the time his mom used to take them to the movies, and all the other good times they had as a family before she started using drugs, and the pain was acute. "Listen, Lameek I know that nigga is robbing you blind. You ain't got to feel bad about not getting crazy on that nigga for all the shit he's doing. I'm here now, and some how some way that nigga is gonna pay. I know you ain't built for what I'm about to do, so I'm not gonna drag you into it cause this shit is gonna get ugly. If you feel you can bust a few shots that will be helpful."

"Bust shots! Man, whatever I can do to take that nigga down you can count me in. That motherfucker got me in a trick bag, he murdered mommy, and he's shitting on folks like it ain't no thing. You motherfuckin' right I'm gonna try to get at this nigga." He paused for a moment as he collected his thoughts. "I'm not trying to make him bigger than what he is, but don't underestimate him. Killer is real strong. This nigga got police, federal agents, politicians, judges, millionaires and even billionaires down with him. If we go up against him, we gotta come right, and we definitely can't let him even get an inkling of an idea that we trying to get at him."

"Can you get access to Hoodaroma bank account numbers?"

Lameek smiled, because he saw where his big brother was going. With enthusiasm he said, "Yeah, I can get them. But how can we hit him in the pockets that way?"

"Let me worry about that." Rasheen could already see Sharon licking her chops with this one, because he was going to suggest that she let her fingers get good and sticky. "You get those numbers and we'll start our campaign."

"I don't know if you know it, but Killer's caught up in a war with the Russians and Italians. We might be able to use that to our advantage."

Rasheen was proud that Lameek was thinking like a strategist. "I heard about it. I read it in the papers and shit. We definitely gonna put that to use. In the meantime, don't tell anybody that I'm out here, especially Crystal." He rose to his feet, causing Lameek to do the same. "I'll drop you back off at the Serenade. Give me your private cell phone number. I'll get in touch with you."

Lameek pulled a pen and a piece of paper from his pocket, wrote down the number, and handed it to Rasheen.

"Another thing; the feds and the Connecticut State police are hunting me. So keep that in mind when I call you." Rasheen gave Lameek a strong brotherly hug and headed towards the car.

After Lameek was dropped off at the Serenade, Rasheen, Ja-King and Willie were on their way to Watts, LA's equivalent to New York's Harlem and Brooklyn's Bed-Stuy. When they pulled up in front of Rooster's raggedy shack, an army of nine gun totting, 40-ounce drinking, handkerchief on the head wearing type of brothers stepped straight to the ride.

Before they were able to get a word out of their mouths Ja-King got out of the car and when the nine gang bangers saw who it was they was enthralled with admiration and delight. They were hugging and embracing Ja-King as though he was truly a part of the family.

Ja-King said, "These are my peeps. They fam through and through." He waved for Rasheen and Willie to get out of the car. Then he said to the leader, Goliathon, "Yo, what's up with Rooster? I need to kick it with him."

Goliathon waved to one of his soldiers and the young banger took off towards the shack and entered it. A few seconds later, the soldier stepped out and waved them towards the shack while shouting, "It's cool!"

Goliathon lead them towards the shack.

Once inside the shack, Rasheen saw this place looked like some shit right out of a Hood horror movie. An old flea-bitten sofa sat in the middle of the floor, 40-ounce malt liquor bottles were shattered everywhere, some were broken, graffiti was on the walls, and the place smelled like piss. The statement, "Long live the all mighty South Central Rangers" was spray painted all over the place. Rasheen gave Ja-King a look that could've killed; there was no way he was going to bring in some disorganized, reckless, drug heads and dope fiends, to run with him on a mission against a multi million dollar adversary. When he saw Rooster come from the back, he was shocked because Rooster looked like he was totally out of place to this busted ass living room. Rooster wore a short Afro with a neatly trimmed goatee; his brown skin was clean and flawless, his clothing was neatly pressed and he reminded Rasheen of a business executive.

After the handshakes and introductions, Rooster escorted them to the back area of the shack. When Rasheen saw the condition of this room, everything started to make sense because this room was neat and clean and Rasheen put the pieces together; the front room was a front. Ja-King introduced Rasheen and Willie. When Rooster spoke, Rasheen saw his assumptions were confirmed; Rooster was a throw back from he earlier 70s militant era.

"Please have a seat." Rooster gestured towards the empty chairs as he took a seat. "Brother Ja-King. Damn G, the ancestors are watching over you."

"Yeah," Ja-King said with a serious expression, because he knew how Rooster liked to do business. "I guess all that love I was showing the people when I was getting a piece of the good life is coming back to a brother." He knew it was always wise to slide in an inconspicuous reminder that he was, to some degree, for the peoples.

"Yeah, Ja, you did show some love. But there's so much work to be done. What you did was just a drop in the bucket. So what brings you here? You said it was something me and SCR wouldn't refuse to get involved in; let's hear it?"

It took Ja-King and Rasheen five minutes to explain the plan to Rooster. During the presentation, Rooster was so focused it appeared as though he had an attitude; his hard, no nonsense screw face could intimidate the most harden criminal.

With an even harder expression on his face, Rooster said, "I'm with y'all on this. You should know I got a special kind of beef with Killer Kato. But I got stipulations. I'm the General when it comes to my people and all SCR activities. SCR move when I say to move. They follow only my orders. From the way it looks, Rasheen is top dog amongst your click. That's cool." He locked eyes with Rasheen and said, "But you don't run shit with me. If you can agree to those ground rules, then you got my sixty-five bangers and me."

Rasheen saw Rooster had a power complex, and was a serious control freak. Since Rasheen was always captain of the ship he commanded, and it was obvious Rooster felt the same way, somebody was going to have to bend. Now he had to decide was it worth all the inevitable clashes. As he and Rooster locked eyes with each other, Rasheen thought he even saw something else in those deep brown eyes. He wasn't sure what it was, but it had a strong resemblance of hatred, envy and jealousy, which were forces that were far more dangerous than the very person he wanted to get rid of.

Chapter Twenty-Two

Killer Kato got out of the limousine, and saw that the fourth level of the parking garage was empty, except for the three or four cars on the other side of the parking lot. It was about 2 o'clock in the morning and most of the city was asleep. Crazy B and his six associates got out of various cars and stood guard. Inside the three Ford Escorts on the other side of the garage, were Aaron Wilson and his crew. In the green Escort was Aaron; when he saw Killer get out of the Limo, he got out of the vehicle. Aaron brought his crew along, so they could get a look at the infamous Killer Kato, Colin Gibson, in the flesh. Aaron viewed his associates as a rainbow coalition because he had an ethically diverse crew. Donald Mooney was white of Irish heritage; Carlos Chavez was Puerto Rican; Eugene Lee was African-American; Bruce Freud was of Jewish ancestry; Ted Glass was from Hawaii and Norman Qing was of Chinese descent.

Killer Kato and Aaron Wilson approached each other as though they were gunfighters, itching to draw their weapons. Killer could never understand why Aaron insisted on having these types of dramatic meetings in parking garages, secluded parks, old warehouses, etc. As he drew closer, Killer Kato saw Aaron had on his old trench coat and black suit. Then again, he realized all federal agents had a thing for dark suits with the whole tie bit. As far as Killer was concerned, it really didn't matter what the hell they wore just as long as they allowed him to purchase their services, everything was fine and dandy. He wondered what was eating at Aaron; he said this meeting was very urgent.

When they were upon each other Aaron said, "I wanna congratulate you on your success with the Italians and Russians. That was no small feat to get them to agree to allow you in the game. That means less money for them."

"Couldn't have done it without you. I hope those bonuses I sent you and your boys were sufficient."

"We can't complain. Things could always be better, you know, but we're content. Hey, Egypt wasn't built overnight, and I've learnt many moons ago that slow money, is sho money. And often it's safer money." He sighed as he saw Killer Kato's impatience becoming visible. "It feels rather odd because I'm here seeking your assistance for a change. I'm trying to put the gloves on a Brooklynite name Rasheen Smith. I got reason to believe you may know this individual. Some associates of mine were rubbed the wrong way by this gentlemen, and I thought you might be able to point me in the right direction."

"Rasheen Smith!" Killer Kato appeared genuinely flabbergasted. "I thought he was in prison in New York. The last I heard he was at Sing Sing."

"I hope you're jerking my chain."

"You know I don't play games," Killer Kato folded his arms over his chest. "So what you saying? He's out of prison?"

"Out of prison! That Negro's been out for the pass two years. So I guess that answers my question as far as whether or not you seen him. What's up with his brother? Didn't he reach out to him?"

Killer wasn't totally surprised he knew Lameek and Rasheen were brothers; after all, he was a federal agent with access to unimaginable amounts of information. "I can assure you that he didn't contact Lameek, at least not that I know of. If you don't mind me being nosy, what did old Rasheen do to rack up the wrath of a force such as yourself?"

Aaron smiled, "You know something, Mr. Colin Gidson." He knew calling him by his government handle would scratch a raw nerve. "You just lost points asking me some dumb ass shit like that." He saw Killer gritting his teeth. "If you don't want me touching a nerve, then don't touch my nerves. You know the rules; never ask about my employers. How would you feel if I revealed your identity or your agendas when motherfuckers start developing a case of nosiness?"

Killer Kato's rage was snuffed out instantly, because Aaron was right. He played himself for asking. "No disrespect intended. It was a mere slip of the tongue. To answer your question straight up; no I haven't seen or heard from Rasheen. Hell, I didn't even know the nigga was released from prison. I thought he had at least five more years to go. And I damn sure didn't know he was on this side of town."

"Keep your eyes open for me. Let me know if he reaches out to his brother. I hope you and scrams don't got any special bonds, cause if you do I strenuously suggest you get over them very quickly."

Killer Kato laughed. "Special bonds? I was about to ask you if you would like me to do the honors of laying that clown ass nigga down for you. He ain't no part of the Hoodaroma family; if anything, the nigga's a threat, since I know he got a bone to pick this way, and there's definitely some shit he wants to get off his chest."

"Hey, if you feel the urge to lay him down, be my guest. Just make sure you get in touch with me immediately when you do. And I'm talking very immediately." He gave Killer a very intense stare down to place strong emphasis on the comment. "Well, that concludes our discussion. Peace out." Aaron turned and headed for his vehicle, while Killer Kato did the same thing.

Several hours later, Killer Kato was standing in the middle of his huge bedroom in his multi-million dollar mansion in Lakewood, talking to Lameek like he was his father, which had Lameek on the brinks of getting violently physical. In the background, rap music and massive partying people could be heard.

"How is it you don't know!" Killer Kato shouted.

"What the fuck! You act like I got a motherfuckin' crystal ball. He ain't contacted me! I thought he had at least five more years to do. What happened, he escaped or some shit?"

Killer Kato started pacing; he realized now he had to find a way to figure out where this nigga Rasheen was. He knew when an associate of the likes of Aaron Wilson asked for assistance, it was a request you go way out of your way to fulfill. He stopped pacing and stared at Lameek, trying to detect if he was lying. When he saw Lameek squared off with his rebellious attitude turned up to full volume, he didn't know what to think since Lameek was always mad at something. All this little nigga did was bitch, complain, fight, argue and make matters worse. "Well, I know from a reliable source that he's not only out of prison, but he's in LA."

Lameek didn't appreciate Killer Kato entertaining the thought that he would be stupid enough to give up his brother. But he was wise enough to stay calm and try to extract and accumulate as much information as possible. "I'm saying, even if he is what's the big fuckin' deal? I know you don't think my brother wanna get at you because you laying dick on Crystal? Why you looking for him, what's up?"

Killer Kato was about to blurt out the fact that he wasn't interested in Rasheen, and that it was Aaron who was looking for him, but immediately caught himself. "I just wanted to know. Ain't nothing up. I figured maybe we could welcome him onto the team. He's family whether we like it or not."

Lameek wanted to tell him to his face that he was full of shit. He sighed, realizing Killer wasn't going to share with him the real deal, so he changed the topic. "Why you worried about rinky dink shit like that when you've taken Hoodaroma somewhere, where no other black man could take an Entertainment company before. Shit, the whole goddamn Hoodaroma family should be celebrating right now, including you and me. Here we are in here arguing about bullshit while you got a house full of folks having a good time; you fucking high with this nonsense. We a worldwide Distributor, man! Let's start acting like it!"

Killer Kato smiled animatedly. Lameek sure wasn't lying about the misdirected splurging of energy. He should be celebrating because he pulled it off. His dream has been partially fulfilled! With explicit underworld approval he was permitted to become an International Entertainment Distributor. All the heavy weights, like Sony, Time Warners, Viacom, etc., were pissing a bitch, but his foot was in the door and he had full intentions of keeping it there. He sighed, "You know something Lameek. You right. Pardon me for hittin' you in the head with this shit at a time like this. I ain't mean to disturb this party atmosphere. It's all good. Come on, let's get back to the party."

As Killer Kato led the way out of the room and back to his huge living room the size of a dance hall, Lameek was wondering how the fuck Killer found out? He wondered did he know that he was talking to Rasheen on the DL? Looking at the way he spoke, Lameek concluded he didn't know; at least he hoped he didn't know. He started getting nervous because he had gave Rasheen Hoodaroma's company bank account numbers. The shit he had to go through to get those numbers was ridiculous and just thinking about it made him exhausted. But he got the three main numbers, passed them onto Rasheen, and felt damn good. As he danced with a fine looking groupie with an ass as voluptuous as Jennifer Lopez's, Lameek smiled inwardly because he knew if the issue of Rasheen being on the west coast got under Killer's collar he could only image the hell he was going to raise when millions of his dollars started coming up missing.

Rasheen was in the passenger seat of the blue Acura Legend; Willie was chauffeuring while Ja-King was in the back seat. They pulled up in front of Rooster's place. After doing some deep thinking Rasheen decided to be the one who would bend; he needed Rooster for the next phase of his plan, and accomplishing the end results was bigger and more important than a little scratch to his ego and emotions. In any event, Rasheen concluded that if Rooster wanted full control over his team, in all fairness such a request really wasn't an unreasonable stipulation.

As Rasheen got out of the car, he saw Goliathon approaching, while the other five soldiers stayed put. He liked the fact Rooster had put his team on point; they had called Rooster earlier and told them they were coming over to discuss their progress. It was 3 o'clock in the morning and he knew it couldn't possibly be standard practice for Goliathon and his crew to be hanging out in front of the crib at this hour of the morning.

Rasheen, and Ja-King approached Goliathon; they shook Goliathon's hand, gave him a hug and entered the shack. Willie remained in the car.

Rasheen, Ja-King and Rooster sat at the table talking.

"That organization you gave me," Rasheen said to Rooster. "It didn't have legitimate 501(c) (3) non-for-profit status. My contacts can only transfer Hoodaroma money to those types of organizations. She…My contacts tried to move money to profit based organizations and ran into some major problems. Give me any organization with legit papers, and we'll make it happen. So far about ten million of Killer's money is tied up in these organizations."

Ja-King cut in, "I know you wanna touch some of that cheddar Rooster, but right now we in the stage where we softening this nigga up for the knock out. If we can put a major dent in his finance, we can weaken him enough to run up on him and do damage. Once we go there that's when we can rob his punk ass in the raw."

Rooster sighed. All this sneak thieving shit wasn't his style. To him it was real girlish, but deep down he knew it was all a part of the art of war. "Yeah, I'm feelin' all this, don't get me wrong. But I was leaning more towards a shotgun blast kind of approach. Hit this nigga from ten different angles all at the same time. That way he doesn't get any time to recuperate from any of the blows we lay on his bitch ass. As it stands, this nigga got so much money it'll take at least a year to wreck havoc enough to cripple him. And since this money-taking thing might eventually get cleared up, once he gets his lawyers on the job, it really boils down to this sneak thieving shit being a futile endeavor. I ain't never been into just blowing steam. I like to hit a nigga and make him feel it for life."

"Naw, bro, you got it twisted, we ain't wasting time," Ja-King said, "We said his lawyer might be able to fix some of the issues with the money transfers to various accounts, but he won't be able to get back all the money." He was about to reveal the fact that him, Rasheen and Sharon had created a fake organization solely for the purpose of getting the lion's share of the transferred money, but immediately caught himself. Once the money was secured, they would dissolve the organization and the fake executive broad would disappear along with the money.

Rasheen was in deep thought. That shotgun blast tactic did have some validity. "Yo', check it. I gotta admit that shot gun thing might be in our best interest. Stepping to Killer the way you just laid it out, Rooster, could work." The reason he really felt this way was because Lameek informed him that Killer had some how found out that he was out of prison and was in LA. Knowing that he no longer had the element of surprise had thrown his whole plan into a tailspin. It was apparently time to come up with a new, highly aggressive approach towards this situation, and maybe the solution could be found within the shotgun blast approach. "I think you should know something else Rooster; Killer Kato some how found out that I'm out here in LA. I can only assume he's gearing up for some vicious drama."

"What happened? Your brother slipped up and told him?" Rooster said.

Rasheen was about to blow up, but figured a tit for tat would be the better way to address the matter. "No! Why would Lameek go there when his life is now in danger? We're trying to find out what happened, and I figured since we a team we should put you on point. Actually, I'm wondering if you got some rats roaming around this rat trap, since this didn't start until we touched base with you."

Rooster was sizzling with anger; he locked eyes with Rasheen. The room became silent as the tension mounted.

Ja-King saw shit was about to get crazy. "Hold up y'all we on the same motherfuckin' team! Now, I hope we ain't gonna start

Meanwhile, Rasheen and Ja-King pulled their weapons; they both were brandishing Berretta 9mms with 18 shot clips; they both had a gun in each hand.

Rasheen shouted, "Big boys! Who's the big boys?"

As Rooster snatched opened the hatch door, and was pulling out heavy artillery in the form of military assault rifles, and sub machine guns, he responded to Rasheen's inquiry. "That's FBI fool! Big boys!" He turned, saw Rasheen and Ja-King brandishing their little pee shooters and shouted, "Nigga get yo' ass over here and get one of these real guns! Hurry!"

As Rasheen tucked his weapons back in the waist of his pants and rushed over to the stash, he wondered how were they going to bang out with the FBI and get away, since he'd learned from pass experience that when they rolled, they literally rolled with numbers that could constitute an army, and they also had access to the same weapons the armed forces used. An answer didn't seem like it was forthcoming, but one thing that was for certain, he was going to use whatever force needed to get away.

Chapter Twenty-Three

"Don't give me that shit!" Killer Kato shouted at Philip Henderson and Crystal, who were cringing in their seats across from him. "How the fuck did that much money get channeled to charity? Crystal, what the fuck are you trying to tell me?"

Crystal sat with a laptop computer sitting in her lap. "I…I'm telling you that these large money transfers were approved by you and they're accompanied by your signatures. Look and see for yourself."

Killer stomped over to the laptop. When his eyes absorbed the information, they almost sprung from their sockets. He saw at least twenty or more large money transfers for hundreds of thousands of dollars of his precious money, all approved with his signatures. They fucked him! They did the oldest trick in the book on him! He grabbed the laptop and was about to hurl it against the wall, but he stopped in mid-motion. With the computer held over his head, a voice in the back of his mind pierced through the dark cloud of rage and told him that breaking up shit would only confirm that the enemy had gain even more control over him. Breathing hard with intense fury, he tossed the laptop back to Crystal, and returned back to his seat behind the desk. After he composed himself, he said, "Phil, can we stop these transfers?"

Philip was trembling because Killer wasn't going to like the answer. "Ah, this is a yes and no answer."

Nigga, don't play no mind games with me! Lay it on me in the raw, the way it is!"

"Yes, we can put a stop on the transfers, but if the recipients have already taken the money, and if these organizations fold, which some have already begun to do so, then no, we will not be able to retrieve the money. For your edification, Killer, this is the work of very powerful people."

"This is certainly the work of rival Distributors." Crystal added. "They made it clear to us that they would not take our entry into the International Distribution market laying down. I would say with resounding force that this is a clear manifestation of that threat."

Killer Kato was seething with rage, anger and something much stronger than fury. He was so hot under the collar he felt the blood vessels in his head throbbing as though they were moments from exploding. They were fucking with his money! Oh hell, fuckin' no! He wanted to react impulsively, run out and start gunning down every possible enemy he could think of, but he struggled not to allow his hastiness to become his guide. That's what they wanted him to do, because it could result in him lashing out on the wrong entity. As he stared at Philip and Crystal, he realized he had to first find out who was behind this attack. He also realized he had so many enemies he didn't know who to start with. He sighed dramatically. "Philip, Crystal, do you value your lives?" His calmness even scared him.

Philip and Crystal were stuck on stupid. They gave each other panic-stricken glances as if to suggest that the other answer first.

"Somebody better say something up in this motherfucker!" Killer Kato said with clinched teeth.

"Yes, I value my life very dearly, Killer," Philip said.

"I value mines also," Crystal said immediately.

"Okay, I thought you did. Now, listen up. I don't give a fuck if you have to hire every specialist or expert on the planet. I want that money tracked down, I want the source of those transfers found, and if you fuck up, the penalty will be very severe, and make sure the next time I see you, which should be in another two hours, you have something good to tell me. I want every able body Hoodaroma employee on this. Now, get out of my sight." He saw them sprung to their feet scurried towards the door. "Tell Crazy B, I need him in here immediately."

They zipped out of the office.

As Rasheen followed Rooster towards the backdoor, the sudden explosion of rapid Uzi fire signaled to them that the federal had stepped to Goliathon and his crew the wrong way. Rasheen had a Colt M16 assault Rifle with four extra clips in his back pockets; Ja-King had the same weapon while Rooster had a ridiculously huge machine gun that looked like it was supposed to be mounted on vehicles and aircraft. Rooster said it was an M 2.50 Caliber machine gun and Rasheen couldn't wait to see that big ass gun in action and to see whether or not Rooster could hold it once that thing started spitting bullets.

Rooster stepped out the back door expecting to be confronted with gunfire, but nothing happened. Rasheen was expecting the same thing. They moved rapidly around the shack heading for the front. Rooster peeked around the shack and saw four Ford Escorts across the street with several men in suits kneeling behind them. Goliathon and his men were kneeling behind cars in stand off fashion.

Rasheen peeked around the shack and saw the situation. This made no sense whatsoever, since these supposed to be federal agents weren't accompanied by an army. They had a mere four cars with about seven men. Rasheen also saw Willie had left the scene, which was a damn good look.

Suddenly, a man yelled from across the street, it was the voice of Aaron, "You have someone inside the house, his name is Rasheen Smith, send him out, and we'll be on our way."

One of Goliathon's men fired a wave of Uzi bullets at the cars in response.

Rasheen's eyebrows crunched up with intense confusion. Dozens of questions attacked his mind, but he knew now wasn't the time for answers, because common sense told him that these agents were dirty; they were apparent engaged in an illegal covert mission, and were on to him.

"I see you the life of the party," Rooster said, "With these corrupt feds looking for you, you got me wondering what kind of bullshit…"

"You can stop wondering cause it ain't shit to wonder about. I'm wondering why every mufuckin' time we come here, I'm suddenly running into all type of drama and shit…"

"Come on, y'all," Ja-King cut in immediately, "Let's deal with this shit first, aight." He examined the situation, recognizing that it was a standoff. "They can't do shit with Goliathon holding them back."

Then, suddenly, police sirens began to materialize; they could be heard at a distance. No one had to be told it was LAPD.

Rooster had to make a fast call. Should he stay and bang out with the police or break out? Since the feds were here for only one person, it was clear that they were up to no good. Rooster could also see that they didn't expect to be confronted with a crew standing out front. Seeing that they couldn't gain anything from banging out with the police and it was apparent that these dirty feds weren't going to pursue them, he decided to break out and fight another day. Rooster unleashed a unique whistle and Goliathon and the other South Central Rangers scurried off as Rooster led Rasheen and Ja-King towards the back, climbing over the fences of neighboring back yards.

Aaron Wilson was furious beyond description. He was crouched behind his car, peering over the hood. He was going to hang Domtar for not warning him that Rooster had a mob right out front and in the back of the house, protecting it from a sneak attack. He was planning on surrounding the shack, rush inside and gun down everybody inside including Rasheen Smith. As he watched Goliathon and his five heavily armed men slide away, he was furious because he couldn't do a damn thing. It was also evident that Rasheen was inside and had apparently gotten away. Aaron waved to his men and they hastily got in their cars and fled the scene just as the first LAPD police car turned the corner responding to a call indicating shots were fired.

Rasheen turned the corner and saw the Acura Legend with Willie in it. This was a good look. It was a pleasure to see Willie had a natural knack for following instructions. He'd told Willie if they had ever ran into a problem at Rooster's place to meet up with them on the street in the back. They all jumped in the Acura and screeched off.

Aaron sat in the passenger seat of the car while Carlos was driving. He knew what he had to do but didn't really want to do it. Now that he revealed his hand, it was almost impossible to get access to Rasheen's whereabouts again. If Rasheen was smart, which all the data confirmed he was, he would seek out the informant amongst the South Central Rangers. As stupid as Domtar was, it was nothing short of a miracle the fool hadn't been discovered by now. Aaron sighed because he had to do it. Plus, time was not on his side. He had 48 hours left to take care of Rasheen since he had to get back to Atlanta to his official post. He also didn't like the fact that he was unable to get this region's Director to approve his pursuit of Rasheen Smith, so now he was not only cutting dangerous corners, but was playing Russian Roulette with his job and the jobs of his crew. Ted and Bruce were already developing a case of cold feet and if he didn't get this ball rolling, he was bound to lose their help on this mission.

Aaron saw Carlos was waiting for a response to his inquiry regarding their next move. With a strained expression on his face, Aaron said, "We're gonna snatch up his brother, Lameek and use him as bate." He pulled his cellular phone, and conveyed the plan to the rest of his mob. None of them had any disagreements.

Rasheen, Rooster, Ja-King and Willie arrived at an abandoned warehouse where the entire South Central Rangers were waiting. The number of gang members, and the way they were conducting themselves with militaristic attitudes impressed Rasheen. They agreed to begin a blitzkrieg upon any and all of Killer Kato's establishments. However, since it was quite late in the morning, they decided to begin tomorrow evening after they all got a couple of hours of sleep.

Lameek was dreaming. He shifted every so often when the dream world images took on a realness that could've fooled every cell in his body. He was having a viciously hot sexual episode with this new girl he'd recently met, named Cadesha. Lameek had both of her legs cocked up high in the air and he was pounding her wet, extremely juicy and tight pussy like an expert jackhammer operator. The vividness of the dream had Lameek's dick hard as blue steel, despite the fact he'd just finish sexing out Aisha (his current bed buddy for the moment) who was lying next to him.

Suddenly, Lameek heard screaming and he felt the dream rapidly dissolving, since his mind told him the screams came from the world of reality. He opened his eyes when he felt himself being roughly snatched to his feet. With wide eyes he saw four masked men. Two of them were manhandling Aisha. She had tape over her mouth and was thrashing wildly as the two men were tying her down to a chair.

Through his grogginess, he felt his mind rapidly clearing up as tape was slapped over his mouth, handcuffs placed on his arms, and he was dragged out of his bedroom. His mind was convoluted with pure anxiety. Whatever he did it was obvious, it was very serious he realized, and he was hoping and praying Killer Kato wasn't going to kill him. He just knew Killer found out about the Hoodaroma bank account numbers, and now he was doing what he did best: mangle, mutilate, maim and murder. The only thing Lameek's inner voice was screaming was "help!" but obviously no one but him heard it.

Killer Kato was pacing as Crazy B sat watching.

"Are you sure about this Crazy B?" Killer Kato stopped pacing, leaned against the bookshelf, and crossed his arms, trying to stop himself from smashing something.

"I spoke to the dude personally, and that's what it is," Crazy B was fiending for a hit of some Jack, but it was too early to start drinking, especially in view of the fact today was going to be a very hectic and eventful day. "They're trying to use Lameek as bate to draw Rasheen out. Actually, it's a good tactic if you ask me."

"What!" Killer Kato's eyes were wide with disbelief. "Lameek is our top money maker. Not only that, Aaron didn't even green light this move with me before he made it."

"He knew what you would say, so instead of wasting time going back and forth he busted his shot. Folks, who are about business, ain't into the habit of sittin' around waiting for shit to happen. We live by that code, and we can't get crazy cause they live by that same code; they stepped to their business, cut and dry. What's all the ruckus anyway, it's about time we turn that little foul mouth, ungrateful ass nigga into a martyr. Just like with Ja-King, that motherfucker is worth more to us dead than alive. The money to be made if he's killed as a result of a kidnapping will push record sales off the mufuckin' chart! We should tell Aaron after he knocks out Rasheen, he should murder Lameek…"

"Nigga, if you don't…" Killer Kato was about to pull his 9mm from its shoulder holster, but realized Crazy B didn't know what time it was. He drew in several deep breaths and let them out slowly to calm down the tension. "We ain't killing Lameek. That ain't gonna happen. No how, no motherfuckin' way. Infact, man the fuck up. Get up and get every hitter we got and some more, cause we going to go get our little million dollar making rapper from these…"

"These cats are feds, Killer," Crazy B couldn't believe Killer was asking him to go toe to toe with Aaron. "All the shit Aaron has done for us, and we gonna flip on him just that quick over some fly mouth nigga who's worth more to us dead than alive."

Killer Kato moved abruptly towards his safe, startling Crazy B. As he spun the safe's dial to its appropriate numbers, he knew it was time to let the cat out of the bag. Crazy B was his ace boom bang, his right and left hand man, and if anybody had a right to know it was definitely him. He snatched the safe door open, rummaged through the stack of papers inside, found what he was looking for, pulled it out, and shut the safe. He handed the document to Crazy B.

Crazy B took the documents with intense confusion dominating his facial expressions, "What's this?"

"It'll answer your questions."

Crazy B started reading the medical document. He saw Killer's government name and some other information he didn't totally understand. The more he read the more he felt a wave of shock grabbing hold of him. Before he reached the clincher info, he sensed what it was going to say. The words "blood test" and "DNA comparison" were the terms that told it all. He couldn't believe it. Lameek was his son! Goddamn! Ain't this about a mufuckin' bitch! Crazy B looked up with perplexed eyes. "Well, I'll be god damn! That little nigga is your rug rat, huh?" He started laughing genuinely; he thought back into time, remembering when they were in their earlier twenties and the memories began to take shape. "I remember when you was hittin' Barbara too. Before them drugs got hold of her, every nigga in the Hood was trying to run up in that." He looked at the date on the blood test report. "You just found this out on 5/16/1999?"

"I've always suspected he was my seed, but you know how shit is. Barbara was fuckin' around on a nigga, so I wasn't trying to hear shit. When she was pregnant, she was saying it was mine. Hey, you know how shit is. When you ain't sure, you gotta wait until you see it before owning it. After he was born I stopped by to check out shorty, and back then that little nigga didn't look shit like me, and I was up outta there. As time went on, I saw he was almost a spitting image of Barbara, but I could see a little bit of me in there somewhere. Finally, after I had this nigga down with my team, I figured I might as well find out for certain. I got Doctor Davis to get some of his blood and I gave some blood. Fucked me up when the results came back."

Crazy B rose to his feet, "Well, I'll get the troops ready. Just know if we go there the repercussions are going to be awesome."

"Well, that's life. I may be a murdering, scheming, cutthroat, making money by any, every and all means possible kinda brother, but you can bet your ass I take care of my family. Not one of my four daughters got a care in the world. I thought I would never make a son, but come to find out, I got one. Right up under my damn nose too. Image me killing my only son, especially when I've been trying to make one for years?"

Rasheen sat on the sofa staring out the glass door of the patio at the pool and the trees in the background. He read the note again. It was supposed to be a ransom note, but it didn't ask for any money. This federal agent wanted him real bad. But why? Was all his mind could repeat over and over again. Then he realized he'd done so much dirt over the years, had robbed and murdered so many people it could be emanating from almost anywhere. After a moment of tossing his options around in his head, it was a done deal. He'd decided to meet up with them at the designated location (Victorville on the outskirts of the Mojave Desert). But he had to find a way to at least guarantee that they didn't kill Lameek even if they succeeded in killing him.

Ja-King was doing some shopping with this gorgeous woman named Marjorie Williams. They were surfing the store aisles trying to find a nightgown for her to wear at their upcoming dinner date. He'd met Marjorie two days ago at the nearby supermarket and they hit it off instantly; their energy gave off a vibe that made Ja-King truly feel as though he had finally found his soul mate. Marjorie was built like a super brick house, had a sweet, babyish voice, and every time he came near her his dick came to life. The plan was to wine and dine her, shower her with whatever materialistic things her heart desired, take her to a hotel room and blow her backside out of the frame. Since they were scheduled to step to the people who kidnapped Lameek tonight at about 9 o'clock, he had the whole day to do his thing, since it was only 11 o'clock in the morning.

As they exited the store, Marjorie said, "Why don't we get us a hotel room, I could use a body massage."

Upon hearing Marjorie's sensuous words, there was nothing else to discuss, and Ja-King drove to the nearest hotel. They entered the room peeling off their clothing. When Ja-King started kissing her in an attempt to diving right into the grand finale, she stopped him and demanded to receive her body massage. As Ja-King's hands massaged her body from her neck down to her calves, and back up, Marjorie brought up the fact that Ja-King looked so much like that famous rapper. When Ja-King said humorously, "Maybe there's a blood relation", Marjorie smiled and suggested that he shower first.

Right then and there Ja-King was stopped in his tracks. A red flag slapped him in the face because if they were so lovie dovie, she should've suggested they shower together. And in light of the fact this shower suggestion came immediately on the heels of her inquiry about him looking like the famous rapper who was on the run, this whole situation was an attention grabber. The Atlanta incident where he had to dump Robin Woods' body in a vacant lot a couple blocks from Capital Projects after they murdered her, re-entered his short-term memory bank and now his sexual fire was rapidly fizzling out.

Marjorie saw it in his eyes. She'd said something that freaked him and she instantly knew it was time to use strong medicine. She laid down on the bed, wiggled out of her panties, cocked her legs wide open, and displayed her bush, knowing it would throw him completely off. She realized what she had just said had almost blew the mission. Now she had to allow herself to be used in order to salvage the situation. As Ja-King started kissing her, she hit a button on her wristwatch and activated the alarm.

Two minutes later, just when Ja-King had got off two penetrating pumps, the hotel room door was kicked off its hinges, and four LAPD plain cloth officers crashed through the door with their weapons pointed. A cacophony of shouts, screams and serious direct orders were launched at Ja-King.

Ja-King rose to his feet with his hands raised high above his head and his condom covered dick standing at full attention as Marjorie scurried away from him. With a venomous snarl, he looked over at Marjorie who was now getting dressed as the cops moved precautiously towards him. He instantly knew he was played and he looked over at his two 9mms in the shoulder holsters dangling from the back of the chair. The urge to go for his guns was very strong, but reality told him if he did it would be a death sentence. With that thought surging through his mind, and the fact that he was looking at life imprisonment or worse, capital punishment, he let his heart be his guide.

Chapter Twenty-Four

As Rasheen approached the secluded town of Victorville that bordered the outskirts of the Mojave Desert, he saw the reason why Aaron chose this place to do the switch. Rasheen was in the passenger seat of the van while Willie was behind the wheel. Three of Rooster's soldiers were sitting patiently in the back compartment. Victorville was a classical no man's land kind of town with family houses scattered about. Just on first glance it could easily be estimated that there was a very small population of less than 2,000 living within the town's perimeters, and because of the surrounding Desert isolation was its good and bad qualities.

At the moment the town looked like a speck on the earlier evening horizon and the glare of the sunset reflected light rays off the glass windows, giving a foreboding feeling to the whole situation. Rasheen was still furious with Ja-King for allowing himself to get caught. It wouldn't have been so fucked up if he had went out with a blazing gun; to get caught butt ass naked while laying pipe to an undercover cop was a disgrace after all the shit they'd been through. He'd warned Ja-King that his dick was going to get him in trouble, and now he was paying to the piper. Immediately upon hearing about Ja-King's arrest and capture on the news, Rasheen did the same thing he and Ja-King had done when Candy ended up in police custody; he hastily moved the buried stash and abandoned the house in Glendale and relocated to Westwood. There was no such thing as being too precautious when dealing with people (Homies or whomever), since people in general were utterly and completely unpredictable.

Rasheen looked at the road sign and saw they were less than a mile from entering Victorville. As Rasheen signaled to Willie to start looking for a place to park, while peering through the side view mirror to make sure the other 8 vans with Rooster and other SCR members were still in formation, he realized inwardly that the only guaranteed thing about people was that the vast majority of them were inconsistent, selfish and forgetful, a sure shot recipe for flipping on family.

About an hour before Rasheen and his crew arrived, a team of 7 heavily armed, masked men entered the Victorville Sheriff's Office as though they were about to rob the joint in bank robbery fashion. Four of the men burst through the front door while the other three came in from the back. After rounding up all the law enforcement officials inside the police station, the masked men stripped the Sheriff and his six deputies, including a female, down to their underwear, handcuffed them and locked them all inside cells. Before exiting the station, they severed the universal phone line, killing every phone in the entire station.

As the masked men got in the van, Capone, the leader of the squad, got on his cellular, and said into the phone with a heavy Columbian accent, "Aaron, we have problem. Two polices are missing. They driving around."

"Track 'em down," Aaron said. "Go back inside and check the transmission log, it should tell you where they're currently located. Remember, no gun play if possible."

"No problemo," Capone said, hung up, instructed one of his soldiers to go inside and check the transmission log.

Three minutes later, the soldier returned with the stragglers whereabouts and the van drove off. Within ten minutes, the two deputies were found, cuffed, dragged back to the station house, stripped naked and tossed inside a cell. The entire Victorville Sheriff's Department paced their cells confused and scared out of their minds; none of them could believe this was happening; their anxiety and stress held firm at unhealthy levels because they were certain about one thing; something very big and terrible was about to happen.

Killer Kato was in the passenger seat of the SUV while Crazy B was behind the wheel. Killer was on his cellular phone talking to the scout he sent into the town several hours earlier to ascertain the best logistical approach to take in order to deal with this matter. Trailing the SUV was a convoy of 8 Jeeps containing 22 soldiers in possession of everything from military weapons to explosives.

Killer Kato said into the cell phone, "Are you sure Rasheen has that many people with him?" He honestly thought Slick had misstated the figures when he said he had 9 vanloads of brothers numbering about 34 strong.

"I'm watching him right now," Slick said from the attic of an unoccupied house. According to the answering machine, the family was away on vacation at Disney World. With infrared, night vision binoculars he watched Rasheen and the others moving about. "These niggas are deep. And they got mad hardware too."

Killer nodded approvingly. This was a good thing he concluded, because he could kill two birds with one skirmish, wipe the slate clean and get a fresh start. "Okay, Slick, you did good. That's a bonus point, bro. We minutes away. Are you sure we can get in on the Westside without any of them seeing us?"

"You can do it on foot," Slick said. "That nigga Aaron got some extra hands. Like I said, I don't know his total body count.

All I saw was 13 people, not including Aaron. Some of them looked like they were Latino, Mexican or something."

This little tad bit of info had Killer wondering what Aaron was up to with the Mexicans? However, he was glad Aaron found a way to get rid of the Victorville Sheriff's Department; this didn't surprise him in light of Aaron's way of doing things in an organized manner. Killer saw the silhouette of the town on the night's horizon. "Okay, the fireworks are about to begin. Keep your eye on Rasheen, aight, I'm out." He hung up.

Ten minutes later, Killer Kato, Crazy B, and the 22 soldiers were moving rapidly through the town on their way to the closed down Bowling Alley within an abandon Shopping Mall in the northern section of the town.

Lameek sat in a chair with his hands bound behind his back; his mouth was gagged and a blindfold covered his eyes. The place he was in was damp and smelly; the sound of a busted water pipe could be heard somewhere in back of him. He knew his abduction wasn't Killer's doing. He heard them mention Rasheen's name several times. And whoever these men were, they were far from amateurs. He wasn't allowed to see them, but from the way they spoke and how they followed the boss man's instructions, Lameek knew they were definitely cops, dirty cops, the kind that did wicked things that could make Hitler's skin drawl with disgust. His guts were growling like crazy, since he refused to eat and they didn't make him consume what smelled like fried chicken. Although they hadn't beaten him, he still felt beat down because his stress was causing massive amounts of acid to bombard his system.

Suddenly, Lameek felt himself being snatched to his feet.

"It's time, Mr. Thug rapper," Aaron said as he dragged Lameek by the collar out of the Bowling Alley and into the parking lot. "Your brother's here to rescue you." He'd just got word from Capone that Rasheen and several other men were heading towards the Bowling Alley. In other words it was show time. "Stand your ass right here and don't move a muscle. If you even sneeze, you will be gunned down. You here me?"

Lameek didn't answer; his trembling was interfering with his voice box.

"Do you hear me?" Aaron shouted.

The shout almost buckled Lameek's knees. "Yeah! Yeah, I hear you man!" He shouted back, more so out of being startled than anything else.

With an 18 shot 9mm in his hand, and an Uzi tucked in his waist, Aaron moved back towards the entrance of the Bowling Alley.

Rasheen arrived at outskirts of what used to be a Shopping Mall. He had an Uzi in each hand, and four extra clips in his special made utility belt. About ten yards in front of him was a burnt down Carvel store, and about 100 or more yards further down he saw Aaron heading back towards the Bowling Alley. When he saw Lameek standing in the parking lot, blindfolded with his hands behind his back, he started closely examining the structural lay out. He didn't want to announce his presence until he got a feel of the layout. About two minutes later, he told Rooster and the others to lay low, and he ran to the old burnt out building that was once a Carvel ice cream store. Once behind the building he shouted, "Yo! Rasheen is here! Whoever you are, I'm here!"

Aaron nodded his head his as he stood near a window with night vision binoculars, watching and listening to Rasheen. He put the binoculars down and shouted out the window, "Walk towards your brother with your hands in the air."

Rasheen couldn't believe these fools thought he was stupid enough to make himself a sitting duck. He looked at his watch wondering what was taking so long for Rooster's people to come up the rear of the Bowling Alley and pop off. Before this thought was fully formulated in his head, the machine gunfire ignited. Rasheen's head turned with panic stricken haste because the machine gunfire came from behind him. He took aim but couldn't return fire because he couldn't see whomever it was picking off Rooster and his soldiers.

Almost at the same moment, machine gunfire came from the direction of the Bowling Alley and Rasheen scurried into the Carvel store as bullets ripped at the walls as he fled. He peeked out of the store and saw dozens of Uzi's being fired on the western side of the Bowling Alley. He shouted to Lameek, "Get on the ground, Lameek! Get down!" He wanted to call him stupid, but he saw Lameek lay down flat on his stomach.

Earlier, Aaron was about to mark the mission off as a victory when he heard and saw Capone and his Columbian soldiers opening fire on Rasheen and his mob. But that all changed when simultaneous gunfire came from the western side of the Bowling Alley. Just as he was rushing over to the area of the gunfire, Aaron saw Ted's head explode from a sharp shooter's bullet. His mind was going crazy with confusion because he was assured that Rasheen's crew had not moved in the direction of the western region. Aaron realized something had gone terrible wrong as he pumped off a volley of bullets at a group of men charging at the

Bowling Alley, dropping two of them. The attackers who weren't struck by Aaron's bullets returned fire, and Carlos and Bruce failed victim to these unknown attackers' bullets when they ripped through the concrete walls. Aaron pulled his Uzi and started sneezing off dozens of rounds.

Killer Kato was unleashing a sheet of Uzi bullets as he and Crazy B ran towards Lameek. They looked like military men embroiled in a special opts mission as they ran in a crouched position spitting sporadic spurts of gunfire at the Bowling Alley and at the Carvel store.

Rasheen saw Killer Kato and Crazy B and impulsively opened fire. Both his Uzi's shook, rattled and rumbled as they sprayed countless bullets per-second. He saw Killer Kato dive for the ground as Crazy B did a vicious dance of death. "Yeah!" Rasheen cheered triumphantly as he pulled back behind the wall realizing he had definitely hit Crazy B's bitch ass. This was emphatically a good look.

Rooster was lying on the ground holding his gut with one hand while the other hand was brandishing an assault rifle. He was firing shots at the Columbians whenever they approached. Twice he cut down several of the Columbians when they thought the coast was clear and were making an effort to get to the Bowling Alley. Rooster was furious by the fact his entire crew was obliterated; he'd watched them being picked off in the same fashion as General Custer and his soldiers were knocked off during that infamous ambush and last stand at Little Bighorn.

Killer Kato saw Crazy B was hit fatally. Seconds earlier, he had felt droplets of Crazy B's blood splattered on his face just as the bullets from the Carvel store rang out. Spraying the Uzi towards the Carvel Store, Killer slid to Crazy B and saw Crazy B was definitely dead from the apparent headshot. The shot tore off a huge chunk of his head, (exposing his brain matter), and Killer Kato had to struggle not to break down in tears. Killer Kato now had to move rapidly; he slid to Lameek, pulled off the blindfold, untied his hands, and said, "It's time to go."

Lameek's grateful eyes told it all. The shock was galvanizing because it was obvious Killer Kato was here to save him. He sprung to his feet and ran behind Killer Kato as Killer sprayed off Uzi bullets at the Carvel store, even though the gunfire had ceased.

Capone and four of his men swiftly moved towards the western region of the Bowling Alley. By the looks of the situation, Capone realized something was very wrong; there were shooters in that region and had apparently attacked Aaron and his team from the blindside. Capone had lost six of his men so far and had signaled his 20 backup men into action about five minutes ago. Just before signaling his backup to the western area, he had picked off virtually all of Rooster's soldiers from specially concealed locations.

As Capone approached the rapid flickering of the sparks from the machine gunfire, he saw the backup team was engaged in a gun battle with these newcomers in the western section. Instead of merging with his backup team head-on, Capone proceeded in a northerly direction, using the wooded area as cover. He strategically slid up on the newcomers' blindside and easily picked all of them off. As the ones who weren't instantly mowed down tried to retreat, Capone slaughtered them all in a most merciless manner.

Killer Kato and Lameek ran down a dark street as they heard massive gunfire going off as though it would never stop. Killer Kato felt bad; it touched his ego knowing that he was running away from a fight. The urge to go back and assist his men was very strong, but there wasn't much he could do to save them, since he saw they were out gunned and out numbered. Plus, in order for him and Lameek to live they had to die. If no one were there to hold them back, they would've easily chased him and Lameek down. Killer Kato believed he was worth too much to throw himself into a suicide mission.

Killer Kato and Lameek jumped in the SUV and got on the highway heading back to LA to his Lakewood Mansion.

Rasheen rushed over to Rooster and saw he was dead. The two bullet wounds to his gut were huge and indicated that the men who attacked him were using Teflon bullets, since Rooster's bulletproof vest was useless against the bullets. On the horizon the flickering sparks and the rapid explosions of gunfire could be seen and heard coming from the western region. Rasheen looked around the immediate area and saw about 15 of Rooster's soldiers sprawled out on the ground in a similar expired state as their General. He saw movement out his peripheral vision and frantically took aim at the bushes.

"Rasheen, it's fam!" Duke shrieked as he came from behind the bushes with his hands up in the air, one of his hands was brandishing a Mac 10. "Be easy!"

Rasheen saw it was two of Rooster's soldiers, Duke and Tony T; he went to them.

Tony T had an assault rifle in his hand and was distraught. "Damn son, they clipped us from behind." He sounded like he was seconds from crying. "They duffed out our whole fuckin' mob! They knocked SCR down! This shit is fucked up!"

Rasheen took charge, "There ain't nothing else we can do here. We outta here. Let's go." He began running towards their vehicles parked a few blocks away that were being watched over by Willie; Tony T and Duke followed him.

Later, Aaron inspected the faces of the men they had just murdered. He was in a very dangerous state of mind; Ted, Carlos and Bruce were dead, three federal agents were murdered and boy was there going to be hell to pay when the Bureau got wind of this. He'd always knew something like this could happen, but he didn't know he would feel this twisted in the mind once it did occur. There was no doubt his life was now dangling from a very thin string. When he saw Crazy B and several of Killer Kato's other very close associates, he realized Killer Kato had crossed the line. He didn't think Killer would go against him over a bullshit gangster rapper, and the realization that he took it there was very upsetting.

Aaron, Donald, Eugene, and Norman reluctantly decided to put phase four into activation. This was the part they all hated about skirting the edges, because it got real dirty, so dirty it made them experience bad dreams, and made them realize that if there was a heaven and hell, they had guaranteed their entry into that place of fire and eternal misery. They quickly repositioned all the bodies in the region to make it look like Rooster's gang killed the federal agents. Aaron, Donald, and Eugene had to standup the bodies of their life long friends in certain positions, fire the bullets from the weapons of their alleged killers into their bodies and allow their corpses to fall accordingly. Norman took no part in the fourth phase clean up because his stomach just wasn't up to it. All the dead Columbians were removed, and secretly transported to Arizona where Gomez would bury them properly.

Twenty minutes later, after they redesigned the crime scene, Aaron and the remainder of his team were cruising down the highway on their way to Killer Kato's Lakewood Mansion. Surprisingly, their whole mission's objective had suddenly changed. No longer was Rasheen the top priority. Obviously, once Killer Kato chose to put his nose where it didn't belong, he traded places with Rasheen Smith.

Chapter Twenty-Five

Killer Kato was gunning the SUV down the highway. Lameek was in the passenger seat in a state of shock. Killer glanced over at Lameek and said, "Hey, life is crazy like that. Believe me, it fucked me up when I got the confirmation."

Lameek was totally fucked up in the head at the moment. Killer Kato was his father! This was too much for him. After escaping a kidnapping and to have this dumped in his lap wasn't fair; the least Killer Kato could have done was let him recuperate from the trauma of the kidnapping before smashing him in the head with this crazy shit. At first he refused to believe it, and thought Killer Kato was trying to fuck with his mind, but after considering the fact that he had rescued him and sacrificed a good portion of his top notch bodyguards in the process, made it highly unlikely that he was lying. Killer Kato was the ultimate king of grime and if he put himself in harms way, it had to be, because it benefited him in some way.

Lameek sighed and said, "Since you my father, I got one thing to say. All them years we was living in the same Hood and you had an idea that I might be your son and you never even show me a single drop of love, don't you think that shit was foul? Now you want me to embrace you as my father!"

"I ain't askin' you to embrace me as your father. I personally don't give a flying fuck what you do." He lied, but he couldn't stop being whom he was. "You don't understand what the fuck happen back then, so either way you look at it, what you think don't really matter." He paused, realizing he was about to go way off the deep end. He thought about his hostility, admit it was unwarranted and decided to bring it down a notch or two. "You know something, Lameek, you right. Back then I was hittin' your mom and I should've known you was my seed. But your mom wasn't no angel in this shit either, cause she was sneakin' with some nigga name I-God." He went into a reverie, and after a moment he said, "Life's a bitch, and we all make mistakes, but with me I take care of my seeds, when I know for sure they mine. That's the reason I went and got your ass, cause ain't no motherfucker in this world can ever say that Killer Kato shitted on his children. And I mean no motherfucker. Now, if you flip or try to kill me, then all bets are off. That's when I'll treat you like any other enemy."

There was a moment of intense silence.

Lameek said, "If you had reason to believe I was your son, you should've had those blood test done back then. You ain't got love for your seeds. You frontin'! You waited all this long to check it out, you ain't really wanna know what time it was."

Killer Kato let it go with that. About a minute later, he saw the highway exit to his mansion, and got off it.

The moment Killer Kato entered his ten million-dollar compound, he was content when he saw the twenty extra bodyguards waiting inside the mansion's courtyard. The minute he escaped the Victorville fiasco he called them up with specific instructions to be at the mansion with every weapon they could get their hands on. His heart, instincts and common sense had told him that this shit wasn't over. He wasn't certain if Aaron was still alive, but from the way the tables had turned on him, it was only logical to assume he wasn't dead. As Killer Kato brought the SUV to a stop, he saw the garage door was open and knew his personal vehicle attendant was working overtime, caring for his fleet of expensive cars. He had a Maserati 3200 GT Coupe, Porsche GT2, Lamborghini Murcielago, BMW Z8, Ferrari 360 Modena, Porsche 99 Carrera 45, 470 Lexus truck, S500 Mercedes Benz, 2004

Corvette and a Dodge Viper, and from the way things were looking he knew he had to turn it up if he intended to continue enjoying these benefits of life.

After he informed his men of the situation, and instructed them on what he wanted them to do, Killer Kato entered the mansion and called Crystal into his office. Crystal was trying to relax her stressed out mind with a late night bath in the Jacuzzi and knew something terrible had happened before Killer even opened his mouth. She had been on edge ever since Killer Kato's backup bodyguard team had stormed the mansion. When he informed her of Crazy B's death, she cried genuine tears. Upon hearing that Lameek was his son, she thought he was playing head games until he showed her the blood test results.

Rasheen cruised around Killer Kato's Lakewood mansion; this time he was behind the wheel of the blue van while Willie was in the passenger seat, and Duke was in the back compartment. Tony T had abandoned the mission, reasoning that he would only follow Rooster or someone who was legitimately deemed the General. It took about ten minutes for Rasheen to conclude that they didn't have enough manpower to step to Killer Kato in a way that would bring this issue to a close. Rasheen parked the van and stared at the front gate hoping an idea would come to his mind. Ten minutes later, he saw a fleet of about five cars and four vans cruise by the van. He and Willie frantically crouched down in their seats the moment they detected the vehicles' headlights.

Peering over the dashboard, Rasheen nearly jumped for joy when he saw Aaron get out of a dark green car, waving to the drivers of the vans and other vehicles while he and several men with Uzi's and assault rifles boldly approached the mansion. As he observed the men moving about, an idea came to his mind with the explosive power of a nuclear explosion. Aaron's appearance on the scene was a super good look. Rasheen explained the situation to Willie and Duke, exited the van, and ran at top speed towards the back of the mansion.

Killer Kato ran for his gun cabinet when the machine gunfire shattered the late night silence. He retrieved his gun he called the Tony Montana. The damn thing had everything but the kitchen sink attached to it. Although he loved that classic movie Scar face, he wasn't stupid enough or twisted out of his mind on drugs to run into a blazing furnace of fire the way Tony had done. He was going to keep running until he got in a position to get the upper hand. Once he killed Aaron things would mellow out, and it would be back to business as usual.

Killer Kato ran into the rooms where Lameek and Crystal were and informed them that if they wanted to live they had better follow him, and as expected they didn't have to be told twice. Earlier, Killer Kato had put the Limo chauffer, Kay Kay on point instructing him to be ready with the Limo if he heard any shots. Lameek had heard Killer Kato tell this to Kay Kay and knew more drama was on the way.

Killer Kato, Crystal and Lameek bolted out of the mansion and saw the Limo waiting. As Crystal and Lameek got inside the Limo, Killer Kato saw a group of men climbing over the elegant white brick wall with a grappling fork; he took aim, but gave the intruders enough time for most of them to get over the fence and onto the lawn. When four of them were over and the other two were about to climb over the fence, Killer Kato unleashed a stream of bullets that chewed at the four men's bodies with savage force. Killer Kato then hit a switch on the gun and hastily squeezed off two missiles from his gun called Tony Montana. When the two missiles made contact with wall, a huge hole appeared while transforming everything within a ten-foot by ten-foot radius into small bits and pieces of debris, including the two men on the other side of the wall.

Killer Kato scooted inside the Limo as the sounds of a massive raid swarmed over the mansion. He tossed the weapon to the floor as the Limo screeched away and sped towards the huge gate that opened at a touch of a button. Killer Kato's compound was so huge, he knew no army, short of the US army, would have enough men to cover all inches of his mansion, so escaping was never an issue once he was out of the mansion and into a moving vehicle. The Limo zipped out of the gate and onto the roadway.

Killer Kato reached for the liquor bar and made himself a stiff drink. He gulped it down in one swallow as Crystal and Lameek looked on with stressful expressions. Killer poured himself another drink, and sighed loudly. He took a moment to appreciate Lameek and Crystal's frighten facial expressions and laughed because he enjoyed the awesome power of fear. As he sipped this drink, he looked outside at the roadway and noticed Kay Kay wasn't going in the direction they had previously discussed. He shouted to Kay Kay, "What are you doing!? You going the wrong fuckin' way!"

Suddenly, the car came to a head-jolting stop on the side of the roadway. The divider window slid down with a loud electrical buzz, revealing a 9mm pointed at Killer Kato. When Killer Kato saw it was Rasheen, his eyes were wide with intense surprise.

"Disarm him Lameek," Rasheen said not blinking once as he grilled Killer Kato. He saw Lameek was indecisive. "Don't worry, La, I got a damn good aim. If he tries some dumb shit, I'll blow his fuckin' top off, bet that. And thanks for that info about Kay Kay." Earlier, Lameek had called Rasheen on his cellular phone and informed him about the Limousine parked in the back of the mansion and of Killer Kato's plan to use it as a vehicle for escape if there was any trouble. Upon seeing Aaron and his team about to invade the mansion, Rasheen knew the old bust the chauffer in the head and take the Limo trick would definitely work.

Lameek confiscated the 9mm from Killer Kato's waist.

"Open the door and get out," Rasheen said.

Lameek slid out first, and then Rasheen. With Rasheen's 9mm aimed at his chest, Killer Kato got out next and then Crystal.

"I guess this is the part where you expect a boss nigga like me to fold up like a little bitch and beg you not to kill me?" Killer Kato said as he wolfed down his drink and tossed the glass. It shattered into pieces on the deserted roadway. "Well, guess what, nigga? It ain't gonna happen!" He squared off and locked eyes with Rasheen; he didn't want to die, but he would take that route if it meant getting on his knees. Suddenly, an idea came to fruition. "Before you shoot, tell him what time it is Lameek. Yeah, tell him."

"Tell me what!" Rasheen said impatiently.

"This nigga is my father," Lameek said reluctantly.

Rasheen laughed. "And you believed him?"
"I saw the blood test document. My Doctor's name and signature was on the report." Lameek felt odd because suddenly he had doubts about his hatred for Killer.

"Documents can be forged..."

"It's the real deal, Rah," Lameek said pointblank.

Rasheen realized with dread circulating through his veins that this was not a good look.

"I bet you, you remember me," Killer Kato said to Rasheen. "You was about five or six years old back when me and your momma was dealing. You used to have this little Spiderman doll that you slept with all the time. You loved that doll so damn much you never went anywhere without it. The way you loved that toy, you probably still hanging on to that thing to this day. Back then y'all was living over on Hart Street." He looked over at Lameek and said, "Your momma probably said your daddy's name was..." He hated his government name. "She used to call me Colly. That's short for Colin. She said your daddy's name was Colin I bet."

Lameek nodded his head. "She said his name was Colin Gidson."

Suddenly, Rasheen's memory made the connection. He remembered his mother used to always say Lameek's father's name was Colin Gibson. But whenever Lameek would ask questions about him, she would basically shut him down and not talk about the subject. He also remembered his father's name was J.D. Dawson, and like so many other brother's from his Hood he'd never met his father. But the clincher that confirmed it, was his mentioning of that Spiderman doll. There was no doubt how much he loved that doll and he was right; he hung on to that doll until well into his teens. So this nigga is Lameek's father. After looking at the whole picture, he decided it didn't matter anyway. "So what you trying to say? Huh? Because you Lameek's old dad, you think that change all the shit you did!"

"Please, Rasheen," Crystal interjected, seeing that her bread and butter was on the line. "Put the gun down! This makes no sense; it's totally uncalled for..."

"Shut the fuck up, bitch!" Rasheen was seconds from putting a bullet in her head. He said to Killer Kato. "I just wanna know a few things. Why did you lie to me about the whole Black Bob situation? Rambo told me everything, so don't lie!"

Killer Kato said nothing as he glared at Rasheen.

"Why did you kill my mother?" Rasheen knew he wasn't going to answer, but he felt it was only right to layout some of the reasons why he was going to blow his top off. This stuff had been festering inside of him for years, and it felt good to be able to finally get all this shit off his chest. "Why did you send me out on kamikaze missions, without a bulletproof vest? Huh?"

Inconspicuously, Crystal slid her hand inside her purse. She saw Rasheen was so worked up he didn't notice her movement. There was no doubt Rasheen was going to kill Killer Kato, and her livelihood in the process. She couldn't standby and let this crazy fool destroy years of hard work because he wanted to keep a bullshit vendetta going. In a flash, Crystal pulled her 32 automatic, and as Killer had instructed her on several occasions, she aimed the gun at Rasheen, pressed down on the trigger and held it in place as the gun came to life as though it was fighting its way out of her hand.

BOW! BOW! BOW! BOW!

From that moment forth, everything seemed to go so fast, that the events that followed were rapidly overlapping each other. Crystal's bullets pounded Rasheen body as he collapsed to the pavement. Simultaneously, within an eye's blink Lameek opened fire on Crystal, blowing two huge holes in her chest, killing her instantly. Killer Kato pounced on Lameek, trying to wrestle the gun from his grasp.

Killer Kato and Lameek fell to the ground, tussling feverishly over the weapon.

"Let the fuckin' gun go!" Killer Kato growled as he strained with all his might. "Nigga, I will..." He was about to say 'kill you', but he realized he didn't have to say it because he almost had the gun out of Lameek's grasp.

Lameek, realizing he was about to lose the gun, decided to squeeze the trigger with hopes that the shots would startle Killer Kato enough to allow him to get a better grip on the gun.

BOW! BOW!

Lameek convulsed with great pain as the two bullets tore through his body like scorching hot missiles. Everything went black as one of the bullets pierced his heart.

Killer Kato was startled, but not by the two shots; he was disturbed by the fact Lameek pulled the trigger when he should've known the gun was pointed at his body. Killer Kato struggled to his feet, and didn't see that he had finally given Rasheen the clear shot he'd been trying to get off ever since he and Lameek started tussling over the gun.

BOW!—BOW!--BOW!--BOW!--BOW!--BOW!--BOW!

Rasheen saw the rapid gunfire from his 9mm was holding Killer Kato up on his feet as the bullets tore at his center mass. Finally, Killer Kato fell lifelessly to the ground. Rasheen dragged himself into position, took aim and fired two more shots into Killer's head; the bullets ripped away half of his cheek while splattering blood every which away.

Rasheen still couldn't believe one of Crystal's bullets hit him in the groin area at the base of his stomach, just a few inches from his manhood. The bad luck part of it all was that the bullet just missed his bulletproof vest. Two of her other bullets hit the vest, but this one fuckin' bullet had to hit him, he sighed in great pain because he could feel that the hot bullet was lodged in the lower part of his stomach. He surmised that the bullet entered the lower base of his stomach, ricocheted off of his hipbone and was now in his stomach. The pain was much stronger than excruciating; it was terrifying beyond description.

When he looked over at Lameek, he cried elephant tears. Instantly, he started blaming himself. He should've shot Killer Kato and Crystal on the spot. But no, he had to do all this talking and jib jabbing. Damn! This is motherfuckin' bullshit! If he had did what he was supposed to do when he was supposed to do it, Lameek wouldn't be laying here dead! He wept hard. Suddenly, a sharp pain jolted him out of his weeping state; this pain spoke loud and clear and it said if he didn't get moving he'd be joining Lameek very soon.

He loved his baby brother, but he wasn't ready to join him. With every drop of strength he could muster, Rasheen pulled up his internal forces and energies from the depths of his soul, powers he didn't even know he had in him. Rasheen dragged himself behind the wheel of the Limo and drove off.

As the Limo swirled drunkenly, Rasheen flashed back to the Livonia Avenue hit where he was in a similar situation. The irony was the first thing to slap him in the face and he couldn't help but laugh out loud. That night Crystal save him from imminent death and now the bitch might be the one who killed him. Life was a bitch! He concluded as he allowed his foot to become very heavy on the gas, despite the fact his control over his motor skills was rapidly deteriorating.

Two minutes later, through blurred vision, he saw the sign that said the exit for the San Bernardino Hospital was coming up next. The thought of rushing to the hospital was very tempting, but he knew that would mean going back to prison, and the thought of returning to a cage was far more terrifying. As the blood poured from his body and soaked the seat of his pants, he wondered was his vow never to return back to prison was worth dying for? After a moment, he convinced himself that Willie was just a few more miles away as he zoomed pass the exit to the hospital. Then his son, Rasheen Junior, came to mind and he wondered would he ever even get the chance to see him? When he nearly fell to sleep behind the wheel, he realized it was a bad idea to have Willie not get involved in his conflict with Killer Kato. Had he at least kept him nearby he would probably be receiving medical treatment by now.

Five minutes later, Rasheen saw the van and he nearly passed out from delight. He brought the Limo to a tire-screaming stop as he saw Willie walking towards the Limo. He struggled to open the door and fell to the street. A vicious sheet of darkness finally gripped him and he gave into it.

Willie saw Rasheen was apparently in serious trouble; it was obviously he was injured and Willie frantically ran to aide him.

Fifteen minutes later, Willie pulled into the driveway of Doctor Myers, who was their backdoor, under the table doctor, who agreed to provide any type of medical treatment, including bullet wounds, as long as the price was right. As Willie pulled Rasheen's limp, lifeless body out of the car, he sensed it was too late, but because of the awesome grip that the money had on his mind, he refused to believe it was over, especially since Rasheen had never told him where any of the stashes were located.

The End

So Real You Think You've Lived It!!

Street Knowledge Publishing
Order Form

Street Knowledge Publishing
P.O. Box 345, Wilmington, Delaware 19801
Email: jj@streetknowledgepublishing.com
Website: www.streetknowledgepublishing.com

For Inmates Orders and Manuscript Submissions
P.O. Box 310367
Jamaica, NY 11431

Bloody Money
ISBN # 0-9746199-0-6 $15.00
Shipping/ Handling Via
U.S. Priority Mail $3.85
Total $18.85

Me & My Girls
ISBN # 0-9746199-1-4 $15.00
Shipping/ Handling Via
U.S. Priority Mail $3.85
Total $18.85

Bloody Money 2
ISBN # 0-9746199-2-2 $15.00
Shipping/ Handling Via
U.S. Priority Mail $3.85
Total $18.85

Dopesick
ISBN # 0-9746199-4-9 $15.00
Shipping/ Handling Via
U.S. Priority Mail $3.85
Total $18.85

Money-Grip
ISBN # 0-9746199-3-0 $15.00
Shipping/ Handling Via
U.S. Priority Mail $3.85
Total $18.85

The Queen of New York
ISBN # 0-9746199-7-3 $15.00
Shipping/ Handling Via
U.S. Priority Mail $3.85
Total $18.85

Purchaser Information

Name: _____

Address: _____

City: _____State: ___Zip Code: _____

Bloody Money ___

Me & My Girls ___

Bloody Money 2 ___

Dopesick ___

Money Grip ___

The Queen of New York ___

Quantity Of Books? _____

Make checks/money orders payable to:
Street Knowledge Publishing

Upcoming Novels From Street Knowledge Publishing

Coming Fall of 2006

The Queen Of New York
By: Visa Rollack

Don't Mix The Bitter With The Sweet
By: Gregory Garrett

Stackin' Paper
By: JoeJoe and DeJa King

Coming 2007

Dipped Up
By: Visa Rollack

Dopesick 2
By: Sicily

Lust, Love, & Lies
By: Eric Fleming

No Other Love
By: "Divine G"

Shakers
By: Gregory D. Dixon

Dirty Livin'
By: Fernando Seirra

The Hunger
By: Norman R. Colson

M.U.C.C.
By: Ronald Jackson

Playin' For Keeps
By: Gregory Garrett

Bitch Reloaded
By: DeJa King